What Reviewers Say About Gun Brooke's Books

Sheridan's Fate

"Sheridan's fire and Lark's warm embers are enough to make this book sizzle. Brooke, however, has gone beyond the wonderful emotional exploration of these characters to tell the story of those who, for various reasons, become differently-abled. Whether it is a bullet, an illness, or a problem at birth, many women and men find themselves in Sheridan's situation. Her courage and Lark's gentleness and determination send this romance into a 'must read.'" -- *JustAboutWrite*

Protector of the Realm

"Brooke is an amazing author, and has written in other genres. Never have I read a book where I started at the top of the page and don't know what will happen two paragraphs later.

She keeps the excitement going, and the pages turning. In a century when marriage is recognized between two adults and gender is not an issue, Brooke shows that love and romance and passion can grow. Likewise, she reveals to us the soft vulnerable side of these two strong, battle-hearty women. Let's just say, I can't wait for the second in the trilogy to see what happens next." -- *MegaScene*

Coffee Sonata

"In *Coffee Sonata,* the lives of these four women become intertwined. In forming fridnships and love, closets and disabilities are discussed, along with differences in age and backgrounds. Love and friendship are areas filled with complexity and nuances. Brooke takes her time to savor the complexities while her main characters savor their excellent cups of coffee. If you enjoy a good love story, a great setting, and wonderful characters, look for *Coffee Sonata* at your favorite gay and lesbian bookstore." – *Family & Friends* Magazine

Course of Action

"Brooke's words capture the intensity of their growing relationship. Her prose throughout the book is breathtaki[...] have you been hiding, Gun Brooke? I, f[...] romances from this author." – *Independe[...]*

T0126248

By the Author

Visit us at www.boldstrokesbooks.com

WARRIOR'S
VALOR

SUPREME CONSTELLATIONS
BOOK THREE

by

Gun Brooke

2008

ISBN 10: 1-60282-020-1
ISBN 13: 978-1-60282-020-3

This Trade Paperback Original Is Published By
Bold Strokes Books, Inc.
New York, USA

First Edition: July 2008

Credits
Editor: Shelley Thrasher
Production Design: Stacia Seaman
Graphics By Gun Brooke and Sheri (graphicartist2020@hotmail.com)

Acknowledgments

Len Barot, aka Radclyffe, publisher and owner of Bold Strokes books, thank you for believing in me, and for the enthusiasm with which you approach every new project. Your continued faith in my writing, as well as the example with which you lead, inspire me.

Dr. Shelley Thrasher, editor and my guiding light. You also serve as the copy editor for *Warrior's Valor*, and your double duties are not going unnoticed. We make such a great team, and I already long for our next project!

Sheri, the cover is awesome. I'm delighted that you thought my 3D painted cover art was good enough to use for this book.

My beta readers and friends, Lisa, Sami, Ruth, Georgi, Jan, and Mary, all helped save me from myself.

Thank you also to the gang of proofreaders and other BSB associates who helped this project along. I think Lori (Andy) deserves special thanks for everything she does for the BSB newsletter and the online bookstore.

Dedication

To William, our first grandchild,
whose birth coincided with the creation of this story.

PROLOGUE

"If this doesn't work, you must avenge my demise, Desmond." Hox M'Ekar, the former Onotharian ambassador, glowered at his manservant.

"Don't worry, Your Excellence. Kyakh, who sold me the device, assured me it's foolproof."

"Let's not waste any time then. No matter how infallible this procedure is, it'll still alert the SC law enforcers. The chip emits signals on a regular basis, and if it's shut off, they'll appear like hawks from the sky."

"We'll be gone from Jasin long before then." Desmond looked convinced, but given the man's youth, M'Ekar wasn't inclined to take his optimistic statement at face value. "Kyakh owns a nearly brand-new Legacy-class vessel, the *Viper*, perfect for escaping SC space. Once we've captured that Jacelon woman, Kyakh will fly us successfully across the border to intergalactic space in less than three days. The SC has never intercepted the *Viper*."

"I hope you're correct, young man." M'Ekar rose and rubbed his neck, a habit he had begun the day that damn SC doctor implanted the lethal microchip in his spinal cord. If he strayed outside his designated area on this godforsaken, mosquito-infested planet, the microchip would receive a signal that released a minuscule amount of a highly lethal substance. It would kill him within a few hours, unless any of the law-enforcement forces that carried the antidote found him.

"I would never trick you, Your Excellence."

When M'Ekar had promised Desmond a glorious career as one of his most trusted aides, the young man had quickly capitulated. M'Ekar's guardian-turned-accomplice wouldn't join him in his escape, however. It almost saddened him to think of Desmond's early death.

It is a necessary sacrifice for me to reach the greatness I was born to enjoy. "Excellent," he said with a nod. "How long?"

"Kyakh's crew is three weeks away from this sector."

M'Ekar stood, motioning Desmond closer. "Then we should prepare." He chuckled. "Not that I have much to pack."

Desmond suddenly looked nervous. M'Ekar knew that a lot depended on his manservant, who was probably realizing what he was undertaking. It was important to reassure him. If Desmond turned on him, M'Ekar wouldn't know how to get in touch with this Kyakh. He placed a fatherly hand on his shoulder. "What would I do without you, son? You have proved that you'll make a fine aide de camp."

Desmond appeared more self-confident. "Thank you, Your Excellence. I look forward to serving with you."

M'Ekar wondered if the sting he felt was one of remorse at the hopeful and admiring expression on Desmond's face, but shrugged it off. People were useful for a moment, and when they weren't—they were expendable.

CHAPTER ONE

You have to recognize the severity of this threat, Your Honor."

"I don't *have* to do anything, Ms. Izontro." Supreme Constellations Judge Amereena Beqq regarded Dwyn Izontro haughtily from behind her desk in the luxurious hotel suite. Outside the window, the Cormanian capital, Corma Neo, glimmered like an enormous jewel. "It's late in the evening, and I'm tired after my journey. You managed to bypass the proper channels and see me directly only because I'm visiting Corma unofficially."

Dwyn knew the esteemed judge was peeved, but butting heads with authorities around the SC for more than fifteen years had toughened her. "I know, and I'm grateful," she said, and wasn't entirely lying. She had half expected the judge to close the door in her face.

"Judge Beqq, the importance of what I have to say makes up for my audacity. The Disi-Disi forest is one of the few untouched territories within the Supreme Constellations, and the Cormanian government has always protected it and its natives from any interference. It sustains the indigenous people who are living as they have for thousands of years, but it also keeps this planet stable. I work for the Aequitas group, a pro-bono activist organization that attempts to save the environment and supports other worthy causes."

"'Justice,' in the ancient Earth language of Latin. Appropriate."

Dwyn couldn't tell if Beqq's words were cynical. Instead she continued. "Aequitas has received credible intel that the Cormanian government already is cutting parts of the forest."

"That would go against the SC decree regarding such measures."

"No offense, Judge, but you of all people should know how greed and the hunger for power make men and women regard a law as merely a suggestion."

"True enough."

"Corma is overpopulated, like so many other worlds within the SC. Lobbyists are pressuring certain Cormanian politicians to pass a bill that allows prospectors to purchase real estate that will diminish Disi-Disi territory. If our intel is correct, the Disians, the natives of the forest, will suffer greatly when their natural habitat shrinks. We risk losing a society that is entirely unique. But the destruction of the forest will also alter Corma's climate and cause tornadoes, hurricanes, inland storms, and plasma cyclones—disasters beyond anything the Cormanians have ever experienced."

Dwyn swallowed her impatience because she knew this woman could best help her deal with this mess. "Lives will be lost, Your Honor, and Corma will experience an uncertain fate. New deserts will form where the land is now lush and green. Glaciers will appear all the way down past the northern hemisphere." As Dwyn rattled her facts, she leaned forward to emphasize the severity of her words. This senior judge of the Supreme Constellations had to understand.

"I know the SC Council has discussed this topic extensively." Beqq spoke quietly and as if she weighed every word that passed her lips. "Possibly someone has offered the Cormanian rulers substantial sums of money to allow various prospectors access to the protected area. Officially, the Cormanians have declined, but if your group is correct..." Beqq looked resolute as she twirled the obsidian-embedded titanium ring on her left index finger. "From what I remember, you've been right a lot lately. We in the court system have also questioned some of your methods."

"Serving the greater good is worth any possible risk."

Judge Beqq blinked. "Really. Well, Ms. Izontro, I'll investigate the situation. I'm not as well connected on Corma as I used to be, but I still have a few strings to pull. Will you be satisfied if you get to see the forest for yourself?"

Dwyn frowned and shook her head. "Depends on what I find, ma'am."

"All right. I'll speak to you as soon as I've taken the matter into consideration and run it by some of my contacts. Hopefully, by then I'll know if it's possible to grant you permission." Beqq laced her fingers loosely and rested her chin on her joined hands. "I sympathize with your concern for this planet, Ms. Izontro. But since you approached me, you probably did your homework well enough to realize that I do things correctly or not at all."

"I know. Guess it comes with the territory of being a judge?" Dwyn smiled slightly.

"It comes with the territory of doing what's right."

❖

"You must be joking, sir?" Emeron D'Artansis dropped her back-strap security carrier on the floor next to her computer console and turned to her superior officer. "Isn't my unit overqualified to babysit some SC hotshot?"

"You misunderstand, Commander," Captain Zeger said gravely. "I wouldn't assign this delicate matter to anyone *but* my best unit. These orders have travelled down the chain of command for a week now, and the commissioner has issued a direct order. Report for briefing tomorrow morning at 0600. You and your team need to be geared up and ready to move out an hour later."

"Sir, yes, sir." Emeron would have huffed, but she respected Captain Zeger too much. And she never let her personal feelings show when she received an order. Still she muttered to herself, "This is crazy," as she sat down and began to read the messages on her computer.

Most of them were work related, but several from her mother were blinking in bright red. Not willing to deal with Vestine D'Artansis while she was trying to come to terms with the babysitting assignment, she marked the messages as "can wait." Emeron had little patience with her snobby family even during normal circumstances. She wished Zeger had informed her of her assignment before she had gone to the gym. Then she could have worked off her frustration there instead of sitting here with it simmering below the surface.

She leaned back in her chair and rubbed her forehead. Her patience wore thinner every day. Even her next in command, Mogghy, had said so to her face after a few drinks at their favorite bar a month ago. Emeron had tried to laugh his words off, but he hadn't smiled. "I've known you too long, ma'am," he'd said, shaking his head. "Something's eating at you and it's driving you crazy, not to mention the rest of the unit. The troops aren't sure what to think."

"What do you mean?" She'd been annoyed, but also embarrassed.

She'd never expected to have this talk with anyone, least of all one of her subordinates.

"I wouldn't say anything if we weren't such good friends outside the force." Mogghy finally smiled. "I have your back, Commander, and I hope you know that."

"I do." His disturbing observation was hard to swallow, and Emeron focused on it for a few seconds before he continued.

"I don't know, Commander. You seem angry, or perhaps frustrated. I could be way off base here, but that's how I see it."

Mogghy wasn't far from the truth. So many things gnawed at Emeron these days. As long as she kept working, she could ignore them, or so she'd thought until now. Her temper, which she'd struggled with since she was a child, was now even more volatile. She had to resort to the many different relaxation techniques she'd learned during her years as a member of the law-enforcement service to keep from resorting to violence. *I'm always angry.*

She sighed. "I'm sorry if I've given the unit any reason to doubt my professionalism. And thanks for letting me know before the speculations go any further. I'll deal with my problem and you won't have to mention it again." Emeron knew she sounded stiff, but she felt uncomfortable. She also realized that Mogghy had saved her a lot of professional grief by not going through the proper channels. "Appreciate it, Mogghy."

"Anything for you and the team, Commander. Always."

They hadn't mentioned this conversation again, and Emeron had consistently performed her duties and assignments flawlessly. Still a cold knot at her core persisted, and she feared she wouldn't be able to suppress her anger much longer. On those occasions when she'd had to quickly back off in order not to let the beast within her show, yet act as if nothing were amiss, she had caught Mogghy's worried glances. Working out was the best way to remain focused and she was in the best shape ever.

"Here you are, Commander. For your eyes only." Captain Zeger placed a handheld computer on Emeron's work console. "A preview of tomorrow's briefing."

"Thank you, sir." Emeron punched in her security clearance code and pressed her thumb on the small pad below the screen.

Reading, she soon realized that her assignment had gone from boring to hellish. *Babysitting an environmental activist.* She could think of few things worse than catering to some saintly woman, who was probably more interested in her own goodness than actually achieving something worthwhile. A picture of a blond woman with finely chiseled features and pale gray eyes appeared, and Emeron read the name underneath. Dwyn Izontro. An Iminestrian name, but Izontro's face belonged to a human. Izontro was thirty-four, but looked younger. She worked for one of those shady businesses that labeled themselves pro bono, but rarely was. They were lobbyists of the worst kind. In Emeron's opinion they'd cause havoc and lobby for any "just cause" in the universe, for a fee.

She scrolled down to other pictures that showed Izontro in action. The woman had targeted several different installations and was clearly fearless in her efforts to draw attention to her agenda. Emeron sighed. Izontro had to be a hardened troublemaker. She browsed through more pictures but frowned as she viewed one of Izontro lying face down on the floor of a police hovercraft. A bulky officer had his large boot placed firmly in the small of her back, and the man's smirk made Emeron cringe. She wondered what the tiny woman could have done to warrant the officer's brutal behavior.

When she finished reading, she flicked the computer off with her thumb and walked over to the latrine. She needed cold water on her face to calm her down. Scanning her own reflection in the metal-mirror above the hand-sanitizer unit, she wasn't surprised to see a dark fire burning in her eyes. Her skin was stretched taut over her high cheekbones, which she recognized as a sign of irritation. She tapped the sensor for the aqua faucet and scooped a cupped handful of water to her cheeks. Drying with a recyc-towel, she didn't have to look into the mirror again to know what subdued annoyance looked like. She had seen it on the face of each of her mothers too many times.

❖

Judge Beqq's dramatic red hair and curvaceous figure attracted the attention of both men and women in the restaurant. Seemingly unaware of this fact, she drove her fork through a double-tailed shrimp and chewed it slowly before she spoke. "I'm glad you could join me for dinner, Ms. Izontro—"

"Dwyn. Please." Dwyn wasn't accustomed to such formalities. Her parents called everyone by their first name, and so did everyone Dwyn worked with in the Aequitas group. "It took you quite a few days to sort things out, but I'm grateful that you climbed out on a limb for me."

"I hope you found a way to occupy your time. Corma has a lot to offer."

"I spent my days at the National Archives and Library, going through the original documents of the Thousand Year Pact." Dwyn smiled. "That probably doesn't sound like much fun."

"Actually, I'd like to peruse the documents myself, one day." Beqq seemed unaffected. "I need to talk to you more, Dwyn, before you set out." She placed a small item on the table.

"A scrambler?" Dwyn frowned.

"Yes. We cannot afford to be overheard."

"All I need is my permit. I'm used to being on my own in the strangest of environments."

"Well, this time, you won't be." Beqq spoke with conviction.

A small flicker of dissatisfaction moved beneath Dwyn's ribs. "I can take care of myself."

Beqq laid an elegant, well-manicured hand over Dwyn's and squeezed. "I know all that. I've studied your files. But this is different. You're going against a potentially very greedy adversary, and if your group's intel is correct, you'll need protection."

"As in bodyguards?"

"As in a team of Cormanian law enforcers. They will accompany you every step of the way. Don't argue." Beqq squeezed Dwyn's hand again. "It took me several days, and I had to use all my accumulated goodwill with the Cormanian Minister of Domestic Affairs to pull this off. The Cormanians wanted to delay any investigation, which in itself is bothersome. But they had to relent when I told them that the SC Council leader was paying this matter special attention."

"You did? I mean, he is?" Dwyn had actually met Marco Thorosac once. He had visited her university, which was apparently his alma mater, when he had been re-elected councilman for a new decade.

"He is now. I also did my own bit of research, and you're correct about the long-term consequences of the loss of this ancient forest. I've deployed the court ship *Dalathea*, and it will arrive in orbit shortly. I don't have to tell you that, with the war effort, everything else is secondary."

"I know. It used to be much easier to motivate the SC public. Now it's nearly impossible to raise funds for any cause not directly related to the conflict with the Onotharians."

"A lot is at stake for certain Cormanians if you prove the intel true." Beqq frowned. "If you fall into the hands of the ones who will gain from silencing you—"

"All right, Judge." Dwyn nodded slowly. "I see your point."

"Good. Here's the address where you will meet your team at noon tomorrow. A Commander D'Artansis will head up your escort."

"Very well. I hope they're all used to hiking. The undergrowth makes it nearly impossible to cross this kind of terrain. And when it comes to the Disi-Disi forest, with all its prohibitions and laws to abide by, you can't cut your way forward with a plasma-pulse weapon. And you can't travel with anything but small hovercraft. It's all part of the Thousand Year Pact."

"I studied some of that last night," Beqq said. "The rights bestowed upon the Disians were extensive. No loopholes that I could find."

"And yet the Cormanians are going back on their ancestors' word and their honor. I'm eager to get out there."

"Use your head and your gut feeling, Dwyn. I don't want this to be our last meeting."

"Fair enough. I'll be careful, Judge."

"Excellent."

They ate in silence and Dwyn began to relax, if only marginally. In her mind and heart she was already on her way to the Disi-Disi forest.

Chapter Two

D wyn pressed the sensor that released the tension in the shoulder straps of her back-strap security carrier and slid it off. The black wire-mesh canvas held everything she needed to document the Cormanian government's potential crimes in the protected forest. Placing the security carrier on the floor next to her chair, she gazed around the mission room. Three women and four men sat in the chairs right next to the podium and had obviously chosen to ignore her.

A tall woman stood by the podium, next to an older man, browsing a handheld computer. Jet black hair framed her strong features, and intense black eyes, very typical of some Cormanians, seemed to analyze and dismiss her in less than a second. Dwyn was used to others perceiving her as an annoyance, at best, or even regarding her with disgust, but something in the woman's eyes made Dwyn clench her jaws. The man looked up and nodded solemnly.

"Captain Zeger, I believe," Dwyn said pointedly with her sweetest voice. The faint coloring of the Cormanian officer's neck proved that her gentle needling found its mark.

"Ms. Izontro, this is the officer in charge of your safety while in the Disi-Disi forest, Commander Emeron D'Artansis." Captain Zeger indicated the woman next to him.

Dwyn had to admit D'Artansis was impressive. At a closer range, D'Artansis's black eyes made an even greater impact. Deeply set, they seemed to reflect no light at all, like wells where sunlight could never reach. Stark, strong features added to D'Artansis's austere expression.

"Commander." Dwyn greeted her politely. "Shall we start?"

A faint look of surprise flickered across D'Artansis's features. "By all means. The sooner the better."

Dwyn didn't think D'Artansis was eager to go on this mission. In fact, she was almost certain the commander regarded it as a waste of her precious time.

"Heads up, people," D'Artansis began, and immediately had her team's total attention. "As you've gathered by now, we're going into the Disi-Disi forest. We don't have to worry about the Disians. They'll avoid us if we don't bother them, but plenty of other things can go awry if we don't stay sharp. Captain Zeger has briefed me this morning on our objectives, and I'm certain this team will act with its usual distinction."

Commander D'Artansis glanced at Dwyn. "Ms. Izontro, who is under the protection of prominent politicians and law enforcers, plans to observe a certain situation. The Disi-Disi forest is beautiful, but also treacherous, unless you know what you're doing. Once we're in the forest, it is up to us to keep her, and each other, safe. Yes, Oches?" D'Artansis indicated a bald young man in the first row.

"What's Ms. Izontro's mission in the forest, ma'am?"

"That's up to her to share, or not." D'Artansis raised an eyebrow in Dwyn's direction.

"I'm on a humanitarian and ecological mission to appraise the keeping of the Thousand Year Pact." Dwyn spoke clearly, enunciating every word so no one could underestimate the importance of this enterprise, no matter what their preconception was. "I will document any potential trespassing, cutting of protected plants or trees, and other signs of wrongdoing."

"And if you find anything like that going on, ma'am?" Oches frowned. "What then?"

"I will try to secure evidence of the perpetrator's identity." Dwyn was pleasantly surprised at the young man's interested tone.

"Sounds like you could use some help. Or are any other members of your team joining us?"

"I need all the assistance I can get. I will be collecting samples, and—"

D'Artansis interrupted. "Excuse me, Ms. Izontro, but such details can wait. We need to finish the briefing before we head out to the Maireesian fields."

Dwyn had never been to Corma before, let alone to the Maireesian fields, but she knew they served as a kind of no-man's-land between the urban expanses of Corma and the Disi-Disi forest. As on most of the

SC planets, agricultural areas were few and strictly monitored. Many people preferred the synthetic alternative to traditional produce and regarded the latter with suspicion. Even some people in the Aequitas group thought they could become sick from eating a vegetable grown in the dirt, rather than the pure synthetic version created in a factory's sterile environment. Still, others, usually the famous and the rich, ate nothing but traditional food, cooked at expensive restaurants.

Dwyn sat down next to Oches as D'Artansis held a straight-forward, detail-packed briefing for her staff. When she paused, Dwyn thought she was done, but instead D'Artansis turned to her. "And you, Ms. Izontro, need to know only a few things. Stay next to me, never go anywhere alone, and don't try to be a hero if anything unexpected happens."

Furious at the patronizing way D'Artansis handed out "orders," Dwyn slowly raked her eyes over the commander. "Understood. Now, is this when I make my requests?"

D'Artansis blinked, and for a second Dwyn thought she'd ignore her. Instead, D'Artansis shrugged and motioned for her to speak. "Certainly." She strode to the back of the room and leaned against the wall.

Dwyn rose and gazed around her. "I won't enumerate the many reasons my mission is so important. But if my intel is correct, your planet's future is at stake. I'm doing this for you, the people of Corma, to mitigate, as much as possible, any repercussions of a potential environmental crime. I was unaware that I needed protection of this magnitude, but it should tell you something. So, let's get going. The faster we get out there, the sooner you can be back fighting, eh…crime, or whatever you normally do."

Dwyn thought she saw an appreciative gleam in two of the young men's eyes, but perhaps they simply liked blondes. More than once, a man had told her that she looked pretty or cute, and she hated such comments. If anyone thought she would be interested in a little fondling behind the habitats, they were sorely mistaken. Hopefully they were merely relating to what she'd just said.

"Very well." D'Artansis pushed herself off the wall. "That's what we need to know for now. Gear up, people, and pull up the hovercraft."

D'Artansis's team scrambled to their feet, except a man who looked older than the rest. As he walked up to Dwyn, he extended a hand in the typical Earth greeting. "Welcome to Corma, Ms. Izontro. I'm Lieutenant Mogghy."

Dwyn returned the handshake. "Nice to meet you, Lieutenant."

"Just Mogghy, please."

"Then call me Dwyn." It was a relief to be on an informal basis with someone.

D'Artansis joined them. "Mogghy is my next in command. If, for some reason, I'm not available during this mission, this is the face you look for. Got all your gear, Ms. Izontro?"

"One bag outside in the corridor. These are my instruments and documents." Dwyn grabbed her security carrier. "I'm ready."

"Good. Mogghy will take you to the hovercraft and make sure you're assigned a seat behind me."

Clearly, D'Artansis was going to monitor her at all times and thus avoid trouble with the brass, Dwyn thought. "See you there," she said, and followed Mogghy.

As they stepped out into the corridor Mogghy said, "The commander is *the* best law enforcer in the capital. You're lucky to have her in charge of your safety."

"You don't have to reassure me." Dwyn hoisted her trunk onto her shoulder. "In fact, most of the time when I'm on a mission, I work alone, or with a local guide or two. I'm used to taking care of myself."

"Apparently someone thinks the situation here on Corma is a little different, Dwyn. And it's wise to be careful. You can't make a difference in the world if you're dead."

"Touché." Dwyn grinned at the amicable man. "How long have you worked with Commander D'Artansis?"

"Oh, the commander graduated from the academy my first year there. After I graduated and got a chance to join her team—she was the XO then—I took it. Haven't regretted it for a moment. We've been through quite a bit together."

"Must be interesting. Do you work planet-side only?"

"No, some of our missions have been in the Cormanian jurisdiction of the SC space."

They stepped outside, where three small hovercraft had pulled up below the stairs. With sleek lines, they sparkled in the sunlight. Each vehicle contained a driver's seat with a double seat behind it and one additional single seat in the back. The storage hatches were still open, and Mogghy showed Dwyn where she could stow her things.

"You'll ride in the lead vehicle with the commander. Ensign Oches will drive the second craft, and I'll follow in the third."

Dwyn wanted to shake her head in disbelief at this large operation on her behalf. "All right, Mogghy. See you when we reach our first stop."

"Safe journey." Mogghy saluted her with two fingers. "Here's the commander now."

"Saddle up, people." D'Artansis walked up to them. "I want you right behind me. You'll sit next to Ensign Noor."

Dwyn climbed into the seat next to one of the women on the team. "Hello. I'm Dwyn."

"Ensign Noor." The look on the black-haired woman's face was standoffish at best.

Ah, no handshakes there. Dwyn didn't respond to the hostile introduction, but focused on the belt. Snapping it closed, she felt a vague humming sensation as the straps squeezed her gently against the backrest. The seat was body shaped and quickly adjusted to her slight frame.

"D'Artansis to Oches and Mogghy. What's your status?"

Two voices answered over the communicator that they were ready to go.

"All right. We're off. D'Artansis out."

A vague whining sound reverberated through the craft, and soon they hovered at traffic level above the ground. D'Artansis expertly maneuvered the craft into the busy traffic paths and kept elevating the agile craft until they sped through the Cormanian capital.

Containing buildings up to 12,000 meters tall, both commercial and residential, Corma Neo was literally bulging, and it was impossible to distinguish the border of the neighboring cities. The Cormanian government had installed oxygen-producing technology at several levels among the structures, which Dwyn's organization considered almost like re-terraformation. Corma was practically without any agricultural areas, and Dwyn feared that before long this planet, once among the most wondrously beautiful ones within the Supreme Constellations, might consist only of urban neighborhoods and industries.

The craft veered off toward the faint skyline north of the city.

Suddenly feeling jittery and alert, Dwyn lifted her chin and watched as they approached the Disi-Disi forest. She had studied almost everything written about this place, and to her it held its own magic, its own amazing wonder.

"What a view," Ensign Noor murmured, sounding reluctantly impressed.

"Don't let that fool you, Ensign," D'Artansis said with obvious disdain. "It's actually a glorified swamp."

Dwyn studied the rigid back in front of her. D'Artansis obviously wasn't all that keen on the forest, but something in her voice had been almost hostile. "I can't wait to experience it for myself," Dwyn said.

"Good for you. As long as you experience it quickly." D'Artansis didn't turn around, but she didn't have to.

Dwyn could easily interpret the other woman's voice and posture. She loathed the protected forest. For some reason, Dwyn was as eager to solve this mystery as to pursue her current task.

CHAPTER THREE

Emeron punched in the commands for a routine flight to the Disi-Disi border, where one of the forest rangers would scrutinize them. Zeger had provided all the necessary credentials and permits, but Emeron knew how bureaucracy worked on Corma—slowly, and if you tried to force anything, even slower.

She glanced over her shoulder and saw Ensign Noor sitting with closed eyes, no doubt following the unwritten rule of the law-enforcement teams—if you have a chance for a nap, take advantage of it, because you never know when you'll get another opportunity to sleep.

Dwyn Izontro sat behind her, apparently deep in thought, and Emeron acknowledged that something about the woman annoyed her more than was justified. Granted, she frowned upon this mission because the assignment took her back to the Disi-Disi forest, a place she'd rather avoid.

"Beautiful, isn't it, Commander D'Artansis?" Izontro said softly, interrupting her thoughts. "Look at the mist hanging over the treetops. Some of them are more than forty-five meters high."

"I know." She wasn't in the mood to chat, but couldn't very well ignore Izontro.

"They grow slowly. It takes them two hundred years to reach that height."

"I see."

"Have you ever been here?" Izontro's breath tickled Emeron's neck.

"Yes."

"I can't wait to experience this place for myself. I can't remember ever wanting to be dead wrong as I do now."

"What do you mean?" Intrigued despite her best intentions, Emeron glanced at Izontro.

"I want to believe that the Cormanian government and the free-market players, the conglomerates of vanguard business, have honored the Thousand Year Pact. I hope they haven't touched so much as a square meter of this area, but I'm almost sure they have." Dwyn sounded sad and a bit forlorn.

"If they have, you'll find traces of it." Emeron made a wry face at her lame attempt to sound encouraging.

"Yes. I will." There was no doubt in Izontro's tone. "I always do."

A small fort at the border of the Maireesian fields appeared, and Emeron began the descent. Very few vehicles were in their traffic corridor and Emeron touched down just outside the gate. A guard approached, her weapon slung casually over her shoulder.

"This outpost area is off-limits." She sounded bored and obviously didn't look closely at Emeron's uniform.

"*Ensign*," Emeron said, "I have permission to enter. But if I had been here on unlawful errands, greeting me with your weapon like that could have been the last thing you ever did."

Snapping to attention and shifting the weapon to the correct position, the woman paled. "Yes, ma'am. Sorry 'bout that, ma'am."

"You better be. Here are my permits and credentials." Emeron produced a handheld computer.

"I'll see to this right away, Commander." The guard hurried toward a booth by the gate. Emeron noticed two figures moving inside and impatiently drummed her fingers on the console before her.

A moment later, the ensign came back and returned the computer. "Everything checks out, ma'am. You are allowed a thirty-day stay within the Disi-Disi forest's boundaries. We added a document listing the rules and prohibitions for the area. You need to familiarize yourself with the five basic ones before you cross the Maireesian fields."

Emeron nodded briskly and placed the computer inside her uniform. "Thank you." She brought the hovercraft up to the lowest ground level of traffic. Out of earshot of the ensign, Emeron pressed the sensor to her communicator. "Mogghy. Oches. Stay sharp while addressing the locals."

"Aye, ma'am." Mogghy and Oches sounded calm, but Emeron knew they had understood.

She kept her eyes on the view screen that revealed what was occurring behind her and relaxed marginally when Oches's and Mogghy's hovercraft lined up behind hers. "We're going to cross the Maireesian fields now, and then we'll enter the perimeter of the forest," she informed Izontro and her two subordinates. "Expect a bumpy ride, since the fields are outfitted with sensor-jamming technology and other sensory equipment to alert the units in charge of protecting the forest."

"How long before we reach the site where I'll gather the samples for my base values?" Izontro asked.

"Approximately ninety minutes."

"Good."

Izontro seemed calm yet intense. Emeron had encountered do-gooders like her before, always caring about the bleeding masses, but with a personal agenda. Nobody did anything for the greater good without making sure the greater good gave something back. Fame of the heroic kind usually motivated types like her. Corruption, from one or more players, sometimes motivated others. Emeron wondered what Izontro's currency was, though she bet the woman probably aspired to sainthood and heroism.

The Maireesian fields billowed beneath them, stretching as far as Emeron could see. Even she admitted that the green with splashes of purple, red, and golden where the flowers grew in groups created a spectacular sight.

"Have you seen this before, Ensign Noor?" Emeron heard Izontro ask.

"No, ma'am."

"Please, call me Dwyn."

Silence.

"It's a fantastic view and a completely unique flora and fauna. These fields were originally created by the government a thousand years ago. At that time, of course, Berenias, the Emperor of Corma, led your government."

"Really." Noor didn't seem very interested in the history lesson.

"Yes," Izontro continued, clearly undaunted. "Berenias was a great ruler, according to the chronicles, far ahead of his time. He considered all men and women equal and was the first to realize how quickly the Disi-Disi forest could be exploited and destroyed unless someone established safeguards to protect it. He and Chief Troboday, the leader of the Disians at the time, signed the Thousand Year Pact, a treaty that would ensure the Disians' right to their forest and prevent deforestation and intrusion. It has been nearly a thousand years now, and the Cormanian government, as well as the open market, apparently thinks it can gnaw at the edges of the pact."

"And why not?" Ensign Noor asked, sounding mildly exasperated. "We need the space. The Disians are...how many? Sixty thousand?"

"Not that it should matter, but approximately two hundred thousand individuals exist. However, the point is—"

"And they should be entitled to nearly a quarter of the southern hemisphere?" Noor raised her voice, and Emeron knew she would have to intervene or the hotheaded ensign might insult the woman they were there to protect. She opened her mouth, but was forestalled by Izontro.

"You should be glad that the forest covers a fourth of this hemisphere."

Noor's total silence confirmed that the change from enthusiasm to forged steel in Izontro's voice had taken her aback.

"It gives you the oxygen you breathe and stabilizes this planet's ecosystem. Without it, Corma would suffer one natural catastrophe after another, not to mention how the buildup of toxic gases would poison this planet. If you don't care about the Disians, look at it from a selfish point of view. If you want to breathe clean air and drink clear water, pray that Aequitas is wrong. Pray that your government hasn't allowed greed to override the law."

"Ah. Well. Never thought of it that way." Noor cleared her throat. "Actually, I've never been to the forest."

"It's hard to get a permit to enter," Emeron added. "Not many regular people ever go there."

"Perhaps that needs to change. It might help open people's eyes." Izontro's voice mellowed. "The seclusion of the Disians is part of the problem."

"The mystique and romance surrounding this race are overrated," Emeron said without thinking. She realized too late that her contempt shone through and wished she had had the sense to shut up.

"What do you mean? The Disians are one of the very few original people within the SC." Izontro sounded bemused. "They live the old-fashioned way, with shamans, with no modern technology, not even electricity."

"And you find that admirable." It wasn't a question, more of an accusation. When it concerned a population who refused to evolve, Izontro was as starry-eyed as most of her kind.

"I do. It's easy to adopt the view of everyone else. Staying true to your beliefs and honoring old traditions—"

"Traditions?" Emeron had to laugh and wondered if Izontro detected her bitter undertone. "Tradition is just another word for stagnation, and it also stands for nostalgia."

"And you have no use for nostalgia." Izontro's voice turned annoyingly mild. "Makes me wonder what you have against these people, Commander. It sounds personal."

"I don't have anything against any individual. But every person should evolve, not hang on to *tradition* and use it as an excuse for not growing or being ambitious." Emeron punched in new commands and flew the hovercraft in an elegant curve, following the outline of tall, dark trees. "We've entered the forest. We will reach our coordinates for the landing site in half an hour." Emeron hoped her tone would ensure that the subject was closed.

❖

Ambassador M'Ekar walked on board the matt black spaceship. A smaller vessel had taken him off-planet and delivered him safely in high orbit. He now admitted this part of the escape had made him nervous. This was a critical moment. He automatically felt the side of his neck where Desmond had used the instrument provided by Weiss Kyakh to configure and remove the insidious implant. The only trace of the chip that would have directed the lethal poison into his carotid artery was a small ridge of scar tissue. He shuddered involuntarily, then immediately straightened and stared inquiringly at the woman before him.

"I am M'Ekar. And you are?"

"M'Ekar. Strange, I somehow pictured you younger." The tall woman stood inside the docking port and regarded him with a crooked smile. Dark brown hair, kept in a short, tight ponytail, emphasized her sharp features. Her deeply set, frost green eyes clearly appraised him, and the fact that she seemed to find him lacking infuriated M'Ekar.

"You have yet to identify yourself," M'Ekar hissed. "Where's Kyakh?"

"You're looking at her."

M'Ekar blinked. "I thought you were older. And male."

"We were both wrong." Weiss Kyakh shrugged and smiled maliciously. "But we don't have time to stand around debating our flawed perceptions of each other. The sensor scramblers can hold off the authorities for a limited time, but let's not push our luck. Come on. I'll show you to your quarters."

"How long before we reach our target?" M'Ekar asked as they started walking down the corridor.

"Five days. The *Viper* is faster than most SC vessels."

"A lot can happen in five days."

"You can always try to get another ride." Kyakh looked expressionlessly at M'Ekar. "Here we are now. Your quarters."

M'Ekar sighed at the sight of the miniscule cabin. The term "quarters" was entirely an exaggeration. This was little more than a bunk bed with walls. "Hmm. Thank you." He tried not to let his exasperation show. Couldn't Desmond have arranged for something a little more in his league?

"I hope you don't mind sharing." Weiss Kyakh motioned to the young man behind M'Ekar. "Quarters are cramped in such a small and insignificant ship, so we have to bunk where we can and share when we must."

"Share?" This was too much. M'Ekar had to object. "Not only am I traveling under deplorable circumstances, but must I share quarters with a servant?"

Desmond's eyes darkened. "I am not your servant, not anymore, Your Excellency," he said, sounding both hurt and angry. "I have risked everything to help you escape and I, if anybody, deserve to stand by your side."

"Now, now, boys," Weiss Kyakh said slowly. "No fighting. Ambassador, cut the "I'm-entitled" act. You're not *traveling* anywhere. You're a fugitive, running for your life, and you have no say in what goes on here. I'm the captain and ultimately everybody's boss until we reach your homeworld and I get paid. On board this vessel, my word is law. The ship's name is the *Viper*, and trust me, the name fits. So, you share quarters, Ambassador. End of discussion." Weiss Kyakh left them and M'Ekar saw her shaking her head as she disappeared down the narrow corridor.

Desmond was obviously sulking. M'Ekar knew he might need more favors from the resourceful, and unscrupulous, young man. "Forgive me, Desmond," he managed. "I didn't mean to sound so harsh. It's been nerve-wracking recently."

Desmond seemed eager to get back on good terms with his former prisoner. "It's all right, sir. This ship is fast, and I'm confident Kyakh will deliver us safely to Onotharat. I will be proud to stand by your side when you regain your title and office."

You fool. "Of course, dear boy. You've been most helpful." M'Ekar never knew when he might have to sacrifice someone else for his own greater good.

The faint buzz under his feet told him the *Viper* was leaving the planet Jasin's high orbit. He sat down on the narrow bed, ducking so he wouldn't bump his head against the top bunk. This journey couldn't go fast enough.

CHAPTER FOUR

Dwyn opened the door to the small carbo-nylon habitat where she'd spent her first night in the Disi-Disi forest. Morning dew lay like transparent drops of glistening syrup on the shrubbery. The air was thick and humid at this early hour and Dwyn drew a few extra breaths, needing more oxygen in her lungs.

"You're up early." The husky voice to Dwyn's left sounded reluctantly approving.

D'Artansis sat on a cubic chair at the table near the cookery unit that the team had placed in the center of the circle of habitats. D'Artansis took out a small cube from a container next to her and tossed it on the ground with a muted pop. It hissed and instantly took on the shape of a cube big enough to sit on. "Have a seat."

"Fantastic trick. Thanks. Normally I love sleeping in." Dwyn shrugged and sat down, determined to not let D'Artansis get to her this morning. These protected surroundings were beautiful, and today she was eager to journey farther. If anyone was exploiting the territory, they were most likely doing it well into the forest, out of sight. "You're always up early, I suppose, Commander."

"Call me Emeron," D'Artansis said, surprisingly. She shrugged in a cynical manner. "We're going to spend time together in this godforsaken place, and I'm not one for formalities."

"You don't like formalities and you're in the military?"

"Trust me, when it comes to my team, I'm prepared to make an exception."

"Then please call me Dwyn." She peered into the pot on the cookery plate. "Cormanian coffee?" she asked hopefully.

"Of course. Help yourself. There's breakfast, if you don't mind military rations."

"Military rations are fine." Dwyn poured coffee into a thermos-mug and grabbed a bar of cereal-nutrients. "How early is it? We the only ones up?"

"Not really. Mogghy and Noor are making sure the hovercraft are in good shape. Never hurts to be extra careful."

Dwyn knew that transportation was vital to her assignment, but something in the way Emeron spoke made her think the outcome of Dwyn's work wasn't what concerned her.

"Expecting trouble already?"

"Not really. But I'd rather be wrong than be caught off guard with no way to get you and my team out of here."

Dwyn took a bite of the tasteless bar and sipped the amazing coffee, which warmed her stomach and rejuvenated her instantly. "You seem as if you could care less about this place. To me it's wondrous."

"It's a forest. Nothing more, nothing less."

"A rare forest. A life-sustaining, one-of-a-kind forest." Dwyn spoke softly, sensing that if she pressed too hard, she'd lose this more benevolent connection with Emeron. She didn't want that.

"I can see its ecological value. I can even understand the anthropological interest some may have in the lives of the Disians." Emeron gestured dismissively with her free hand. "I simply don't admire its inhabitants. There's nothing to admire about a people who make a point of being different, of being *backward*."

Dwyn blinked. "Backward?" Certain she must have misheard or misunderstood, she searched Emeron's pitch black eyes. "The Disians aren't backward at all. A famous Earth anthropologist recently called this an amazing society with traits many people would do well to emulate."

The blackness in Emeron's eyes cooled as she slowly placed her mug on the table. She snarled quietly, "I don't agree with some enamored Earth anthropologist who views these natives through a romantic filter. They're nothing but a stagnated people, caricatures of 'sons and daughters of nature.' Once you see them for yourself, you'll be disappointed." Emeron tossed what was left of her coffee into the bushes. "I understand why Corma needs this forest intact, but trust me, Corma doesn't need the Disians. They contribute *nothing*."

Emeron's opinion stunned yet intrigued Dwyn. The words "backward" and "caricatures" showed more than indifference. Such language revealed disgust and contempt.

"I disagree," she said softly. "Without the Disians, this forest would be in even greater danger of extinction. They're one with nature, both flora and fauna, and their mythical reputation ensures that no one blatantly violates the Thousand Year Pact. Without them, Cormanian exploiters would have leveled this paradise centuries ago."

"God, you're blind." Emeron sighed, obviously frustrated. "Finish your breakfast, Dwyn. It's time to wake the others and break camp."

Within minutes, the camp buzzed with activity as the team collapsed the habitats and quickly stowed everything in the back of the three hovercraft. The men and women paid Dwyn little attention, and she knew not to get in their way by trying to help. Instead she readied her sample kits and handled her own gear. She had learned the hard way to never rely on or expect anybody else to carry her personal equipment.

She stashed the daypack behind her seat in the hovercraft and sipped the last of her coffee, then refilled her mug. Glancing over at Emeron's stark features she knew she would need all the caffeine she could find.

❖

Weiss Kyakh stood behind her helmswoman who, during the last twenty years of avoiding SC authorities, she had come to trust with her life. She heard shuffling from behind, combined with M'Ekar's annoying yet well-modulated voice. Already exasperated with the pompous man, she focused on the reward waiting after they kidnapped the woman M'Ekar would then deliver to the Onotharians. Weiss would be happy when they finally reached intergalactic space.

"Are we there yet?" M'Ekar asked as he entered the small bridge.

"The Keliera space station is only fifteen minutes away, Ambassador. We're right on schedule," she said, suspecting that her impatience with this petulant man shone through.

"And your sensors say that Jacelon's ship is there?"

"*Yes.*" She swiveled and glowered at M'Ekar. "Take a seat over at the navigation station. There's an extra chair."

"Thank you." The ambassador clearly chose to take her order as a polite offer.

"Keliera is hailing us," the ops crewman said.

"Audio." Weiss sat down in the captain's chair. "Keliera, civilian vessel *Viper* here, on a humanitarian mission, needing to dock to purchase supplies."

"*Viper*, Keliera gatekeeper here. What's your final destination?"

"Gatekeeper, we're on a medical mission to the minefields of Hordonia Prime, just outside the border." She smiled. Hordonia Prime was a desolate planet of outlaws who worked the mineral mines there and made a fortune that they burned just as fast, gambling and using drugs that were illegal within the SC. No one would question anyone on a medical mission to this hellhole, merely pity them.

"Good luck on that one," the gatekeeper said predictably. "Sending coordinates for automatic docking at port 43. Welcome to the Keliera Station. Gatekeeper out."

"Receiving coordinates, Captain," the helmswoman said. "Initiating approach."

"Excellent." Weiss turned to M'Ekar. "So far, so good."

"So far." He did not seem impressed.

The ops crewman punched in commands. "Captain, the luxury cruiser is docked two levels directly above us. It won't take long to hack into the gatekeepers' roster."

"Good. Report to me when you succeed. In the meantime, Ambassador, make yourself invisible. Your young fellow as well. No one seems to have noticed your escape yet, but obviously some people aboard this station know you personally, if I understand the situation correctly."

"You do." M'Ekar spoke through clenched lips.

"You'll soon have whatever revenge you're after." *And I'll get the money I need.*

"I'm in, Captain," the ops crewman said triumphantly. "They sure don't have many safeguards in place."

Weiss grinned. "But we're not going to tell them."

"The luxury cruiser is due to leave in ten hours."

"That doesn't give us very much time." Weiss opened her communicator. "Ms. White. Time to move."

"Can hardly wait, Captain," a female voice purred. Gilda White, wanted for crimes on sixteen different homeworlds, was Weiss's head of security. The tiny blonde, with hair color to match her name, made others want to protect her, especially men. It didn't take them long to realize she was as lethal as she seemed innocent.

"See you at the airlock."

❖

"Did you talk to Rae and Kellen today?" Chief Diplomat Dahlia Jacelon asked Armeo O'Saral M'Aido, the boy who had become her grandson after her daughter married his guardian. At age thirteen, the young Gantharian/Onotharian hybrid possessed a natural maturity that Dahlia could relate to. Sometimes their easy relationship made her feel guilty that she had never been able to experience this type of closeness with her daughter Rae when she was a girl.

"Yes," Armeo said, bubbling with enthusiasm. "They said they can't wait to see me. And Granddad too. He said he had a job for me when I get to Corma. They all miss me."

"Of course they do. It's been two months, child." Dahlia refrained from ruffling Armeo's hair. Having traveled through space on a luxury cruiser for weeks, they were now strolling down the main commerce street at the Keliera station, and Dahlia knew that even if Armeo didn't mind a quick hug in public, there were limits to how grandmother-silly she was allowed to be. "And you've been a very pleasant traveling companion." Dahlia turned her head and smiled at the young woman who walked behind them. "You too, Ayahliss. You've been a great help."

Ayahliss blushed faintly at the praise, and Dahlia stopped and put an arm around her. She was aware of the young Gantharian woman's idolization of Kellen and herself. Ayahliss was barely recognizable as the angry twenty-four-year-old woman who had come to stay with the Jacelons on Earth five months ago. Proper health care, nutritious food, and the comfort of a beautiful home had transformed Ayahliss. To look at her now, wearing red slacks and tunic, with her short black hair boasting a healthy shine, it was difficult to believe she had been one of the Gantharian resistance's most lethal members.

"I feel like I've known you much longer than I actually have," Dahlia said.

"If I had gone to the refugee camps with the rest of the resistance fighters, my life would have been totally different. I owe Kellen everything for taking me to stay with her family."

"Ayahliss, she sees something in you, most likely something of herself. She knows what it's like to be orphaned at a young age. That's why you're here and not on Revos Prime."

"But Rae doesn't perceive me that way." Ayahliss sighed.

"Rae will, once she understands how far you've come and how hard you're trying." Dahlia knew Rae was wary of having a volatile young woman in Armeo's presence, though she disagreed with her daughter. She had seen firsthand how Ayahliss had come to adore the young prince with every beat of her heart.

"I doubt it," Ayahliss spat. "She won't be impressed just because I've learned to use the proper fork."

Dahlia knew Ayahliss hid her worry behind her sarcasm, a trait she and Rae had in common. "Rae and I aren't always on the best of terms, and that has often been my fault." Dahlia kept her eyes on Armeo, who was a few steps ahead of them, looking in the windows. Four security officers were nearby, but she never lowered her guard when it came to this child. "Rae was so different from me, and so like her father, but both my husband and I still managed not to know her, or the woman she became. Trust me. Rae won't make the same mistake. To begin with, she may try only for Kellen's sake, but eventually she'll see what an amazing young woman you are."

"Really?" Ayahliss asked quietly, and Dahlia knew that anyone seeing her like this would assume that she was a beautiful, bashful woman out shopping with her grandmother. Dahlia chuckled at the thought. Ayahliss was as lethal as Kellen was, and ten times more unpredictable. Having grown up as a street child, and later highly educated by monks who possessed unusual gifts, she was a raw diamond, with hard corners and jagged edges, in the process of being polished.

"Really. I don't see any reason—"

"Armeo, watch out." Ayahliss threw herself forward, launching her thin, wiry body against a tall man who was about to corner Armeo. Her heel landed in the man's midsection, sending him staggering backward into a flower arrangement. The pots fell to the floor and broke into several pieces, dirt raining over all of them.

Plasma-pulse fire blazed repeatedly through the air, hitting two security officers. They fell to the floor, blood gushing out of their chests.

"Armeo." Dahlia screamed and leapt forward as well, reaching for him. At the same time, hard hands pulled her back, away from Armeo and Ayahliss.

"Not so fast, Jacelon," a female voice rasped in her ear. Something hard pressed into her ribs as the tall woman restrained her. "If you don't calm down, this plasma-pulse will make a big hole in you, and the pulse would go straight through and could hit the prince. We can't have that." More people moved in on both sides of Dahlia and she tried to glimpse them as she struggled to free herself. Two burly looking men and a diminutive woman stood with weapons raised, aiming at Armeo, Ayahliss, and the guards.

The woman pulled Dahlia back and halfway through a door in the station's bulkhead. Dahlia fought with all her strength, but she wasn't a young woman anymore, and the plasma-pulse weapon was shoved so hard against her back, she feared it had cracked a rib.

"Grandma. No!"

To Dahlia's horror, Armeo was running toward them, the security officers barely able to hold on to his shirt. More plasma-pulse fire singed the air to Dahlia's left as the small woman covered her capturer's retreat.

"Armeo. No," Dahlia croaked. "Stay away, son."

"But, *please*, Grandma, they're hurting you." The boy struggled furiously to free himself from the protecting arms of his guards. "Leave her alone. Let her go. I command you to let her *go*."

A whirlwind of something red approached, which Dahlia barely recognized as Ayahliss in her red outfit. Much taller than the stranger, Ayahliss emitted a high-pitched battle call and sent the woman sprawling into the bulkhead. Dahlia stumbled backward as the woman holding her hauled her down the metal stairs. The bodyguards rushed forward and grabbed Ayahliss, tugging her away from the woman she'd floored.

The last thing Dahlia saw before the door closed was Ayahliss breaking free from one of the remaining bodyguards and lunging toward them.

CHAPTER FIVE

Admiral Rae Jacelon looked up from her computer as three people rushed into her office, located within the SC military base on Corma. One of them was her wife, Kellen O'Dal, accompanied by Rae's father, Admiral Ewan Jacelon, and his aide de camp.

"Did I forget dinner again?" Rae asked, and looked first at Kellen and then at her father. Kellen seemed guarded, which was normal, but her father was pale and his features stern. Rae knew the expression. "What's happened?" She wondered if the Gantharian-Onotharian conflict had suddenly escalated.

"We just got word from SC headquarters on Earth, Rae," Ewan said. "It's your mother. She's been kidnapped."

"What?" Rae blurted after a moment's shocked silence and sprang from her chair. "How the *hell* did that happen?"

"We're not sure, though another piece of intel might explain it," Ewan continued. "M'Ekar has escaped. The timeline fits."

Rae remained standing for a few seconds before her knees gave way. She sat down with a thud. "Oh, damn it." She dug her fingertips into her computer console so hard they must have left permanent indentations.

"He probably bribed one or more of his guards to help him."

"He has no assets to use as bribes," Kellen said. "According to intel, the Onotharian leaders confiscated his entire estate when the SC sentenced him."

"He could have used something other than monetary offerings to persuade someone," Ewan said. "Promises of power, glorious careers, for instance."

"Where is Mother? What about Armeo and Ayahliss? Do we have

a clue? Surely the implanted chip must have rendered M'Ekar harmless by now."

"We think he found a way to disarm the chip. The Keliera space station confirmed our intel from headquarters. Keliera is operating at complete lockdown." Ewan sighed.

"What about Armeo?" Kellen's voice vibrated with an underlying dark tone.

Ewan seemed at a loss for words and his aide de camp took over. "The prince is safe, ma'am. The young woman traveling with Diplomat Jacelon was hit by plasma-pulse fire, but managed to keep the prince from being abducted as well."

"How badly?" Kellen snapped, and held on to the backrest of the visitors' chair she stood behind, her knuckles slowly blanching with the tension.

"Not life-threatening. Unfortunately, two of Diplomat Jacelon and the prince's security personnel were killed during the ambush. That's as much as we know, currently."

"We have to go there." Kellen looked taut and barely contained. Rae knew she must act or her wife might hijack the closest shuttle.

Ewan cleared his throat. "I've already ordered the Keliera station to allow the luxury cruiser they were traveling on to continue toward Corma. We'll have more ships rendezvous with them, to make certain they're travelling with the safest vessel possible. We'll know more when they arrive."

"For stars and skies," Rae muttered. "Damn it, Father, weren't there any indications? What about the security detail? They were traveling with an entire entourage, and their whereabouts were on a need-to-know basis."

"I'll keep in touch with SC headquarters and also inform our Cormanian hosts. The council is concerned, of course. If M'Ekar has your mother…" Ewan glanced at Rae, his lips thin and pale. "You know as well as I do why this is potentially disastrous, not only for our family."

"Yes, Father." Rae understood what he meant, but she could think of nothing but the safety of her mother. They had just begun to communicate, after years of strained, formal attitudes between them.

"I want to take a shuttle and rendezvous with Armeo and Ayahliss." Kellen stood stiffly next to Ewan, her ice blue gaze alert and not revealing the turmoil Rae knew she was experiencing. As Protector of the Realm, Kellen was the last member of the Gantharian royal family's guardians. Kellen never let Armeo out of her sight, unless her duty as a lieutenant in the SC military kept her from him.

Ewan took a deep breath and visibly controlled his own worry. "I'm not about to let you go off alone in a shuttle when M'Ekar and his cronies could be anywhere." His voice softened. "We should prepare for the children's arrival. Their ETA is tomorrow morning."

"I can't sit idly by when Armeo might be in danger and Ayahliss is injured." Kellen stormed by both admirals, forcing the aide de camp to flatten himself against the wall.

Ewan put his hand up. "Let's find out what's going on first. As soon as we know more, we can take appropriate action."

"You don't understand," Kellen hissed. "This is about *Armeo*."

"But I do understand." Ewan didn't avert his gaze. "This is also about my wife."

Ironclad wills clashed as Kellen's crystalline blue eyes met Ewan's dark gray ones.

"Kellen. Father." Rae rose and circled the desk. "We're wasting time. We can use the new long-range scanners to perform initial searches for traces of any vessel leaving the Keliera space station moments after the kidnapping. If it *is* M'Ekar, I bet he's traveling with a civilian ship, and we might recognize its signature."

Rae fought to think clearly, to remain as by-the-book as she would have been if this were an incident regarding a stranger. *Incident.* Rae wiped her palms against her uniform-clad legs. The word suggested something minor, but her *mother* was missing. If Dahlia was in the hands of the man who had everything to gain—and nothing remotely important to lose—by abducting her… Rae cleared her throat to loosen the forming lump. "Kellen, please, darling, listen to me. I promise, as soon as we know what we're dealing with here, we'll go get Armeo and Ayahliss."

Kellen drew long even breaths, a technique Rae recognized. Her wife's volatile nature didn't surface often, but now, when the child she regarded as her son might be in danger, the beast tore at its tethers. "Very well, Rae. I will do as you suggest. For now."

"For now." Rae returned her attention to her father. Ewan's dark eyes met hers, and his piercing stare reminded her that, under certain circumstances, he could be as deadly as Kellen. Kidnapping his wife of almost fifty years was one of those situations. "Sir, Kellen and I should join you in the mission room to monitor the progress."

"I agree. You know M'Ekar better than anybody, except perhaps Dahlia, and you might be able to anticipate his actions."

Rae dragged a hand through her hair. "His motives aren't hard to guess. He wants to combine business with pleasure, in a manner of speaking. Mother is privy to classified SC information because of her level-one security clearance. He plans to make her talk."

"What good would that do him?" Kellen asked, sounding calmer.

"He could use her information in many different ways," Rae said. "He'll most likely try to regain the trust of the Onotharians and thus get his old life back."

"There's only one glitch in such a plan," Ewan added.

"Mother would never talk. Ever." Rae was as sure of that as she was of her love for Kellen.

"You're right." Ewan cleared his voice, his lips pale and tight. "She wouldn't."

Rae fought to remain calm as horrific images of her mother remaining stoic and silent under one torture session after another flickered through her mind. Any method was possible. Physical assault, brain scans, truth serums, other mind-altering drugs, unscrupulous telepaths. Or all of them.

"So that leaves us only one option," Kellen said gravely. "We have to get her back. Quickly."

Heading for the door, Rae turned to look at Kellen, who seemed every bit as determined to pursue M'Ekar as Rae herself was. "You'd better clear the way with headquarters fast, Father," she said abruptly. "Because no matter what, Kellen and I are going."

The forest had become denser after Emeron and her team parked the hovercraft and stepped off the trail to escort Dwyn farther. They all carried heavy back-strap security carriers with enough supplies to spend two nights without the habitats.

Emeron shoved vines out of her face, annoyed that she couldn't simply use her sidearm and cut them with a well-aimed plasma-pulse ray. She cursed the Thousand Year Pact for prohibiting such methods.

Instead, she had to make sure she didn't harm any single plant or animal within the Disi-Disi forest. The natives believed the trees had souls, as well as other superstitious garbage. Emeron briefly remembered Briijn—large, deeply set brown eyes in a furrowed, wise face—and then she slammed an inner door shut around the twitch of familiar pain. "Superstitious garbage," she repeated to herself.

"Excuse me," a clear voice said, as Dwyn closed the distance and stopped next to her.

"Nothing. Is this spot good enough for you?" Emeron pointed at the small clearing ahead of them.

"Perfect." Dwyn surveyed the area. "We can make camp over there and I can use this section for samples. I found traces over an hour ago that suggest someone has tried to cover their tracks around here."

"Really?" Emeron raised an eyebrow. "Are you sure? The undergrowth is as dense here as everywhere else." It was their fifth day in the forest, which to her looked undisturbed.

"It takes a trained eye, but I've documented the signs thoroughly. And I wouldn't be surprised if we discover even more obvious ones here."

"I thought you were looking for actual structures that someone built unlawfully. So far I haven't seen as much as a straw bent out of shape."

Dwyn shrugged. "You don't know what to look for, but that's all right. I do."

Emeron refused to huff out loud, but she was definitely not used to anyone talking to her like this. Dwyn was self-assured in a way that few people were around her. Though Dwyn appeared to be physically frail and ethereal, she was surprisingly stubborn and cocky when it came to her job.

"Let me show you." Dwyn knelt just inside the clearing and motioned for Emeron to join her. Carefully she parted the knee-high, silky grass. "Here. Can you see the color of the soil here?"

"Brown." Emeron looked indifferently at the dirt.

"Look closer."

She felt silly, but couldn't very well refuse. She slid nearer to Dwyn. Something mild and fruity filled her senses, and at first she thought it was the vegetation, perhaps some flower, but soon realized the scent came from Dwyn. Perplexed at herself, she inhaled stealthily.

"Well?" Dwyn prodded.

"Eh…brown, with dark streaks?"

"Exactly. Good." Dwyn smiled brightly. "This means that soil, which should be dark brown, is now infused with a foreign substance. If we dig very carefully…" Dwyn produced a small spoon-like object. "Aha." She held up a piece of the dirt and, to Emeron's surprise, the black streaks were dark orange inside.

"Even I know that orange-colored dirt isn't normal."

"No, it's not." Dwyn emptied the spoon into a small canister and tucked both items back into one of her many pockets. She looked up as they rose, her silver-gray eyes sparkling, most likely from the joy of being correct. "Visible orange, in this case, means that the underground constructions have gone far. Way too far."

"Underground? Weren't you looking for traces of deforestation? I mean, above ground." Emeron had lost track of where Dwyn's thoughts were taking her.

"In order to build the vast structures that become a tiered city, as in Corma's two largest metropolitan areas, you need a foundation that stretches farther down than the ancient bedrock. And the width of the underground foundation must equal the height of the central part of the structure."

"Are you saying that developers are defying Cormanian laws and working underneath us to create a foundation for a new tiered city?" Emeron stared at Dwyn, uncertain what to think. Surely she was merely making an educated guess.

"That's exactly what I'm saying."

"And how would they achieve that?" Emeron brushed off her hands on her pants. "You couldn't hide a tiered city right in the Disi-Disi forest."

"Oh, so you're under the impression that someone trying to break Cormanian law is doing this?" Dwyn wrinkled her nose, and her expression showed clearly her disdain and cynicism. "The Cormanian government is actually our prime suspect. They could easily tunnel into the forest from outside, working in secret."

"That's ridiculous. Why would the Cormanian government give you and your organization permission to investigate, if they were the guilty party?" Emeron was angry now.

"Two reasons. Some people among your rulers possibly aren't happy with these covert incursions of the Thousand Year Pact. Also, the Cormanian government initially denied my organization the right to investigate. Eventually, they had to concede, much to their annoyance, when the chairman of the SC Council intervened." Dwyn shrugged. "Proves very handy to have connections in high places."

Flabbergasted and annoyed at Dwyn's deductions, which seemed maddeningly plausible, Emeron thought of something acerbic to say. "I am here to uphold the law and to keep you safe. I personally think you are in more danger of being sued for spreading false allegations than anything else, but—"

The air filled with a bright green light and the unmistakable scent of plasma-pulse fire. The air crackled, and Emeron reacted instantly. "Down!" She threw herself on top of Dwyn, knocking her sideways to the ground. "Keep your head low." She pulled her sidearm and pressed the sensor, setting it to kill. "Who the hell is firing on us?"

She glanced around and spotted something moving to their left. Two round objects hurled through the sky, which she recognized as floater bots. Law-Enforcement Command used them for surveillance. The first one twirled and emitted a plasma-pulse beam continuously, hitting tree trunks and shrubbery. Smoke billowed from the scorched plants. She yanked her communicator from her shoulder pad to her lips.

"D'Artansis to Mogghy. We're under attack. Where are you?"

"Mogghy here. We're five minutes behind you."

"So far no individuals, only floater bots."

"We see a few here too. They haven't engaged us in combat."

"They might. Use caution." Emeron tucked Dwyn under her arm, shielding her as she pulled her beneath a massive tree as the bots circled the clearing. She was infuriated that she hadn't seen this attack coming.

"What's going on?" Dwyn gasped, peering through the dense branches.

"Floater bots. Someone's monitoring us."

"I'd say they're doing more than that. Watch out." Dwyn tugged Emeron toward her as one of the metal orbs hovered closer, its luminescent green rays scorching everything in its path.

"Shh." Emeron allowed herself to be pulled back. "Their audio sensors might pick up our location."

"Are they operating automatically, or are they remote controlled?" Dwyn whispered.

"You tell me. From the way they're moving, I'd say they're fully automatic." The bots swept back and forth throughout the clearing, farther and farther from where they hid. Emeron let a few seconds pass after the bots were out of sight, then took a careful step out from under the tree.

Suddenly a movement to her left flickered at the outer perimeter of her field of vision. Emeron grabbed her plasma-pulse laser weapon and took aim, but too late. A bright, green ray pierced the air, and she heard, more than felt, it singe her left arm. Next, something incredibly forceful hit her lower abdomen. She landed on her back on the ground. The force of the impact created a vacuum in her lungs and she struggled to gasp for air.

"*Geoschad jam, Padmas. Geoschad, Padmas Briijn.*" *I am sorry, Grandmother. Sorry, Grandmother Briijn.*

The words tumbled over her stiff lips like a prayer before she attempted to raise her weapon again. When her arm failed a second time, she knew she wouldn't make it. Her life-journey would end in this place, forsaken by all deities.

CHAPTER SIX

Emeron." Dwyn watched in horror as the blast threw Emeron halfway across the clearing. As she darted toward Emeron's dropped weapon and grabbed it with sweaty hands, she dared to glance at the motionless body in the grass. Breathing. Good.

A humming, screeching sound behind her made her swivel and raise the plasma-pulse weapon. Her fingers slipped on the controls. Frantically, she managed to aim the weapon toward the closest bot—there were four—and shoot. The plasma-pulse reverberated through the heavy firearm and pierced the air with a distinct hum. She kept her trembling fingers on the firing controls as she clutched the weapon hard to keep it level.

Dwyn squinted at the closest bot. It approached her on a steady trajectory and at first she thought she'd missed. Her heart beat furiously and sweat poured into her eyes, but she refused to blink it away, scared to let the machine out of her sight for a nanosecond. Suddenly it veered to the left and spun into a sapling. Smoke billowed from its openings and loose components cascaded in a circle around it.

The next bot fired at her and Dwyn ducked, then lost her balance and fell to her knees next to Emeron. She risked another glance at the still body. Barely noticeable movements betrayed life in Emeron.

"Hey, Emeron, can you hear me?" Dwyn yelled, hoping Emeron was coming to. She fired at the second bot repeatedly and watched it veer off and out of sight. It didn't reappear, and she hoped she'd taken it out.

"I could use some help here," Dwyn shouted, but Emeron didn't respond. Her heart raced even faster. Was Emeron seriously or, worse, terminally injured?

She blazed repeatedly at the bots, hitting two more and transforming them into a cloud of smoke. A whining sound made her look up to her left. A fifth bot approached much faster than the others, and she knew, as she moved, that she couldn't shoot quickly enough at this much-larger one. Red beams crackled repeatedly around her, and she acted without thinking. She threw herself sideways on top of Emeron and aimed above them, but missed.

A roar near the smoking bots startled her and apparently the large one as well, which turned and directed its green scanning rays against this new threat. Rumbling loudly, Mogghy ran into the clearing, hoisting a shoulder-held plasma-pulse field weapon. "Over here, you piece of shit." He fired and the impact tossed the large bot backward. It tumbled to the ground and rolled into thick shrubbery, where it exploded in a gush of sparks and metal parts.

"Mogghy. Emeron's hurt." Dwyn crawled off the bleeding woman beneath her and looked in horror at the wounds in her lower abdomen and left arm.

"Let me see. We have to get out of here. Whoever sent those damn bots has more up their sleeve." Mogghy kneeled next to Emeron and pulled out a medical scanner. Running it along her, he sighed deeply. "Thank the stars. The pulse wasn't deep enough to do any real damage. No head trauma either."

"But she's unconscious."

Emeron's husky voice startled them both. "Not anymore. You're sitting on my hand, Dwyn."

She shifted hurriedly. "Sorry. How are you feeling?" She bent over Emeron and met her eyes. Emeron looked a little dazed, but she managed to sound as sarcastic as usual, which was probably a reassuring sign.

"Sore. Mogghy. Make me well." Emeron grimaced and shifted on the ground. "And let me sit up...oh." She fumbled to get an elbow underneath herself, but only managed to sway to the side and land with her head on Dwyn's lap.

Dwyn instinctively wrapped her arms loosely around Emeron. "Hold on to me while he treats you. It won't take long."

"Get on with it then, Mogghy," Emeron muttered, turning her head toward Dwyn's stomach. "And make it quick."

"Yes, ma'am. Good to see you so chipper." Mogghy winked at Dwyn as he pulled out another medical instrument. "You may feel a slight tingle. Tell me if it starts burning or hurting."

"All right, all right. I know how it feels to have a wound closed. Just do it. Hurry."

Mogghy sighed and ran the instrument over the wounded area in Emeron's abdomen. "Have you seen this procedure before?" he asked Dwyn. "It's the latest SC-issued derma fuser."

"I've seen older versions of a derma fuser, but nothing like this. Can you show me how it's done? Next time, you may not be around."

"What do you mean, next time?" Emeron said. "It's not like I have a habit of getting injured—"

"Thou shall not speak the untruth." Mogghy moved the instrument in small circles, about one centimeter above the skin. "You set the fuser alignment according to the size of the wound," he told Dwyn. "The one on the left arm is a five. The one on her abdomen is a twelve. If the wound is deep, rather than wide, like here, you set this control to a slightly higher value. This sterilizes the wound at the same time as you repair it, lessening the risk of infection." Mogghy closed the wound next to Emeron's bellybutton, then handed the derma fuser to her. "Here. You do the one on the arm."

"What? Oh, stars, I'll end up with a scar the size of the Maireesian fields." Emeron shut her eyes.

"Never mind the commander." Mogghy grinned. "She always gets cranky when things like this happen."

"Mogghy..." Emeron spoke quietly. "Watch it."

Mogghy apparently knew when it was time to shut up.

Dwyn moved the instrument in the same pattern she had observed Mogghy make. Slowly, the wound on Emeron's arm healed.

"Good, you're a natural. It will be red at first, which is normal. Sorry, Commander. No scar to write home about." Mogghy tucked the derma fuser away. "Let's get out of here before they send new bots after us."

"No. We're not leaving." Emeron sat up and then stood, looking pale but in full control of herself. "That's what the people behind the bots expect us to do. Instead, we're going to build old-fashioned natural shelters to camouflage us. If we line the shelters with the same type of antisensor sheets we use to cover our vehicles, we can make them practically impenetrable for bot sensors. We'll be invisible. Find trees no more than two years old, and cut them down. Don't use your sidearms. They pollute too much. Use the axes in your survival kits."

"What about the rules?" Dwyn asked. "We're not supposed to—"

"Cut down trees for our own benefit," Emeron snapped. "We're saving our lives. That means more than any stuffy old rule."

"A rule that I'm sent here to protect."

"The rules were meant to keep people from ruining this forest for arbitrary reasons, or for greed. No one expects us to sacrifice our safety for a few trees."

Dwyn caught the long tresses of her hair that had escaped the metal-mesh chignon and tucked them back in. "Okay. Let's get on with it then. I have to protect my samples."

"Now there's an argument I should've thought of."

Emeron winked, which startled Dwyn into action. She hadn't expected to see Emeron's humorous side and was uncertain why such a nice trait in the stern officer would send tingles through her.

"Don't worry, Dwyn," Mogghy said, and smiled broadly. "Oches and I will perform the killing of the trees. You won't have to sacrifice the little plants yourself."

Normally, such a ribbing would have sent Dwyn into a scathing temper tantrum, but Mogghy's smile was charming, and she suspected she had somehow earned his respect. *Most likely for saving his commanding officer.* "All right. I'll mark out the best places to build the shelters." She tried to sound casual. "I learned this the hard way in the protected rainforest on Earth."

"Fine." Emeron glanced at her chronometer. "We have less than two hours before sundown, and something tells me there might be backup bots not far from here. We better move." She turned as if to start walking back to the hovercraft. "Hey, Mogghy, nice." She motioned toward the bots at the other end of the clearing.

"Those? That wasn't me. Thank Dwyn."

Emeron seemed speechless, then slowly bobbed her head. "I'm impressed. You saved us."

"Not really. I mean, not alone. Mogghy is being humble." Dwyn's cheeks warmed in the most annoying way. She fiddled with her chignon again, securing it firmer around her hair. "I'll start clearing some ground over there. There are nine of us, so five shelters, right?"

"No, just four. You'll have to bunk with me. And until I can keep a personal eye on you again, take this. You obviously know your way around a weapon. I don't want you to be without one of your own from now on." She handed Dwyn a sidearm, smaller than the one she had fired earlier. "It's my spare."

"Oh. Thank you." Dwyn closed her fingers around the weapon. Emeron was right. She did feel safer, but it wasn't just because of the plasma-pulse weapon. "I'll take care of it."

"Good." Emeron's black eyes drilled into her again. "Let's get to work."

❖

Kellen stood by the huge view screen, her arms folded over her chest. Behind her, the mission room at the SC headquarters bustled with activity. She let the background noise filter through her as she focused on the part of space scanned by long-range sensors. Stars glimmered inside the sensor grid, and at any other time, the beauty of outer space would not have been wasted on her. Now, when all she could think about was Armeo and his safety, she wanted to leap right through those sensors and be by his side.

And then there was Ayahliss, the young woman she and Rae had rescued from an Onotharian asteroid prison. Ayahliss was a remarkable, if a bit unruly and volatile, woman whom Kellen had grown very fond of. She wasn't sure if her feelings were maternal or sisterly, knowing that Ayahliss had been half-trained in the art of gan'thet fighting, a skill and honor bestowed only upon individuals born to hold the title of Protector of the Realm. For a young, orphaned woman to possess such knowledge surprised but also worried her. It was dangerous to merely know the martial-art technique. If a person were not equally trained in restraint and patience, she could become too dangerous, for the art of gan'thet was as deadly as it was beautiful to watch.

Kellen had persuaded Rae that they should bring Ayahliss to live with them, and Armeo adored her immediately. Worried, initially, Kellen had watched a special friendship unfold, and before long, she knew that Ayahliss loved the young prince. She made sure he was safe and taught him the dirtier hand-to-hand combat of street fighting. As much as this had appalled Kellen, it had amused, and even impressed, Rae. "You never know when he might need these less 'classical' means of self-defense," Rae had said, and kissed Kellen.

"Less classical? She teaches him to bite his opponent if all else fails."

"That's what I'd do—if all else failed." Rae had nudged her wife toward the bed. "And thinking of that, Armeo will be occupied for the next hour or so. Could I interest you in some recreation of our own?"

Brought back to present time, Kellen blinked at the lights of the Cormanian capital that spread as far as she could see outside the window. She swallowed hard at the bright memory from not so long ago and willed her thoughts to remain in the present. What if they never had the opportunity for some lighthearted banter in the midst of their family again? What if that scum M'Ekar killed Rae's mother?

"What's going on inside that brilliant mind of yours?" Rae's voice interrupted Kellen's dark thoughts. "I know that look by now."

"I'm trying to convince myself that long-range scanners will pick up their ship's signature any second. But it will be hours before they reach this point." Kellen pointed at the star-grid on the screen. "It seems so long. Too long." Her throat hurt as she spoke.

"Darling." Rae spoke mutedly. "I know."

Kellen wished they had been somewhere more private so she could have hugged Rae. Whenever she trembled like this, like a propulsion system ready to hurl a ship into space, it usually helped if Rae held her tight. "It kills me to do *nothing*."

"I know that too. But I have good news, all things considered. Armeo's vessel has passed the outer marker. No use in standing here, though. They rendezvoused with a caravan of ships from the Guild Nation. They all have cloaking capability."

Air gushed from Kellen's lungs. "He's safe."

"Yes. For now he's safe, and so are Ayahliss and their escort. ETA is eighteen hours. Why don't you go get some sleep? You'll need your strength once they arrive."

"And you?"

"I have to stay here. Father is trying to remain professional and objective, but he… I never thought I'd say that my father looked frail."

"Dahlia is a strong, resourceful woman," Kellen said. "She will prevail."

Rae paled a few shades. "I hope so. And I fear her strength too."

"You're afraid she will be tortured because she won't fold." Kellen knew firsthand how ruthless M'Ekar was. If the people who had sprung him from captivity were as callous as he was, Dahlia Jacelon would be in deep trouble.

"We'll find her before that happens." Rae squeezed Kellen's hand stealthily. "For now, they're too busy running from the SC forces to have time to interrogate her."

"Then we have to keep pressuring them, pursuing them."

Rae nodded, her eyes slate gray. "I won't ever stop."

CHAPTER SEVEN

The four small shelters beyond the perimeter of the clearing were almost invisible, unless you knew where to look. Emeron nodded approvingly to herself as she inspected her unit's hard work. They had braided large *geshto* leaves into the sides and the sloping roofs, together with branches and vines from different trees.

Emeron glanced at Dwyn, who had been working as hard as any of her team, and knew it hadn't been easy for her to witness Mogghy and Oches returning with the saplings. Dwyn hadn't said a word about it, but handled the narrow logs with apparent reverence.

To Emeron's surprise, she wasn't as annoyed as she had expected to be. Instead, she had stood speechless for a moment when even Ensign Noor followed Dwyn's example as they tied the logs together into walls and roofs. Noor was otherwise the most blasé and arrogant of her team, and to watch the cocky young woman carry dead wood as if it were a living thing was miraculous.

Dwyn stood next to the shelter they would share. Removing her carrier, she set it gently inside, obviously mindful of her precious samples. Emeron thought her care was appropriate, since they were all out here risking their lives because of these samples and this woman.

"Time to contact headquarters, ma'am," Ensign Oches reminded her, and she nodded after she checked her chronometer. To be able to use a secure line, they needed to communicate with headquarters only at a certain time every day, on a specific channel, unless it was a matter of life and death.

"Set it up at the other side of the clearing."

Oches nodded and grabbed his carrier. He was responsible for the communication amplifier, a device required within the Disi-Disi forest since the Thousand Year Pact prohibited the installation of any amplifiers within the protected area.

"Emeron?" Dwyn suddenly appeared at her side. "When I looked for material to build the shelters with, I saw some signs of disturbed soil about a hundred meters due east of the clearing. Can I borrow Mogghy to help me gather more samples?"

She was pleased that Dwyn realized she shouldn't go alone. "Yes, but be quick about it. It'll be completely dark in an hour and we can't risk having any lights on. And if you notice anything remotely looking like a bot—"

"—we'll hide. And we'll take antisensor blankets. We had some spare ones left."

"Good." Emeron motioned to where Oches was waiting. "I have to place a call."

"All right. See you later." Dwyn hurried to her carrier.

Emeron walked over to Oches. "All set?"

"Yes, ma'am. Headquarters is online."

Emeron donned the earpiece and Oches left her to carry out the briefing. She told Captain Zeger about the bot attack, and he was immediately concerned about Dwyn's status.

"She's fine, sir. Actually, she knows her way around weapons and managed to take out a few bots after they injured me."

"You're telling me a civilian saved your ass, D'Artansis?" Zeger said incredulously. "You must be joking."

"Negative, sir." Emeron cringed at her commanding officer's reaction. "She's a good marksman. Some of those bots move quickly."

"And you've decided to tough it out and trick whoever sent them?"

"Yes. I looked at the downed ones for markings, but any identification tags were scraped off. They were obviously not official law-enforcements bots."

"What made you consider that possibility in the first place?" Zeger asked.

"Just trying to keep an open mind and figure out who has the most to gain by not letting Dwyn—Ms. Izontro—complete her investigation."

"Good point. Let's change the time for our daily communications to noon."

"Affirmative. Will call in tomorrow, sir. D'Artansis out." Emeron closed the connection. Captain Zeger had apparently been stunned to hear about the attack. Both of them had expected this assignment to be uneventful, but they had been wrong.

She walked back to the shelters, handing the communicator to Oches, who was opening a self-heating food pouch. "Can I get you anything, ma'am? I know this is emergency rations, but with some *trestos*, you wouldn't think so."

Emeron grimaced at the thought of pouring trestos, a hot, peppery spice that many Cormanians swore by, on the rations. She found the stuff vile. "No, thank you, Ensign. I'll settle for some dry-frozen soup." She poured water into a small canister, then pressed a sensor on it, which heated the soup instantly. Taking a few sips, she sat down on a large rock next to the shelter she would share with Dwyn.

Thinking about Dwyn made her frown and check her chronometer again. She and Mogghy had left forty minutes earlier, and though Emeron had no real cause for concern, not yet, it would be completely dark in twenty minutes. They hadn't spent a night this far into the forest before, and Dwyn probably had no idea how utterly black it became beneath the massive trees. Not even the moonlight filtered through, which helped make this clearing safe. Mogghy would know, she thought. He'd been in the forest before.

When only minutes remained until complete darkness and she saw no sign of them, she stood, impatient and worried. "Where the hell are you?" She tapped her communicator and hoped the missing two would be close enough to pick up the signal without the help of amplifiers.

"D'Artansis to Mogghy. Respond." Only faint static sounded from the communicator. "Mogghy, Dwyn. What's your status?" First, more silence, then a muted voice.

"Mogghy here. On our way, ma'am. ETA one minute."

"You're cutting it close." She wanted to yell at him to move faster, but he'd sounded unexpectedly out of breath. Were they running?

Suddenly she heard a bustling sound at the north end of the clearing. Two figures appeared, carrying something between them. Something heavy. The other team members joined her and they circled Mogghy and Dwyn.

"Look." When Emeron reached them, Dwyn gasped and pointed at the item after she let go of her end. "Now *that's* proof even you can't deny, Emeron."

"What is it?" The object was roughly 1.5 meters long and 0.4 meters in diameter.

"I think I know," Mogghy said, and placed his end on the ground. "It's a drill bit."

"What? This big, and this far into the forest?" Her jaw momentarily went slack. "A drill bit?"

"We better cover it up, ma'am," Oches said, and ran toward the shelters. He returned with an antisensor blanket. "Here we go." He spread it over the drill bit. "I suppose we can examine it more tomorrow."

"Good thinking. We still have a lot to do tonight. We can discuss the importance and potential implications then." She turned to Dwyn. "That was too close."

"It was important," Dwyn said. "I felt safe with Mogghy."

"That isn't the point. Not even Mogghy can see in the dark." She was annoyed and had just realized that soon they would share very cramped quarters. "The crew has erected a makeshift latrine behind the largest tree. Can you find your way, or do you need me to escort you?"

Dwyn drew a very audible breath. "I think I can find my way to the toilet."

"Good. Don't wander off. Ours is the shelter in the center."

"All right. See you there."

It was so dark now that she could barely make out Dwyn's contours as she disappeared toward the latrine. In the meantime, Emeron made one more round among her crew. She needed to use the facility as well, and then she would climb into a bedroll next to Dwyn Izontro.

❖

Dwyn ran a portable sanitizer over her upper body, fatigue making the small rod nearly slip in her hands. Kneeling on the bedroll, she wanted to eradicate the grime that had accumulated during the eventful day, and she tried to hurry, expecting Emeron to join her in the restricted shelter any minute. Stiff and aching, she put the rod down and pulled a retrospun linen shirt from her back-strap security carrier, shivering now in the cool night air.

A rustling sound behind her made her flinch and hold the shirt in front of her, suddenly shy, which was unusual for her. She had grown up on a spaceship inhabited by at least ten people at a time, all very casual about nakedness and what they considered natural. Only when she left for Iminestria to continue her studies had she found out the hard way that people in general weren't that open-minded.

Recalling how she'd walked through the dormitory with only a towel around her waist, and the stares and whispers that followed, still made her wince. The dormitory matron had even lectured her, the woman clearly appalled at Dwyn's "immoral display," as she put it. Matron insisted that she make a public apology, since the university had strict rules of conduct and an even stricter dress code. She would rather not dwell on this complete humiliation, but it still affected her. She now held the shirt in front of her and kept her back to Emeron.

"Oh, sorry. You all right?" Emeron's husky voice seemed an octave lower as she crawled onto her bedroll. "Thanks for arranging stuff in here." Emeron squinted at Dwyn. "You look tired. Long day, huh?"

"Yes." *How the hell am I going to get the shirt on without embarrassing her?*

"I'm pretty exhausted too," Emeron admitted, and tugged at the fastening of her uniform. The jacket was buckled with heavy metal clasps and, to Dwyn's surprise, it lost all cohesion when the clasps were undone and literally fell off Emeron's broad shoulders. Underneath, she wore a black, form-fitted, retrospun linen shirt that emphasized her upper body. She was muscular, yet lean, with long arms, and carried herself with lethal grace. *Utterly sexy.* Dwyn groaned at her undisciplined thought process and fiddled with her shirt.

"You sure you're all right?" Emeron focused her glance. "What's that on your back?"

She leaned in to look and Dwyn inhaled her scent—musk, something fruity, and a deep indistinguishable fragrance that she couldn't identify. "I don't know," she managed, and turned her head to try and see what Emeron was talking about.

"A large bruise. It even broke the skin. We need to take care of this, Dwyn." Emeron crawled toward the opening. "Don't go to bed just yet. I'll be right back."

Dwyn sighed. *Now what?* She pulled the shirt over her head, grimacing at the pain, and acknowledged for the first time that she must have injured herself when fighting the bots.

Emeron returned a moment later with a medical scanner and a derma fuser. "I borrowed these from Mogghy. He was already asleep. Oches and Noor have the first watch." She sat down next to Dwyn. "Why did you put your shirt on? Now I can't see your entire bruise."

"I was cold." It wasn't a lie, exactly.

"All right. Here." Emeron tugged at the thermo blanket and wrapped it around her. "I'll just pull the strap down like this." She slid the strap down Dwyn's shoulder, which effectively locked Dwyn's left arm against her side.

Emeron ran the medical scanner over the bruise. "Thank the stars. You don't have any deep tissue damage or fracture. I didn't think so, but you're so tiny, we have to take extra care of you. Today was a rough day on all of us, and even harder on you."

"Tiny?" Dwyn raised her voice and stared at Emeron. "I'm not tiny."

"Depends on who you compare yourself with. In the present company, you're tiny. Miniscule." Emeron seemed in an unusually good mood, teasing her like this, and Dwyn couldn't help but smile.

"What are you then? Humongous?"

"Exactly." Emeron's voice gave away that she was smiling. "You'll feel a warm tingle now. Ready?"

"No problem. This is hardly my first bruise, or my first derma fuser." Dwyn paused. "But it is my first ultra-modern derma-fuser experience."

"What kind of injuries did you experience before?" Emeron's free hand on her waist steadied Dwyn, and the warm touch sent shivers throughout her belly. She shifted nervously and tried to remember if she'd ever reacted like this to anyone.

"Let me see," Dwyn said slowly. "The last time I needed a derma fuser, and a bone knitter for that matter, I had fallen inside a volcano on Earth. I fractured three ribs, my left wrist, and had contusions on my head, back, and...well, bottom."

"Oh, stars. What the hell were you doing there? I mean, by the volcano?"

"Protesting along with other nonprofit organizations."

Emeron didn't answer at first, but administered the derma fuser precisely, as if she was preoccupied with something. "Protesting against what? And why?"

"Rare birds, pilgrim falcons, protected by the EDA, Environmental Department Authorities, have made this inactive volcanic area their home for over two hundred years. The SC Science & Development Center was conducting tests there and disturbing the hatching season. Their actions threatened an entire generation of falcons."

"You risked your life for a flock of birds?" Emeron looked incredulously at Dwyn. "You're joking, right?"

"I risked my life because the SC thought they could break the law and endanger an already near-extinct species," she spat, annoyed at how Emeron dismissed the importance of her work. "A flock of birds may not seem much to you, but a flock of birds today, and then they extend this approach to include a flock of people, or worse—"

"Are you suggesting that the SC would stoop to genocide?" Emeron raised her voice too, placing the derma fuser back in its casing. "Are you crazy?"

"No, I'm not. And if you read all aspects of SC history, back to before any of our people conquered space, you'll see that our worlds have committed countless atrocities."

"That was then. We live in enlightened times. Our council wouldn't sit idly by—"

She shook her head slowly, exasperated and sad at Emeron's attitude. She wasn't the only one who thought the SC Council could do no wrong. "Emeron, *that's* a very naïve and shortsighted statement. Are you really that gullible?" She withdrew from Emeron and scowled. "And here you have the audacity to act as if I'm a misguided child."

Closing the small bag with angry gestures, Emeron tossed it into a corner and backed away from her. "You're calling me naïve?" She sounded baffled and furious. "You go from planet to planet and cause trouble with your gang of do-gooders. You tie up an entire unit and keep us from doing our job."

"As in 'real work,' catching bad guys and being decorated with flashy medals," she hissed. She shivered, but refused to avert her eyes to try and find her sweater.

"If you didn't have people like my team and me to catch 'bad guys,' you'd be in deep trouble and so would a lot of other people," Emeron said slowly. She glowered at Dwyn. "Don't you dare dismiss what I do for a living."

"Why not? You dismissed me and the work I do before you even met me. Just listen to yourself."

Emeron stared at Dwyn, her eyes hard and her gold-speckled black irises burning like hot coals, with an amber glow simmering just beneath the surface. She looked ready to slice Dwyn into thin shreds, but then she faltered and refocused her dark eyes. "You're shivering."

She blinked. The change of mood was dizzying. "It's cold." Unable to stop trembling, she rubbed her arms.

"Hold still," Emeron said, feeling her forehead. "You look pale." She let go of Dwyn and reached for the medical scanner, then ran it along the back of her head and down her spine. "You have something on your lungs. Weird. Looks like damaged tissue. How the hell did that happen?"

"The smoke from the bots I blasted was pretty thick."

"You inhaled it?" Emeron stopped scanning. "And didn't tell me?"

"When should I have done that? We've been busy all day." She pivoted where she sat and nudged the scanner in Emeron's hand away from her. "Surely you noticed that I haven't sat down until now?"

"Have you eaten?"

"Yeah. One ration bar."

"Don't bite my head off." Emeron pulled a small chromed canister out of the med-kit bag. "Here." She tapped a setting into it. "Inhale."

Dwyn raised her eyebrows, but inhaled the medication. It stung a bit, and she coughed, long deep coughs that shook her body. "Happy?" she managed after finally catching her breath.

"For now. You have to inhale more tomorrow. We don't know what substances the burning components consisted of. My scanner isn't that sophisticated."

Dwyn's chest constricted at the thought of permanent lung damage. "But it doesn't even hurt to breathe," she said slowly.

"That's a good sign. I'm sure you'll be fine, but we better take precautions, just in case."

"All right. Just in case." She turned to crawl into her bedroll but felt a strong hand on her arm. She looked questioningly at Emeron.

"Tell me if you're feeling worse." It wasn't a request.

"I'm sure it—"

"Promise me."

Dwyn suddenly lost her breath, and it had nothing to do with her lung damage. Emeron was hovering over her, half a head taller than her as they sat there. "I promise," she said, willing her voice to sound steady.

CHAPTER EIGHT

Emeron watched Dwyn climb into the bedroll. She was still pale, but a quick scan had proved the medication effective. Not a person to suffer from false pride, Emeron was truly grateful that Dwyn had saved her life during their encounter with the bots. Still, she experienced a strange feeling resembling remorse that Dwyn had been physically harmed. Dwyn had more guts than she'd given her credit for. Petite, almost ethereal, she evoked a strange feeling of protectiveness, which Emeron immediately considered part of the job. An irritating inner voice insisted it was much more than that.

"Emeron? You all right?" Dwyn asked quietly.

"I'm fine. Time to get some sleep." She followed Dwyn's example and slid between the thermo-blankets. Their bedrolls lay next to one another, and when she turned on her side she was close enough to Dwyn to feel her breath against her face.

"I'm tired, but I'm not sure I can sleep," Dwyn murmured. "I can't stop wondering who the hell sent those bots after us. Me."

"We're one step ahead of them right now. You don't have to worry. My unit is prepared. They won't catch us off guard again." Emeron injected calm assertiveness in her voice.

"I don't doubt your team, Emeron." Dwyn rose on her elbow. "I simply don't want any of you hurt because of me. Again." Her voice trembled faintly.

Emeron could hardly breathe. Somehow, the air inside the shelter was thick and refused to fill her lungs. "Part of the job," she said, her voice hoarse.

"I guess. But that doesn't make it any easier for me." Dwyn lay down. "My job is to help preserve our planets and ultimately help make them as habitable as possible. I simply can't see life go to waste."

"You're passionate about what you do, but so am I. Don't worry about—"

"But I do." Dwyn rose on her elbow again and touched Emeron's arm with her free hand. "How could I not, since all I can think of is you bleeding to death on the ground only hours ago." Dwyn's breath was ragged as fury and something unreadable shone from her eyes.

Dwyn's touch burned like fire against Emeron's skin. Gasping, she stared down at her hand, as if trying to will it away with the blaze of her glance. "Dwyn," she said warningly.

"Oh." Dwyn snatched it back.

She looked at Dwyn and saw something entirely unexpected. Where normally Dwyn's eyes projected confidence and persistence, now they were filled with surprise and…innocence? *Damn it. She looks terrified.*

"Emeron?" Dwyn reached out again, halfway, but then her hand hovered between them. "What's wrong?"

"A lot of things." Something inside her snapped. She had no idea if the molten feelings had erupted because she'd barely cheated death or because she had a stunningly beautiful woman practically in her bedroll. She grabbed Dwyn's hand and tugged her close. Dwyn ended up on her back halfway on Emeron's bedroll, her silver-gray eyes huge. "*You* are wrong. The wrong woman at the wrong time and, damn it, in the wrong place." She buried her face in Dwyn's long hair where it had escaped the chignon.

Dwyn whimpered and grabbed her by the shoulders, digging her fingertips in. Emeron was sure Dwyn would push her away, out of anger or fear, but instead, Dwyn held on as she slid one of her hands up and touched the back of Emeron's head.

"I thought you were dead." Dwyn's soft murmur deflated Emeron's rush of emotions.

"I'm fine. Thanks to you." Knowing she sounded far too formal, she tried to free Dwyn of her weight, but Dwyn didn't let go.

"Yes. You are." Dwyn allowed her to lift her head enough for their eyes to meet, but kept her hand around the back of her neck.

All the arousal rushed back, flooding her, and she couldn't take her eyes from Dwyn's delicate features. Her pale, curvy lips were parted slightly, and the quick glimpse of small white teeth behind them sent tremors through her.

"Emeron?" Dwyn was out of breath and still looked confused.

"Forgive me." She moved off Dwyn with the last of her

determination. "This is highly unprofessional, and it won't happen again."

"Isn't it normal to feel a little rattled after a brush with death?" Dwyn reached toward her again, but she ducked.

"It is. I'm trained to ignore such emotions."

"Oh." Dwyn seemed not to know what to do with her hands. She was still half lying on Emeron's bedroll. "I see."

"I don't know what happened just now, but you can be certain that I will *not* forget my position again." She could hear how cold she sounded, but didn't know what else to say—or do.

Dwyn's features stiffened and her marble skin looked as cold and rigid as its color suggested. Emeron watched with fascination how an emotional shield slid down over Dwyn's eyes, not allowing any feelings to permeate. "Of course. I appreciate that." She slowly crawled over to her own bedroll and curled up in it. "Good night, *Commander*."

Emeron winced at the pointed use of her title. She had behaved unprofessionally and lowered her guard since she assumed this was a mere babysitting job. She had also offended the person she was ordered to protect by allowing her libido to surface. She crept into her own bedroll and sighed. All in all a rather lousy day.

❖

"The shuttle from the Guild Nation vessel has landed, Admirals, Lt. Commander." An ensign gestured for Kellen, Rae, and Ewan Jacelon to follow him. After stepping into the VIP room at the shuttle-gate area, Kellen waited impatiently the two minutes it took the passengers to disembark. The door opened and her handsome boy with olive skin and dark eyes, a heritage from his father, appeared. Even though he looked mostly Onotharian, Kellen thought he looked more and more like his mother, Princess Tereya of Gantharat, her childhood friend and protégé.

Kellen had loved and cared for Armeo since he was born, and when his mother was assassinated when Armeo was five, Kellen became his sole guardian. Now she wrapped her arms around him and felt him go rigid for a few seconds before he clung to her waist. She knew he might be embarrassed later, but she needed to feel the beat of his heart and listen to him breathe. "Gods of Gantharat. You're safe," she murmured, and tipped his chin up to examine his face.

Armeo was now nearly thirteen human years old, but looked younger since Gantharians' average life span exceeded humans' by thirty-some years.

Rae said huskily, "Let me look at you, son," and stood by Kellen's side. Without thinking, Kellen wrapped one arm around them both and held them tight. This was her life, her family. Without them, she was nothing.

At first, Rae's affection for Armeo had been the only redeeming quality of a woman who had held both of them captive. Now, Rae's love for them, her willingness to risk her life, not only for Armeo, but for the freedom of his and Kellen's homeworld, Gantharat, was only one reason Kellen loved her.

"Hey, Kellen, you're crushing us," Armeo objected, and blushed as he looked at Ewan Jacelon. "Save me, Granddad."

Ewan came over and hugged the boy briefly, a man-to-man kind of hug that apparently Armeo approved of. A moment later, his eyes darkened. "Granddad, I'm so sorry." He cast his eyes downward, but just as quickly raised his gaze again, looking both afraid and brave as he spoke. "I wanted to save her from the kidnappers. I tried."

"Shh, son. It wasn't your fault."

"People at the space station whispered that M'Ekar has escaped. Is it true? Is it him?" Armeo's voice cracked at the end of the sentence.

"We don't know, not for sure, but it's likely, Armeo," Rae answered in her father's place. She still stood in Kellen's embrace.

Kellen winced at the pain and fury on Armeo's face. "I hate that man. I hate being related to him. I despise what he's done in the past and what he's doing to Grandma now." Armeo's eyes glowed like scorching rings of fire.

"I know, Armeo, we all feel the same way." Kellen knew this wasn't the time to hug him, no matter how much she wanted to wrap him in her arms and shield him from life's harsh truth. "We will find your grandmother."

Armeo nodded, jaws clenched. "They hurt Ayahliss. After they took Grandma away, Ayahliss took several of the bad guys out, even when our guards tried to restrain her. She used her gan'thet skills, and the bad guys had to shoot her to stop her. Even when she was bleeding, she limped after them. Then they fired at her again, and she didn't get up a second time." Armeo's voice was monotonous as he retold the horrible event. "She's doing a little better now."

"A lot better, kid," a youthful voice said from the doorway. Ayahliss, pale and obviously in pain, stood proudly without holding on for support. Behind her, a medic watched her closely.

"Ayahliss," Kellen said as she approached her.

"I beg your forgiveness. In my effort to keep Armeo safe, I failed Ms. Dahlia. I tried to...I tried." Ayahliss's face contorted, and for a moment Kellen thought she would see her cry for the first time, but she jutted out her chin and straightened where she stood.

"You and Armeo are not at fault," Rae said behind Kellen. "You're going to fall over any second, Ayahliss. Come here."

Ayahliss looked truly surprised as Rae guided her to a couch. Kellen understood Ayahliss's consternation. Until now Rae had kept her distance from her. Reluctant to trust the volatile young person, she had been suspicious about her friendship with Armeo. Now she helped Ayahliss sit down and joined her. She looked at Rae as if she were an imposter, her expression almost humorous, despite the serious situation they were all facing.

"Ma'am. Uhm, Admiral..." she began.

"Call me Rae."

Her mouth fell open before she tried again. "Rae. Once I see the physicians and they perform the last procedure, I'll be able to join the hunt for this *tremasht*."

Rae briefly touched her arm and looked over at Armeo. "You two have an even more important mission," she said gravely. "Until Armeo is of age he can't join an armed team, but that doesn't mean he isn't valuable. When it comes to you, Ayahliss, keeping Armeo safe is the most important thing, and I've realized you're totally dedicated to this task. When you're well again, I trust you to stay close to him, no matter what happens. You'll have your own security detail, as before, but you're more than his mere bodyguard." She looked steadily at Ayahliss. "You're his friend. Nobody can be a better companion for him."

Kellen blinked. She hadn't been aware that Rae had given Ayahliss so much credit for keeping Armeo safe on the Keliera space station.

"Thank you. I won't fail you, ma'am—Rae." Ayahliss paled further and pressed a trembling hand against her midsection. "I have to confess, though, that I'm in pain."

"We need to get you into bed. Father, we need a gurney. She can't walk all the way to the hovercraft."

"Of course." Ewan moved toward the door on the other side of the room. In passing, he smiled at Ayahliss. Soon, he had summoned the ensign that helped them earlier and informed him of the situation.

"Is the young lady going to the hospital?" the man asked.

"Her location will be classified information." Ewan frowned. "I need a vehicle, but I'll pilot it myself."

❖

Weiss ran to the bridge, ducking at every bulkhead opening in the corridor with measured dips of her head.

"What the hell's going on?" she yelled, and held on to the railing that led down a short flight of stairs to her captain's chair. The *Viper* lurched under her feet and sparks erupted from two computer consoles.

"All our systems are malfunctioning and I have no clue why. Probably a series of burned relays and melted gel manifolds," Weiss's next-in-command yelled.

"We need to land, Captain. I can't hold her." The woman at the helm struggled with the console, furiously entering commands.

"Nearest habitable planet?" Weiss snapped her head around toward her ops officer.

"Corma."

"Damn. Set her down, as remotely as possible, if possible."

"Aye, ma'am." The helmswoman frowned as she entered the new coordinates. "I need more power."

"Redirect from any system necessary. Even life support, if that's what it takes." Weiss kept her voice calm as she clung to the armrests of her chair.

"Captain Kyakh. What are you saying? We can't land within SC space," M'Ekar shouted over the blaring alarm klaxons. "Can't this woman get us to the border?"

"If you mean my helmswoman, you'll have to settle for her being able to get us down in one piece at all. Don't worry. I have contingency plans for most scenarios." Weiss was confident because she spoke the truth. She'd been untouchable in this business of mercenaries and space pirates for many years. As the *Viper* bucked and lurched its way toward Corma, she fought an annoying little voice that had become more insistent lately. *The longer it is before you get caught, the more likely it is that you will.*

She shook her head and grabbed her armrests harder as they approached Corma. If they could break orbit and find a remote area, they had every chance of escaping the authorities and making the last little jump over the SC border into intergalactic space.

"How much longer?" she asked.

"We reach orbit in less than five minutes. Our success depends on whether I can maintain a correct angle. If not, we'll become space debris."

"That's not an option. Not a very fitting end for the esteemed ambassador," Weiss said. "Get us down in one piece. We can worry about the rest later."

❖

It took some effort to help an increasingly pasty-pale Ayahliss into the hovercraft. It was an elongated version, lean and black, and once they were all inside, Ewan pulled out into traffic.

"Father, are you comfortable driving in these conditions? Traffic is horrible." Rae spoke quietly. She knew her father was exhausted from worry as well as all the intel he'd sorted through since the kidnapping.

"I'm fine. Make sure the kids are all right." Her father sounded gruff, but Rae knew this was only stress talking.

"They're fine—"

"Headquarters to Admiral Rae Jacelon. Headquarters to Admiral Ewan Jacelon. Please report on secure audio channels ASAP." The metallic voice echoed throughout the vehicle.

"We're almost there." Ewan punched in new commands on the console before him. "Take over the controls, Commander O'Dal."

The formality of how he spoke was alarming. Kellen nodded briskly at Rae and moved forward between the seats and took the co-driver's seat. "I have the controls."

"Good. Are we secure?" Ewan asked Rae.

"Getting there. Kellen, please erect a privacy wall." An opaque wall rose soundlessly between them and the back area of the hovercraft. Rae cleared her voice, suddenly nervous. "Secure channel Alpha-Alpha-Jacelon-6. Admirals Jacelon and Jacelon present. We are safe to talk."

"Rae, Ewan, we have news regarding Dahlia," a familiar voice said over the communicator.

"Alex. When did you get here?" Rae exclaimed, relieved and surprised.

Alex de Vies, captain of the flagship while Rae was in command of the Gamma VI space station, was also one of her best friends. Alex's wife Gayle had been wonderful to Kellen from the start, and Dorinda, their daughter, was Armeo's best friend.

"I got in an hour ago. When I heard the news I asked the command group for an express transfer. I'm so sorry about Dahlia." Alex paused. "As I said, we have news."

"Ewan here, Alex. Report."

"Sir, Cormanian sensors show that a small vessel, identical to the one escaping from the Keliera station, has crashed into the Disi-Disi forest."

"Crashed." Rae mouthed the word but couldn't make a sound.

"Its status?" Ewan asked, his voice steady in contrast to his white lips.

"Disabled is our best estimate, sir," Alex said. "Corma doesn't allow for extensive scans of the area, so we have no way of knowing precisely. You know this forest is protected by an ancient pact—"

"My mother might be injured, or worse. I don't give a damn about any ancient pacts." Rae found her voice and thundered on. "We're going to make sure the children are safe, and then I want to talk to the Foreign Minister. Make that happen, Alex."

"I'm on it. But be careful, Rae. The Thousand Year Pact isn't just any document. It stretches back into Cormanian history and right up to modern day. Just so you know what you're up against with the minister."

"Thanks. See you soon. Jacelon out." Rae closed her eyes briefly, then looked at her father.

"At least there aren't any hard surfaces in the jungle, or are there? No tall buildings or..." Rae had to swallow twice to be able to continue. "Kellen. ETA at the hotel?"

"Two minutes." Kellen spoke calmly, but Rae, who was familiar with every nuance of Kellen's voice, knew she was ready to explode into action.

Rae sat straight, breathing in the relaxation pattern that usually worked. *Mother. Be all right. You have to. You simply have to.*

CHAPTER NINE

They had hiked for hours, going much farther into the Disi-Disi forest than their application to enter had stated. Emeron remained in the rear, convinced if the bots attacked again, they would come from the rear. Dwyn had started out behind Mogghy, but had gradually fallen back and was now walking in front of her.

"Are you getting tired? Do we need to rest?" She tapped Dwyn's shoulder. Dwyn jumped, obviously having been lost in thought. "Sorry."

"No. I'm fine." Dwyn looked stubborn rather than defeated, and Emeron knew she wasn't used to the pace they'd kept to get as far away as they could from potential bots.

"All right, but we could all use a break and, what's more important, something to drink." It was humid this deep into the vegetation beneath the tall trees, despite their temperature-sustaining underwear.

"If you insist." Dwyn looked like she was doing Emeron a favor as they all formed a circle and sat down on their carriers.

Emeron pulled out a box from her med kit and passed it around. "Grab a capsule each, people. We need to make sure we're in good shape if we run into those bots again."

"What are they?" Dwyn asked, wrinkling her nose. She held the yellow capsule as if it were poison.

"It's a multivitamin and also contains the equivalent of a day's worth of minerals, glucose, and salts. Don't worry. It's designed to suit multiple species." She placed her capsule in her mouth, pulled the hose from her carrier that held her water, and took a sip. "There."

"All right." Dwyn did the same, then bent forward, her elbows on her knees. "How far before we can get back on track? I need to reach my coordinates as soon as possible to get my last readings of the soil and observe the forest's perimeter for signs of—"

A loud, repetitive beep interrupted her. "Incoming emergency message." Oches pulled out the communication antenna. He punched in a few commands and nodded to Emeron. "You're ready to proceed, ma'am."

"Thanks." Emeron rose and walked far enough into the vegetation to be out of sight and earshot. The signal had been unmistakable. The message was urgent and confidential. She plugged an earpiece into her communicator and pressed the sensor that linked it via a satellite scrambler to the antenna in Oches's back-strap carrier. "D'Artansis here. Go ahead." A slight crackle of static, then Captain Zeger's voice came through.

"Commander D'Artansis, we've had some disturbing developments. A space vessel harboring enemies of the Supreme Constellations and a kidnapping victim has crashed not far from your position. Since you're the closest unit, you are to scan for the crash site and potential survivors. It's a matter of galactic security that we rescue the victim. Her name is Dahlia Jacelon, and she's an important senior diplomat, with a level-one security clearance. We believe that the kidnappers intend to interrogate her and sell any information they might extract to the Onotharian Empire."

Emeron's head spun with several potential scenarios. "And she'll go through a living hell before they kill her," she said in a flat voice.

"Exactly."

"Are reinforcements on their way?"

Captain Zeger sighed. "You know our government and its maddening bureaucracy. We have some influential military people here, but the location of the crash site makes it difficult for them to get permission to enter the forest. Dahlia Jacelon is the wife of an admiral and the mother of yet another one, but that doesn't seem to pull any weight with our ministers."

"You've got to be kidding me, sir."

"Well, both Admirals Jacelon seem ready to hijack a shuttle and leave on the spot, but their hands are tied."

"So, sir, if we come across the kidnappers and Diplomat Jacelon, we're on our own?"

"Yes. For now."

Emeron rubbed the back of her head. She was already reviewing various tactical scenarios, but no matter how clever they were, the odds weren't stacked in her favor. "All right, sir, is it possible to download the latest intel into my receiver? Or are we going in blind?"

"My aide de camp is already transmitting what we have to Ensign Oches."

"Good. I'll keep you posted, sir."

She broke the transmission and walked back to her team, all of them sitting in a circle propped up against their carriers. Glancing at Dwyn, she wondered if things could possibly get any more complicated. She couldn't possibly take a civilian on such a dangerous mission.

"Listen up, people. There's been a new development." Without giving away too many details about the status of the kidnapping victim, Emeron described their situation. "We are to proceed to the crash site, which means I have to delegate two of you to escort Ms. Izontro out of the forest."

"Absolutely not." Dwyn stood up and her eyes flashed angrily. "I've come too far to turn back now. Besides, you can't afford to reduce your unit by two heads, Commander. And I think I've proved myself under fire."

"You don't understand. This is a top-secret mission. We cannot have civilians present."

Dwyn stepped closer and Emeron realized she wouldn't give up easily. "Are you sure that two of your people will be enough if we run into one of those hostile bots? We've traveled four days to come this far into the forest, and it'll take us even longer to get back since we can't very well travel along known paths."

Grudgingly, she had to concede that Dwyn had a point. Still, it worried her that it would be twice as hard to keep Dwyn safe during this new mission. She had no idea how many criminals were aboard the crashed ship or how many of them had survived and were still able to fight. She saw that Dwyn planned to say something more and held up her hand to forestall her. "All right. You're coming with us, but only because you're right. It *is* too dangerous for you to turn back with only two junior officers to protect you. But I want you to stay even closer to me unless I tell you differently. No heroics on your own, all right?"

Dwyn brightened. "Got it. I'll carry out my own assignment as inconspicuously as possible."

She obviously hadn't grasped the seriousness of the incident. Emeron resigned herself to the fact and turned to Oches instead. "Has the intel downloaded yet?"

"All set, ma'am." Oches handed over a small handheld device.

Reading through the information, Emeron knew the situation was even worse than she first thought. No matter how she looked at it, the outcome would be disastrous whether the kidnappers managed to break Dahlia Jacelon or not. The list of criminals aboard the downed ship included mercenaries that any thug with money could hire.

The thug in this case apparently was the infamous Ambassador M'Ekar. Everyone within SC space knew who he was. Many people on Corma blamed him for the escalation of the conflict with the Onotharian Empire. Emeron realized there was more behind the impending war with Onotharat, but if Ambassador M'Ekar had been on board the crashed spaceship, she fully intended to apprehend him before he could cause any more trouble. She closed the intelligence document and tucked the device into her own back-strap carrier. She suspected she would receive several more reports soon.

"Listen up." She waited a few seconds until she had everyone's attention. "We'll head due north, and Ensign Oches and I will take the lead. Mogghy, you bring up the rear." She nodded at Dwyn. "Stay near, all right?"

"All right." Dwyn shrugged.

"You have your weapon?" Emeron spoke pointedly. She recognized the stubborn look on Dwyn's face.

As Dwyn hoisted her carrier onto her back, she patted a pocket on the side of her pants. "Yes, I'm all set."

"Keep a low profile and take your cue from me. From now on, we can expect the bots to attack and will have to engage the enemy when we locate the space vessel."

Dwyn buckled her carrier and it conformed to her slight frame with a buzz. "I understand." She produced a long-bladed laser knife and stuck it into her right boot. "I'm ready."

"I hope so. I can't promise that I'll be able to babysit you—"

"Don't even try to start that old tune again." Dwyn stepped up to her. "Remember who rescued whom yesterday."

She shrugged. "Keep close to me," she said, pretending she didn't hear Dwyn snarl. She did hear Dwyn sigh as she stepped in behind her and they began to make their way through the undergrowth. Emeron knew this mission would be dangerous, but part of her was excited. After all, law enforcement was her job.

❖

The mission room seemed unusually quiet as the four individuals stood at the main screen. Kellen studied the other three. Rae was exasperated, and rightfully so, as she tried to communicate with the infuriating Cormanian official. Ewan Jacelon appeared stricken, and though he could still be forceful, he seemed content to let Rae take the lead. Alex de Vies stood next to Rae and seemed every bit as annoyed with the man on the screen as Rae did.

Kellen clasped her hands behind her back, a familiar gesture that instilled calmness in her when she was furious and craved revenge. This was not the time for that, not yet. Instead, they needed to execute a flawless plan to rescue Dahlia and capture M'Ekar.

"This is absurd." Rae's voice, a low-register growl, filled the entire mission room, making it clear to Kellen and everyone else present exactly what she meant. "I won't let any puny little bureaucrat keep me from going after M'Ekar."

"That may be, Admiral Jacelon," the Cormanian civil servant on the view screen said, his condescending tone obviously infuriating Rae further. "The Cormanian law holds the Thousand Year Pact in high regard, and nothing, I repeat, nothing, can be considered an exception."

"You fail to understand that this is a matter of Supreme Constellations security," Ewan Jacelon said, briefly touching his daughter's arm.

"I thought this was a personal request regarding your spouse, Admiral?" The Cormanian official looked disdainful.

"Have you even read the intel we sent with the request for backup?" Rae spat. "For the love of the stars, we're dealing with two of the most wanted people within the SC."

"As it happens, yes, I have. I forwarded your request to the Cormanian Law-Enforcement Service, and they have a unit present in the forest right now."

"How large is this unit? How well equipped?" Rae leaned forward, her body language familiar to anyone who had ever seen her consumed with fury.

"I don't have that particular information here, but—"

"Then I suggest you get it, fast. I also need to be able to communicate with this unit. They have no idea what or who they're up against."

"Strict regulations also govern communications in the Disi-Disi forest."

Rae slammed her hand into the computer console. "Damn it, is *anything* not strict or difficult on this planet?"

Kellen hurried to Rae's side and touched her stealthily. They couldn't afford to alienate the irritating man completely. She sought Ewan's gaze and he appeared to understand the wordless communication.

"I'm sure you'll do your best to have us talking with the commander of the unit in the forest within an hour," he said firmly. "In the meantime, we will use our own intel and equipment to assess the situation further."

"I'm sure the situation will be resolved to everybody's satisfaction." The Cormanian looked relieved not to talk directly to Rae anymore.

"I hope so," Ewan said, his voice an octave deeper. "If not, I'll contact my very good friend, Council Leader Thorosac, and several other high-ranking SC officials. If we're still no closer to a solution, they're not going to like it and they'll give me a mandate to act as I see fit."

A few shades paler, the Cormanian official nodded briskly. "I'm sure we'll have resolved matters before that point, Admiral."

"Good. Jacelon out." Ewan closed the view screen and faced the others. His face didn't betray his emotions, but the lines around his mouth and nose had deepened.

"So they have a team there already, for whatever reason." Rae spoke slowly. "I want this information instantly. Alex, get in touch with the Cormanian part of our forces. Find out if any of them have responded to this situation yet." She glanced at her wife. "Kellen, I need our best people on this. Contact Owena Grey and Leanne D'Artansis. If I'm not mistaken, they're planet-side."

"Right away." Kellen moved to the closest computer console and began to punch in commands. She knew very well that Owena and Leanne, two of their best friends, were on Corma, Leanne's home planet. She wondered if Rae had forgotten *why* they were on shore leave. After all, they had attended the couple's wedding only three weeks ago.

She thought of Armeo and Ayahliss, now resting comfortably at one of the luxury hotels on the SC base. Available only to SC dignitaries and their families, the hotel boasted a top-level security force. They had arranged for Ayahliss to get acute medical attention at the hotel, since Kellen knew that private commercial stations such as Keliera didn't have the best medical personnel on staff, certainly nobody with specific knowledge of Gantharian physiology.

She was surprised how Rae had taken time to personally ensure Ayahliss was taken care of. She had been prepared for Rae to leave that to her, since she had never quite accepted Kellen's determination to bring Ayahliss with them to Earth. The young woman herself had seemed even more stupefied at Rae's obvious concern. When Rae held Ayahliss's cheek and promised her she would be fine, she had blinked several times, clearly fending off tears.

"How are you doing over there?" Rae asked.

Kellen jerked back to present time and tapped the screen before her with quick fingertips. "I've ordered Lt. Commanders Grey and D'Artansis to check in with headquarters."

"We better hope they check their messages during their honeymoon." Rae smiled wryly. "No, I hadn't forgotten, Kellen."

"I don't think Owena is far from her computer," Kellen said. "Her sense of duty surpasses most people's."

"She's even more a stickler for protocol and regulations than I am, isn't she?" Rae patted Kellen's hand. "Let me know as soon as you hear from them." She glanced at Alex. "Anything from the team in the forest?"

"Not yet, ma'am. I'm waiting for a cadet to find a Captain Zeger for me. I think I scared that poor kid."

"If that's what it takes." Rae returned her attention to Kellen. "We need to deploy a small, covert unit to the forest. Start making arrangements and, for now, keep it confidential. The Cormanians could have all sorts of reasons not to want us to enter the forest. The longer they think we're playing by their rules, the better."

"Understood." Kellen began her task, but found it unusually hard to focus. Now that she no longer feared for Armeo's immediate safety, she thought about Dahlia. Rae's mother possessed a laser-blade sharp intellect and was as resourceful as her daughter, but she was in the hands of one of the most unscrupulous people Kellen had ever known. Only her old archenemy Trax M'Aldovar outranked M'Ekar as the most hated person in her life.

She drew a deep breath, then slowly exhaled between clenched teeth. If she had one more opportunity to apprehend M'Ekar, she wouldn't fail. He would meet the same destiny as Trax M'Aldovar. Death.

CHAPTER TEN

D wyn walked behind Emeron, grateful that she pressed the low branches aside carefully. They stayed off the trail and she suspected Emeron had a specific goal in mind.

"With the risk of sounding like a child, are we there yet?" She raised her voice.

"What do you mean, there?" Emeron glanced at her.

"Wherever we're going. It's been four days and now you've scanned the area at least ten times in as many minutes. If you scowl anymore at the poor, innocent instrument, it'll self-ignite."

Emeron smiled and shook her head. "I wasn't aware I was scowling."

"Perhaps obvious only to me. I don't have anything else to do but keep walking and study what's in sight." Her cheeks warmed. "Ahem, well. You're the nearest thing. And Lt. Mogghy went to reconnoiter and hasn't returned. Makes me think we're approaching something, or someone."

"You're right. We're getting close." Emeron frowned. "And I confess that my scans concerned me. A Disian village is coming up. Actually, it's more than a village. It's their equivalent of a capital. So, large village."

"And? For stars and skies, you don't think these people are there? Wouldn't they hide in the forest?"

"We'll see."

"How much farther?" Dwyn hoisted her carrier up and lengthened her stride to be able to walk next to Emeron. "I think I smell smoke."

Emeron stopped and scanned again. "The village is near." She waved at Oches, who immediately neared. "We have to be prepared. Who's carrying the med kits?"

"Noor. I'll have her distribute them among us."

"Good."

Mogghy joined them. "I managed to get a good view of the village without being spotted, ma'am." His face looked like it was carved from stone. "It's bad. A whole neighborhood is on fire."

"Good sense of smell there, Dwyn." Emeron's face was just as devoid of feelings, but her black eyes reminded Dwyn of half-burned-out ashes.

Noor approached, and Dwyn accepted a set of bandages and a derma fuser. It was larger than the one she was used to and was also a bone knitter. The fact that she was in charge of it made her stomach churn with nervousness. She hoped she hid it well. Tipping her head back, she could see drifts of smoke between the trees.

"We can safely assume by now that the space vessel crashed into the village." Emeron raised her hand. "The Disian leaders are no fools and are well aware of the technology used outside their territory. But a lot of the common people will be traumatized, especially the children, who know nothing of modern technology."

"Some of them could also be orphaned at this point," Mogghy said. He rubbed his neck quickly. "We should move in from the south and make sure the locals know we're not the enemy, but here to help."

Dwyn nodded, automatically standing next to Emeron. "Will they attack us if they believe we're responsible for the crash? They might think it's some sort of aggression."

"No. They won't," Emeron said. "They don't do things like that. Besides, they use their weapons only for hunting."

Dwyn hoped Emeron was right. She wasn't looking forward to being anyone's prey, mistakenly or not.

"Let's go." Emeron motioned for Dwyn to keep close to her.

They walked fast, now following a much wider path where Dwyn saw traces of narrow wheels. Someone had driven a vehicle here. The smoke made her cough, and soon Emeron ordered everyone to pull on their facemasks. Relieved, she drew a couple of deep breaths. Her head became clearer, she could focus better, and now she saw the outline of Disian structures.

The wooden houses at the edge of the village were stunningly beautiful, with elaborate ornaments carved in the logs. The windows were golden, and the doors shimmered in every vibrant color imaginable. However, there were no people in the street at the outskirts of the village. They jogged toward its center, and as they approached they encountered a dense crowd. Villagers were shouting over the noise, but just as many were standing still with their eyes closed and their hands pressed together, palm to palm, as in prayer.

Dwyn couldn't help but stare. Very few images were available of the Disians. The pact made it impossible for news crews or anyone else to bring cameras into the woods. The surveillance bots could be used, but normally only along the perimeter. Not sure what she had expected, she scanned the people standing nearby who seemed oblivious to Emeron's team.

The Disians were tall, if the ones she saw were average for their race. Both men and women wore their black hair long, and it ran down their backs like waterfalls when it wasn't tied back in a braid or ponytail. Their garments ranged from white to tan, embroidered with softly shining pearls and beads.

Suddenly the large crowd parted and an older woman limped toward them, her long hair almost white. On her hip, she carried a little girl, perhaps two years old, whose hands were wrapped in bandages. The woman spoke in a guttural voice.

Mogghy shrugged helplessly and pointed in Emeron's direction. The woman turned around and paused briefly. She held the child and merely looked Emeron up and down. Dwyn had no idea what the wordless exchange could mean.

Emeron bowed marginally, a mere dip of her head, and took off her mask. "*Ylams, herona Pri. Hordos avasti.*" She gestured toward Dwyn and the rest of her team. "*Megos foshme, deos avasti.*"

Staring at Emeron, Dwyn realized that she had spoken to the old woman in Disianii. It didn't make any sense, and everyone else in the unit except Mogghy stared at Emeron as if she'd just fallen from the sky.

The old woman nodded slowly and replied in flawless Premoni, the official language of the SC. "*Imer-Ohon-Da.* It has been too long. And now you return when mayhem has struck us."

"Pri. Yes, it's been a long time. I'm here to help. Show us the crash site, please."

"Nobody is left to save."

Emeron shifted and her body tensed. "Nobody? Everyone on the ship died instantly?"

Pri shook her head and hoisted the child farther up. She looked tired, and without thinking, Dwyn reached for the child. Growing up in a collective had ensured she was not only used to dealing with children, but also prepared to pitch in whenever needed. The little girl looked at her with huge black eyes, but allowed herself to be lifted by a stranger. Dwyn hugged the little one, tucking her in under her chin.

"Thank you. She was becoming heavy," Pri said.

"I'm happy to help." Dwyn motioned with her chin toward the origin of the smoke. "How long ago was the crash?"

"Dear child, our concept of time would mean nothing to you. Enough time for us to count our dead and wounded. That is all I can say."

Dwyn didn't know how to reply and was grateful when Pri refocused on Emeron.

"To answer your question, Imer-Ohon-Da, no, everyone did not die. Some of them walked through our streets on foot, carrying weapons and firing at the ones trying to put out the fires. They dragged some of their wounded along. Still, I suppose they could have left dead comrades inside the ship. They appeared to be without honor, and it is likely they would not care to tend to the dead."

"Do you remember how many of them? In what direction—Pri." Pri swayed, and Emeron managed to grab her before she slumped to the ground. "You are exhausted. Direct us to someone we can help organize a search-and-rescue unit."

"Amiri. Over there," Pri said, and pointed at a woman striding toward them. "We have elected her to succeed me as our speaker."

"Does she speak Premoni?" Emeron asked.

"Yes."

A man and a woman arrived, and the man placed his arms around Pri, helping her stand. They looked at Emeron with curious eyes, but didn't say anything.

"Are you the reason this has happened to our village?" Amiri stood before them, hands on her hips. Her black hair lay in unruly tresses around her shoulders, and her anger and frustration were evident in her voice.

"No. We were in the forest on an assignment, abiding by the pact, when my superior officer issued an order for us to pursue a fugitive and his mercenaries."

"How do I know you're telling the truth?" Amiri was obviously not impressed.

"Pri can vouch for me."

This statement seemed to get through to Amiri, who blinked a few times and looked at the old woman, who was now sitting on a crate a few steps away. "Pri?"

"Yes, Amiri. You can trust her. She is one of us."

Dwyn had begun to suspect Emeron and the Disians were connected, which made her animosity toward this place and its people even more intriguing.

"Very well." Amiri motioned for them to follow her. "This way. The vessel crashed into several homes down this street."

Dwyn had almost forgotten that she was carrying the little girl and let go of her only when a man approached, nodding for her to pass the child to him. She followed the rest of the team, grateful for the mask. She couldn't imagine what it must be like for the Disians, who apparently didn't own, or use, such equipment.

The farther they went, the harder her heart hammered at the sight of the burned homes. Disians were still digging through what remained of the wooden houses, and the sight was so tragic, she had to swallow bitter tears and force herself to keep walking.

"This is as far as I can go, without breathing protection," Amiri said, and stopped, coughing. "We have attempted to recover our dead, but some of them are merely ashes." Sorrow and fury were etched on her strong features. "If you are one of us, you know how this desecrates our beliefs. We need to clean and bury our dead the first night. Their souls will roam and not—"

"Yes. I know all about your beliefs," Emeron said with disdain, then turned to her unit. "All right, people. As gruesome and tragic as this is, we have to go in. I want Noor and two more to go back with Amiri, to help with the wounded. The Disians are skilled at internal medicine, but since we brought our med kits, we're better with trauma. Dwyn, I want you to go with Noor—"

"No. I go where you go. If there's a toxic spill, I know more than you ever will about how to deal with it." She didn't wait for a response but handed over her medical equipment to Noor. She thought she glimpsed admiration in the stern ensign's eyes. "Good luck," she murmured.

"You too."

"All right. But stay *close*." Emeron's tone made it clear this wasn't a suggestion.

They slowly advanced down the street, and Dwyn pressed her mask tighter to her face. She had seen some terrible things in her life, but this was one of the worst. She walked next to Emeron, unwilling to show any weakness. Emeron needed her expertise whether she realized it or not.

The nearer they got to what Emeron called ground zero, the less there was left of the structures. "It's miraculous anyone in the spaceship survived, if the crash site looks like this," she murmured.

Emeron shook her head. "We don't know what kind of ship it was. If it had the latest dampeners and crash-stabilizers, who knows? Make sure your weapon is easily accessible."

"All right."

Two large trees lay across the street, and Dwyn climbed over them, the massive trunks almost as tall as she. She slid over the second one, her heart pounding so hard she felt the pulsations all the way from her chest to her temples. Glowing, smoking debris lay everywhere, and she saw no traces of any Disians on this side of the tree trunks.

"Over there." Emeron pointed to their left. "It looks intact, though charred."

The space vessel was far larger than the shuttle-size ship she had envisioned, at least eighty meters long and perhaps twenty-five meters tall. It had ploughed through several houses and now rested against a dense grove of trees where it lay slightly askew, the half-open hatch on its belly clearly visible.

"It's a state-of-the-art cruiser, ma'am," Mogghy said, and pulled out his scanner. "Its hull is outfitted with mirror-ceramic alloy, which makes it hard to trace via long-distance scanners. No wonder the SC had problems finding it."

"But that's used only on prototypes." Emeron frowned.

"And for good reason," Dwyn added. "The composite used to attach the mirror-ceramic is highly poisonous. The facility where it's manufactured and used has to be extremely cautious, which makes it almost impossible to get permission to produce it."

"But when you're operating outside the law and under the radar, it's not undoable." Mogghy moved in and Emeron followed suit. Dwyn stayed behind them as the rest of the unit fanned out on either side of her.

"These criminals must be well connected," Dwyn said, out of

breath as she tried to keep up with the others' longer strides. "If they can outfit their ship like this, undetected, there must be quite a covert operation going on."

"Probably on some of the pirate-infested asteroids. Who knows what they have buried inside them," Emeron said. "It's their latest scheme. They pretend to have a legit mining company and work the asteroids, and what do you know—a weapons storage facility or a place to modify illegal ships."

"Wouldn't surprise me if this ship is tachyon-mass-drive capable." Mogghy frowned as they had to stop. The heat was unbearable at this distance, and Dwyn wondered how the people on board this ship had managed to get away.

"Tachyon-mass drives are illegal as well," she said. In fact, the propulsion in question made it possible for the vessel to travel at an unfathomable speed through space. The drives, however, polluted space in irreparable ways, which had caused the SC to ban them.

"Bet that's at the top of Aequitas's list of things to keep track of," Emeron said, crouching as she tried to get closer to the ship. "Damn it, this is too hot. If we go any farther our suits will be burned off our backs."

"Is there any way to contain the damage to this area?" Oches asked as he joined them.

"It's fairly contained. The Disians must have cut down those trees to create a barrier of sorts." Emeron surveyed the area. "Until the ship cools off, we can't investigate it. We should go back to the center of the village and see what we can find out from witnesses, and also help where we can."

"Shouldn't we go after the culprits who did this?" Mogghy gestured toward the ship. "They could be a long way from here by now."

Emeron smiled joylessly. "I don't think so. You noticed how much slower we traveled compared to normal circumstances? They're wounded, or at least some of them have to be. They're not moving fast, and they're not used to this forest."

"And they'll leave traces all over the place," Dwyn said. "I agree. We should stay here for the night."

Emeron looked surprised, which Dwyn found puzzling. Perhaps because they usually argued?

"Agreed, then. Noor and the others should have assessed the situation in the village by now, so let's join them. Oches, we better communicate with headquarters and report our findings."

"Aye, ma'am."

Dwyn was so tired when they began to walk back, she was afraid she might not be able to climb the tree trunks. She pulled herself up, but slipped twice. She was about to fail a third time when Emeron extended a strong hand and hauled her up. Trembling now, she slipped twice more trying to climb the second tree trunk and clenched her teeth in annoyance at this sign of weakness. She dug deep and found the strength to grasp Emeron's hands and managed to stand. Tree sap made the logs slippery and she clung to Emeron, who wrapped an arm around her waist.

"Easy now. I've got you."

As they slid down on the opposite side, she found herself pressed against Emeron's chest. They stood together as Dwyn got her bearings, her heart hammering again, this time because of how Emeron felt against her. Confused, and more intimidated than she cared to admit, she realized Emeron was moving her hand in tiny circles at the small of her back. Her normally stark expression had softened, and her mouth was relaxed with slightly parted lips.

"I'm fine," Dwyn croaked. "We…eh, we should go?"

Emeron let go of her as quickly as if she'd burned her hands. "Of course." She cleared her voice, her dark eyes shuttering her emotions. "Let's hurry, people. We've still got a job to do."

Dwyn gathered the last of her energy, knowing that the Disians were much worse off than she was right now. She tried not to think about the way her body had responded to Emeron. It had been so much more than a physical reaction. For a moment, she had looked into Emeron's eyes and experienced something entirely new.

CHAPTER ELEVEN

Dahlia coughed. Her lungs stung, and she knew she had suffered smoke-inhalation damage. She wasn't the most injured, though. Several of the gang of mercenaries had died on impact. Only the fact that she was kept locked in tiny quarters in the center of the ship's belly had prevented her from being seriously burned.

The forest was thick around them as she, M'Ekar, and the sixteen mercenaries struggled through the undergrowth. There had probably been a path here once, but it was overgrown with vines and tall grass, slowing them down.

M'Ekar had complained from the beginning, insisting they follow one of the wider paths leading out of the village they'd left behind more than a day ago. The leader, unscathed and quite impressive, hadn't paid much attention to the former dignitary's whining. Dahlia had tried to listen for names or anything that might define this group and reveal their plans.

"Halt," the female leader suddenly barked. "Our fearless ambassador needs more painkillers. "Ms. White. Bring the med kit."

"We can't waste all of them on him, Captain." White moved with such silent grace that Dahlia couldn't hear the rustle of the undergrowth as she neared the makeshift stretcher bearing M'Ekar. "He's slowing us down."

"He's also the reason we're getting paid." The leader nodded toward Dahlia. "So is she. All we have to do is get to a clearing big enough for the *Viper* II to land, and we'll be on our way."

"I still say we leave him behind and give them her." The blond woman dug around in the black bag containing the medication. She haphazardly gave M'Ekar a shot of something and the tall, rigid body of Dahlia's enemy slowly relaxed.

"I may be wounded, but I'm not dead," M'Ekar said. "If you don't deliver me to the ship waiting for me by the Onotharian border, you won't get any reward whatsoever."

"Enough bickering," the leader said, and motioned for everyone to get to their feet. "Time to continue. This forest is protected from interference from the outside world. But for her sake," she pointed at Dahlia, "I'm sure they're prepared to make an exception."

"We've been on our feet all day," White groused. "I say we make camp."

"We will. After we put more distance between that village and our position."

"You're being overcautious." White grimaced, but took up the rear as the man in charge of guarding Dahlia nudged her. "Move."

Dahlia counted the remaining ambulatory mercenaries again. Sixteen. They carried two on stretchers, M'Ekar and a young woman who hadn't spoken or shifted once since they hurried through the village. Two men limped between their shipmates, hanging onto them as they became increasingly pale.

"All right," she muttered to her guard and rose. Her right hip ached, as if it had been pulled out of its socket and shoved back in again. *Guess I'm not seventeen anymore.* Settling in behind the man carrying the foot of M'Ekar's stretcher, she continued to do what she'd done ever since they left the Disian village. She stealthily broke a twig here and there, when she was sure her guard wasn't paying attention. She let tiny pieces of her Iminestrian *ymlertite* bracelet fall to the ground. If anyone scanned the area, the non-indigenous material would make their sensors scream.

"You. You look annoyingly intact, *Madame.*" M'Ekar's scornful voice broke her out of her reverie.

"Justice comes in many ways. You should try to learn from that fact." She saw with satisfaction that M'Ekar's blood pressure rose, indicated by his color change from an olive tint to a dark purple.

"Bitch," he managed, and tried to rise, causing the men carrying his stretcher to nearly buckle under their burden. "You self-righteous—"

"Lie still, Ambassador," the mercenary leader hissed, and strode up to him. "If you want to survive this, you shouldn't let her goad you."

M'Ekar coughed and slumped back. "Weiss, you better put her in shackles. She's planning something. Don't take your eyes off her."

"I won't. What do you think I am? A novice? And if I put her in shackles, she'd only slow us down more."

"Weiss? So that's your name?" Dahlia hid the bracelet in her hand. "We haven't been formally introduced."

Weiss looked at her with an expression of reluctant admiration and exasperation. "The idea of such silliness didn't even occur to me."

"No, I would imagine that niceties like that are redundant when you deal in murder and kidnapping." Dahlia fought to remain calm. "I wonder how you sleep at night after firing against innocent children."

"Innocent? Are you talking about that wildcat at the Keliera station? It took some effort to calm her down."

"What do you mean?"

"Oh, I guess you couldn't see when my friend back there, Ms. White, took a shot at her. She was furious to have a kid defeat her. Nobody ever beats her at hand-to-hand combat."

Dahlia nearly stumbled, but managed to conceal her reaction. "No, I didn't realize Ayahliss was hit." She swallowed hard. "So, you actually do shoot children."

"Personally, it's not my method of operation, but White…well, White is another matter. She's a special sort. Handy in a pinch." Weiss shoved Dahlia's side. "Keep walking."

"Don't touch me." Dahlia spoke quietly, furious at the other woman's callousness.

"Or what?" Weiss asked, feigning horror. "Should I be scared now?"

"Yes. If you're half as clever as you think you are, you ought to be. If you don't harm me, or even touch me, you may live through this. People are already looking for me, whose dedication you cannot even begin to fathom."

"Oh, you have no idea what kind of people I've been up against." Weiss smiled, but her lips looked stiff.

"No, perhaps not. But you haven't come across anyone like Kellen O'Dal, Protector of the Realm. Nor her wife, who happens to be my daughter. Or my husband. Any of them is formidable and together…" She paused to emphasize her threat.

"You're good. A good diplomat who knows how to use words." Weiss shrugged. "That's all they are. Words. Whoever may or may not come after you will be too late. If you don't think I have backup plans, several, you're completely mistaken."

"Oh, I do." Dahlia smiled easily. "But, just so you know, such plans are futile." She could tell that her persistence was wearing on Weiss, even if she was acting casual and confident.

"Shut up." White hurried up to Dahlia and pressed a laser-knife against her neck. It vibrated lethally, and she could tell from the stinging sensation that it had broken her skin.

"That wasn't very clever." She kept walking, not even looking at White, the knife edge chafing her more with every step. She spoke in her infamous blistering tone, using every bit of her courage to sound menacing. "You're assaulting a civil servant of the SC with a deadly weapon—again. You're as good as dead, Ms. White. As good as dead."

❖

Emeron stood in the doorway to the Hall of Worship and took in the situation inside. People spoke in hushed voices as they wrapped wounds, comforted small children, or prayed with the ones who wouldn't survive. Flashbacks of her childhood, of having been in this exact structure with one of her mothers and her grandmother, made her press her tongue firmly to the roof of her mouth to keep from crying.

"She seems to be in her natural element, doesn't she?" Mogghy said from behind her, making Emeron snap her head around.

"What are you talking about?"

"Dwyn. Look." Mogghy pointed to the left.

She couldn't see Dwyn at first, merely heads bowed in worship around a set of cots. Only when she moved farther to the left did she discern a curtain of white-blond hair glimmering in the dim light. Dwyn knelt next to one of the cots, holding a young female as a Disian woman held a sculptural array of crystals above the injured person and murmured inaudible words. *A healer.* Emeron knew the Disians honored and revered their healers. She regarded them with dismay.

Dwyn raised her head and gazed up at the crystals. Her eyes were darker than usual, her pupils dilated in the poor light, and the crystals reflected in them. Her delicate features seemed even more ethereal than normal, and with her hair fallen out of its usual chignon she looked like

WARRIOR'S VALOR

one of the forest creatures Emeron's grandmother Briijn had told her stories about.

"And they come out only at dusk, child. During the day they hide behind trees and bushes, and under shrubs, but when the sun begins to set, and everything is golden from its last rays, the elfins come out. They are the most beautiful little creatures. Blond hair and white skin, dressed in leaves and spiderwebs. If they let you see them, you fall instantly in love with them because they are so precious. Nobody who has seen a real elfin has been able to remain indifferent. They demand you love them, merely by being so wonderful. And you do, child. You have no choice, so you do."

Emeron gasped at Briijn's voice, so clear inside her head. Half expecting the long-gone most beloved member of her family to be there, she walked over to Dwyn and stood behind her, prepared to say something scathing about the Disian methods of healing, something she'd once regarded with childlike awe. She opened her mouth to speak, but at that moment Dwyn stared up at her with tear-filled eyes. "Isn't it wonderful? Look."

There it was, the elfin beauty Briijn had spoken about. The rays of the setting sun played with the prisms in the crystals, casting a glow over Dwyn's pale face. The tears clinging to her long blond eyelashes looked like tiny perfect diamonds, and the glitter that shimmered in her eyes took Emeron's breath away.

"Look, Emeron. Look." Dwyn turned her head toward the Disian healer. The crystals spun now within her hands and seemed to defy gravity. The young woman on the cot was trembling. Fine tremors reverberated through her, and not sure why, Emeron knelt next to Dwyn, telling herself she was about to pull Dwyn away from this quackery.

Instead, Dwyn took her hand and placed it on the patient's thigh. "Feel."

The small tremors resembled the ones she experienced when she was cold to the bone. She didn't expect anything more, but after a few moments, she sensed something else—an underlying rhythm, like a distant drum beating to a different pace. The healer didn't say a word now, merely moved her hands in small circles, making the crystals dance between her hands.

• 91 •

Suddenly the young person drew a deep breath and opened her eyes. She sat up, or tried to, and a woman who had crouched by her other side pulled her into an embrace. *"Yhja. Megos dansa."*

"What does that mean?" Dwyn asked, her voice only a breath.

"My daughter. Her name is Yhja." Emeron was shocked to hear that her voice was just as breathless. "What is…was wrong with her?"

"She had been thrown from the crash site almost to the center. She lived in the house directly where the ship landed. It's a miracle she's alive to begin with."

"Who told you this?"

"Amiri." Dwyn glanced around her. "I don't know where she went. I suppose search parties are still out there working."

"Yes. Oches and Noor are heading up our unit. Mogghy and I came to appraise the situation here. You weren't supposed to wander off on your own, you know."

"But I was safe here. Besides, I had to do something. I couldn't simply ignore all these injured people." Dwyn shrugged. "I'm not used to having my own bodyguard. I'm used to complete independence."

Emeron was still dazed from the experience with the healer and not ready to deal with the multitude of questions that welled up inside her. She had absolutely no time for old, painful memories right now. "And now Yhja is all healed. A miracle," she said, unwilling to let go of the sarcasm in her voice.

"Yes." Dwyn challenged Emeron with her eyes. "She suffered from a serious concussion and inner bleedings. Her skin was blotched, her respiration shallow and fast, and both shoulders were dislocated. The healer set her joints first, the softest maneuver I've ever seen, and trust me, I've seen that done several times. Twice on myself. And look at her now." Dwyn gazed at Yhja with eyes that welled with new tears.

"I see her." And Emeron had to concede that she didn't act or look as if she were concussed with inner bleedings. "Did you scan her?"

"Yes. As a matter of fact I did. The healer told Amiri it was all right, that it could actually help her adjust the crystals."

This piece of information stunned Emeron and made her stand up so quickly she nearly knocked Dwyn over. "This is utter nonsense, and you should know better." Furious, and unable to stop herself, she towered over Dwyn, who looked startled. "If you truly believe that waving crystals over an unconscious kid does anybody *any* good, then you're even more delusional than I thought. You work for a company that does nothing but encourage so-called civil disobedience. You claim to be on this heroic mission to preserve the old worlds that have no appreciation for new technology and the sacrifices people make for the sake of human evolution." She growled, "I won't sit here and watch you look all radiant because someone made an unexplainable recovery. As soon as we're done here with the search-and-rescue operation, we're back to doing what we came here to do. Catch the bad guys and get the hell out of here."

Red mist clouded Emeron's mind and she almost lost control completely. She didn't look at Dwyn again, but stomped out the door. Staring at the sunset, she wished she'd never set foot in this godforsaken place again.

CHAPTER TWELVE

Dwyn walked past the long line of Disian men and women who stood outside the House of Worship waiting to hear about their friends and loved ones. Their heads were bowed as they prayed or meditated.

"There's a reason for her outburst," Mogghy said from behind her. "Don't judge her too harshly, Dwyn."

Dwyn didn't answer right away. Her ears still rang from Emeron's loud eruption, and she felt numb. She didn't care about losing face in front of the Disians. But the torment, the *anguish* behind Emeron's words, and the fact that she had lost control in a manner Dwyn had thought impossible, concerned her deeply. "I don't judge her. How could I?"

"Well, she probably thinks you do." Mogghy neared her, his huge body towering above her. He had the kindest eyes she had ever seen, and an honesty that told her what she needed to know.

"I wonder where she went." She gazed around them, but saw only the Disian crowds. "She disappeared so quickly."

"I can tell you, child." Pri appeared at Dwyn's elbow so unexpectedly that she jumped. "When Imer-Ohon-Da was a little girl, she used to go down to the waterfalls."

"Why do you call her that? Immeron—"

"Imer-Ohon-Da. It is her name, pronounced the Disian way. It means 'as sung by the people.'"

"Emeron has a Disian name? I don't understand."

"You must ask her, child." Pri spoke softly. "There is much hurt with Imer-Ohon-Da. She is aimed for greatness and has yet to find her path. She is by the waterfalls. You must go to her."

Dwyn frowned, uncertain what the old woman meant. Mogghy seemed to concur and motioned for her to start walking.

"I'll show you the waterfalls. I saw them earlier. Come on."

She didn't seem to have any choice. Sighing, she followed Mogghy as he maneuvered through the crowd. The Disians moved to the side like a parting sea, allowing them effortless passage. Dwyn became more nervous with each step. She had no idea what mood Emeron would be in, and she was almost certain that she herself was the last person on this planet Emeron wanted to talk to right now. Still, both Pri and Mogghy, who clearly knew Emeron much better than she did, seemed convinced.

The eastern part of the village was framed by slender trees and uneven rocks, which created a magical scene. Short, soft grass grew between the trees, and a wooden path, lit by oil-fueled lamps, led down to a small lake where a twin waterfall created a hypnotic sound.

"There she is. I'll leave the two of you alone, all right?"

"Ah...sure." Dwyn slowed her steps. More oil lamps circled the lake, and the sand on the shore clung to her boot-clad feet. She couldn't resist the urge to get out of her boots. Unbuckling them, she pulled them and her socks off and placed them at the beginning of the lake path. Then she stood for a moment, digging her bare toes into the sand. The waterline was only a few meters away and she dashed down, dipping her feet in the cool water. Now the sand clung to them as she began to walk along the shoreline of the lake.

The twin moons were out, and when she squinted, she could vaguely see the outline of the vast military space stations that orbited the smaller moon. Off-limits to civilians, such installations were foreign to her, but she didn't envy the people who lived and worked there. She knew what it was like to be on an endless space journey with no place, other than an old space vessel, to call home.

A dark shadow out on a small pier drew her attention. Emeron sat with her boots at her side, dangling her feet just above the waterline. Dwyn felt a bit better that they had done the same thing. "Water's lovely, isn't it?" she called, and began to walk on the pier. It was made of wood and wobbled.

"Yes." Emeron didn't look around, but Dwyn kept on.

"I thought I'd make sure you're all right."

"I'm fine."

"Yes, I can see that." She took the last few steps up to Emeron and nudged her boots out of the way, sat down, and rinsed the sand off her toes.

"You didn't have to come."

"Yes. I think I did."

"Why?" Emeron turned her head and gazed at her with emotionless eyes.

"Because you said things, to me and about me, which suggested that you not only despise me, but that you think I have ulterior motives."

Emeron flinched and redirected her eyes toward the water. "Sorry."

"I didn't come for an apology either." She touched Emeron's hand briefly. "I came because I care, and I think it's important to discuss things."

"What *things*?"

"Oh, for instance why one moment you seemed impressed, in awe even, with what was happening with Yhja and vehemently dismissed it the next." She was careful to speak softly and not sound accusing.

"God, you don't mince words, do you? You go straight for the jugular. You'd make a good soldier," Emeron said bitterly.

"I disagree. I'd be charged with insubordination so fast I'd spend most of my career in the brig."

Emeron stared at her for a second, then laughed. A short bark of a laugh, but it was a start.

She smiled and shrugged. "It's the truth."

"Somehow I don't doubt that." Emeron dipped her feet into the water and let them dangle. Water drops glistened in the light of the moon and the lamps. "You're too honest, and too independent. You'd better stick to your current job."

"You called me terrible things just now." She dangled her feet as well.

"Yes. I did. That was unfair. I apologize." The strangled words came out sounding authentic. They seemed torn from Emeron's throat by sheer force.

"Apology accepted. But I still need an explanation. Pri suggested that you've been here before, that you're somehow connected to this place."

Emeron stopped moving her feet and merely sat there, as if she held her breath. Perhaps she was trying to figure out how to avoid having to explain everything. She certainly had every right to, Dwyn thought, but was adamant about knowing the truth.

"My grandmother, Briijn, was Disian."

"What?" That wasn't what Dwyn had expected. "But the Disians… they never leave the forest. That's one of their rules. They're true to their heritage and revere the forest and their traditions."

"No rules without exceptions." Emeron lifted her right leg and hugged it to her with both arms. "Briijn was curious about the outside world. In every generation some choose another path. Briijn belonged to the ones with a tremendous amount of curiosity. She dreamt of exploring the Cormanian world and perhaps even traveling off-world one day. She ended up doing all that before she died."

"She must have been extraordinary."

"She was the one soul in my life who gave a damn about me. Briijn loved me like a mother should, when my own mothers didn't. Or couldn't." Raw with emotion, Emeron's voice came out staccato.

"And when she died, you had nobody."

Emeron blinked. "You're very perceptive. Most people at the time said I was still fortunate to belong to the nobility among the all-women dynasties."

"So, your grandmother, Briijn, was married to another woman. What happened to her?"

"She divorced Briijn after only a few years and left her to raise Vestine, my birthmother, alone. When my other grandmother passed away a few years later, her parents found Briijn working in the docks at a shuttle station, with my mother strapped to her back, which is the Disian custom. They wanted the little girl, their grandchild, to grow up in their midst so they took them both home. I have to give them that. They never mistreated Briijn. At least not deliberately. But they never understood her, and she was the most interesting, amazing woman among them. When I was born, she insisted she'd take care of me, like she had done with Vestine, which my relatives found curious since it was customary to employ nannies. She was more of a mother to me than my birthmother or my names-mother."

Rather stunned at Emeron's long speech, Dwyn boldly took her hand. "What happened that made you so furious with your heritage?"

"She died."

"I realize that. But—"

"And the Disians didn't do anything to stop it, even if they were supposed to know how. They stood by and let her die. There was certainly none of that crystal-swinging magic then."

"How old were you?"

"Fourteen." Emeron's voice sank to a whisper and she squeezed Dwyn's hand hard. "Briijn developed a life-threatening condition from a dormant illness that appears in many Disians when they reach a certain age. The only treatment consists of local herbs and some of their *magic*. I call it quackery." Emeron sighed. "My mothers didn't realize what was happening, and when they finally brought her here, apparently the Disians refused to interact with someone who had crossed over to modern life. They didn't help her. She died. That's it."

"A piece must be missing. The Disians seem enlightened and caring, from what I've seen."

"And you've been here half a day." Emeron didn't sound scornful, merely sad. "Pri, who is actually my grandmother's cousin, and the others, squabbled when they could have done something immediately. My relatives also acted too late. The bottom line is these people, my Disian brothers and sisters, are proud and regard any other culture but their own as inferior, when actually they're the ones lacking. They could have moved out a long time ago, contributed to society and not merely been a bothersome—"

"So that is how you see us, child? Bothersome people who don't contribute?" Pri's voice from behind made Emeron jump up and turn around.

"Yes. That is how I see you and the rest of these people. Only the children are innocent, and they don't know anything about the outside world. But the rest of you? Some take the opportunity to attend schools and get an education, but then they return home, here, to this charming but unproductive village."

"Your misconceptions have caused you much suffering, dear child. You are my kin, and I would like to explain a few things to you, if you are ready to listen."

"It's too late for explanations." Emeron grabbed her boots and shoved her feet back into them.

"I disagree. I don't think you've been ready until now." Pri gestured toward Dwyn. "Now that you've brought your *hesiyeh sohl* with you—"

"She isn't mine. That should show you just how wrong you are. Dwyn means nothing to me personally, and the fact that she's here..." Emeron shrugged, "is coincidental."

Emeron's words reverberated throughout Dwyn and caused a dark, dull pain. Afraid that her agony would show, she stumbled to her feet. "I should let the two of you work things out. You obviously have a lot to talk about. See you later, Emeron."

She hurried along the wooden pier and ran down the path to where she'd left her boots. She thought she heard Emeron call her name, but didn't stop to make sure. Tears burned behind her eyelids, and if she had to face Emeron right now, she'd break down and cry out of sheer humiliation. To think she had begun to believe that she could reach that cold-hearted automaton. Angry as well as humiliated, she grabbed her boots and hurried to the area where Oches and Noor had set up camp. Four makeshift tents of varying sizes outlined a rectangle with a fire burning in the center.

"Which is mine?" she asked abruptly.

"The one by the low-hanging trees, over there." Noor pointed toward a group of trees full of dark purple flowers, which were closed for the night, and their retreat mirrored Dwyn's desire for solitude. She murmured her thanks, then crawled inside the tent and into her bedroll, not even bothering to put on clean clothes. So what if she smelled of smoke? All she wanted was to fall into a dreamless sleep.

❖

Emeron stared after the disappearing Dwyn, still furious with Pri for her assumptions. "Was that necessary? You upset Dwyn."

"Did I?" Pri shook her head. "By speaking in a language she doesn't understand?" She shook her head, looking sad. "I hope you realize that your words caused the little one's sudden departure."

"*My* words?" Emeron almost shouted. "You were the one who embarrassed her by assuming I brought her here for a reason that doesn't exist."

Pri frowned. "Use your heart as well as your head, child. Your own words, when you stated so angrily that she meant nothing to you, hurt her. You obviously are important to her."

Emeron winced. "Damn." How had she expressed herself? Wanting to assure Pri that she was wrong, she'd said what was necessary to get through to the stubborn old woman. *Without regard for how my words sounded to Dwyn.* Groaning, Emeron clasped her forehead with both hands. "Damn it all."

"We should have our talk another time. I am sorry that my intervention caused such a reaction. The little one is an innocent,

I believe, and she has just begun to admit the attraction she has for you."

"What? What are you talking about?" Emeron looked at Pri, bewildered.

"The little one. The woman you call Dwyn." Pri spoke slowly, patiently. "She is an innocent when it comes to love. If you look carefully at her, you will see it too."

"Dwyn is a highly professional and capable woman, who's traveled throughout the SC all her life. She's by no means what you think." Emeron wondered what made Pri so sure.

"She has seen too much of humanity's decadence and selfishness, that is true, Imer-Ohon-Da. I am concerned about the things she has never allowed her heart to see, or her hands to touch. She is not experienced enough to see what lay behind your harsh words, child."

Emeron wanted to lash out at Pri, but knew her distant relative didn't respond to her intimidation like her unit members did.

"You should reassure her. Without delay." Pri looked in the direction Dwyn had disappeared. "Or the damage could fester and become irreparable. This is the second time today that you have lost your temper around her."

"I often lose my temper. That doesn't mean I should have to grovel because she misunderstood something." Emeron sighed and shook her head. "It's not up to me—"

"You care about this woman. You cannot hide your feelings, child. It is up to you, indeed, to reassure her. Once you care about another soul, you are obliged to treat that person kindly. Your words were not meant to hurt, but they did. They were not kind."

Emeron shoved her hands into her jacket pockets. "So, I'll grovel. Damn."

"It is not easy to—how do you put it—grovel. You set yourself up for potential hurt."

Emeron began walking back to the shoreline. "Then why should I do it?" She stopped and turned around, both hands on her hips.

Pri caught up with her and briefly touched Emeron's temple with her fingertips. "Because it is the right thing."

Chapter Thirteen

Rae?" Kellen stepped into Rae's office, where she found her gazing out the window at Corma Neo.

The dark aqua night above the capital and its six billion citizens was lit up by the vast city beneath. The tall buildings were impressive, some 12,000 meters at their tallest point. Cormanian engineers, known for their advanced technological solutions, had over the last two hundred years constructed such buildings, boasting up to 3,400 floors. Nanocarbon technology, paired with the use of transparent aluminum, had made this feat possible, as had the way they had managed to create foundations for the buildings, which reached far underground.

Rae's office was located on the 1134th floor, but the SC military base in which it was housed stood on a hill in the north of the city, which made their vantage point still among the highest in the city.

"Yes, darling?" Rae answered distractedly, not taking her eyes away from the view.

"How are you holding up?" Kellen stood behind Rae and wrapped her arms around her waist. "I'm worried about you."

"Oh, I'm fine. If anything, be concerned about my mother." Rae's voice was noncommittal, which Kellen recognized as Rae's way of coping. *Don't think. Do.*

"Of course I worry about Dahlia. But I'm also anxious about your father. He's not handling this very well."

"No?" Rae turned around within Kellen's embrace and met her slate gray eyes, now creased with small wrinkles. "He seems the same."

"He's pale and probably hasn't eaten or slept since we learned of Dahlia's kidnapping."

"Oh."

"And neither have you." She brushed her lips along Rae's temple. "Why don't you lie down on the couch in here, and I'll keep an eye on things. I promise to wake you up the minute there's any news."

"No, I can't. I appreciate it, darling, but I can't settle down. I'll try to eat something if it makes you happy."

"That's a start. Why don't we go back to the hotel and have dinner with Armeo and Ayahliss?"

Rae hesitated. "I'm not sure... All right. Why not? They'd probably feel better for having spent time with us. And I've missed them."

"Even Ayahliss?" Kellen asked carefully.

"Ah, well, yes. I'm warming up to our hothead." Rae smiled faintly. "She grows on you, I suppose."

"It took you some time to warm up to me too," Kellen said before kissing her gently.

"Oh, but when I did," Rae breathed against her lips, "I overheated instantly."

"Mmm. I agree. You did."

"And so did you."

"True."

They stood in each other's arms for a moment. Kellen hadn't known how much she'd missed holding Rae like this, to comfort her and distract her with teasing banter. They'd been thrown into one chaotic situation after another, and this time, the stakes were higher than ever. She knew Rae wouldn't buckle under the pressure, but she also knew the toll it took for her to remain professional and objective.

"Admiral, ma'am. Oh. I'm sorry."

Kellen looked at a startled ensign by the door. "Enter." She let go of Rae and witnessed the familiar transformation as Rae turned into Admiral Jacelon. It was as if she grew centimeters taller and her persona took up more space than her body did.

"Report," Rae said, and sat down behind her desk.

"Ma'am, the Cormanian officials have sent the necessary permits for you to form a search-and-rescue team to enter the Disi-Disi forest."

"What? Already? You sure about this, Ensign?" Rae rose immediately.

The ensign gulped, probably from being under the scrutiny of the admiral's now-brilliant blue eyes. "Yes, ma'am. Also, Lt. Commanders D'Artansis and Grey have arrived at headquarters and are on their way to the conference room." The young man cleared his throat. "I took the opportunity to alert Admiral Ewan Jacelon and Captain de Vies."

"*Excellent* thinking, Ensign. You saved us valuable time."

"I'm on duty for the next twenty-four hours if I can do anything else to help," he said, looking flustered.

"Good to know. Dismissed."

"Finally, a step forward," Rae continued, new energy in her voice. She circled her desk and pulled Kellen into a full embrace. "We're going to get her back."

"Yes." Kellen had already prepared herself, but didn't plan to tell Rae of her gan'thet meditation session earlier. She knew this mission would be difficult and she would have to prepare her body, mind, and soul for the upcoming task. The most important thing was to rescue Dahlia, but Kellen was aware that in order to reach this goal, she might have to take a life—again.

"Let's go find Owena and Leanne. They might forgive us for destroying their honeymoon once they hear what's going on." Rae slowly let go of her. "My turn to ask. Are you all right, darling?"

"My turn to reply, I'm fine, Rae." She took a deep breath and assumed the smile she knew had to be in place to satisfy Rae. "Time to go."

As they left Rae's office, Rae let go of her hand, and she felt the lack of touch as a physical pain. They were on their way to carry out a new mission, one where personal happiness was at stake. Kellen let her thoughts barely graze the memory of her meditation. She had seen dark clouds form at the horizon as she had focused on the low hum when her gan'thet sticks aligned on the floor before her. Dark clouds were foreboding, and in her experience they never represented anything good.

❖

"Leanne. Owena. I'm so glad you're here." Still outside the conference room, Rae could allow herself to address her friends casually. Once inside, she'd be the admiral, their commanding officer.

Leanne, the more spontaneous of the two women, rushed toward Rae and hugged her fiercely. "Rae, Kellen, we're so sorry to hear what that idiot M'Ekar has done. You must be beside yourselves with worry. Once I get my hands on him—"

"—unless I get to him first. As my brand-new wife says, we're here to help in any way we can." Owena, introverted and brooding, joined them. She was as tall as Kellen and as dark as Kellen was blond. "We'll find Dahlia."

"Now that you're here, I feel even more confident. Right, Kellen?" Rae looked at Kellen, who now waited for Leanne to embrace her.

"Absolutely. Hello, Leanne. My apologies regarding your honeymoon."

"Hey, we can always go back. This is more important."

Leanne D'Artansis was the only native Cormanian among them, and her pale skin, combined with her dark red hair and slender figure, suggested a certain frailness, though nothing could be more inaccurate. Rae had seen Leanne take on huge male soldiers in one-on-one combat exercises and, most of the time, the men found themselves on their back within seconds.

"Aha, a reunion." Rae's father joined the group of women, and Owena and Leanne immediately snapped to attention.

"Good evening, sir."

"Commander Grey, Commander D'Artansis. Time to devise a plan. I believe my daughter and Kellen have one ready for our perusal."

"Aye, sir," Leanne said, and opened the door into the conference room. Inside, Alex de Vies was already working at the main screen, pulling up charts of the Disi-Disi forest.

"Ma'am, sir, I have the latest satellite intel here. The Cormanians didn't like the fact that I used a military satellite and redirected it toward the forest, but I finally convinced them that this is a special occasion and that the SC has no desire to spy on the Disians."

"Good. Let's get on with it." Ewan sat down, followed by Rae and her colleagues.

She took a few moments to gaze at the faces around her before she spoke. "We have heard from the Cormanian team already in place within the forest. They have reached the largest Disian village, popularly described as the Disian capital, and the conditions are bad. The *Viper* crashed into a residential area, causing mass casualties. The team leader, Emeron D'Artansis... Yes, Commander?"

Leanne had leaned forward, studying the screen with narrowing eyes as Rae had started the briefing.

"Sorry to interrupt, ma'am, but did you say Emeron D'Artansis?"

"Yes. I noticed her name right away, but had no way of knowing if your last name is common on Corma."

"It isn't. My family, well, it's considered part of the old nobility. I come from an all-women family, and Emeron *is* a relative. Unless I'm mistaken, our great-grandmothers were sisters. She's considered an outsider in the family, much like I am."

"Ah, can you tell me anything else about her?"

"She's been in military law enforcement since she left home before she was twenty. She rose rapidly through the ranks. Emeron is the sort happiest when she's working. And she's good at what she does. I haven't seen her in more than five years, though. Oh, and one more thing, she has one advantage. She spent some time in the forest when she was an adolescent. She knows the territory. She's one-quarter Disian."

"Really? That's unusual." Rae waited while Alexis noted the information. "Thank you, Commander D'Artansis. Hmm. This name issue could become confusing."

She returned to their main topic. "Emeron D'Artansis has been heading a unit of nine, including herself and a civilian, to perform some survey of the protected forest. Her unit was deployed near where M'Ekar crashed, then redeployed to provide intel. Seems they stumbled right into the mess. They're currently conducting search-and-rescue operations and collecting evidence. The Disians reported that several of the passengers on board the *Viper* survived and left immediately after the crash."

"How far do we estimate M'Ekar and his mercenaries have made it?" Ewan asked.

"Here, sir." Alex pulled up a satellite image of the forest. "They crashed at these coordinates." He pointed to the east of the forest. "We have no way of knowing exactly which direction they took, but considering the testimonies given about where they were headed when they left the village, and the fact that some of them were injured and carried on stretchers, we figure they are within this area." He drew a circle using the computer. "At least four major paths—I wouldn't call them roads—lead from the village in this direction. Perhaps they even stayed away from the paths and made their way through the undergrowth."

"Not something I'd recommend, but damn it if I know how these criminals think," Ewan said. He seemed to consider something, then spoke again, his voice tense. "Any intel on my wife in particular?"

"I went through Emeron D'Artansis's latest notes and, so far, nothing. They haven't been able to enter the *Viper*. It was still too hot from the massive fire at the crash site."

Ewan paled and Rae had to press a hand against her midsection. The thought of what might have happened to her mother sickened her, but she couldn't allow fears of a worst-case scenario to hinder her efficiency.

"How do we rendezvous with Emeron D'Artansis and her unit?" Rae asked when she knew she had her voice under control.

"As it turns out, there are twenty-one clearings in the Disi-Disi forest where it is legal to land a vessel, or drop supplies, in case of an emergency. Council Leader Thorosac did quite some arm-twisting before the Cormanians would let us employ one of our shuttles for this purpose. However, we can't use anything larger than a Beta shuttle, thoroughly inspected by the Cormanian section of this military installation."

"That doesn't allow us to take much backup," Owena said. "A class-Beta shuttle carries only six people, including the pilot and navigator."

"I know, but this was the best I could do, given the time constraint."

"It'll have to do." Rae spoke quickly. "I'll head up the team and will take Commanders O'Dal, D'Artansis, and Grey. Two marines will accompany us, and Captain de Vies will be our liaison with the base and the Cormanian authorities." Rae turned to her father, whose gray complexion suggested his age for the first time, but she knew she couldn't show him any pity or compassion in public. "Admiral, we need you to use your connections within the SC Council. And they have to put more pressure on the Cormanians. I don't know why they are so reluctant to cooperate, but we can't have M'Ekar slip through the cracks because of them."

"Agreed. I will keep Marco Thorosac posted, and Captain de Vies will keep me informed of every development. When is your ETD?"

"We'll leave as soon as the shuttle is equipped according to our needs and the Cormanian law, which should be interesting." She stood. "This is a matter of great importance for the SC, as well as a personal matter. My mother is privy to confidential information that could damage us significantly if it ended up in the wrong hands. Knowing my mother, she would rather risk her life than give them anything. But you know as well as I do that mind-altering drugs can make a person do things completely out of character."

"Oh, stars," Leanne whispered, and Rae˙ saw Owena squeeze Leanne's arm.

She didn't acknowledge that she'd heard anything. "We need to save my mother before she's harmed or somehow forced to compromise the SC and its plans. We have to stop M'Ekar, apprehend him, and incarcerate the people that facilitated his escape. It's a lot, and it's up to us."

Rae finally looked at Kellen and saw cold determination in her eyes. Something was going on. Kellen had locked the door to her office for an hour earlier that day, and she wondered why.

CHAPTER FOURTEEN

E meron hesitated outside the tent. Noor had motioned toward it when Emeron appeared, and the frown on her face had not been encouraging. Did everyone think she was to blame here? What about Dwyn's stubborn self-righteousness? Surely her unit members hadn't forgotten their exasperation, only days ago, when they learned of this trivial assignment?

Pushing the tent flaps aside, Emeron ducked inside and held her breath, not sure what to expect. At first she was relieved to see Dwyn curled up inside her bedroll, apparently asleep. Determined not to disturb her, Emeron turned around to leave. She had her hand on the tent flap when she halted again. Something about the very still form wasn't right. She remembered how Dwyn had inhaled the poisonous smoke from the bots she'd destroyed. What if her lungs had deteriorated from the smoke around the Disian village?

"Dwyn?" Worried, Emeron crawled up alongside her. "Are you all right?"

"Go away," she said quietly, but Emeron heard the forced indifference in her tone and knew what it meant.

"Dwyn, I'm sorry." She was surprised how easily the words came out. "I can be such a bitch."

"You meant what you said. You don't have to apologize. It is what it is." Dwyn didn't move. Curled up, nearly in a fetal position, she still didn't look at Emeron.

"The thing is, I didn't. I mean, I was furious at what's going on here—still am." She shifted and sat down more comfortably next to Dwyn. "I guess it's no secret that I resent certain aspects of my heritage." She touched Dwyn's hip outside the bedroll and let her hand remain there as she felt distinct tremors. "I shouldn't have involved you. When Pri called you my *hesiyeh sohl*, my woman of the sun, I was angry."

"Don't worry. I got the message."

"I know. But it wasn't true. I mean, I'm not as indifferent to you as I sounded. And Pri called me on it. She gave me a piece of her mind after you left."

"What do you mean, it wasn't true?" Dwyn stirred and sat up, her blond hair mussed in a silver cloud around her. She had obviously jumped straight into her bedroll without using the portable sanitizer. The dark, vertical streaks down her cheeks showed where tears had revealed clean skin. *She's been crying. I made her cry.*

"Yes, well. I gave the impression that I'm indifferent to you. That you don't matter." She studied the pattern of dust and stains on her uniform pants. "It wasn't…isn't, I mean…true. I do care about you. About your safety."

"You do your job well, *Commander*." Dwyn sighed, gesturing with her palms up. "I have no complaints. You don't have anything to worry about."

"That's not what I meant." Frustrated, she clenched her fists. "I do worry. I mean, I care."

Dwyn looked into her eyes, apparently searching for something. "You care? How?"

Cornered, she wanted to retreat, but told herself she had never acted cowardly and this wasn't a good time to start. "I care. About you, I mean. I told Pri you didn't matter, but that's a lie. I said it because I resented her being presumptuous. I never stopped to think how it would seem to you."

"And what do you think now?" Dwyn's voice didn't give anything away.

"You would feel as if you were invisible and insignificant." Emeron found it difficult to speak, and when the words were out, she sighed and shook her head. "Please, forgive me."

"But you don't know me. You don't even *like* me. Why would it bother you how I feel?" Dwyn still sounded detached, but her trembling hands and the thin lines around her eyes gave her away.

"I don't know everything about you, but I know a lot. You are courageous, passionate, heroic, and, more than that, you are dedicated and a believer. I envy you that."

"A believer?"

"Yes. Someone who still believes in her cause, in her fight. You look at the universe through a completely different window than I do. You see other things, and you value them whereas I merely shrug."

Dwyn rose onto her knees and squeezed Emeron gently. "I could almost think that you admire me, Commander." Whereas Emeron's title had sounded insulting before, Dwyn spoke it with a gentle tease in her voice now. "That's quite a switch."

"Still true." Emeron licked her lips, at a loss suddenly on how to proceed. Dwyn's proximity stole her breath, and she had to remind herself of what Pri had said about Dwyn's innocence. *Just how innocent are you? Innocent, period—or innocent when it comes to women?* The thought of Dwyn in the arms of a male lover, *any* lover, disturbed her. *Damn it, I have to stop this.*

Dwyn traced Emeron's jawline with light fingers. "I know what we should do," she said huskily. "It's way overdue."

"It is?" Emeron swallowed.

"Yes." Dwyn blushed faintly. "We both need to use the sanitizer. Clothes, skin, teeth. The lot."

Relieved, and disappointed, she took Dwyn's words literally and reached for her carrier that Noor had placed above her bedroll. "We can use mine."

Dwyn's smile showed relief as well, but somehow another, more contented kind. "Would you start with my hair? I have to harness it into a braid, and it's much easier if it's clean."

The thought of touching the silky mass dried her mouth again, and she had to attempt to speak twice before she succeeded. "All right. Turn around."

Dwyn pivoted and sat with her back to her. Her hair lay in long tassels, more gray than blond from the smoke.

"Wait." Dwyn rummaged through the carrier, then handed her a small ampoule. "Here. I use this sometimes."

Emeron regarded the tiny object under raised eyebrows. "Apple blossom?"

"Yes." Dwyn shrugged, looking embarrassed. "It's a childhood thing. The scent is comforting. Perhaps because Mom used to make me apple-cinnamon tea. I don't know." She shrugged again and sat still, a little hunched over.

A few days ago she would have scorned Dwyn. She would have mocked the use of perfume on an assignment without any regard for Dwyn's reasons. Now, she slipped the ampoule into the little compartment in the handle of the sanitizer and ran it along Dwyn's hair. "Mmm. Smells nice."

"Really?" Dwyn's hopeful tone tore at her.

"Really. Can I borrow some? If you'd do my hair?" *Did I just ask to use perfume in the field? Mogghy's never going to let me live that one down.*

"Sure."

She kept working on Dwyn's hair and had to lift the silvery masses to reach all sides of it. It was like a live entity. Flowing and falling between her fingers, it twirled around them and pulled her in. Finally, it was clean and she had the daunting task of sorting out all the knots.

"What do you use, a comb?" She looked in her own carrier.

"No, that'd get stuck. I use this." Dwyn pulled out a hairbrush unlike any she had ever seen. Its strands were white and soft, and the back and handle were made of silver. An intricate pattern of swirling flowers was engraved on the back, an alien monogram in the center of the pattern.

"This must be very old. It's beautiful."

"It's a family heirloom. I'm probably more superstitious than I care to admit, but I never go on an assignment without it. My mother is a very prosaic woman, but the fact that she and all the women before her kept this, and used it, every day, means a lot to me. I believe it's from the nineteenth century."

"Really? Amazing." She began to run the brush through Dwyn's hair and found it easier to get rid of the knots if she started at the ends and worked her way up. She made sure she held on tight above the knots, so she wouldn't yank Dwyn's scalp. "Let me know if I hurt you." She spoke before thinking and groaned inwardly at her words. She'd already done her best to hurt this woman today.

"You're doing fine." Dwyn leaned closer and the apple-blossom scent filled Emeron's senses. "I remember crying sometimes while my mother brushed my hair when I was growing up. She wanted to cut it short, shorter than yours, for practical reasons, but I refused."

"Have you ever? Cut it, I mean?" It was soothing to talk about everyday things in the middle of this disastrous situation. She couldn't remember ever brushing anyone's hair, not even when she'd tried to woo a woman when she was younger.

"Only the ends. Other than that, no. I know I'm not very feminine, but my hair is sort of a signature."

"Hey, what do you mean? Not feminine? What are you talking about?" She pushed Dwyn sideways so she could meet her eyes.

"Well, I'm not girly. I never was. My profession has hardened me, I suppose."

"But you're the most beautiful and feminine woman I've ever seen," Emeron blurted, momentarily shocked by her own words. It was too late to take them back.

Dwyn stared at her, her lips parted. "What? Are you blind? I'm sitting here in dirty coveralls, and you think I'm feminine?"

"Very." She smoothed the last tress. "And I think it's time to clean up our act, coveralls and all. Want to go first? I can wait outside."

"All right." Dwyn regarded her shyly. "But you don't have to leave."

She had no reply, merely sat and watched Dwyn disrobe. She had slender, yet wiry, arms, narrow shoulders, and a boyish, thin torso. Tiny, bluish freckles covered the back of her neck and ran downward in an arrow shape. Inherited from her Iminestrian father, no doubt. Emeron couldn't look away from Dwyn's small breasts, so perfectly proportioned to her slight body. Her mouth wasn't dry anymore. In fact, it watered instantly at the sight of Dwyn's small, dark red nipples.

"Let me help you." Emeron changed the setting on the sanitizer to skin and removed the ampoule. She ran it over Dwyn at a two-centimeter distance and watched the flesh come to life beneath it. The cleansing process made it almost impossible not to bury her face against Dwyn's neck.

"Thanks." Dwyn's voice was hoarse, and she fumbled as she reached for a clean linen shirt.

"You're welcome." Emeron lowered the sanitizer and watched in horror-filled delight as Dwyn donned the garment, then slid off the lower part of the coveralls. Her hips were as slim as her chest, and still there was nothing boyish about her.

"I'm not making you uncomfortable, am I?" Dwyn halted as she stuck her hands down the waistband of her underwear.

"No. No. Why do you ask?" She licked her lips.

"Because you're staring."

"Oh. Sorry. I…" She shifted her gaze and fiddled with the sanitizer.

"It's all right. Just as long as I don't freak you out. I'm used to a non-privacy kind of environment. I figured you'd be desensitized from all your years in law enforcement."

"I am. Well, I mean, I was." Furious at her own stuttering, she cleared her throat. "I didn't mean to stare, but you're just so damn beautiful."

Dwyn had pulled her underwear down halfway and now she stopped, blushing faintly. "Oh."

Emeron acted without thinking. She placed the sanitizer on her bedroll and covered Dwyn's hands with her own. Slowly she slid the last items of clothing along Dwyn's legs and off her feet. Grabbing the sanitizer, she ran it along Dwyn's legs and around her hips. Dwyn accommodated her, trembling, her blush more saturated as she parted her legs. Emeron was sweating now, her hands shaking as she ran the device between Dwyn's legs, not touching the skin, but right next to it. When she was done, Dwyn rose to her knees, her eyes narrow and dark, and began to unfasten Emeron's coveralls.

"Your turn." Her words came from a deep place in her throat, a guttural sound that barely resembled her normal speech.

Emeron tore off her clothes, so turned on it hurt to wear them. Dwyn ran the sanitizer along her, carefully cleaning her hair and not missing a spot. The hum from the device ignited fires along hundreds of thousands of nerve endings, and she knew she'd be buzzing soon too.

Dwyn placed the sanitizer back into Emeron's carrier, then merely sat there, looking at her. "You're stunning," she said. "Absolutely stunning. Like a work of art."

"Dwyn." She touched Dwyn's chin. "Have you forgiven me? For this evening?"

Dwyn blinked. "Oh." She scooted closer. "The way you've touched me, or not touched me, rather, says more than any apology. So, yes. I have. I do believe you care."

"Having you near me like this is something I never thought would happen."

Dwyn smiled. A sweet, lopsided smile. "I never thought I'd be in this situation with you."

"Pri said you're an innocent when it comes to intimacy."

Dwyn pulled back, only a few centimeters, but enough for Emeron to see the change in her demeanor. "Why would she say that?"

"Because she's very perceptive."

"And I'm clearly a totally clumsy fool, who—"

"No. You're not. Not at all. But Pri told me to be careful. That you have little or no experience."

"What did you say to make her warn you like that?" Dwyn didn't avert her eyes, even if she spoke in a shaky voice.

Emeron felt a blush creep up her neck. "I really didn't say anything."

"But, as you said, she's perceptive."

"Eh, yes." Emeron knew she was navigating a minefield and wondered, not for the first time, how she'd become caught up in this.

"And you have, of course, experienced physical intimacy," Dwyn said casually. "Many times."

"I've shared quite a few beds, that's true. Until a few years ago, I was on the prowl at every opportunity." Somehow, she knew if she was anything but honest with Dwyn right now, her words would come back and slap her in the face.

"What happened to change that?"

"I was unhappy." She had never admitted that out loud, but knew it was true as soon as she said it. "I felt empty, and lonelier than when I was actually alone."

Dwyn's eyes softened. "So, I haven't missed anything? Is that what you're saying?"

"No, no, not at all." Emeron tried to explain. "There's nothing wrong with two people sharing a moment. For me, in the end, it was more like scratching an itch than sharing something wonderful with someone. The problem lay with me, not the women I was with."

"I see." Dwyn's eyes took on a shade of shining silver. "And now, when you've recognized this problem, have you given up hope of ever finding a soul mate?"

Dwyn's words startled her. *Soul mate.* "Eh, I've focused on the job, mostly. You know what I do for a living. If I don't concentrate, people get killed." Determined not to be the target of more difficult questions, she quickly said, "And why have you kept to yourself so much? You're a beautiful, intriguing woman. You couldn't have been without offers, so to speak." Unable to resist the surge of desire that accompanied her words, she cupped Dwyn's neck under the heavy hair.

"You making me one?" Dwyn's smile was tremulous. "But no, I

haven't had that many offers. Apparently my job situation is like yours. So, same reason, pretty much."

Emeron lost the last of her breath and, gasping, embraced Dwyn. She laced her fingers through Dwyn's hair, guiding her head back. "Dwyn." Hungrily, she pressed her lips onto Dwyn's, and the soft sweetness was almost too much for her inflamed senses. She groaned and knew she had to taste Dwyn, devour her mouth and put this overwhelming desire to the test. She slid her tongue between Dwyn's lips and expected her to reciprocate.

It took her a few seconds to realize that Dwyn was completely rigid and certainly didn't return her kiss. She pulled back and let go, mortified and embarrassed. "I'm sorry. I'm so—"

"Don't." Dwyn was pale. "You don't have to say anything."

"I shouldn't have…" She pulled the bedroll up, intending to cover herself, but looked at Dwyn, who sat shivering in her sleeveless shirt. She changed her mind and wrapped it around her instead. To her surprise, Dwyn sobbed once and rolled into her arms.

"*I'm* the one who's sorry." Dwyn buried her face against Emeron's neck. "So stupid."

She closed her arms around Dwyn, bedroll and all, and held her tight against her breasts. *Damn, she's an innocent, and I kiss her, for the first time, when she's half-naked.* "Shh." She merely embraced Dwyn, not moving at all. "You're all right."

"Today has been too much for me." Dwyn sighed. "I just can't seem to respond as I want."

"What do you mean?"

Dwyn pulled back and met her gaze. "When you kissed me, I wanted to respond. I really did. Somehow I'm stiff and frozen, and I have all these images in my mind—of the burned Disians, and the dead people…"

Cursing her own libido and lack of sensitivity, she groaned and hugged Dwyn. "You're reacting in a much more natural way than I am. I'm too hardened." *And too horny, obviously.*

Dwyn felt wonderful in her arms, and even though Emeron desperately wanted to kiss her, she was content to simply sit like this for a while.

"Aren't you cold?" Dwyn asked.

"You're joking, right?"

"No? I... Oh." Dwyn pressed her hot face back into Emeron's neck. "I see."

"Should we try to get some sleep? I have a feeling we'll be very busy tomorrow."

Dwyn nodded and they arranged the bedrolls and climbed into them. Emeron lay down, and before she could move onto her side, Dwyn slid up next to her.

"Do you mind?"

"Not at all. Come here." She pulled Dwyn onto her shoulder. "There you go."

"Thanks."

"Try to get some rest." Dwyn relaxed against her before she finished the short sentence, and she knew without checking that Dwyn was already asleep. Just before Emeron drifted off, she realized that, for the first time, she was content to merely hold someone as she slept.

CHAPTER FIFTEEN

Dwyn watched Emeron disengage the secure channel communicator. Her stark features gave nothing away, but it wasn't hard for Dwyn to interpret the steely resolve in her eyes.

"We have new orders." Emeron stepped into the circle of her unit. "Our headquarters is teaming up with the SC military installation. A unit of senior officers is en route to the nearest drop zone."

"Drop zone?" Dwyn hadn't thought there were any such things in the forest. "Are they big enough to actually land a ship in?"

"Yes, I believe so. They're strictly for emergencies, of course, and are located in natural clearings."

"Natural clearings? How can they stay open when you can't even break off a twig in the forest?" Mogghy asked.

"I don't know why, but the dirt appears infertile to larger plants and trees in these areas. To my knowledge, they've been used as drop zones for no more than a hundred years." Emeron shook her head. "I suppose there's never been an emergency such as this."

"So, where's the nearest drop zone?" Mogghy asked.

"About four hours' walk from here, if we take the less-known paths. I'll ask Pri for help. We need indigenous guides if we're going to reach the clearing in time."

"How many people does this unit contain, ma'am?" Noor hoisted her plasma-pulse weapon. "I hope they bring enough to help us catch M'Ekar and his cohorts quickly."

"As I understood, six. Four senior officers, and by that I mean *senior*, as in one admiral and so on."

"An admiral, you say?" Mogghy whistled. "There must be a lot at stake here."

"Evidently." Emeron began to leave. "Break camp. I'll go talk with Pri. Dwyn, you're with me."

"Aye, ma'am," she murmured without malice and lengthened her stride to keep up. Emeron had woken up only an hour ago and had looked completely energized. Dwyn was by then grateful that the tent was still fairly dark, since she had curled up almost under Emeron during the night. Not sure what to say, she had laughed nervously, which in turn had made Emeron hug her, quickly and fiercely, before leaving their tent.

"About our backup, did things just get better, or…?" She peered at Emeron as they hurried to the center of the village.

"Better, I hope. But Mogghy's eerily correct. A lot more than a fugitive and kidnapping is at stake here."

"What do you mean?"

"Well, since headquarters wouldn't brief me even over the secure comm channel, I'd say it's a matter of constellational security."

"That sounds ominous." She wondered what could have been aboard the crashed vessel to warrant such actions. Or whom. "And as I understand it, until these high-ranking officers get here, we're it."

"Correct." Emeron stopped at a small intersection in the village and turned left. Three houses down the narrow path, she hesitated briefly before opening the gate. "This is Pri's dwelling."

"You've been here before." Dwyn didn't make her words a question. It was clear to her that walking among the Disian houses wasn't easy for Emeron.

"Yes."

"They're not called houses? They're…dwellings?"

"Yes. The Disians don't see the house as a property, but a place to stay. They might live in the same dwelling all their life and still see it as a shelter given to them by the forest deities, one not to be taken for granted."

"All right. Let's see if she's in." She took the initiative since Emeron hesitated at the gate. "Do I knock?"

"Yes." Emeron blinked rapidly a few times, then joined her on the small cobblestone area outside Pri's front door.

Pri opened it and gestured them inside without a word. She guided them into what Dwyn guessed was the equivalent of a living room.

"Thank you for seeing us, Pri," Emeron said in Premoni. "I suppose you could sense us coming and know what I plan to ask you?"

"That, and the neighbor's little girl told me you were on your way. It wasn't hard to figure out why."

"And why do you think I'm here?" Emeron spoke politely, but the underlying curtness of her tone didn't escape Dwyn. She wondered if Pri noticed. Probably.

"You are here because you need *trei-kas*, guides, in order to travel with speed through the blessedness."

"You are right, as always." Emeron's face didn't reveal any sarcasm, but her voice insinuated as much. "Handy things, these Disian traits."

"Traits which you possess, if your pride would not deny—"

"Leave my pride out of this."

"Your grandmother—"

"Briijn is definitely off topic here."

"Please. Stop it." Dwyn couldn't be quiet any longer. The old Disian woman looked as if she could crumble at any second, and the loathing with which Emeron stared at Pri scared Dwyn. "Pri, we've come to ask if you could help us. Apparently you've already guessed, or somehow seen, what we need. Even I didn't know exactly what Emeron was going to ask of you, so clearly there's more going on than I understand." She drew a new breath, not taking her eyes off the two surprised women. "I realize there's history between the two of you, and one day I'm sure you'll have it out with each other. But today, this instant, isn't the time."

"Your hesiyeh sohl speaks her mind. That is a good sign. You need that," Pri said abruptly, but the fire in her voice was gone. "We should listen to her."

"She's not…" Emeron stopped. "Yes, she always seems to speak her mind. So, will you help us? We need two guides, since they have to take turns in order to remain alert and accurate."

"Yes. I have already chosen the two. The young woman you saw in the House of Worship, Yhja, and a young man, Trom. They are ready to join you."

Dwyn stared at Pri. "But she was dying when I saw her yesterday. She's in no shape to venture into the forest."

"Yhja was placed in a Cage of Prayer last night, and when the sun rose, all that ailed her was gone. The *Antahk* force is strong, and it gains more strength in times of adversity and need. Our deities do not let us down."

GUN BROOKE

"Nonsense. Your so-called gods sure pick their fights then." The anger and resentment were back in Emeron's voice. Her eyes simmered with hostile emotions, and Dwyn was afraid she would launch a full-scale verbal assault on Pri.

"You still harbor too much anger, Imer-Ohon-Da." Pri sighed. "We did what we could for Briijn."

"You ought to have been able to save her." Emeron raised her voice as she flung her hands into the air. "My family took her into the forest so you could do just that. I was *here*. I saw how you squabbled and then did nothing."

"You were very young and saw something you misinterpreted." Pri reached out to Emeron, palms up. "Briijn was in the last stage of the *idjus-kanh*. Had they not waited, but brought her instantly, we would have been able to save her. It broke our hearts that your grandmother, who was unique, no longer was among us. We tried every chant, every ceremony we could think of. It was too late. Briijn had traveled on to the next world."

"You say my Cormanian relatives were to blame?" Emeron asked, her voice menacing.

"No. They did what they thought was best. They took her to different doctors, and when the disease, so common among our people but unknown among outsiders, was finally diagnosed, they hurried her here."

"But too late."

"Yes, child." Pri stepped closer. "No one is to blame, child. No one."

Emeron stood still and seemed frozen in time.

Dwyn interrupted and briefly touched Emeron's hand, hoping to help her stay focused. "Yhja is going with us. Amazing."

"Yes. Yhja is an intuitive huntress who knows every part of the forest surrounding our village. Trom, who happens to be Yhja's betrothed, is a trader. He travels to our sister villages frequently and has also become an excellent tracker."

"Good," Emeron said flatly. "Are they on their way to join the unit? If so, we should leave. The team will have broken camp by now."

"They are prepared." Pri hesitated, suddenly appearing a decade older. "Imer-Ohon-Da, look out for them. They are but young people, and they know little of your technology. I have told them about the dangers and how death can come quickly if one of your high-technology weapons is fired upon them. I fear that they still do not understand fully, so please. Watch out for them."

Something seemed to soften marginally within Emeron. She didn't touch Pri, but she nodded. "Naturally. I give you my word that I will do my best to make sure they're safe."

"Thank you."

Pri walked them to the door, her steps heavy. Dwyn realized this woman must have been on her feet since the crash and was exhausted.

"Please, ma'am," Dwyn said shyly, "try to get some rest. You've done so much to help others that you've depleted your own strength. You must tend to yourself as well. Show yourself the kindness and thoughtfulness you've shown others."

Pri looked surprised. "Thank you, child. You are a kind and thoughtful soul, and it's such a joy that Imer-Ohon-Da has found her hesiyeh sohl."

Behind her, Emeron groaned, but when Dwyn turned to face the source of the sound, Emeron didn't look exasperated at all.

"If you say so, Pri," Emeron said softly. "We better go now. *Siendesh.*"

"*Siendesh, Imer-Ohon-Da.*"

Dwyn and Emeron hurried back along the paths, and Dwyn had to run to keep up with Emeron's strides.

"I didn't want to ask in front of Pri, in case it wasn't proper," she said, "but what's a Cage of Prayer?"

"What it sounds like. A wooden cage, cut out of a single huge tree trunk of the ancient trees. The sick or wounded person is placed inside, while a priestess, or a healer, leads the mourners in prayer."

"The mourners?" Dwyn didn't understand. "What do you mean?"

"They mourn the loss of the soul that will happen *if* the person in the cage does die after all." Emeron slowed down. "Sorry, didn't realize you had to run. Anyway, the mourners chant softly, urged on and inspired by the healer. He or she, mostly it is a woman, is trained in the art of inspiring people to reach that ecstatic phase when they are as one in voice and mind. I saw this many times as a child."

"And yet you don't believe in it?"

"I do," Emeron said sharply. "It's their choice, of when they use it and on whom, that I have a problem with."

"Whom?"

Emeron shook her head. They were approaching the camp where Mogghy had stored everything in their back-strap security carriers. "I don't want to talk about that. Perhaps later."

"I'm sorry. I didn't mean to pry—"

"You didn't. They're valid questions." Emeron smiled briefly. "Don't worry about it. It's history now. Ancient history."

"All right." Dwyn returned the smile. She didn't believe Emeron, since everything she'd witnessed proved that history wasn't ancient at all. It was alive in Emeron's soul.

Yhja and Trom shyly stood next to Mogghy. They both wore light green and brown pants and shirts. Yhja had tied her long black hair back into two braids, and Trom wore his in a tight, low ponytail, adorned with brown-and-white speckled feathers. Their feet were clad in skins, laced with something resembling thin intertwined vines.

"Report," Emeron said, her eyes gliding easily across the faces of her unit members.

"We're all packed, ma'am," Mogghy replied smartly. "We're ready, and it seems these two are prepared to join us."

"Yes, so I understand." Emeron looked at Yhja and Trom before she redirected her glance. "Oches, Noor, I want you to protect Yhja and Trom, since they're coming along to help us find our way faster through the forest. I want to return them in one piece, is that clear?"

"Yes, ma'am," Oches and Noor echoed.

"Good." Emeron grabbed their carriers and tossed one to Dwyn. "Time to head out."

The group began to hurry in the same direction that M'Ekar and the mercenaries had taken, with Yhja and Trom directly behind Emeron and Dwyn.

❖

"Don't worry, Admiral," Ayahliss said, moving up onto the couch where she'd been resting. "I'll take care of Armeo."

"I know you will." Rae sat next to her and pulled Armeo down on her other side. "And it's important that you two follow safety protocol. Hopefully Kellen and I won't be gone long, but we don't know for sure. Your grandfather will be here, but he has to work and run things from the mission room."

"Can we page him?" Armeo asked, with a familiar smile that revealed his concern.

"You'll have your own set of communicators with your own private channel to Granddad." She ruffled Armeo's hair, even though she knew he disliked it. The fact that this gesture made him curl up under her arm spoke volumes. They had left him twice before, and she hated doing this to him again.

Kellen emerged from their bedroom and sat down on Armeo's other side. "We will send word through Ewan. It won't be like when we were on Gantharat. We will at least be on the same planet."

"I'm glad Ayahliss will be with me."

"So am I. She's good at looking out for you." Kellen smiled at Ayahliss, who nodded solemnly.

"No, well, yes, she is, but that's not it." Armeo sighed. "It's just so boring to be with grownups all the time. The security officers are nice, but—"

Rae blinked. "Boring?" She looked at Kellen and was hard-pressed not to laugh. "Well, I suppose we can't expect them to be both good at the job *and* funny."

"I guess." Armeo didn't so much as stir under her arm. "Rae?"

"Yes?"

"You and Kellen need to look out for each other too. This one woman, the one Ayahliss kicked, she looked evil. You know. She laughed as she was firing at the guards."

She squeezed Armeo firmly. "I promise we'll be very careful. Leanne and Owena are going with us, and the best marines we could find." She didn't tell him there was only room for two marines.

"All right." Armeo had apparently snuggled enough and rose from the couch. "How long before you have to leave?"

"Two hours," Kellen said.

"Then Ayahliss and I should get to choose what we do until then."

"All right. What do you want to do?"

"Play the new holo-game." Armeo didn't stop to check if Ayahliss agreed, but ran off to the other room to get it.

Kellen shook her head with a smile and followed him.

"Admiral?" Ayahliss pulled a leg up and clasped her hands around it. Resting her cheek against her knee, she still looked tired.

"Please, Ayahliss, call me Rae. Are you all right?"

"Yes. Thank you."

"What were you going to say?" She frowned as something almost resembling fear flickered across Ayahliss's face.

"I want to be able to protect Armeo, but in my weakened state, I'm afraid I can't perform as I should."

She was stunned to realize how sincerely Ayahliss took her self-appointed job as Armeo's guardian. She had nearly died trying to save him, so Rae knew how adamant she was. She deserved a serious reply.

"Listen to me, Ayahliss." She spoke slowly and with emphasis. "I believe you'd sacrifice your life for him. You've proved that. I also want you to relax, since the kidnappers are far away from here and you're safe inside a military installation."

"There must be something, a medication or *something* I can take to regain my strength." Blue tears of fury formed at the corners of Ayahliss's eyes, and in that instant, she reminded Rae so much of Kellen, of how she'd looked the first time she saw her. Furious, wounded, scared, and with blue tears streaming down her cheeks. Swallowing her pity, Rae channeled her feelings into what Ayahliss needed to hear right now.

"There isn't anything you can take, but there *is* something you can do. It will be painful, and tiresome, but if you're prepared to do it, to fight, you'll regain your strength much quicker."

"What?" Ayahliss sat up straight, wiped quickly at the treacherous tears, and looked at Rae attentively.

"I'll have the base chief medical officer devise a schedule for physical training. You'll need to document each day's progress in a journal, and if you have setbacks, I want you to document them too. You can keep an eye on Armeo at the same time by making him your trainer. He can time you and keep count of repetitions."

"You seem to know a lot about these things."

"I was badly wounded on Gantharat the first time I was there, and I nearly died. Kellen saved my life, like you helped save Armeo." She took Ayahliss gently by the shoulders. "I know you can do this. I followed a strict training schedule and if I, a much older person and somewhat more badly injured than you are, can do it, so can you. I'm ready to bet you can accomplish it in two weeks."

"Are you going to be gone that long?"

"Hopefully not. But you will be well underway when we get back, no matter what. What do you say?"

"Oh, Rae." Ayahliss lit up and, to Rae's astonishment, threw her arms around her and hugged her fiercely. "I'm going to do it. You'll see. You just get yourself and Kellen back, and I'll prove to you that Kellen didn't make a mistake when she brought me to live with you."

She felt a sharp twinge of remorse about how she'd treated Ayahliss. She hadn't been able to trust her or see beyond the wild and unpredictable, no matter how Kellen had guaranteed that Ayahliss's heart was true.

"I know you will, and you've convinced me with your own actions, and your own words, that Kellen made the right choice." Rae returned the hug. "Now, listen to me. There's one more thing. Armeo's grandfather isn't doing too well. I'm sure he's so worried he'll forget to eat. Can you try to make sure he has a meal with you and Armeo at least once a day? I know it'll be hard, because he'll come up with excuses. You and Armeo can think of something, I'm sure. Use anything. Guilt, if you have to."

Ayahliss pulled back and stared at her with huge eyes, then began to laugh. "We'll do our best. Your mother says I can be very persuasive."

Rae nodded. "She's probably right."

"Here. Found it." Armeo rushed into the room and placed the humming game on the coffee table. "Who should go first?"

"You, Armeo," Ayahliss said indulgently. "You thought of it, so you get the first chance."

"Thanks." He beamed.

"Enjoy it while it lasts," Ayahliss continued, "because when it's my turn, I'm going to incinerate you."

Rae had to laugh at Ayahliss's words and the look of surprised determination on Armeo's face as he reached for the controls. The game was on.

CHAPTER SIXTEEN

M ove."
Dahlia stumbled as the nozzle of a plasma-pulse weapon hit her lower back. White's hiss of a voice was meant to intimidate her, but Dahlia found it merely irritating. She didn't kid herself. She knew White was lethal and unscrupulous, and it was wise not to antagonize her at this point. Dahlia had stealthily dropped small parts of her gold bracelet along their path, but now, two days later, she had to fight the doubts that multiplied with every passing hour. Was anyone looking for her? Did they know *where* to look? Ewan must realize by now that someone had kidnapped her and wounded Ayahliss.

The thought of the courageous young woman made Dahlia dig deep for hidden pockets of strength. What if Ayahliss had been terminally injured? *Damn, I was naïve regarding our safety.* Furious for second-guessing herself, she willed the fatigue away and counted every step in her head. As far as she could tell, they were still heading northeast, and she wondered how far they had to go and where they were going.

"Surely you can walk faster," White snarled, and shoved the weapon into Dahlia's back. The pain nearly sent her to her knees, but she managed to stay upright, clutching the last ten pieces of her bracelet in her hands.

"Damn it, White. Cut it out." Weiss Kyakh strode up to them. "How many times do I have to tell you this one is going to make us rich? If I detect one mark on her, and trust me, I will keep looking, you'll regret it."

"She's slowing us down on purpose. She's up to something."

"What the hell could she be up to? She's old and not used to marching through uncharted terrain like this. What do you expect?"

"It's not that. I've been watching her." White shoved her face up under Dahlia's, glaring at her. "Remember, she's the brainy type. Her sort always tries to be too clever for their own good."

Dahlia squeezed her gold hard, then willed her hands to relax, not to draw attention to them. She wanted to shove them into her pockets, but knew that would look suspicious.

Weiss seemed to consider White's words. She looked appraisingly at Dahlia, then shook her head. "You're not doing anything that would make me mad, are you?"

Dahlia's diplomatic training made it possible for her to sound just as tired as she was, and then some. She donned a frail voice and, she hoped, an exasperated expression. "No. I wish I was. I wish I had more strength, instead of having to stumble along behind *him*," she said, and pointed at M'Ekar's stretcher. "It's enough with this heat, these flies, and *her* ranting." The last part was directed at White. Dahlia couldn't help but stick it to the infuriating woman.

"Can't say I blame you for that. You can be exhausting when you let your mouth run, isn't that so, White?" Weiss grinned evilly and grabbed White around the back of her neck. "Behave."

"Yeah, yeah." It was clear that White was only accommodating Weiss, and Dahlia expected the woman to slap her head or shove her back again soon.

"I mean it." Weiss stopped smiling. "I don't want to be forced to choose between profit and an insubordinate employee."

For the first time, White looked shaken by Weiss's words. "I said I'd behave. Don't worry."

"Okay." Weiss turned her head to the front of her group. "Let's go, people. It's another few hours before we can rest."

Dahlia began walking, determined to keep her distance from White. At first she found it puzzling why Weiss let White be in charge of her, but assumed that White was Weiss's best and most ruthless member if she were to try something.

The forest became increasingly dense and she noticed she wasn't the only one who was exhausted. Several of the others were still coughing from the effect of the smoke inhalation, and the men carrying M'Ekar's stretcher were buckling under the weight.

"Captain," one of them finally called, "I can't do it anymore. He has to walk for a while. Surely you don't expect us to drag his sorry ass the entire time?" The man, young and thin, perhaps in his early twenties, was pale, and sweat poured down his forehead and the back of his neck.

"I can't walk. I'm injured," M'Ekar said, his voice surprisingly strong.

Weiss strode back to them and examined M'Ekar. "You look better. Try to stand up."

"You don't understand. I'm not a young man anymore and I've been incarcerated—"

"In a luxury suite," Dahlia said. They weren't moving fast with the men carrying M'Ekar, but perhaps they'd be even slower with him stumbling in front of her. Also, with a little clever maneuvering she might be able to trip him.

"Shut up." M'Ekar began to sit up, his face contorted with rage. "Don't listen to that bitch. She was the one who sent me to that mosquito-infested planet, not even fit for animals."

"You had a big house, servants, and permission to wander throughout your neighborhood." She smiled mildly at the enraged man.

"Shut up, I tell you. My *servant* was killed in the crash. *You* are my prisoner—" M'Ekar reached for her, though she stood well out of range. His sudden movements made the stretcher twist within the carriers' hands, and the thin young man dropped his handle. The others weren't prepared and had no time to compensate for the shift in weight. The stretcher tipped over, sending M'Ekar flying headlong into the undergrowth.

"Ow," he howled, as he rolled over on his back, clutching his shoulder. "That bitch. Look what she did. She's trying to kill me. Don't you see, Kyakh, she needs to be shackled and gagged."

"Quit whining, *Ambassador*, and get on your feet. You hurt your arm. Not very impressive if you look at my employees over there with third-degree burns and high fevers." Weiss gestured to the carriers. "Get rid of the stretcher. If we need a new one for him or someone else, we'll build one." She directed her attention to Dahlia. "And you, Diplomat Jacelon. I've just about had it with you. I'm beginning to think White wasn't exaggerating. You could be up to something, but remember, you're not going to succeed, no matter how clever your plan is. So keep walking and stop trying to stall things."

Dahlia hid a triumphant smile. Weiss might be on to her, eventually, but right now the *Viper*'s captain had no idea that M'Ekar had just played into her hands. She quietly kept walking with two mercenaries between her and M'Ekar. Soon she would have another opportunity to sabotage this hike. Clutching her gold, she took deep breaths of the sticky air. She had to stay alert.

❖

"Descending to low-corridor altitude." Kellen piloted the armed hovercraft with Leanne D'Artansis at her side. "We're crossing the Maireesian fields now."

"Good." Rae poked her head forward between them. "Keep low. I don't want to alert more sensors than we have to. We have permission, but let's not push it. You never know how well the Cormanians briefed their forestkeepers. From the intel I had time to read, they show no mercy toward trespassers. We're breaking quite a few rules with the armaments on this vessel."

Kellen agreed with Rae's caution. She had also done her homework, probably even more thoroughly than Rae. The keepers, all military people, used technology that had been especially approved to guard the border of the Disi-Disi forest. It was interesting that this part of the Cormanian military did not report to the SC military. Once this mission was over and Dahlia rescued, this situation needed to be investigated.

She was focusing every cell in her body on the ongoing assignment because they simply could not fail. Leanne and Owena seemed just as goal oriented. From the way Rae had briefed the two marine corporals, now thoroughly checking equipment, it was clear she didn't intend to return without her mother.

Kellen squeezed the controls. While the mission centered on the rescue of Dahlia, she was also determined to eliminate M'Ekar, one way or another. Her gan'thet staffs were hidden beneath her uniform. She had managed to squeeze in a practice session before they left, and they had felt familiar in her hands, even if her busy schedule didn't give her time to train like she used to.

Leanne interrupted her thoughts. "Look at that outline of trees. God, it's amazing. I haven't seen this since I was a child. It's like, you know it's there, but you're not allowed entrance. And when you rarely hear about it, you forget about it. Sounds strange, I know, but…" She shrugged. "This is so beautiful."

"Don't let that fool you, love," Owena said, joining them. "Any forest is beautiful in the same way a predator can be. It shows itself in all its glory, but it creates traps and captures you in ways you never dreamed, not in your worst nightmare."

"For the stars and skies, Owena, you sound like a horror story." Leanne looked up.

"I didn't mean to, but it's true. A forest is fine as long as you have a guide. That's why we can't go in blind. We need someone like your relative Emeron D'Artansis."

"It's going to be interesting to see her again. I've met her only a few times, long ago. Her mothers are as snobbish as my own, so I can understand that she keeps to herself, if she's as independent as they say. Just the fact that she chose a career in military law enforcement ought to have ticked her mothers off."

"And she's part Disian?" Rae asked.

"Yes. A quarter. Her grandmother, Briijn. I was only a baby when she passed away, but there was a big uproar in the family. At first she was more or less shunned, my birth-mother told me, but later she generated interest from our leaders, giving her an interesting, though hardly flattering, position within the family. They still felt the same about her, but she elevated the family from being noble to being noble *and* famous."

"Why did she gain such fame?" Kellen asked.

"She was a healer. She would chant and work with crystals, and sometimes just place her hands on people, and they recovered. When modern medicine failed, her healing powers didn't, and she started to get high-profile clients. Ministers, business tycoons. She never charged for her healing, which ticked my relatives off, and insisted on helping the less fortunate, which they thought should be beneath anyone in the D'Artansis dynasty." Leanne shrugged.

"So they liked the fame she brought, but she was still persona non grata because of her heritage and working with poor people?" Owena asked.

"Yes. Briijn was angelic, but no coward, from what I could read between the lines." Leanne blinked rapidly and tears clung to her lashes. "She never spoke ill about anyone, but she stood up to them, and she took care of Emeron. She loved that child and kept her away from the family's usual nannies. Her own daughter, Vestine, was under the spell of my snobbish relatives, but Emeron still adored her until the day she died. I'm not sure how that happened. A lot of silence regarding that situation, so I'm sure there's a story there that doesn't look good for my kin."

Kellen wanted to squeeze Leanne's hand, but knew it was inappropriate while on a mission, and besides, comforting Leanne wasn't her duty. It was Owena's.

"You're nothing like them, love," Owena said in a soothing voice. "You don't have to feel ashamed."

"I know. Yet I do."

Rae stood behind Kellen and touched her inconspicuously by running gentle fingertips along her neck. "I can understand that too. I have a sense of shame for not having a good relationship with my mother until recently. We've just begun to get to know each other again, and this happens. I'll never forgive myself if…"

Kellen didn't think. She pressed the command for autopilot and pivoted in her chair. The obvious pain in Rae's voice made her disregard protocol, and she wrapped her arms around Rae's waist and looked up at her. "Dahlia's aware of how you feel about her, and she's grateful."

"How could you possibly know?" Rae sounded angry, but her eyes were a soft aqua with hardly any gray as she gazed down at Kellen, her hands framing Kellen's face.

From the corner of her eye, Kellen saw Leanne and Owena move to the back of the hovercraft. Rae sat down in the co-pilot's seat, and Kellen held her hand.

"Because she told me," Kellen said.

"What?"

"A while back, I asked her how she felt about your relationship. You didn't know what you felt at the time, because you were recovering from your injuries on Gantharat."

"And?"

Rae's short tone was alarming, but Kellen didn't mind the interrogation. It was only fair. Dahlia was Rae's mother. "She said that nearly losing you, and being in charge of Armeo at the same time, opened her eyes." She spoke softly, careful to let her sincerity be obvious. "Dahlia said that her job had taken precedence, that she had left you with employees most of the time. She regretted it and had hardly slept while we were gone. She felt she wasted your childhood and youth, and was afraid she'd never get a chance to tell you how she felt or ask your forgiveness."

"I see." Rae didn't take her eyes off her for several long moments. Then she gazed over the Disi-Disi forest, seemingly admiring its beauty. "So that's what she meant."

Kellen waited patiently for an explanation while Rae digested the information.

"She embraced me when we deployed again and left Ayahliss and Armeo with her. She said, "Please forgive me, child. I owe you so much." I had no idea what she meant, I didn't have time to ask, and later I forgot about it. Mother was asking my forgiveness for my childhood?"

"I think so."

"And I said nothing, *nothing*, to alleviate her guilt."

"That can actually be a good thing."

Rae flinched and her eyes grew darker. "What? How could that possibly be good?"

"Motivation." She ran her thumb along Rae's lower lip. "You didn't answer her directly, and since she's so preoccupied with this guilt, the notion that she needs your forgiveness means she'll fight to stay alive and find ways to escape or leave traces for anyone trying to rescue her."

Rae didn't move. Her breathing was labored. Eventually a beeping sound from the helm's computer alerted them and broke them out of their reverie.

"All right," Kellen said. "The coordinates are coming up." She punched in a new command. "All hands, secure all equipment, return to your seats, and prepare for landing." Her voice carried throughout the ship as she returned the controls to manual.

Rae did her part, going through a checklist of procedures provided by the Cormanian authorities. They descended farther and the vegetation appeared impossibly dense. Kellen had never seen such impressive trees. They were so tall, lush, and varied. Some were in bloom and others bore unknown fruit.

"You're absolutely correct, darling," Rae whispered. "Thank you. That was what I needed to hear, and now I can focus on the assignment."

"Good. It was easy for me to assess." Kellen kept her eyes on the forest and saw the clearing just as it appeared on her computer screen. "We're about to touch down. It's going to be close."

"You'll do fine."

Her fingers danced over the controls, as if the hovercraft propulsion system was one of her beloved musical instruments destroyed in the fire that took her home on Gantharat. She compensated for a heavy wind and landed the hovercraft in the center of the small clearing.

Setting the controls on standby, she made sure they were ready for instant departure. "I should conduct a preliminary scan."

"Yes. Make sure there are no beasts, humanoid or animal, out there."

Kellen nodded briskly. "If there are, I'll take care of them too."

Rae hesitated before she spoke. "Just be careful. I'll cover you from the airlock. Owena, you use the escape hatch on the port storage compartment, and Leanne on the starboard one."

"Aye, Admiral," they echoed, and with the use of Rae's title, Kellen knew they'd put their private friendship aside. From now on, the deployment was all about being professional.

She surveyed the clearing from the airlock. Nothing moved, and she assumed that if Emeron and her team had made it here ahead of time, they'd be just as cautious. She stepped out, her plasma-pulse sidearm in one hand and a handheld sensor in the other. The screen blinked twice and she stared at it.

"Nine humanoid formations surrounding the clearing," she called to Rae. "They're moving in on us."

"Take cover, Kellen. Get back inside." Rae's voice was hardly audible as the wind howled in the trees.

Suddenly something singed past her, above her head. A red beam hit the hovercraft's fuselage with a resonant tone. She ducked, clasping her weapon tighter while staring at the sensor. "They're firing from the stern."

"Get inside."

She tried to fall back, but another beam stopped her.

"Stay where you are," a deep, husky voice yelled, obviously having no problems carrying above the loud wind. "Identify yourselves."

"We're here on a mission from the Supreme—"

"Emeron. It's me, Leanne. Do you remember me?" Leanne appeared at Kellen's side, her hands in the air to indicate she was unarmed. "I'm your relative, Leanne D'Artansis."

There was a long silence, and even the wind seemed to hold its breath.

Suddenly Kellen heard a loud, sarcastic laugh. "Well, what do you know—another outcast." A woman stepped into the clearing, her weapon lowered but obviously ready to engage. "What a team this'll be."

Chapter Seventeen

Emeron stood at the base of the ramp that led up to the hovercraft door. The tall, blond woman who had appeared first kept her weapon raised as Leanne approached. Emeron vaguely recognized her from younger days.

"Don't sell us short, cousin," Leanne said seriously. "Where's the rest of your unit?"

"Strategically placed, in case you aren't who you say you are." She scanned the blond woman with the sensor attached to her weapon. "She's neither Cormanian nor human."

"I'm Gantharian." The blonde approached her. "My name is Lt. Commander Kellen O'Dal."

"Lt. Commander within the SC? A Gantharian? Sounds implausible." She waited, having learned from experience that this approach, provoking people enough to annoy them, made them display their true nature. The only person it hadn't worked with was Dwyn.

"Just as plausible as a woman of Disian descent being a commander in the military law enforcement." Kellen O'Dal spoke promptly and without emphasis.

Emeron frowned. She hadn't expected the immediate comeback. Kellen, with her long hair in a tight braid and wearing the SC's gray mission coveralls, her skin faintly blue, looked so beautiful she nearly hurt Emeron's eyes. It wasn't until she was close enough to gaze into her ice blue eyes that she saw her strength.

"Enough with the niceties," Leanne said, and approached her with a broad smile. "It's been too long, Emeron, and we have a lot to catch up on. That will have to wait, since we have a job to do, but we have more in common than you think. It's good to see you again." She embraced Emeron, who stood frozen in place within the much-smaller

Leanne's arms. Well aware that Dwyn and her unit were watching from their positions around the clearing, she didn't want to look as awkward as she felt. She returned the hug quickly. "You too," she murmured.

"If we're all sure who's who now, perhaps we can continue according to our plan?" a throaty voice said. Another petite redhead appeared, this one with fiery, short hair and a commanding presence. "I'm Admiral Rae Jacelon, and you've already met my spouse, Lt. Commander O'Dal. This is Lt. Commander D'Artansis's spouse, Commander Owena Grey." Jacelon pointed to the right of the ramp.

A woman who could have been Emeron's twin, with her dark hair and stark features, emerged from the port airlock, followed by two large SC marines. Emeron nodded briskly at the new arrivals and motioned for her unit to show themselves. Immediately, they circled the hovercraft. Dwyn walked behind Mogghy, as instructed, with Yhja and Trom.

"Civilians?" the admiral asked, and Emeron couldn't judge if she was displeased.

"Yes, ma'am. Dwyn Izontro is an environmental activist who, you could say, got caught in the line of fire by being with my team. We were on a completely different assignment when our new orders came through. Yhja and Trom are our scouts. They know this part of the forest better than anyone."

"All right." Jacelon greeted the military members of Emeron's unit, who saluted her smartly. "We have a job to do and a lot hangs in the balance. A team of mercenaries has kidnapped Dahlia Jacelon, my mother. They also helped Hox M'Ekar, a former Onotharian ambassador guilty of war crimes, among other things, to escape. We have no way of knowing, yet, who on board the *Viper* survived. For now we're assuming that both my mother and M'Ekar did. We've brought the latest cutting-edge tracking and scanning equipment, which we hope will enable us to catch up with them. Hopefully, we'll then be able to devise a rescue plan."

"We've come across their tracks a few times, Admiral, but since we had to make the rendezvous time here, we could only place beacons. Hopefully the trail won't be too cold."

"Good thinking, Commander." Jacelon looked at each of them, and Emeron had to admit that it felt better to have someone to share the responsibility with. Being in command of this mission had weighed on her mind the last few days. And as the danger level escalated she became increasingly concerned about Dwyn's safety, which threatened to distract her from her ability to direct her unit.

"I'll brief you regarding what you need to know to carry out your duty successfully and safely," Jacelon continued, addressing the whole group. "I don't care if you catch M'Ekar dead or alive, and neither does anyone within the SC. When it comes to my mother, we must retrieve her alive and well, since she is invaluable to the SC, both when it comes to the war effort and our internal affairs. We cannot, and I repeat, *cannot*, allow her to be taken off this planet and across the border into intergalactic space."

"Aye, ma'am," Emeron said. She couldn't detect any pain in Jacelon's voice over her mother's fate. Jacelon and she were apparently similar, able to drop everything personal and simply do the job. *Well, that's how I've been until lately.*

"As for the crew of the *Viper*, they've committed a capital offence under the law of many of the SC worlds, including Corma, and I for one would like to see all of them stand trial."

Jacelon continued to brief them in greater detail before giving the order to move out. "I want you to take the lead with your scouts, Lt. Mogghy. Commander D'Artansis. Damn it, this is going to be confusing. Two Commanders D'Artansis in the same unit." Jacelon rubbed her temple.

"Why don't you call me by my first name, Admiral?" Leanne suggested. "After all, we know each other well, and I'd react as quickly to that as to my title."

"All right. Everyone clear?" Jacelon glanced around her. "D'Artansis, you will bring up the rear with the marines. Okay. Let's go."

Everyone gathered their back-strap security carriers, and Yhja and Trom led, followed by Mogghy and Noor, while Emeron and Dwyn went to the back. The marines walked behind them.

She glanced at Dwyn, then returned her focus to their surroundings, as well as the scanner on top of her weapon. "You haven't said a word since they arrived." She thought it strange that Dwyn quietly strode beside her, not even attempting any conversation or small talk.

"Well, I'm not used to being around celebrities. I'm a simple kind of girl."

"What are you talking about? Celebrities?"

"Yes, and two of them at a time are a bit much." Dwyn wrinkled her nose and laughed softly. "I'm joking. Not about the celebrity part, of course, but the intimidation. I never thought I'd even be on the same planet as a Gantharian protector. Let alone two."

Emeron felt like she had stepped off the real world and into the middle of a fairy tale where she had missed the opening chapter. "What the hell are you talking about?" She was careful not to raise her voice. "Protectors? Of what? And where?"

Dwyn looked like she was going to stop, and Emeron placed a hand in the small of her back to urge her to keep moving.

"You're joking," Dwyn said. "Or you haven't you been watching any news broadcasts for the last year?"

"I normally don't watch those things unless they directly influence my job. The news isn't very uplifting, and I see enough hardship in my line of work." She felt silly for being so defensive, but Dwyn's slight frown indicated that not watching the news was not only strange, but somehow reproachable.

"Surely you know why we're rattling weapons on our side of the border and the Onotharian Empire is rattling right back from its corner."

"Of course. The unlawful occupation that's lasted for twenty-five years."

"And?"

"And the fact that the SC finally has proof of crimes committed toward the Gantharian people."

"And?"

Annoyed at this game, she shook her head. "Why don't you just tell me?"

"Who provided the SC with that intel?" Dwyn wasn't easily swayed and was apparently set on making this into a riddle.

"Some SC commodore."

"Now promoted. Now married to a Gantharian, who happens to be a Protector of the Realm. A guardian to the last member of the Gantharian Royal Family."

Emeron paused, astounded that she was heading up a unit under orders to assist the two women responsible for more political bombshells than she could count. Not to mention that they were living proof of the mythical stories about the protectors. Glancing behind them, she saw the marines nod. All was well back there. She relaxed marginally.

"And just when I thought my life was turned upside down as it is.

Totally weird. Completely and utterly crazy." She groaned and ran a hand over her face.

"You calling me weird and crazy?" Dwyn wrinkled her nose. "A bit on the rude side, if you ask me."

"Rude?" Certain she sounded like a repetitive *gomesk'a* bird, she refused to groan again. Instead she reset her brain, the way she would do if facing an impossible tactical dilemma while in a code-red situation. She cleared her mind of all unnecessary information and sorted the important facts into neat compartments. Now calm, she felt like serenity personified.

"Well, not rude, perhaps. Your words give you away, you know." Dwyn shattered her calm with one look, a long curly tress escaping her usually tamed hair and caressing her jawline. "You can be so transparent sometimes." Mischievousness sparkled in Dwyn's eyes, and Emeron didn't know whether to be angry or exasperated. To her surprise, she couldn't help but smile.

"Transparent, huh? I think I can still surprise you, maitele."

Dwyn drew a deep, shaky breath and stumbled. "I should know better than to challenge you, I guess. You can never resist the competition."

"You're flirting with me, *maitele*." She held Dwyn's elbow and made sure they kept walking, not slowing the others down.

"Not really. I mean, only a little." When Dwyn glanced quickly at her, the fire in her eyes made Emeron lose her breath. "What does 'maitele' mean?"

"I'll tell you some other time." Emeron fought to keep her focus. She needed to keep an eye on her sensors.

"I'll take that as a promise." Dwyn winked discreetly as she moved up to walk in front of her, since the path had narrowed suddenly.

Concentrating on the march through the increasingly dense forest, Emeron was sure Dwyn wouldn't give up until she knew what the word meant. She scanned the area again, thinking how foolish she had been to call Dwyn "darling" in Disianii.

❖

"We *cannot*, Armeo." Ayahliss injected all the authority she could muster into her voice.

"But we can. You heard Kellen and Rae. We're safe here at the hotel. We're inside a military base, Ayahliss. And we won't leave the hotel."

"Your grandfather will punish us." *Especially me.* She folded her arms across her chest. "And we promised to follow their instructions."

"We will. We'll just do it down in the lobby where all the stores are. I saw them when we arrived. They have so many interesting things there. If Kellen and Rae were here, we'd have explored them *ages* ago."

"They aren't here, and we're not going to explore—"

"Ah, come on, Ayahliss, just half an hour. The guards won't even know we're gone. We can slip out the back door to the suite."

"I didn't know there was a back door." She frowned. "That's a security issue in itself."

"There's one behind the walk-in closet in Rae and Kellen's bedroom."

"You sneaky little—"

"Hey. You're talking to your prince, remember." He laughed and threw a pillow at her. She caught it and grimaced at the pain in her side.

"Please, Ayahliss," he said, apparently changing tactics. "I'm going crazy being locked up in here. Just half an hour."

"We shouldn't…" She felt her resolve diminish.

"It'll be so much fun. I have credits. Granddad gave me some Cormanian currency. He said I could spend it later. Well, later is today."

Her heart melted at Armeo's apparent joy. It was so obvious that he needed a little distraction. His mothers, and his grandmother, were in danger, his grandfather had to work most of the time, and all he had was her, who loved him and would die for him. Surely she could take him safely to the store he wanted to visit? "All right," she said, and regretted her words almost instantly. "Let's go downstairs for fifteen minutes. Not a second more."

"Oh, thank you." He threw his arms around her. "I promise, I promise."

She put on shoes and they crept down the hall to Kellen and Rae's room. The guards were in the sitting room, playing some game on the main screen. They had started only a few minutes earlier and would surely be occupied with it for several hours.

Armeo pulled her toward a narrow, nearly invisible door, decorated seamlessly to match the wall next to it. She took over, opening it just enough to peek outside. The corridor was empty, the glass and mirror hallways seemingly abandoned. She took Armeo by the hand and they ran over to the elevator.

"Armeo, it needs a pass." She stared at the door that had closed behind them.

"And here it is." He produced a small glass card interwoven with a thin strand of a yellow metal alloy. "Like so." He swiped it across the sensor and the elevator door opened.

"The lobby with the stores was on the eightieth floor, right?" she asked as she perused the control panel.

"Yes. There." He pointed, pressing the sensor before she had a chance. She had to smile at his eagerness, and again her heart swelled with sisterly affection. It wasn't hard to guess that he was lonely sometimes, especially when all the grownups around him were busy with politics and military affairs. He had spoken of his best friend many times, Dorinda de Vies, a girl his age. But he hadn't been able to spend any time with her for quite a while. He was brave, and more mature than any boy his age, or even older, but he was a kid, after all.

"We're here." Armeo was about to jump out the door as the elevator stopped, but she prevented him, making sure nobody was standing just outside before he exited. A few people were window shopping, and others, some in uniform and some civilians, were inside the stores.

"Oh, look at that." Armeo's dreamy voice caught her attention and she joined him at a window. A set of four hovering miniature assault craft floated inside with blue and yellow rays piercing the air.

"You'd enjoy playing with that?" she asked, uncertain how that could possibly be fun. "They aren't the real thing. The weapons, I mean."

"Oh, Ayahliss, of course they aren't." He laughed, a contagious sound that made her join him, even if she felt a bit silly for her assumption that he hadn't realized this. "They're toys, and you can play with four people, guide them by remote as you're firing on each other. The vessel that takes the most hits loses, of course."

"Of course." She answered automatically as more people were now sauntering through the commercial area of the hotel. Some had turned their heads as Armeo laughed, and a few of them were pointing.

"Armeo, we should leave." Her heart thundered. Something was wrong.

"No, it's only been three minutes. Five at the most." He dragged her toward the store entrance. "I have to go ask if I have enough Cormanian currency."

The murmur from the group of people who had just pointed at Armeo grew, and some of them began to walk toward him. Ayahliss knew if they entered the store, they'd be trapped. "Armeo, come on." She pulled back, but her side hurt and she could hardly hold on to him as he yanked her in the other direction.

"No. Just this one store."

"Prince Armeo." A loud female voice pierced the noise around them. "It *is* him. Oh, Gods, look. It's the Gantharian prince."

Armeo heard and understood this time. Suddenly pale, he clung to Ayahliss's arm as the crowd moved closer. The faces were not unkind, and Ayahliss tried to convince herself that the people were merely curious since Armeo was such a celebrity, but she knew that an enemy could be hiding within the multitude of people.

"Ayahliss." Armeo backed up against the window, and the people neared. Men, women, and children all came out of nowhere, it seemed, to look at him.

"I have you. I'm not letting go. Just smile and say hello." Perhaps that would defuse things.

He smiled politely, a tremulous, nervous smile. "Hello. Nice to meet you. I have to go now."

"Why are you on Corma, Prince Armeo?"

"Who's that young woman with you?"

"When are you going to Gantharat?"

"Where's your protector?"

Questions assaulted them, and the voices drowned out any answer Armeo tried to give. When finally a woman tried to touch his hair, Ayahliss had had enough. She kept hold of Armeo's hand, but grabbed the woman's arm and the stranger wailed, "She's hurting me."

The people around them fell silent, but Ayahliss didn't let go. "Move away from him," she demanded as forcefully as she could. "Can't you see you're scaring him?"

"I suggest you do as she requests," an unfamiliar voice said. "That arm looks like it could snap any second."

CHAPTER EIGHTEEN

Judge Beqq," Armeo gushed, and the look of relief on his face told Amereena Beqq that she'd arrived just in time. She had walked through the entrance of the hotel, on her way to her suite, before returning to the orbiting *Dalathea*, when the crowd caught her attention. She had debated whether to investigate, but a woman's cry decided for her. The last thing she expected to see was Prince Armeo without security, being protected only by a Gantharian-looking woman.

"You know her?" the woman asked Armeo, her Premoni tinged with an unusual accent that sounded like Kellen's.

"She's Judge Beqq, the one who awarded Kellen and Rae custody of me." Armeo tugged at his companion, who finally let go of the woman's arm. Rubbing her wrist fiercely, she glowered at Armeo's friend.

"She should be arrested for assault," she hissed, and the man next to her nodded.

"Yes, let's call security," Beqq agreed. "We can ask them to investigate how all of you mobbed a member of the Gantharian royal family and, by doing so, endangered his life."

"His life?" the woman said in falsetto. "We haven't endangered anything. We were just—"

"Curious? And, by that, drawing attention to a boy you ought to know is always in danger of kidnapping or attacks from political opponents."

"If he's in that much in danger," the man next to the upset woman sneered, "then why is he running around the shops without an escort?"

"Good question." Beqq turned to Armeo, who blushed deeply. "I think it's time we went back to your suite and found out." The crowd dispersed as Beqq guided them to the elevator, where Armeo quietly swiped his pass. "And who are you, my dear?" she asked Armeo's fierce escort.

"I'm Ayahliss." There was a tone of despair in Ayahliss's voice and something else, something Beqq couldn't interpret.

"You're Gantharian, aren't you?" Beqq asked as they entered the elevator.

"Yes, ma'am."

"And you came back with Ms. O'Dal and the admiral after their latest visit to your home planet?"

"Yes, ma'am." The monotonous answer didn't give anything away, but Beqq thought she could see tears glitter in Ayahliss's eyelashes.

"And you, young man, are out on an adventure without your security detail. What is going on?"

"It's my fault," Armeo said passionately. "Ayahliss tried to talk me out of it, but I was so bored and thought perhaps I had enough money to buy—"

"Surely you know better," Beqq said. "I have just been briefed about what's happened to your grandmother. I expected more from you, since we work very hard to keep you safe."

"Don't talk to him like that," Ayahliss said, eyes flashing with anger and her fists tightened by her sides. "He's just a boy, younger than he looks to you, and it's hardly a crime that he wanted to go look at some toys."

Ayahliss's defense of Armeo was interesting, but Beqq had to prove a point. "He's not simply a boy. He's the heir to the throne of a country that's at war with a very dangerous adversary prepared to go to any extreme to get the upper hand. Armeo, you have to learn to take all precautions and not to test your friend's loyalty like this. Do you understand?"

Armeo nodded, slumping a little, but he didn't avert his eyes. "Yes, Judge."

"Good. Now we're going to talk to your grandfather. I also have a few words to exchange with your security detail."

"It's not their fault either, ma'am," Armeo said. "We sneaked out."

Beqq tapped his chin with a gentle finger and couldn't hold back a strong wave of affection for the boy. This child obviously stole everyone's heart. "Oh, son, that's where you're wrong. This situation is very much their fault. Your guards were left in charge of you." Beqq was furious and looked forward to having them stand at attention while she gave them her opinion before sending them back to their commanding officer.

❖

The forest was almost quiet just before dark. The scents seemed stronger, and every plant glowed as it bathed in the setting sun's rays that filtered through the trees. Dwyn rested against a rock and watched Emeron's unit work with the marines to make camp. She had offered to help, but the marines had politely declined, one insisting on calling her ma'am and treating her as if she were frailty personified. If she hadn't been so exhausted, her lungs burning with every breath, she would have shoved the big marine away and still done her bit. As it turned out, she was happy to sit and simply focus on breathing.

"Hi, I'm Leanne D'Artansis. I know we were introduced before, but we haven't had a chance to say hello properly." Uninvited, Leanne sat down next to her and pulled out a bottle. "You look like you need a drink."

"Thanks. Mine's empty." Grateful, and charmed by Leanne's friendly manner, she sipped some water. "Mmm. Just what I needed."

"Then why didn't you ask for a new bottle? You've been sitting here looking more and more parched."

"I didn't want to bother everyone while they're setting up camp. I was going to get one later."

"All right. But you know, when we're in the bush, this far from civilian territory, you shouldn't risk getting dehydrated." Leanne's gentle criticism hit home.

"I know. And it wasn't that bad. You're right, though."

"Trying to prove to Emeron that you can keep up the pace?"

She flinched. Was she that transparent? "I'm not sure what you mean."

"Well, it's sort of obvious how she looks at you. Concerned. Worried about you. A bit more than just carrying out her duty to protect you."

"It is?"

"Only because Owena and I went through a period like that. Doubt. Self-doubt. Intrigue. Stuff that can't be denied." Leanne shrugged. "It took us a while to eliminate the barriers. Especially Owena. She's more like Emeron than I am, even if Emeron is my relative."

"She doesn't talk about her family much."

"That's not a bad thing. Our family is snobbish and a bit of a nuisance when you want to stay independent. They like to keep everyone neatly inside the fold." Lines appeared around Leanne's soft, full lips. "They can make it hard for you if they want to. Emeron and I try to stay under the radar as much as possible, each in our own way."

"I know more about that than you think. I had to go through a pretty bad break with my parents before I managed to gain my independence. They wanted me to follow in their footsteps and live a nomadic life in space."

"And you?"

"I wanted to work for a worthy cause, make a difference, but on my own terms. I'm based on Earth but travel a lot. Guess I became something of a nomad after all."

"At least you have a home, a constant, to return to." Leanne patted her hand. "Owena and I are discussing where we'll live once we decide to cut back on work." She wrinkled her nose. "Not on Corma. I showed Owena my favorite spots on this planet, but I don't want to live here."

"Your family has long arms?"

"Very long." Leanne looked broody for a moment, but then she lit up, her good-natured temperament taking over again. "But not long enough to reach inside the Disi-Disi forest."

"That's good." Dwyn grinned and felt some of the fatigue leave her. Leanne was a nice new acquaintance, and it was impossible not to respond to her. She began to laugh, but the laughter turned into a coughing fit. She sipped some more water to mitigate the attack, but her lungs crackled and burned. When she tried to inhale, the pain in her chest created nauseating images in her mind of how her lungs must be burned to a crisp.

"Oh, Dwyn. Are you all right?" Leanne's voice reached her, but she couldn't answer. She could only cough and wheeze.

"What's wrong?" Another voice, was that the protector?

Dwyn looked up, but the asphyxia was blurring her vision. She tried not to cough, but her body had other ideas. Her field of vision shrank as she tried to control the convulsions. "Em-er-on. Em…" Dwyn knew she was slipping into unconsciousness and found herself floating above her own body. She watched as Kellen O'Dal and Leanne pulled her flat onto the ground and began to resuscitate her. *Resuscitate? Am I dying? Or already dead?* She was relieved that the pain was gone and she didn't have to cough anymore. She was fully intending to let go when she saw Emeron running toward the small group of people around her.

"Dwyn, Dwyn."

❖

Emeron shoved the others aside, not caring that the famous protector was one of them. "Mogghy, the med kit."

"On my way, ma'am."

Emeron breathed oxygen into Dwyn while she waited for Mogghy. Her cold fingertips slipped on Dwyn's sweat-slicked skin, but she felt a tiny, fluttering pulse.

"Here, ma'am. The imbulizer."

She injected the medication directly into Dwyn's jugular, not daring to detour around deep muscle tissue. A few seconds ticked by, endless moments while she held her breath.

"Look. She's breathing," Leanne said, relief in her voice. "What was in that thing?"

"Her lungs were damaged twice." Emeron followed every breath, intent on how Dwyn's chest moved slowly up and down. "We haven't been able to treat them properly. This alveoli stabilizer is temporary. I'm afraid she may need a transplant."

"I'm sure the SC will get her the best-quality synthetic lungs," Leanne said. "She's coming to. Hi, Dwyn. Take it easy. You fainted."

"Ridiculous," Dwyn muttered, her voice thick. "I never faint. Water."

"Here." Emeron pulled Dwyn up onto her shoulder and helped her take small sips. "I gave you some more medication, to hold you until we get back. We should have you extracted—"

"No." Still sounding dazed, Dwyn was as stubborn as ever. "Not leaving."

"All right, all right. Just relax." Emeron held Dwyn tight to physically prevent her from making her condition worse. "Evacuation's probably impossible anyway, at this point."

Someone knelt next to them, and Admiral Jacelon cupped Dwyn's chin in her hand. "You look better. A good night's rest, four hours' worth, will put color back in your cheeks."

"Yes, ma'am."

"She's tough, Admiral," Emeron said. She had misjudged Dwyn's strength and didn't want the admiral and the protector to do the same. Besides, she needed the reassurance too.

"She looks it," Kellen said, surprising her. "I believe your tent is erected over by that group of trees. Yhja will share with Ensign Noor, and Trom with Commander Mogghy and Ensign Oches. I understand it's important for the Disians that things are conducted properly, even under these circumstances."

"Yes, they insist on enforcing their traditions," she said, without her usual sarcasm. "The youngsters can't sleep in the same tent."

"Well, it's all taken care of," Leanne said from above. "Dwyn, Emeron, can we help, or—?"

"We're fine," Dwyn murmured, and tried to get up.

"Stop that." Emeron rose and pulled Dwyn with her, lifting her with one arm around her back and the other under her knees. "Thank you, everybody. I'll let you know if we need anything." She walked over to the tent and guided Dwyn inside. Seeing how exhausted she was, Emeron began to undress her and assisted Dwyn as she reached for the thermo-coveralls. "Good choice," she said. "It'll probably be cold tonight. There aren't any clouds to keep the heat accumulated in the forest today from irradiating."

"You'll be here, right?" Dwyn sighed. "We can share."

"What?" Her heart fluttered.

"First rule of survival in cold and hostile terrain. Shared bodily warmth."

"Oh, that." She kissed Dwyn's forehead as she tucked her into the bedroll. She was so grateful to Leanne and Kellen for keeping Dwyn breathing until she reached them. Losing this amazing woman was unthinkable. The future waiting for them when this assignment was over was fuzzy, but she didn't want to dwell on it. Dwyn was as dedicated to her career as she was to her unit, and their opposing points of views regarding so many things were too depressing to consider right now.

Closing her mind to these speculations, she didn't bother to change. She briefly ran the sanitizer rod over herself and then over Dwyn's clothes. She poked her head out and watched the camp calm down. One of the marines and one of her junior officers were taking the first watch together. Everything was quiet as darkness fell among the tall trees. The marine had a pot steaming over a plasma heater, and Emeron knew they should have eaten something, but she was too tired and still too upset. They'd make up for it by having energy bars and a vitamin shot before they headed out at dawn.

She crawled back, slid into Dwyn's bedroll, and pulled her own on top of them, creating a warm cocoon to keep Dwyn from freezing. Dwyn shifted restlessly in her sleep and suddenly rolled over on her other side, facing Emeron. She curled up under Emeron's chin and drew a deep breath that—Emeron thanked every single mythical Disian forest creature she could think of—was clear and free of wheezing.

"Imer-Ohon-Da…" Dwyn nuzzled Emeron's neck where her collar left some skin available. "You really are, you know, a hesiyeh sohl. Sleep tight, maitele."

She couldn't listen to the tender words any longer or her heart would implode. She pressed her lips to Dwyn's, which prevented Dwyn from talking but didn't reduce the uncontrolled feelings that made her taste so sweet.

❖

"I assume Judge Beqq has already told both of you why this was dangerous and shortsighted?" Ewan Jacelon squinted as he stood in front of Armeo and Ayahliss. "We can't afford another risk like that."

Armeo cleared his throat. He had never thought he'd disappoint the man he admired more than any other male figure. Remembering how he'd felt when Rae's father gave him permission to call him Granddad, Armeo wanted to cry, but was determined not to. He glanced briefly at Ayahliss, who stood rigid by his side, looking like she was prepared to be punished. No, it was more than that, he realized. Ayahliss's expression was that of someone who'd lost everything. If his granddad hadn't been looking at them so closely, Armeo would have squeezed her hand to offer comfort.

"You can't stay here," Granddad continued. "The situation is too dangerous."

"I see, sir. I understand," Ayahliss whispered, her voice hollow.

"I'm glad one of you does. You'll be moved before word spreads that the Prince of Gantharat is on Corma. Judge Beqq has offered a very good option that will keep you safe and prevent anything like this from happening again."

"If I am permitted to ask," Ayahliss said, and Armeo flinched at her pained voice, "how long do I have, and where am I going?"

"I'm not sure I follow," Granddad said. "We should get you out of here ASAP. Within an hour, at the latest."

"May I say good-bye to the prince, sir?" She was trembling now, and blue tears rolled down her cheeks. "I know I failed him. I failed you and all the trust Kellen and Rae put in me. I repaid you badly for the kindness your wife has shown me, but please, if I could just have a chance to say good-bye to Armeo—"

"What's she talking about, Granddad? Where's she going? Are you sending her away?" Dread filled Armeo and he threw himself at Ayahliss, who steadied him as she hugged him fiercely.

"No, no, no. We're not splitting you up. Whatever gave you that idea?" Granddad's voice seemed to come from far away, but finally reached Armeo. He gazed up at Ayahliss's tear-stained face. "Did you hear that? It wasn't what you thought. Did you hear it?"

"Yes." She nodded quickly. "I heard. Gods of Gantharat, I heard."

Granddad walked over and wrapped his arms awkwardly around both of them. Armeo giggled at the look of astonishment on Ayahliss's face, which set her off, since she could never remain serious when he laughed. Granddad blinked and looked utterly confused before he smiled back at them. "Crazy kids. What did I do to deserve you?"

"Probably all those sinful days in your youth, Admiral," Judge Beqq said from the door. "Glad I missed all the drama. I don't do tears very well. Are they ready yet? The *Dalathea*'s captain assures me that the guest quarters are fully stocked with games and literature age-appropriate for Armeo's age, and Ayahliss's too."

"We're going with you to a ship in orbit?" Armeo asked. "But what about Granddad?"

"I'm coming too. I'll be working with the *Dalathea*'s sensor-array technicians to look for your grandmother that way."

Armeo held on to the people most precious to him after his mothers. He couldn't remember when he'd started to think of Kellen and Rae like that. He only knew it felt right. "Thank you."

"Don't scare your old granddad like that again."

"I won't."

"And take better care of Ayahliss."

"I will." Armeo realized now that Ayahliss had paid the highest price for their adventure. "I will."

"Good." Ayahliss blinked the last tears away and hugged Armeo before she dug her fingertips into his ribs and tickled him until he screamed for mercy.

CHAPTER NINETEEN

The searing sound was strangely familiar. Kellen let go of Rae enough to get on her knees inside their tent. "Rae. Wake up." She pulled on her coveralls and grabbed her sidearm. "We're under attack."

Rae was already sitting up, reaching for her weapon. She had slept in her coveralls and now shoved her feet into her boots. Kellen did the same and then carefully opened the tent flap. The air was heavy with morning mist, and multicolored beams crisscrossed the clearing.

Kellen could hear loud voices inside the other tents, but what drew her attention was Ensign Noor's still body in the center of the circle of tents. "One down," she reported to Rae.

"Who the hell is firing on us? And from where?"

"They've surrounded us, whoever they are." Kellen tucked her weapon into one of her back holsters and glanced at her scanner. "I don't detect anything on sensors. This doesn't make sense. I'll check on Ensign Noor."

"Damn it. I'll try and reach Oches's tent where the communication device is."

Kellen crawled outside, her body flat to the ground as she hurried over to Noor. At first she feared the worst, but when she pressed two fingers to Noor's neck, she found a strong and steady pulse. She signaled to Rae, who'd made it halfway to Oches's tent by now.

"Commander O'Dal," someone called from Kellen's left. Emeron D'Artansis was advancing toward her. "This isn't the mercenaries. We've been attacked once before by spy bots, and I'm certain whoever's sent them has launched more to try and finish the job."

"You've been attacked before in this forest and never bothered to let us know?" Kellen glared at Emeron.

"I made the mistake of thinking they wouldn't venture this far. Someone trying to destroy Dwyn's investigation has probably programmed them. Also, last time we were able to pick them up on sensors. This stealth mode is new."

"They're after Ms. Izontro and taking us out one by one in the process." Kellen motioned toward Noor. "We need to drag her out of the line of fire."

"Is she—?"

"She's alive. So far." She helped Emeron pull Noor over to one of the tents, where the two marines hauled her inside. The two men then joined her and Emeron as they crawled just within the perimeter of the circle of tents.

"The tent's protective mesh-alloy should deflect this type of fire," she murmured, "but we can't be certain."

"Their blue rays can cut through almost anything. I've seen it," Emeron said. "Let's hope you're right, though."

"Yes." She also hoped that Rae had reached Oches's tent and the communication center. The bots were impossible to see when they weren't firing, and she guessed that once they did and revealed their position, they immediately moved to another location and began blasting again. Blue, yellow, and green beams pierced the morning air, and together with the mist rising from the damp undergrowth, they blinded her as she tried to pinpoint their origin.

"Here." Emeron tossed her a scanner, which Kellen gratefully accepted. She worked it in a circle around her. "We're definitely surrounded. I read sixteen bots, and they're constantly shifting positions."

"So they actually outnumber us." Emeron reached into the back of her jacket and pulled out a second sidearm. "Not very good odds, but I've seen worse."

"Me too." Kellen recognized some of her own steely resolve in the way Emeron allowed an emotional visor to slide into place. "And I have a way to deal with them all at once."

Emeron eyed her with doubt. "Really?"

"Yes. I have to get to Commander Grey's tent. This may damage some of our gear, but I can't see any other way out."

"All right. Come on." Emeron proved again to be a woman of action and few words as she started to run, stopping only to duck when bots hovered closer and scorched the ground around them.

Kellen felt a searing pain in her left calf, but clenched her teeth to stop her moan. Aware that the bots probably had both heat and motion sensors, she kept going. If she stayed near the warm ground her body signature wouldn't be as easy to detect. Kellen didn't think she was bleeding, since the beam from the bot had probably cauterized the wound. Some grass straws were laser-knife sharp as they whipped at her face. She hadn't had time to pull on her gloves, which she regretted now, as perspiration made her lose her grip on her weapon.

"Emeron. Are you all right?"

"Dwyn. Stay down and take cover inside the tent." Emeron suddenly sounded frantic, not the impersonal soldier at all.

"I can't. Some of the beams are getting through it. My bedroll is destroyed."

"Are you hurt?" Emeron began to crawl faster, getting up on hands and knees. Kellen pulled her down next to her.

"Don't. You'll reveal your position."

"I'm all right," Dwyn said, and now they could see her, huddled by the entrance to her tent. Though tousled and her face smudged with dirt, she looked unharmed.

"Kellen, what the hell are these things?" Owena joined them, pressed to the ground too.

"Spy bots. We need to emit a pulse." She wasted no words.

"They just pierced through the tent and took out our communication center. I hope yours is intact," Owena said, looking at Emeron.

"Me too," Emeron replied through clenched teeth.

"That isn't good." She pointed up. "At least sixteen bots are circling the camp."

"Fourteen. I just took out two."

"Good." In fact it was incredible that Owena had managed to get a lock on the elusive devices. "We should get back to your tent. We need to inform Rae about the communication center."

"What'll this pulse do?" Emeron asked as they crawled back.

"It'll destroy any unprotected electronic equipment and weaponry within a two-hundred-meter radius," Owena explained. "Even gear that's been outfitted to withstand regular electromagnetic pulse. Our weapons have shields against this, and of course there's a remote risk that the bots have similar defense. However, this is newly developed, so I doubt it."

"Our gear doesn't have that protection either."

"Your government sent you on a mission with inferior equipment?" Kellen asked, nonplussed.

"This was never meant to be a high-profile search-and-rescue mission." Emeron glared at her. "Merely a routine security-detail assignment in a low-tech area."

"Low tech?" Owena gazed up, her face lit by a green beam piercing the dissipating mist. Soon they would be more visible to the bots' ocular sensors.

"We have to share the protected weapons." She was determined. "We don't have a choice."

"I agree." Rae spoke quietly from Kellen's right.

Kellen quickly explained the situation regarding their communication center.

"Damn it," Rae said. "But go ahead with the plan, Commander O'Dal."

Dwyn interrupted. "Have you considered that we won't have any communications?"

"She's right," Emeron said.

"Damn," Rae said softly. "Ideas, anyone?"

Kellen cursed inwardly at the bots for hitting their communication center. There had to be a way to keep the Cormanians' comm system safe from the pulse.

"Admiral?" Dwyn said, and crawled to Rae. "When I was on a mission on the Beranta asteroids, they protected their gear from a natural phenomenon that wasn't exactly an electromagnetic pulse, but nonetheless destroyed all their electrical circuits."

"Really?" Rae said. "You paying attention, Owena?"

"Yes, ma'am."

Dwyn had opened her mouth to continue when a multicolored beam hit the ground in front of her and Rae, sending up dirt, grass, and sparks. Rae rolled to her left, covering Dwyn with her body. "Get down," she hissed. "I'll be damned if a gang of tin cans will kill me."

Kellen fought a sudden urge to giggle at her angry words, but she felt the same way. She hadn't survived situations more dangerous than this to die here, killed by unknown adversaries hiding behind cowardly technology. There was no honor in such an end.

"Go on," Rae urged Dwyn as she rolled off her.

"Well, it was simple, really. They used a fine metal mesh, not sure which alloy, but they had constructed entire rooms lined with this mesh, even the door system."

"So, a metal mesh?" Kellen tried to think of what they had that could function as a shield against the pulse.

"Like the one that lines the outside of our bedrolls, Commander?" Emeron slid into the closest tent and returned with a bedroll. "This is a fine metal mesh. Look."

She examined it, then turned to Dwyn. "What do you think?"

"Yes, that looks like it could work. I don't think we have anything that would do better."

Rae issued the orders rapidly. "Wrap three of them around the communication center and as many of your unprotected weapons and medical instruments as you can fit in there. In the meantime, get the pulsator ready."

"Aye, ma'am." Owena crawled back to her tent.

"I'll sweep the perimeter and make sure Noor and the rest of my unit are all right." As Emeron turned to leave, her coveralls' leg rode up and Kellen saw a deep, blackened cavity on her calf. "You're injured. Let your...Dwyn clean your wound and I'll scout the perimeter."

"Ma'am...Protector, I'm fine—"

"Get it taken care of. You should know better than any of us what can happen to a wound like that in this humid environment."

"All right," Emeron responded, and crawled toward Dwyn. She tore a med-kit package from her pocket and threw it at Dwyn, who deftly caught it and went to work.

Kellen began to worm herself around the line of tents.

"Aw, come on, Emeron. Hold still..." was the last thing she heard before she was surrounded by bots firing a multitude of beams at her. Knowing that she had been detected, probably because of the lifting morning mist, she jumped to her feet and ran, doubled over, to the nearest tent. She threw herself inside and nearly floored Ensign Oches.

"I got one of them, ma'am," he yelled above the loud hissing noise. "There's so many of them this time."

"I know. We're dealing with it. Get down." She pulled him back with her as a bot passed only centimeters from the ground, then raised her sidearm and aimed. Firing, she hit the bot and watched it twirl and begin a crazy dance, bouncing on the ground. It flipped over and its small antennas, which resembled undersized wings, twirled like they were searching for the one audacious enough to harm it.

Frowning at how she had nearly thought of the bot as a living entity, Kellen fired at it again, sending it into a new spin. This time it bounced against a small rock, which propelled it in their direction.

"Move!" She pushed at Oches, who scrambled backward, trying to get away from the thing. She moved even faster, throwing herself sideways. She had no idea what would happen if the bot exploded on top of them, but she was sure it wouldn't be pretty.

"Ma'am," Oches called, his tone high and shrill. "You have to get out of here."

She stared. The bot had rolled in and wedged itself between Oches and a tree trunk outside the tent. Smoke was billowing from one of the antennas, and, like Oches, she realized that any minute it would explode and kill him in the process.

"I'm not leaving you," she assured the pale ensign, who was sweating profusely. "Lie very still. Let me scan it."

"Don't, ma'am," he implored. "You don't know what will set it off, now that it's injured and unstable."

She noticed that Oches said "injured" and realized that he, like her only moments ago, looked upon these bots as entities. "I won't do anything to destabilize it. I promise. Lie still."

"No problem. Be quick, please, ma'am."

Kellen adjusted the parameters on her scanner to their lowest settings. Running it over the bot at what she hoped was a safe distance, she tried to make sense of the readings. On the one hand, it looked as if their blasts had neutralized the bot, but she was afraid it would explode soon. She was sure that would happen even faster if they tried to roll it off Ensign Oches.

"It's not looking good, ma'am, is it?" Oches tried to smile, but only managed a faint tremor in his lips. "Damn, I never expected to go down like this."

"Don't you dare give up, Ensign. That's an order."

"All right." Oches's tone wasn't convincing. He relaxed against the trunk now and wasn't even looking at the bot.

"Let's see if this can't buy us some time." She reached into her breast pocket and pulled out the small canister that she'd picked up from the ground after Dwyn Izontro's collapse. "This is Izontro's medication. It's an aerosol, with a potent cooling agent in it."

"You're going to spray it with medication?" The look on Oches's face would have been humorous if his situation hadn't been so dangerous.

"Yes."

"How cool can it be, since it's supposed to be inhaled?"

"Not very, but enough, combined with the miniscule aerosol drops, to keep the bot's circuits in contact with each other. This way it'll think it's not so broken after all and won't self-destruct quite yet."

"Ah. Clever." He closed his eyes as she scanned one more time before she administered the aerosol. "There."

"Is it working?"

"You're still here."

He smiled faintly. "I sure am."

Suddenly the bot gave a soft beep and wound down at the same time. Kellen took a sharp breath, expecting it to self-destruct in a deadly blast.

Instead, nothing. The bot lay there, snug against Oches, and appeared lifeless.

"Everybody all right in here?" Rae poked her head in between the tent flaps. She blanched at the sight of the bot. "Stars and skies, what happened here?"

"It...eh...chased us in here, ma'am," Oches said, a half-grin on his face. He gently nudged the bot off him and edged over to Kellen. "If the protector hadn't given it Ms. Izontro's medication, I'd be dead, most likely."

"Medication?" Rae blinked. "You gave the bot medicine?"

"Yes. Healing it so it lives until we kill it permanently, you could say."

Rae shook her head. "You're going to have to explain that to me later. We need to head out now. This adventure delayed us."

They left the tent and Kellen turned and fired on the bot, just to be safe. It went out with a small puff of smoke. She looked at downed bots littering the clearing. "Casualties?"

"Ensign Noor, Commander D'Artansis—Emeron, I mean—and one of the junior officers in D'Artansis's team. Apart from your injury, only minor cuts and bruises. No fatalities. The Disian youngsters stayed low and aren't harmed." Rae stopped in the center of the clearing. "To think this can be such an idyllic, beautiful place one minute and a living hell the next."

"I know." Relieved that nobody was hurt badly, Kellen wrapped her arm around Rae. "I'm grateful you're all right."

Rae's features softened and she melted into the touch for a few moments. Resuming her professional stance, she dragged both hands through her short hair and drew a deep breath. "Let's go find out how much of the Cormanian equipment we managed to kill. I hope we still have communication capabilities."

She spoke with irony, but Kellen knew that if they couldn't communicate, they might be too late to save Dahlia.

CHAPTER TWENTY

Dahlia woke, cold yet clammy, shivering as the morning mist seeped inside her clothes. She had worn the same outfit for almost eight days, and she frowned at it. Dirt, smoke, and blood created new, ugly patterns on her former off-white caftan, and she'd stepped on the hem of her pants so many times, they looked like tattered lace around her ankles. Insects, particularly mosquitoes, had bit her exposed skin and drunk her blood. She shuddered at the thought of what biological hazard they might transfer to her. It wasn't like Weiss Kyakh had a state-of-the-art med-kit box with her to tend to her prisoners.

"I need new dressings," M'Ekar moaned as he lay propped up against a tree trunk. "My bandages are oozing."

Dahlia could care less, but she wasn't going to stoop to the others' callous actions. She looked at the bandages that White had wrapped haphazardly around his arms and legs, and also around his forehead. His head wasn't too bad, but both his shins were in terrible shape.

"He's right," Dahlia said, raising her voice. "He may be contemptible, but he's rotting away."

"God, woman." M'Ekar made a disgusted face. "No need to be crude."

"It's the truth." She swatted at some flies that hovered around his bandages. "You're nearly gangrenous."

"Oh, damnation, I'm going to lose my legs, Kyakh, because of your incompetent assassin-turned-medic."

"Calm down," Weiss Kyakh said, and knelt next to them. "You're making too much noise to be dying."

"Joke all you want, but look at that," Dahlia said, and pointed at the soggy bandages. "You need to make camp and tend to him and some of the others. That man over there," she pointed, "has even worse-looking wounds. Even if you don't give a damn about M'Ekar, and frankly who could blame you, your own crew member should be a high priority."

Weiss glanced at her people, and her face still didn't give away any emotions. "All right. White, the med kit."

The small box, now looking as dirty as they did, magically appeared, and Weiss opened it with quick fingers. She stared into the box. "Where the hell's the rest of the stuff?"

"I've used most of it," White said expressionlessly. "This is our emergency kit. There wasn't much in it to begin with."

"She certainly didn't use it on me," M'Ekar complained. "If she had, I wouldn't look like I had the Typperline Plague."

"Never heard of it. Be quiet now." Weiss rose and waved a young man over. He and she were the only ones unharmed. All the others suffered from burns, trauma, or smoke inhalation. "Take care of the *ambassador's* wounds."

"Yes, ma'am."

"No," M'Ekar said, and pointed at Dahlia. "I want her to do it."

The young man looked between Dahlia and Weiss. "Captain?"

"Fine with me."

Tossing the med kit box into Dahlia's lap, Weiss walked away with her crewman in tow. Dahlia opened the box and saw a few imbulizer ampoules and a portable disinfector almost without power. There were only five dressings left. "I'll do what I can." As she moved over to M'Ekar, sickened to have to be near the man responsible for killing so many people and hurting members of her own family, herself included, she shrugged. "I can't imagine why you'd want me to help you."

"You detest me, but you have a conscience." He sounded tired and his hands trembled as he tried to brush some of the dirt off his coat. "Deplorable circumstances, but I'll do anything to regain my freedom."

"Even kill innocent people."

"I didn't know Weiss's helmswoman was so incompetent." He raised his voice.

"I'm not talking only about the Disian casualties." Dahlia kept her temper in control as she began to unravel the bandage on his head. "I'm also talking about the people on Gantharat whom you threatened, tortured, and killed, and I'm talking about how you hurt my family."

"And you, Madame, incarcerated me solely because you and that daughter of yours wanted custody of the prince." He groaned as she ran the disinfector over his wound. "Damnation, that stings."

"Just grin and bear it." She worked slowly, since this was a great opportunity to find out more about his plans. "These are superficial flesh wounds, but if you don't sit still and let me clean them, you're in big trouble. I don't have to tell you what happens if gangrene spreads."

"No." He paled further. "I'm grateful for the mildness of your touch, Madame."

"You're being awfully polite," she said sardonically. "Usually you think of me as a royal bitch."

"We're in a serious situation. I didn't think my escape would be like this." He obviously tried to mimic her tone, but they were the same age, even considering that Onotharians' life span was more than thirty years longer. Dahlia also realized that even without his serious flesh wounds he wasn't in shape for this type of "adventure."

"And neither am I," she murmured, and kept working with the pitiful dressings.

"Madame?"

"Nothing. Simply a reflection on age and how much I'd rather be at home, tucking in my grandson and reading a good novel."

A joyless smile grazed his dry lips. "Or having a glass of Dhakaria wine in front of a holo-fireplace, listening to the latest recording by Thoros Kolos."

"You enjoy opera?" Dahlia didn't understand how this conversation with a most despicable man almost comforted her, but talking about something resembling normalcy gave her new emotional strength.

"It is *the* art form, Madame Dahlia. Have you listened to our great national hero on the opera scene?"

"Not a lot. I've heard of him, though." She wrapped the last of the bandages. "Have you listened to any of our opera companies from Vitaporta Prime? Opera is a lifestyle itself on their homeworld."

"Oh, yes." M'Ekar's face softened, and she had no problem envisioning how dashing he'd once been. He'd probably charmed his way into the Onotharian nobility with ease and married a young woman in the M'Aido dynasty. She knew he came originally from simple circumstances, and if he'd used his driven personality for the greater good, he could have made an impact for the better. Instead, he had remained scheming and opportunistic, always putting himself first, ever ambitious.

"As a young man I always wanted to go to Vitaporta Prime," he continued. "I even dreamed of a career in music." He smiled self-deprecatingly, and she was mesmerized that he could be so charming, even disarming. She considered herself a shrewd, even hardened diplomat who, after a lifetime in the SC diplomatic corps, could see through any hidden agenda and outsmart any adversary. Still, when he talked eagerly about his opera dreams as a mere teenager, she could easily picture him then—tall, striking, and no doubt with a good voice. Even to this day, it was resonant and pleasing.

"Why didn't you?" she asked spontaneously.

"Why, I... Oh, that wasn't for me. It was only a dream." His smile faded, and his dark eyes lost their light. "I was destined for other things. My family trusted me to be the one to succeed. They sacrificed everything to send me to the finest schools and to literally buy me a ticket to the finer social functions on Onotharat. You found all this out from your spies while you were interrogating me, no?"

"Yes, some, at least." She pictured the young M'Ekar, carrying the hopes and dreams of his entire family, as well as the burden of striving for success. *He took it a bit too far, I'd say.*

"You done yet?" White's cold voice interrupted the exchange.

Dahlia was annoyed with herself for not having pried more useful, tactical information out of M'Ekar. But she was sure the information she had obtained instead might be handy when it came to understanding him.

"Yes," she answered to White's question.

"The captain says you should hang onto the med-kit box."

"Sure. I need something to carry it in."

White stopped one of the crewmen nearby and made him remove a small pouch from his large back-strap security carrier. "Here."

Dahlia attached the pouch to her belt and carefully tucked the few remaining items into it. She knew she would have to use it again soon.

"All right, people. We're moving out." Weiss stalked along the line of crew members and stopped by M'Ekar and Dahlia. "You look like you could be best buddies if you put your differences away," she said scornfully. "Don't become too chummy, M'Ekar. We still expect to get paid."

"And you will, handsomely, if you get me across the border in one piece."

"Don't count on it, Hox," Dahlia said, deliberately using his first name. Now she knew why it had been such a good idea to be personal with M'Ekar. Even if she didn't trust him for a second, she could keep Weiss guessing and off balance. "The SC would never treat even their worst enemy this way, so be careful whom you trust."

Weiss towered impressively over Dahlia, who wasn't short. "Shut. Up." Weiss's tone was menacing, but it took more than that to intimidate Dahlia.

"You don't need to sound so harsh," she said innocently.

"Don't think I'm not keeping an eye on you, and so is everyone else."

"Very flattering for a woman my age." She didn't look away and finally Weiss broke eye contact first.

"Move out."

They resumed their journey through the protected forest. Just before they left the clearing, Dahlia took her hand out of her pocket and released her last small piece of gold.

Ayahliss stood by the transparent aluminum view port, looking down at the planet Corma as the *Dalathea* hummed very faintly beneath her feet, where it lay in low orbit. The shuttle had delivered Armeo and her, with Judge Beqq, only an hour earlier. She glanced over at the couch where Armeo had fallen asleep while he browsed through the games and other entertainment.

The guest suites onboard the legendary court ship were very luxurious. Ayahliss had understood from Judge Beqq that the *Dalathea* was one of the first of her class to travel throughout the Supreme Constellations space, enforcing the unification law and solving disputes between planets, or planets' leaders, when local laws weren't enough. It was obvious that Judge Beqq was proud to be a supreme judge of this vessel.

Ayahliss pressed her forehead against the cool, nearly invisible surface and sighed deeply.

"What's the matter?"

She pivoted, her hands positioned in the classic gan'thet stance. Judge Beqq raised her hands, palms forward. "Lost in thought?"

Flustered, Ayahliss lowered her hands. "Yes. A bit."

"You look sad." Judge Beqq tipped Ayahliss's face up with a soft hand under her chin. "Have you been crying?"

"No." She automatically wiped her eyes, and to her surprise, they were moist, which made her furious. She didn't want to display such weakness in front of this woman. Judge Beqq had to be the most striking woman she'd ever seen. Red hair billowed down her back in wild curls, only kept in check with a big, ivory-colored bow at the nape of her neck. The black shroud she wore while working only emphasized her beauty and style. Ayahliss forced her jaw forward, her skin still tingling where the judge had touched her. "I'm fine."

"I know. Can I make a guess?"

She nodded, certain her voice would tremble if she spoke aloud.

"You're concerned for Rae and Kellen. You're homesick for your planet, for Gantharat." Judge Beqq caressed her cheek. "And you hate being cooped up here when you'd rather be down there, in the Disi-Disi forest, helping them rescue Dahlia Jacelon. As much as you love Armeo, he's a child and you're a woman."

Utterly stunned, she stared into Judge Beqq's brilliant blue eyes, searching for the truth and for the reason why this woman, a stranger, cared enough to say these things.

"I don't know what you mean," she said. "My place is with Armeo. Kellen and Rae trust me to keep him safe."

"I know, and I admire your loyalty. I'm not saying you shouldn't do your duty toward them and him. I was merely observing why you looked so forlorn when I entered the room."

Ayahliss blinked to cure the burning sensation behind her eyelids. "I'm perfectly fine."

Judge Beqq, whose eyes had been brilliant blue only moments ago, looked at her with golden speckles dancing in her irises. Mesmerized, she wondered if this phenomenon was common among her race. Judge Beqq looked human, like Rae, in many aspects, but some subtleties suggested she might have mixed blood. "If you insist," Judge Beqq said softly. "I merely thought you might need a sympathetic ear since I don't have anything pressing to attend to."

"Well…" She regretted sounding so uptight. This woman was obviously powerful and it might be wise to befriend her, if her situation changed. Kellen and Rae might disagree with Ewan Jacelon and Judge Beqq and think she'd endangered Armeo and shouldn't be around him. "I do feel homesick sometimes." It hurt to admit the truth.

"You're far away from home. Are your parents alive?"

"No."

"How did you live on Gantharat?"

"On my own. I moved out of the monastery when I was seventeen and joined a resistance cell."

"You've lived in a monastery?" Judge Beqq sat down on a small couch below the view port and patted the seat next to her. Ayahliss sat too, inhaling a foreign but intoxicating scent that she realized was Judge Beqq's perfume. The soft, appealing odor emanated from her long, red curls and engulfed her so completely that she stumbled on her words.

"Yes. All my life, since I was a baby. I was orphaned when I was only weeks old, the monks told me. They raised me and taught me everything I know."

"The martial-arts skills as well?"

"Yes."

"Amazing. And you've been on your own, without any family ties, since then." Judge Beqq sounded astounded. "It's even more incredible that you survived."

"The alternative didn't sound very appealing," Ayahliss said, and grimaced. "And I love my homeworld. I'd die for it, just like I'd die for Armeo." She was eager to explain. "I mean, it's not only because he's our prince who will one day return to claim his throne. It's because I *know* him now. I know him for the great boy he is. I've never had a friend like Armeo. Sure, he's younger, but he can also be mature, and I—" She knew she was blushing. "I suppose I sometimes come across as immature and not very trustworthy."

"I don't see that at all." Judge Beqq cupped her chin now. "I see a brave young woman, passionate about whatever she does, who is ready to fight to the death for her principles and, most of all, the ones she loves."

It was impossible to stand firm before such kindness and such praise. She had felt Rae's disapproval and trepidation ever since they had returned to SC space from Gantharat. And even if Rae seemed to have warmed up to her now, she was sure their latest adventure would make her change her mind. It was unfathomable that Judge Beqq, who resembled Rae in her demeanor and her commanding presence, would gaze at her with appreciation and something more, something indefinable. It was tempting to bask in Judge Beqq's words and let them go to her head, but one hard fact remained. She hadn't fulfilled her duty toward Armeo, and this would certainly be obvious when Kellen and Rae returned.

She thought about Dahlia. More guilt enveloped her like a cold, wet cloak, and she sagged where she sat.

"Ayahliss? What's the matter? You look so pale."

"Just thinking of Dahlia. I mean, Diplomat Jacelon." She refused to shed tears. Instead she forced her spine to straighten. "I did not fulfill my duty as a *vhaksamh*."

"Vaxen?" Judge Beqq's pronunciation of the Gantharian word made her smile despite her strong feelings of self-reproach.

"Vhaksamh means guardian, or giving shelter."

"And you feel that to justify the Jacelon family's trust in you, for bringing you back to stay with them, you should have protected Dahlia, saved her." It wasn't a question. It was exactly how Ayahliss felt.

"I can't remember ever having any other purpose than the greater good. When I studied the art of gan'thet, and other martial-art forms, the monks chastised me for being too hotheaded, too harsh. They said I lacked the necessary humility that a person needs to execute it properly. I'm too intense and, despite always being attentive, I still missed the signs that we were followed aboard the Keliera Station. You see?"

"I see. And I don't see." Judge Beqq held her by her shoulders in a steady grip. "Listen to me. You are, well, what are you, twenty years old?"

"Twenty-four."

Judge Beqq looked surprised. "Really. You look younger, even for a Gantharian. However, you were one woman, formidable as you may be, against a team of trained, ruthless mercenaries driven by greed."

"But I—"

"Listen. When Rae and Kellen get back, preferably with Diplomat Jacelon in one piece, they'll tell you the same thing. You can't expect to have been able to overpower them. It's unreasonable."

"It may seem so to you," she said quietly, feeling her palms burn, as if they needed to make contact in a gan'thet way. "The monks taught me well, even if they never quite 'soothed my soul,' as they put it."

"I think your intensity and your soul are just fine." Once again,

Judge Beqq's eyes shimmered with the golden speckles, and her pale complexion became faint red. Intrigued, and mystified, Ayahliss tried to interpret these reactions. She assumed it was impolite to inquire as to their origin, and still she wanted to know, very badly.

"Mmm, 'Liss?" Armeo sat up on the couch on the other side of the room, rubbing his face. "Oh, Judge Beqq." He looked drowsy for another ten seconds before his head apparently cleared. "Ma'am. Is there any news? Have you heard anything from Kellen and Rae?"

"I'm sorry, Prince Armeo, but—"

"Just Armeo, please." Armeo blushed, much like Judge Beqq had just done.

"Very well, then you, and Ayahliss, must call me Amereena, or Reena, when we're in private like this."

"So, no news, Reena?" Ayahliss asked, speaking the judge's nickname slowly, tasting it.

"Not yet. Your grandfather is with the *Dalathea*'s captain in the mission room. We'll hear as soon as he does, I'm certain."

"Yeah, Granddad will be here soon," Armeo said, and walked over to them. He sat next to Ayahliss and leaned against her, not heavily, but obviously seeking contact. "And he'll have something good to tell us. I know it." He glanced up at her, his eyes shiny and his face still flustered after his nap. "He has to, hasn't he?"

Her heart twisted in her chest at his pleading look, and she wanted to assure him that everything would be fine, but she knew he'd see right through such clichés. "I know that Kellen and Rae are the right people to go rescue your grandmother," she said softly. "I also know they have the best people possible with them. They make a great team with Commanders Grey and D'Artansis."

"Ayahliss is right." Reena wrapped her arms loosely around both of them. "I have an idea. Why don't we walk down to the mission room? I'll ask the captain if it's all right for you two to spend some time in there. Besides, the exercise will do you good, and we can pick up something to eat on the way."

"Yes." Armeo stood so suddenly, he nudged Ayahliss toward Reena.

There it was again, that special scent that made her dizzy. Ayahliss lost her breath and pulled back, staring at Reena, who straightened her caftan and didn't meet her gaze. When Reena finally looked up, she stood and motioned toward the door. "Let's go, then."

Ayahliss followed Reena and Armeo, with no clue what had just happened. It wasn't important, not really, but something had connected and then snapped, and it had been as real as a dry twig breaking in the woods.

Or perhaps it was only her imagination.

CHAPTER TWENTY-ONE

Dwyn inhaled the medication and glared at Emeron for standing over her while she obeyed her orders. "You don't have to bully me into doing this," she muttered. "I feel fine."

"You weren't fine yesterday," Emeron said firmly. "The medical scans show that your lungs have permanent damage. Unless you use this continuously... You know it's the truth."

Dwyn drank some water to rinse away the bitter taste. "All right. I suppose it's not smart to have me risk slowing down the whole party."

"That might be everyone else's main concern," Emeron said, "but not mine."

She looked up at Emeron where she hovered over her. "No?"

"No." Emeron didn't elaborate, but her short-cropped words made something warm and glowing reverberate inside Dwyn.

"All right. I'll be good. Maybe the medication works so well that it makes me feel cocky about my health." This could definitely be true. Raised to ignore any physical weakness, Dwyn usually ignored both pain and illness. Her idealistic parents had never been over-sympathetic toward her, or anyone else ill while living in their ship collective. She had internalized their slight disdain for humanoid frailty and showed empathy more easily to others than to herself.

"We're moving out," Admiral Jacelon said from behind. "All set? You all right, Ms. Izontro?"

"Yes, ma'am. And please, call me Dwyn, like you did before. All these military ranks and salutations are enough. I'm a mere civilian and I like to go by my first name."

"Very well, Dwyn." Jacelon smiled quickly. "Let's get out of here before those damn bots show up. We can't afford to lose any more time."

"Aye, ma'am." Emeron grabbed her gear. When she also slung Dwyn's security carrier onto her back, Dwyn tried to object, but she shook her head. "You'll be able to walk farther and faster this way. It's only logical." She moved as if the added weight didn't bother her at all.

"Perhaps I should ask you to carry *me* instead," Dwyn murmured, half laughing. "You're the most stubborn person I've ever met."

"Oh, really. Well, that's good. I like to be the best in everything."

Dwyn swatted her arm as they resumed their long walk. The farther they penetrated the dense forest, the taller the trees became. Dwyn walked in front of Emeron. The narrow, barely visible, path didn't let them walk in pairs. She wasn't carrying anything but an SC plasma-pulse sidearm, and the protector had suggested she wear fortified alu-carbon body armor under her coveralls. The garment didn't make Dwyn as hot as she'd feared. In fact, it helped keep her cool in the humid forest.

When she asked Emeron if she was wearing one, she shook her head. "It's almost certain the bots are after us, and besides, the only ones we have are the ones the SC people brought. I'd rather my junior officers wear them."

"All right." Dwyn wasn't happy that Emeron wasn't wearing the same protection. "You stay behind me if there's trouble, then."

Emeron guffawed. "Not likely."

Dwyn shrugged and kept walking. "We'll see."

Birds, which had been silent for a long time after the bot attack, began to chirp as they walked. Keeping a sharp eye on her surroundings and listening for the telltale whine and buzz of the bots, Dwyn still enjoyed the fresh air and the smell of exotic flowers that blossomed high above them. It was dark, since the trees cut out most of the sunlight. But the cooler temperatures were delightful, and Dwyn greedily inhaled the sweet-scented oxygen.

They walked undisturbed for another couple of hours before Jacelon signaled for everyone to stop. "Let's take a few moments to rest," she said, and approached Oches. "Ensign, I need to use the communication device to be sure the pulse didn't disturb our instruments and send us off course."

Oches pulled off his back-strap security carrier and set up the portable communication center. "There you go, ma'am." He stepped away to give her privacy.

"It's all right, this isn't classified." Jacelon motioned for everybody to sit on fallen trunks and rocks around her. Dwyn gratefully sank onto an impressive trunk and rested against a broken branch. Closing her eyes, she listened to Jacelon and the protector begin the procedure of reporting in to SC headquarters.

"SC HQ, come in. I repeat, SC HQ, come in." The protector repeated the command several times, receiving only static. "Perhaps we're too far into the forest, Rae."

Emeron joined them and said, "Keep trying. I'll adjust the frequency. It's old technology, and it has its quirks."

"Really." Jacelon looked in bemusement at the communication center.

Emeron adjusted the settings several times before the protector finally received a slightly garbled response.

"Lt. Commander O'Dal here." The protector leaned closer. "Come in, HQ, try again."

"SC HQ here. Over."

"That's better." Jacelon grabbed the microphone and spoke quickly. "Admiral Jacelon here. Are we on a secure channel?"

"Scrambling now." There was a brief silence. "We're secure. Go ahead, ma'am."

"Alex. Good to hear your voice. We've had some adventures here, since we left the Disian village." She described the bot attack and the measures they had taken to defend themselves. "We were slightly delayed, but we've made good time today. I need to verify our position via satellite systems and sensors."

"Stand by, Admiral. Verifying."

Jacelon bent forward as a chirping sound emanated from the communicator. "Is it supposed to do that?" she asked Emeron.

"Yes, ma'am. Sorry. It's old."

"As long as it works."

"Admiral. Your position is 40-33-64-10-10 point 32. From where we're sitting, that puts you right on track. We've seen movement about eight hours in front of you. If that's the mercenaries, they're traveling slower than before. Perhaps their injuries are taking a toll."

"That's plausible," Jacelon said quietly.

"Oh, damn it, Rae, I'm sorry. I hope Dahlia is all right." The "Alex" on the other end sounded mortified. "I didn't mean to sound so callous."

"Don't worry about it. I hope some of them are incapacitated, which might make it possible for us to catch up."

"Everyone on your team in one piece?"

"We have mostly minor injuries. However, one of the civilians has damaged lungs and may need an emergency MEDEVAC if her condition worsens. I don't care about the Thousand Year Pact in this instance. If we signal for a MEDEVAC I want it here within an hour."

"Yes, ma'am."

Jacelon glanced at the protector. "How are the kids doing?"

"Eh, ma'am. I was getting to that." The trepidation in Alex's voice was clear even to Dwyn, who saw Jacelon and the protector exchange frowns and worried glances.

"What's going on?" Jacelon demanded.

"There was an incident at the hotel. Everyone's safe and secure, but we flew the young people and your father to the court ship in orbit."

"Who authorized that?" Jacelon barked.

"Judge Beqq suggested it to the admiral, and he agreed. Young Armeo's curiosity got the better of him, and a crowd spotted him."

"Where was Ayahliss?" the protector asked.

"Right there with him, shielding him fiercely. Luckily for all, Judge Beqq found them before she took someone out with her gan'thet techniques."

"Gods of Gantharat." The protector sighed.

"But they're all right?" Jacelon's knuckles tightened on the hand that held the microphone.

"Yes. Don't worry about Armeo or Ayahliss. Things are under control."

"Okay. We're staying on our present course. Keep a sensor lock on us, to make sure we don't deviate from it. If so, try to page us. And let my father know that we checked in."

"Affirmative, ma'am. Already sent him a message."

"Good. Jacelon out." The admiral tucked the microphone away and handed the communication center to Oches. "You heard. We're on track and hopefully going to reach M'Ekar and the mercenaries within the next twelve hours or so. We're not sure how many of them survived, other than what the Disians estimated. They probably outnumber us, but because they're injured and probably not so well armed, we should have the advantage."

"And the element of surprise," Emeron added. "They can't be certain someone's on their trail."

"True."

"Ma'am," Ensign Noor called from the other side of the small clearing. "Over here, ma'am."

Jacelon rose and hurried over to the excited ensign, followed by the protector and Emeron. Dwyn joined them as they stared at the sensor readings Noor had just obtained.

"That's not an indigenous metal." Noor lowered her sensor device. "I've seen this reading before, but it just occurred to me that it may be related to our mission." She made a wry face. "I'm sorry, ma'am."

"We can check the memory buffer on your sensor and see how many of these you recorded." Jacelon knelt and lowered the sensor until it gave a distinct, high-pitched tone. She felt around in the undergrowth and, with a triumphant smile, held up a small golden link, which to Dwyn looked like part of a bracelet or necklace.

"My mother wears gold jewelry all the time," Jacelon said, looking up at the protector. "If she's dropping hints, she must be doing fairly well and hoping we'll be able to rescue her."

"Dahlia is resourceful," the protector said, a faint smile on her face.

Dwyn had never seen the protector smile, and if she had been arresting in all her serious aloofness, much like Emeron, now she was stunningly beautiful. It was clear why Jacelon looked at her the way she did.

"Set your scanner to search for this exact metal, Ensign." Jacelon rose and brushed herself off. "Now we have one more way to make sure we're on track. Also, look for signs of wounded people." She dragged her hand through her short red hair, a thoughtful expression on her face. After a moment, she turned to the young Disians.

"How is the tracking going?"

"I have lost the trail a few times, but not Yhja. She is better than I am," Trom said shyly. "She can find the smallest creature very quickly."

"I see. Do you agree that we are on track, Yhja?"

"Yes, Admiral." Yhja's voice was sweet and nearly inaudible. "We are tracking somewhere between fifteen and twenty people, both male and female, some injured."

Dwyn looked at Yhja with surprise. The young girl, so shy and so petite, even next to Jacelon, who wasn't very tall, seemed suddenly very sure of herself.

"Excellent. Is there any trace of anyone being dragged, killed, or otherwise in trouble?"

"On several occasions, there have been signs of frequent stops, as if they needed to rest. And some of them are injured. Some are dragging a leg, some are making very uneven imprints as they walk. I have seen traces of blood and other bodily fluids also." Yhja looked very matter-of-fact, but Dwyn could see her reach for Trom's hand. "The one taking the lead is most likely female, since her tracks are smaller than those of many men."

"Good. Let's not waste any more time. Those of you who haven't eaten yet will have to down a ration bar or two as we move out. Come on, people." Jacelon motioned for Emeron to take the lead, followed by Trom and Yhja. Dwyn walked right behind them, chewing on a dry, tasteless bar. Emeron glanced back at her every time the narrow path took a new turn or the terrain shifted.

Dwyn tried to read the expression in her eyes, but decided that Emeron was probably being thorough and carrying out both her assignments at the same time. Still, a part of her warmed to the quiet concern in Emeron's eyes, and it was hard not to respond with reassuring smiles. Instead, she acted as if she didn't notice Emeron's glances and kept her weapon raised and ready in case they stumbled into trouble again. She didn't want anyone to worry that she couldn't take care of herself.

❖

"Not again," White exclaimed, and stomped over to where M'Ekar had collapsed with a thud. "He's slowing us down too much. I say we get rid of him and take our chances that *she* will be worth enough to help us escape this hellhole." She glared at Dahlia, who'd caught M'Ekar as he fell, preventing him from hitting his head against a fallen tree trunk.

"You're out of line, White. Back off." Weiss had joined them and stared at M'Ekar with narrowing eyes. "You better not be trying to fool me, Ambassador."

"I can't walk any farther." He gasped. "My leg is killing me. It's burning like fire, and I've lost feeling in some parts of it."

"He's in bad shape, Weiss," Dahlia said seriously. "I'm afraid gangrene has set in. We don't have any more clean bandages. I have one more dose of the medication left and one more of painkiller. You should leave us behind and try to reach your goal without us. I'll take care of him."

"I don't think so." Weiss grinned joylessly. "As much as I hate to admit it, White has a point. You're the valuable asset here. M'Ekar's future in the Onotharian Empire is questionable at best. You, and the intel you're privy to, however, are priceless. So, no, we're not leaving without you. My men have rested and can carry him for a bit." Weiss motioned to the two men who'd transported M'Ekar earlier. "Construct a makeshift stretcher, quickly. We need to reach our rendezvous point within ten hours. I don't have to remind you all that we won't get a second chance."

"Aye, Captain." It took the men only a few moments to cut down two long, narrow branches and braid some strong ferns between them. They placed the groaning, now semiconscious M'Ekar onto it and lifted it effortlessly. Dahlia surmised that they'd recovered better than most of the others.

"He's in terrible condition anyway." She knew she had to be the voice of reason, even if nobody listened. "Is this how you show allegiance to the one who's paying for your mission?"

"His contribution is minor. Nice, but humble, I suppose you could say," Weiss said, and produced her trademark unfeeling smile again. "You are another matter. But don't think that allows you to get away with anything. If you try to run, I'll shoot you in the back."

Dahlia had come across her fair share of callous people, but this comment, uttered with such indifference to humanoid life, was one of the most frightening things she'd ever heard.

"You would, wouldn't you?" she said, her own voice just as cold as Weiss's. "You would shoot a woman for personal greed and not think twice about it. What a prize fool you are. What a sorry excuse for a living being. What a waste of a keen mind. I feel sorry for you." She easily injected all the contempt she felt for Weiss Kyakh into her voice, making sure she spoke loudly enough for all the other mercenaries to hear.

Weiss stared at her, fuming, obviously at a loss for words. Recovering quickly, she looked scornfully at Dahlia. "You're entitled to your opinion, Diplomat Jacelon, but once you're in Onotharian hands and I retire with enough assets to keep me in a very comfortable lifestyle, I'm sure I'll get over the fact that you don't regard my character highly."

Dahlia filed several things away for future reference. Weiss planned to retire. Why? Had she had enough of her renegade lifestyle? Had she accumulated enough wealth or power? Unless she was mistaken, the outlaw looked faintly haunted. Not someone to romanticize anyone so despicable, she was still curious why. There was, however, no reason to doubt Weiss's intentions. She would easily sacrifice M'Ekar the next time his condition slowed them down, and she was determined to hand her over to the Onotharians for a very handsome reward.

Dahlia sighed as she stood, but only after breaking a few twigs behind her back and tying them into a neat bow. She had no way of knowing if any of her signs had been detected or, if so, by whom, but she had to keep trying. The thought of ending up in an Onotharian interrogation room, knowing more than she cared to about their methods, didn't appeal to her.

CHAPTER TWENTY-TWO

Rae ducked under a low branch, trying to keep to one side of the narrow forest path. The soggy ground made walking difficult. The mud sucked at her feet like a thousand greedy leeches, but she was determined to catch up with the mercenaries and her mother before dusk. Checking her chronometer, she found that they had less time than she thought. The terrain had been unforgiving, but she knew the kidnappers were in the same situation. They had discovered two more pieces of gold, and Trom and Yhja had pointed out broken twigs, some even turned into knots, which had raised Rae's hope of finding her mother.

"We need a short break," Emeron D'Artansis said just behind her. "Several of the junior officers' boots are filled with this damn mud, and their feet are hurting. If we don't stop to remedy that—"

"—they'll be in trouble farther along the line."

"Yes."

"How's Dwyn doing? I heard her cough earlier." Rae admired the stamina Dwyn displayed as she kept pace with the rest of them despite her injured lungs.

"She insists that she's fine, but it's clear to me that she's struggling to keep up."

"One more reason for us to take a moment," Rae said. "If she crumbles—"

"She won't." D'Artansis spoke somberly.

"Okay." Rae raised her fist in the air, signaling for everyone to stop. Kellen joined her, glancing at D'Artansis, who now hovered over Dwyn.

"Is she all right?" Kellen nodded in Dwyn's direction.

"Yes, I think so. D'Artansis is keeping an eye on her. Something tells me Dwyn isn't the type who complains about her own wellbeing."

"She reminds me of someone else," Kellen said, and looked pointedly at Rae. "Perhaps all humans minimize injuries or illness."

"Oh, well, perhaps." Rae knew that her own track record spoke for itself. She was a terrible patient, infamous for having exasperated almost every medical officer who had attempted to treat her or even perform a physical.

Rae pinched Kellen surreptitiously as she walked past her toward Owena, Leanne, and the two marines. "I want you to scan the area for any signs of nonindigenous substances or materials."

She turned to the young Disians next. "Yhja, Trom, survey the small clearing west of the path and, also, the rocks on the other side. If we're having problems walking in this water-soaked clay, the mercenaries are too, especially if they have wounded."

The marines pulled out their scanning devices and began to sweep the immediate area. Noor and Oches accompanied Trom and Yhja without Rae having to order them to. Owena and Leanne helped the most junior of D'Artansis's team fill up everyone's water container. The water purifier turned the muddy clay clear and drinkable, a process that always amazed Rae.

"Admiral?" Dwyn said, and approached Rae after she sat down on a log to study the latest intel the SC HQ had sent to her handheld computer. "Is it all right if I disturb you for a moment?"

"Sure. What's up?" Rae studied Dwyn's pale features. Everything in her face was small, except her large, silver-gray eyes. Her transparent skin held a grayish undertone, which suggested she wasn't doing entirely well. The strong sense of character that shone from her shimmering eyes showed no weakness whatsoever. In fact, something within this young woman reminded Rae of her younger self. Perhaps it was the desire to prove herself to those who judged her—by her size or by her family's position. She believed everyone should do things by the book and that there was a right and a wrong way to do them. These convictions permeated every cell in her body. *That was before Kellen came blasting into my life. Literally.*

"Everyone seems to be watching me, wondering when I'll drop dead or at least become ill enough to cause delays and other problems."

The directness in Dwyn's words surprised her, though it shouldn't have when she reconsidered their similarities.

"We're concerned for you, naturally. The condition of your lungs is serious. We have limited ways to help you out here, if you become worse."

"Ah." Dwyn sucked her lower lip between her teeth. "That's just it. Your concern slows everybody down, and ultimately it's not going to change a damn thing."

"What do you mean?" She didn't like the way the conversation was going.

"I mean, no matter what, if I deteriorate, you're helpless. If my lungs give in, clog up, or whatever can happen to them, no one can do anything. It's only logical to conduct this mission as you would have if I was unharmed or not part of it. You never bargained on having a civilian along, much less an injured one. It's bad enough for you to have to worry about your mother, Admiral." Dwyn smiled wryly. "I realize what's at stake. I may be working in a totally different field, but it's also my job to stay aware of the current political climate. Politics directly impacts our worlds, their inhabitants and environments.

There was nothing coy or martyr-like in Dwyn, merely a raw honesty, emphasized by her direct gaze and sincere voice.

"I assure you," she said, choosing her words carefully, "that if I thought it necessary, I'd find a way to continue our mission without you. However, we can't risk your life by leaving you behind to wait for a MEDEVAC unit with just a junior officer to ensure your safety. We don't know how many bots are deployed to scout for you. And, as important as this mission is, we also need to figure out who's prepared to go to such extremes to stop your survey of the Disi-Disi forest."

"Surely the risk of losing information to the Onotharians is more important?" Dwyn shook her head. "My mission is vital to Corma, at least, but I'm not indispensible."

Dwyn's words cut deep, and Rae felt she had to explain. "What you don't realize, since you don't know my mother, is that there is no risk of any intel falling into enemy hands."

"But—"

"None."

"Oh." Dwyn blinked, and Rae knew she had understood what she meant. "Your mother won't talk. No matter what they do to her. Oh, damn."

"Exactly. So this mission is all about rescuing her and capturing M'Ekar, if either of them is still alive, and also apprehending the mercenaries."

"I see." Dwyn moved her foot, and the mud underneath made a wet sound against the sole of her combat boot. "And the hostile bots?"

"Because they attacked SC personnel, we need to investigate their origin."

"Will that mean taking my mission more seriously?" Dwyn folded her arms in front of her. "What I mean is, will the SC finally realize that we won't have an area of space, or live planets, to go to war over, if we don't start taking our environmental issues to heart?"

"I don't disagree with your concerns, Dwyn," Rae said, knowing full well that Earth had its own problems when it came to protecting its remaining wildlife. "The war with the Onotharian Empire is coming. That's no secret. I have no idea how much you know about the Onotharians, but they're invading other sovereign worlds primarily because they've poisoned their homeworld so badly it's becoming uninhabitable."

"And when we win the war against them, what happens to the Onotharian population? Do we evacuate them from a dying world?" Dwyn's eyes shone like white gold as their topic energized her from within.

"Good question. And thank you for your trust in the SC military forces." She smiled at how Dwyn had taken for granted that the SC would defeat the Onotharians. "What's your theory on the matter?"

"My theory?" Dwyn looked slightly shocked. "I don't presume to know anything about an operation that size. How many people live on Onotharat?"

"Approximately twenty billion."

Dwyn's mouth formed a perfect "o" as she whistled. "Oh, my."

"Exactly."

"Is their planet beyond saving?"

"I'm not the right person to ask about that, but when we get out of here—*all* of us—I can put you in touch with experts at the SC headquarters on Earth or Iminestria."

"You think I can really make a difference at that level, Admiral?" Dwyn relaxed marginally and drew a deep breath. Rae could hear a faint crackling sound as she did, which reminded her of Dwyn's serious condition. Not sure why, exactly, Rae knew that Dwyn evoked feelings of protectiveness. She oozed an integrity and strength that everyone she spoke to seemed to recognize.

"I do. Now, I can tell you're not feeling well, so this isn't a request. It's an order. I don't care if you're in my unit or not. I still order you to conserve your energy and be candid about your health situation."

"Hear, hear." D'Artansis approached them. "We're ready to continue, ma'am. Yhja and Trom have found traces of at least fifteen individuals, perhaps eighteen. Like us, they've been trying not to walk directly on the soggy path, but on the grassier sides of it. We found this." She handed over a small item, glimmering in the faint light among the trees.

"A piece of a used bandage," Rae said. "They've obviously got wounded people, and presumably they've sustained smoke-inhalation injuries too. There's a chance we'll find them sooner than we thought."'

"We just might," D'Artansis said briskly. "Yhja and Trom told me there's a vast clearing only a few hours from here. I asked how big, and according to them, at least a hundred meters, diagonally."

"A perfect landing site for an evacuation vessel..." Rae's mind whirled. "We have no way of knowing if they managed to get a message to any backup crew, but it seems logical that criminals this accomplished would have not only Plan B, but also C, D, and E. Damn it." She stood and waited a few seconds until everyone paid attention. "We need to go faster, people. I know the terrain is bad, but it's no better for our adversaries."

"Aye, ma'am," Rae's and D'Artansis's units answered in unison before they began to hoist their back-strap security carriers and connect them to their belts. D'Artansis carried both hers and Dwyn's as before.

"All right, people," Rae said, as she grabbed her own gear. "Let's get going. We'll rest again in two hours and also contact SC HQ." She began to walk next to Emeron, her plasma-pulse rifle in her hands.

"We need a solid plan once we reach the clearing," D'Artansis said. "Providing they're still there."

"Yes. Commander O'Dal is best suited for concocting a last-minute stealth attack. That, together with Yhja and Trom's knowledge of the terrain, should help us succeed. Why don't you talk to her while we try to make it through this damned undergrowth?" Rae jerked some stubborn vines that blocked her way.

"Yes, ma'am. I need someone else to keep an eye on Dwyn."

"I'll do it." Rae could see that her ready offer surprised D'Artansis. "I'm impressed with her courage, Emeron," she said, using the commander's first name deliberately. Emeron obviously had personal feelings for Dwyn and wouldn't be able to focus entirely on hatching a plan unless she knew someone capable was looking out for her.

"Thank you, ma'am."

"Join Commander O'Dal and work with her en route. I know it's not ideal, and it has to be verbal only, but it'll have to do. We can't afford to stop and do it the formal way."

"No worries, ma'am. I think best on my feet. Literally."

Emeron stopped, Kellen caught up with her, and soon they were deep in conversation. The similarity between them, more of character than of looks, didn't escape Rae. Cool demeanors on the surface, volcanic lava underneath. *Yes, very alike.*

Rae walked behind the marines and the Disian youngsters. Dwyn was three steps behind her, and every time Rae glanced back at her, she saw how Dwyn moved her lips as she walked. Eventually, her curiosity got the best of her and she waited for Dwyn to catch up.

"I have to ask. Are you singing, or praying, as you walk?"

"What?" Dwyn's head snapped up. "Oh, no, nothing like that. It's a trick my father taught me when I was young and we were traveling through challenging terrain on one planet or another. He told me that when you're tired, count your steps. That way you know the next step is a new one and you won't have to take the old one again. It's already over and done with. Each step brings you closer."

"That's a new way of looking at it, at least for me." Rae smiled. She was fascinated by Dwyn, but also constantly aware of her surroundings. She knew how quickly an ambush could occur and carried her brand-new, experimental plasma-pulse launcher in her hands.

"Well, I've been in this field ever since I can remember, Admiral. I've walked through more forests, climbed more mountains, and squeezed through more caves than you can imagine. I lived in a cooperative on a spaceship. My parents still do, and my father is the captain. My mother is the activist leader, and they're never short of willing members for the next cause."

No wonder Dwyn was so dedicated. She'd been doing her job almost from the day she was born. "Seems like we have a lot in common," Rae said. "My father is an admiral in the SC fleet and my mother, of course, is a senior diplomat in the SC corps. I thought I rebelled when I joined the Academy, but in fact, I followed precisely in Father's tracks."

"About your mother, ma'am. We'll get her back." Dwyn's voice was soft and she looked so convinced that Rae had no trouble believing her.

"I know. There simply is no other option."

They walked in silence for the next hour, and Rae listened to Dwyn's breathing become increasingly labored. "Are you all right?"

"Yes. Thank you." The answer was short, and breathless.

"You have your inhaler?"

"Yes."

"Use it, Dwyn."

"I'm afraid I'll run out and not have any left when I *really* need it, Admiral."

"Let me see." Rae took the vial attached to the inhaler and checked it. "Yes, I see what you mean. But trust me, we're not far from our goal, and I need to keep up this pace. You have four doses left. Take one now and one when we're in place. We'll make sure you're out of the way and safe before we engage the enemy, and then you'll have two doses to hold you until I can arrange for a MEDEVAC. I'd evacuate you instantly if we had time to wait for a hovercraft, or if we could risk alerting the mercenaries that we're in pursuit."

"I realize that, Admiral," Dwyn said softly. "But if they hear a hovercraft or anything else approach, they might break up into smaller groups. Then we'd never know which one of them had your mother with them."

Rae's admiration for Dwyn grew even stronger. "I'm glad you understand that I'm not unsympathetic to your situation."

"I do." Dwyn exhaled deeply, then inhaled the medication. After a moment, she drew another deep, much clearer, breath and smiled at Rae. "A lot better."

"Very good."

Kellen and Emeron jogged up next to them. "We have a plan. Simple, but doable," Kellen said.

"Excellent. Fill me in." She let Emeron and Dwyn walk a few steps in front of her and Kellen.

"We assume that the mercenaries have no clue that we're right on top of them. They couldn't know that a unit was in such close proximity when they crashed, or that we could obtain both fresh intel and Disian forest guides."

Rae nodded. "I agree."

"The surprise factor is key. We surround them, and we execute our plan perfectly. We fire at everyone around Dahlia and take them out, and also capture M'Ekar and the leader of the mercenaries alive. I have her description. The Keliera space station transmitted everything they had just before we deployed. This woman has many aliases, but she used the name Weiss Kyakh when they docked at Keliera. The vessel's designation was the *Viper*. The only other name of any of her crew is the more cryptic and anonymous 'Ms. White,' who has quite a record despite such a bland name."

"Ms. White." Rae nearly stopped walking. "I've heard of her, but not Weiss Kyakh, though she may have changed her name recently. When I was stationed on Gamma VI, before you arrived, our main objectives were the pirates. Among them, certain names stood out and White was one of them. She's infamous. Completely merciless. I believe she originates from a wealthy family on Audisai. She's built a reputation for ruthlessness and for being a hired gun."

"Have you met her?"

"I nearly captured her, or my intelligence officers did, when we were en route to negotiations not far from Iminestria. Her ship, she was her own boss then, needed repairs, and when we offered to help, she engaged her tachyon-mass-drive engine to get away. Since such propulsion systems are illegal, it wasn't hard to figure out we were dealing with pirates or other criminals. She played cat and mouse with us for days before we could hand the chase over to local law enforcement."

"We have another advantage now." Kellen stayed with Rae as she scanned the surrounding forest. "Dahlia has had time to work on these individuals, and we shouldn't underestimate her ability to drive a wedge between them. She's also good at exasperating and angering her subjects."

Rae had to force back a cynical laugh. Her mother was the queen bee when it came to driving people crazy. She had infuriated M'Ekar during the interrogations, and Rae's childhood and adolescence had been full of situations where she'd clashed with her mother. *What I wouldn't give to have her rip me apart with her opinions right now.*

Since Rae had married Kellen and added Armeo to the equation, their small family unit had never been closer. She knew that Dahlia had become attached to Ayahliss as well, and even if a small, petty part of her had resented that affection momentarily, Ayahliss needed a mother figure and Dahlia needed a second chance to be a mother, to get it right. Because of that and so many other factors, failure wasn't an option.

CHAPTER TWENTY-THREE

The *Dalathea* had moved into low orbit and Amereena Beqq stood by the view port in her study. She looked thoughtfully down at Corma, wondering how Kellen and Rae were faring deep in the Disi-Disi forest.

Reena had dined with Ewan Jacelon, Armeo, and Ayahliss, and she knew that the absent family members had been present in everyone's mind. Armeo had alternated between chatting about mundane everyday things and being pale and quiet, and Ayahliss had eventually risen and told him it was bedtime. Reena had seen a change in Ayahliss then. She was still an intense loose cannon, who would take on the world in a heartbeat to keep Armeo safe, but now she displayed her more low-key side, nurturing and protective.

Reena turned and walked toward her desk. She was about to resume working on a contractual issue for a conglomerate of entrepreneurs on Corma when the computer alerted her that someone was at the door.

"Enter."

The door opened as Reena walked into the living area. A slightly disheveled Ayahliss stood just outside, her hands clenched.

"Ayahliss?" Reena strode up to her. "Is something wrong? Armeo?"

"No. I mean, yes. Armeo's fine."

"Come in." Reena gestured toward the couches just beneath the panoramic view port at the other end of the living room, but Ayahliss remained where she was, her hands opening and closing repeatedly. "Please. You look like you need to talk and have something hot to drink. Tea?"

Ayahliss slowly stepped inside far enough for the door to close behind her. Standing motionless for a moment, she softly cleared her voice. "I can't stay here."

Frowning, Reena took Ayahliss's arm and led her to the couch. "Tea. You definitely need tea." She stepped over to the sideboard and poured a mug of Cormanian silk tea. After handing it to Ayahliss, she sat down next to her. "Drink."

Ayahliss sipped the hot beverage, her eyes a cloudy midnight blue. She clung to the mug and stared into it, as if trying to read her future in the golden liquid. "I have to do something. I didn't know it would be so hard to sit idly by on this luxurious vessel while Kellen and Rae are on a dangerous mission. That, and the fact that my countrymen are either incarcerated, in camps, or fighting a losing battle." Blue tears of obvious fury rose in her eyes and she swiped at them with angry, jerky movements. "I know it's been only two days, but I'm well now, and it's driving me crazy."

"Oh," Reena said, her heart aching for the anguish on Ayahliss's face. "But you're needed here—"

"I love Armeo. I'd give my life for him, but he's *safe* here. He's aboard the safest ship in the whole SC sector." Ayahliss drank more tea. "I can't babysit a boy forever while the fight goes on without me. I can't believe Kellen intended this when she took me to Earth."

"Probably not, but she didn't know this would happen. You're more than a mere babysitter. You're like Armeo's sister, someone he can trust and rely on, no matter how physically safe he is aboard the *Dalathea*. He needs the stability you provide."

"He has his grandfather." Ayahliss spoke starkly, placing the mug on the ledge behind the couch. "He has his family, his *real* family. I'm not part of that."

"What brought this on? You're fiercely protective of that boy, I know that. You said you'd die for him, if necessary."

"I would." Ayahliss flung her hands in the air. "I *would* die for him, but instead I'm stuck here playing games and eating food that none of my countrymen have ever tasted and never will. I'm living this cushioned existence, but the monks reared me to be a *warrior*."

Reena knew then what was wrong. Ayahliss was more like Kellen than she'd realized. The same fire burned in their blue blood, but whereas years of training had harnessed Kellen's zeal, Ayahliss's restraint was new and quickly wore thin. Now, as she sat opposite Reena, her slender body seemed about to rip apart at the seams if she didn't find an outlet for the energy trapped inside.

"Tell me about it," she suggested, hoping this would take Ayahliss's mind off her frustration. "What was it like?"

"It was home." Ayahliss drew a trembling breath. "The monks, all men, took children they found abandoned or orphaned during their travels to a magical place within secret caves hidden at the end of a chain of mountains. We lived there, in seclusion, and the monks taught us everything they knew about a wide variety of topics. I was the only one they taught the art of gan'thet." She rubbed her forehead. "I didn't know how rare this type of martial arts is until Kellen explained its tradition to me. When we were on the way to Earth from Gantharat, she trained me further and said I'm a natural. She finds this curious, since this affinity is usually passed down through protector dynasties."

"Do you know anything about your birth family?" Reena leaned sideways against the backrest, not taking her eyes off Ayahliss.

"No. I was very young when the monks took charge of me. They told me they found me just in time. During the first years after the occupation, Onotharian mine owners sometimes ravaged the orphanages like the one I belonged to, trying to find cheap labor."

"That's beyond terrible," Reena said, outraged. "Child labor?"

"Yes. Many Gantharian children grew up in Onotharian mines, both on Gantharat and on Onotharat, the monks said. That was one of the things I focused on during my time in the resistance. We liberated many of these children and found new homes for them, but nowhere near all of them."

"Yet another crime to add to the long list of Onotharian offenses."

"Yes."

"So you set out into the world and wanted to fight for Gantharat."

"Fighting, physically or strategically, is what I do best. When my unit was ambushed and I was caught, I would've been killed if Kellen hadn't reeled me in. I allowed my temper to get the best of me."

"Kellen is your mentor now. She relies on you to safeguard the person she's destined to protect for the rest of her life. When she left Armeo in your care, no matter that you both had an entire security detail, she expected you to carry out your assignment with both heart and good sense."

"I know. I know all that. And I'd never fail Armeo. It's just that since we came aboard the *Dalathea* and I know that he's safer than he's been in a long time, I'm restless, agitated. I don't want to take it out on him, and I didn't know how to bring up my frustration with his grandfather."

"You did right to come to me." She put her arm gently around Ayahliss. "This is another sign of maturity. You talked things through with a friend instead of acting before thinking. Kellen would be proud. She has battled the same impatience, you know."

"She has? And is she really proud?" Ayahliss's eyes darkened further. "And are you my friend?"

Reena knew it had been a mistake to get too close to Ayahliss. She wasn't sure what was going on, why this young woman, half her age, affected her so much. Trying to act casual, she let go of Ayahliss and resumed her relaxed pose. "Yes. I'm a friend, Ayahliss. You can always turn to me, no matter what."

Ayahliss raised her hand slowly, and for a moment, Reena thought she was going to caress her. Instead, she captured a long tress of curly, red hair between her fingers. "You have the most amazing hair," she whispered. Blinking, she let go and hastily pulled back with a polite smile. "I'm sorry. That was too personal."

Reena's heart pounded. "Don't worry about it." Though normally not a soft-spoken woman, she didn't want to alienate Ayahliss. For some unfathomable reason, she wanted to wrap her in her arms and comfort her, show her that other people apart from the monks cared, that she wasn't alone. "More tea?"

"No, thank you. I've imposed enough. I need to get back and make sure Armeo doesn't talk his grandfather into playing another game." Ayahliss stood and looked down at Reena, her features softening marginally. "Will I—we—see you tomorrow?"

"Of course." She rose and walked Ayahliss to the door. "And tomorrow, we may have some very good news. Let's stay positive and visualize that possibility."

Ayahliss nodded, suddenly looking flustered. "Good idea. Good night, Reena. Thank you for listening."

She ran quick fingers along Ayahliss's jawline. "Always, Ayahliss. Good night."

❖

"Out of my way," White snarled. "I don't have time for this."

Dahlia staggered sideways and fell against a tree trunk. She could feel her ribs bending and waited to hear them crack any moment. Glaring at the woman responsible for shoving her, she saw White also nudge aside the men carrying M'Ekar on the makeshift stretcher.

"What's up?" Weiss met White halfway and Dahlia thought she saw a glimpse of exasperation in Weiss's eyes.

"This isn't working." White gestured toward M'Ekar. "We have to leave him behind. I know that's cutting our losses, but we'll make a nice profit from her." It was obvious that White was talking about her.

"We've been through this. We're not leaving him. He knows too much, for one thing, and we need to complete the mission. This is a high-profile job. Do you really think our reputation will survive if potential clients are afraid we'll leave them to die?" Weiss raised her voice. "And just as a reminder, White, *I'm* in charge here. Not you. If you want to assume command of your own team again in the future, fine. But for now, get back in line and carry out your orders."

White paled and Dahlia knew the two women had reached a crossroads. If White persisted, her actions would be mutinous, and it was clear Weiss wouldn't allow any such thing.

"You're risking everything," White hissed, her lips thin and whitening.

"So are you, by wasting my time, *our* time, like this." Weiss stared down her subordinate. "So, for the last time, take your position."

"Fine. For now." White pivoted and stalked back along the path.

Dahlia pushed herself away from the tree and couldn't hold back a moan as her bruised ribs sent arrows of pain through her chest.

"What's wrong?" Weiss asked, and neared her. "Are you injured?"

"I'm fine." She didn't even look at Weiss, but got back in line behind M'Ekar's stretcher. "You should be concerned about your subordinate. She sounded angry and frustrated."

"Let me worry about White. I think I'll keep you up front with me." Weiss grabbed her by her upper arm and shoved her forward. She glanced at M'Ekar when she passed him, concerned about his grayish pale coloring.

"He's in bad shape," she said. "Please, let me check his wounds."

"No time. We'll take care of him aboard our vessel once we've rendezvoused with our backup."

"You've planned for every contingency, haven't you?" Dahlia struggled to sound impressed. In a way she was, but her animosity toward her kidnappers made it nearly impossible to pretend.

"All part of the job."

"I'm curious why you ended up as an outlaw. You strike me as an educated and accomplished woman."

"We all have our motives." Weiss sounded indifferent.

"I suppose, but you must have really strong ones to become an enemy of the entire SC."

"I could care less about the SC or what they think of me. I live by my own rules."

"You sound rather defensive," Dahlia said, her legs aching from keeping up with Weiss's longer strides. "I think something happened to you, and you saw no other solution but to choose this dangerous path."

"This conversation isn't leading anywhere. Shut up and focus on walking."

"I suppose I could do like M'Ekar and refuse to walk any longer." Dahlia examined Weiss's expression to judge her reaction.

"I wouldn't try that if I were you. If you cause any trouble, I won't hesitate to kill M'Ekar and have one of the men carry you, even drag you by your hair." Weiss's matter-of-fact tone made Dahlia shudder. Seasoned enough not to let her feelings show, she shrugged.

"For someone who isn't prepared to implement Ms. White's idea of ditching the ambassador, you do a good job of *trying* to sound sincere in your threats," she said.

"Oh, trust me, I'm sincere." Weiss gazed at her crew. "And I only have to give the word for any of my men, or Ms. White, to get rid of M'Ekar. She will welcome such an excuse to release some stress."

Dahlia knew that Weiss wasn't exaggerating. White was a ruthless sociopath, and it wasn't difficult to imagine the glee on her face if Weiss indeed gave such an order. Dahlia shuddered and dwelt on less harrowing things. Rae and Ewan had to know by now what had happened. If Ayahliss had survived, she and Armeo must have reported the kidnapping. More unwelcome thoughts surfaced, visions of being a prisoner on Onotharat at the mercy of a ruthless interrogator. She felt faint for a second, but decided to attribute it to hunger and lack of fluids rather than fear. She perceived herself as utterly fearless. Now wasn't a good time to let any cracks in that image appear.

"I have no idea who you're talking about," she answered casually. "I'm confident that you're not only in over your head, but you can't control your own crew. You might as well face it, Weiss Kyakh. This mission will ruin you in more ways than one."

Fury, coupled with a faint trace of apprehension, traveled across Weiss's features. She raised her fist and her crew stopped as if she'd nailed them to the forest path. Snapping her head toward Dahlia, Weiss grabbed her around the neck with a strong hand and slammed her against a tree.

"I won't tell you again, so listen." Her voice was menacing and her eyes scorching as she focused her rage on Dahlia. "If you say one more word, unless you're spoken to, you'll regret it. I don't make empty threats. For your own good, I don't recommend that you test me." Weiss squeezed her neck so hard she couldn't speak or breathe.

Dahlia nodded wordlessly. She did her best to look intimidated, but in fact she was pleased. She'd managed to get under Weiss's skin and rattle her.

"Good." Weiss let go and shoved her onto the path.

Dahlia surreptitiously let the bark fall from her hands. She had clawed the tree when Weiss lunged at her and hoped potential rescuers would notice the scratches. As she walked quietly behind Weiss, she thought of her family, so important now when she finally understood enough to prioritize differently. Was she so self-absorbed that it took a criminal act like this for her to realize that all she wanted was to go home?

CHAPTER TWENTY-FOUR

*H*erona Jacelon, *herona* O'Dal," Yhja said shyly, and bowed. "We must be very careful now."

"What do you mean, Yhja?" Kellen asked. Emeron and Dwyn joined them where they were taking a few moments to wolf down an SC ration bar.

"We are approaching the Sacred Space of Light." Yhja moved her hands gracefully as she explained. "It is the clearing you wanted to reach. Many solar leaps ago, our ancestors, the Revered Disianii elders, came to the clearing once every double-full lunar night to worship the spirits of our Traveled people."

"Traveled?" Kellen looked between Yhja and Emeron.

"Dead," Emeron said. "The Disians don't believe in death. They see life as only a small station on the life journey. Death is a transitional thing, like a shuttle port, before we depart for our next level of existence."

"Go on, Yhja," Rae said. "How far are we from the clearing?"

"If we continue at the same speed as before, we might reach it before dusk." Yhja looked over at Trom, who nodded somberly. "There will be a great disturbance in the clearing since we understand that you mean to engage this enemy of yours in battle. It is not without danger for anyone uninitiated to do so."

"What are you talking about, Yhja?" Kellen asked.

"This is my belief, something that has been natural for me all my life," Yhja said shyly. "Therefore it is hard to explain in detail. Perhaps Imer-Ohon-Da can clarify." She gestured gracefully with her small hands toward Emeron.

"Let's see," Emeron said. "The Disians believe that after all the thousands of years of worship in the Sacred Space of Light, every prayer, every thought or word of worship has grown into a force in itself. Almost like a living entity. Since thoughts and prayers are the most powerful thing they know, they think it would be like firing a plasma-pulse volley into an explosives storage."

"Any reason for us to take this at face value?" Kellen tried to wrap her brain around this spiritual approach to life.

"If you'd asked me a week ago, I would've said no, but now..." Emeron shrugged, her eyes dark and brooding. "I wouldn't be that presumptuous."

"We sure didn't take explosive prayers and worship into consideration before we came here," Kellen said matter-of-factly.

"Exactly." Rae rubbed the bridge of her nose. "Do we have anything on our scanner yet? Mogghy?"

"My new set of scans shows a cluster of humanoids two kilometers from here."

Kellen could sense Rae, who stood next to her, become energized, even though they'd been attacked by bots, then walked for ten hours.

"Finally," Rae said. "We can get down to business." She pulled out a handheld computer and tapped in a few commands. "I've revised the plan and find only a few things that we need to change." Rae held the computer up for her perusal.

"I agree," Kellen said. "We need a base camp for the civilians."

"Good. Kellen, calculate where we can set it up without compromising safety. We have to send a reconnaissance team to determine if they have scanning capability and to collect tactical data."

"We have to be close enough to act instantly, but far enough away to keep our civilians safe." Emeron seemed to be thinking out loud, and nobody interrupted her. "Also, I doubt any of their sensitive equipment survived the crash, and if it did, according to the Disians there wasn't any time to take much gear because they had to leave the ship so fast."

"But we can't be sure," Mogghy added. He tucked his scanner away. "All they had to do was to keep an emergency case handy."

"True," Emeron said. "Still, we have to approach them in order to get our hands on Diplomat Jacelon and M'Ekar. If they have scanners, that will be a problem, but they're weakened and probably not as well armed as we are."

"It only takes one weapon directed at Dahlia for them to have the advantage," Kellen said darkly. "We need to isolate her and M'Ekar, but he's expendable."

Rae squinted at her. "Let's stick to the plan. I want you, Owena, and Emeron to join me in the reconnaissance party. The rest of you will follow until you reach these coordinates." Rae showed Mogghy and Leanne a spot on a map on her computer. "Leanne will head up the base-camp team with Lt. Mogghy as her XO. I want the civilians in a safe place. Ensign Oches, page the SC HQ and report every thirty minutes. We need them to keep MEDEVAC units on standby, as well as military backup."

"Aye, ma'am," Oches said, and began to arrange his equipment.

"Ensign Noor, you're responsible for the junior officers on your team." Rae turned to her marines. "Corporals, I want one of you to join Ensign Noor and the other to assist Ensign Oches with communications." Rae stopped, and the team waited patiently for her to consider further measures. "All right, people. Keep your local communicators handy. Unless I issue other orders, carry out radio silence from now on."

A unison "aye, ma'am" started a storm of activity. Kellen checked her weapons and tucked her gan'thet rods into her belt. She enjoyed the feel of them in her hands. They were more natural to her than any modern weapon. The rods hummed when an expert such as Kellen wielded them, and they seemed to her like extensions of her arms and hands.

"I see you're ready." Rae looked challengingly at Kellen.

"I am."

"And when you have this intense look about you, I know you are unstoppable." Rae lowered her voice. "I want you to be careful. Mother isn't helped by you going in full force at the wrong moment."

"I won't." Kellen knew Rae was right, but it offended her that she felt she had to voice her concerns at this point.

"I'm your commanding officer during this operation," Rae said, her tone firm. "I need to be sure that my team members are ready to follow my orders." Her expression softened. "I know you're afraid for Mother. So am I. We have to stay focused and count on her to know how to stay safe during the circumstances."

"I will try, but I swear, Rae, this is the last time M'Ekar causes our family grief. One way or the other, I'm going to take him down, along with the people who are helping him. He'll regret ever coming up with this plan." Kellen spoke low, but fiercely, and she knew she had done little to reassure Rae of her ability to follow orders.

"Just as long as we stick to *our* plan." Rae shook her head. "Work with me, Kellen, and above all, don't get yourself killed." She paused and a shadow traveled across her face. "It would destroy me," Rae whispered.

Kellen tensed at the pained words, and then slowly relaxed. Looking at Rae, nobody but Kellen could have seen how she had just slipped out of her command mode for a few seconds. Feeling Rae's conflicting emotions pierce her, Kellen knew Rae had finally gotten through to her.

"I will not disobey orders, Rae," she said gently. "And I will not get myself killed. We'll rescue Dahlia. Besides, I have so much to live for, haven't I?"

Two blinks later, Rae was back behind her command mask and nodded approvingly. "We all do, Kellen. Thank you." She glanced at the gan'thet rods at her belt. "Those new?"

"No, only enhanced." Kellen touched the rods briefly. "I had a metallurgical expert outfit the ends with an alu-carbo alloy when we were on Earth. I didn't tell you since you sometimes seem uneasy regarding my gan'thet skills."

"Oh." Rae looked stunned. "I never knew you felt that way. I'm sorry."

Kellen noticed Rae had not denied it. "It's part of who I am."

"I know. We're going to have to talk about this when we get back." Rae tugged at her weapon's harness. "Right now, I'm not oblivious to the possibility that your gan'thet skills may give us the edge we need to make this mission a success."

"I'm ready." Kellen grabbed her plasma pulse rifle and moved to Rae's left side. Rae's concession was small, but it would have to do for now. She looked around to assess everyone's status. Owena was ready and leaned against her modified plasma-pulse rifle, one arm around Leanne. Her weapon was a prototype—thin, 130 centimeters long, and able to fire at great distances with high accuracy. It could cascade plasma-blasts and was also equipped with a laser-knife at its tip.

Owena gazed down into Leanne's eyes, and the way Leanne returned the naked glance made Kellen long for Rae's embrace and at the same time feel annoyed with herself for letting personal thoughts and longing surface. She looked away. Theirs was such a private moment in the midst of the ongoing madness.

On the other side of the path, next to a fallen tree, Emeron seemed to be trying to hold Dwyn in place. Towering over her, Emeron shook her head with an expression of total frustration that made her stark features even more chiseled.

"You heard the admiral, Dwyn," Emeron said. "All civilians must be kept safe and that means you too."

"I won't be left behind while you go risk your life." Dwyn spoke in an almost menacing tone. "I'm *not* going to sit here and hide."

"I know you don't want to, but Admiral Jacelon made it clear. Besides, you're in no condition to travel as fast as we have to, to make it there in time. I'll come back for you as soon as—"

"Don't you dare patronize me. I've walked just as fast as everybody else—"

"For stars and skies, Dwyn."

Kellen studied Emeron's face and realized that her frustration bordered on anger. She strode over to them. "Commander, Dwyn, it's almost time to go." She looked calmly at Dwyn's flustered face. "Dwyn, I know you're not feeling well, but we need you to do something."

"You do?" Dwyn frowned. "I mean, of course."

"Oches will be on standby with the communicators and will need assistance. Make sure that you, Yhja, and Trom are well hidden and safe with enough ration bars and water. I want you to handle the short-range communicators, be a relay station of sorts, for when the admiral decides to end radio silence. You won't be far behind us. We expect you to advance to these coordinates," she said, and pointed at the map on her handheld computer.

Dwyn hesitated, and for a moment Kellen thought she'd refuse and demand to be part of the reconnaissance team.

"I see," Dwyn said, finally. "I don't think that'll be a problem." She began to turn, only to stop and look at Kellen. "I'll do everything I can to help Ensign Noor keep Yhja and Trom safe."

"Do you have a weapon, Dwyn?" Kellen asked.

"Yes. The pulse didn't affect my sidearm."

"Excellent."

Dwyn looked at Emeron with a stern expression that softened

only when Emeron briefly touched her arm. "You will be careful, won't you?" she whispered.

Kellen turned her back to them, knowing that yet another personal moment was unfolding.

"Yes," she heard Emeron murmur. "I will, if you'll do the same. Promise me."

"I promise." Dwyn's voice was so filled with emotion, she hardly sounded like herself. "I better get ready."

"Listen up." Rae hoisted a small back-strap security carrier onto her shoulders. Like all of their packs, it held only ammunition, water, meds, and med kits. Her own contained the same. "Reconnaissance team is moving out and base team will follow shortly. You all know your duties and I can tell you this. I'm certain we'll be successful. To be absolutely clear, unless I break radio silence, no communication."

"Yes, ma'am," both teams echoed.

Kellen walked up to Rae, who'd begun to head out as soon as she finished speaking. "If we're not delayed, we can reach the Sacred Space of Light within forty-five minutes. The terrain seems to be dryer and the path is widening."

"It might be smarter to stay off the path, but that will delay us unnecessarily. It might mean the difference between failure and success. For us, for Mother—"

"I think speed is key," Kellen agreed. She glanced back at the others and saw Owena and Emeron walking in silence next to each other a few steps behind, both of them holding scanners and keeping track of their surroundings.

"All right, let's pick up some speed." Rae began to jog down the path, her lithe, compact form moving easily despite the fact she'd been on her feet for so many hours already. Kellen joined her, and behind her she heard the other two women do the same.

❖

Weiss had made them wait at least half an hour before she returned to guide them into a large clearing. Surprised to see an empty space in the middle of the jungle, Dahlia sank onto the silken grass, her aching legs refusing to cooperate any longer. The grass smelled of something between lavender and lemon, and she inhaled the invigorating scent deeply.

The two men carrying M'Ekar put the stretcher down next to her, half in the shade, and she looked with concern at the once-so-formidable man. His face was a blotted pattern of pale and red. She felt his forehead and yanked her hand back with a gasp. He was burning up and tremors reverberated through him. He obviously had a high temperature, and if he was shivering, it was climbing still.

"He needs water." She rose to her knees and waved at Weiss. "Kyakh, you have to give him some water."

"There's no water left. He'll have to wait with the rest of us until our backup arrives."

"Are you telling me that nobody has a single drop of water?" Dahlia was parched too, but she wasn't dying of gangrene.

"Yes. That's what I'm saying. I distributed the last among you half an hour ago."

"Big mistake," Dahlia muttered. "I certainly didn't get any, and neither did he or anyone else. If you question your precious *Ms.* White, I'm sure she'll say she gave it all away, but you know as well as I do what a ruthless liar she is."

The calm expression on Weiss's face darkened, and she strode toward White, who sat in the shade of a tree. A muted, but obviously heated, discussion followed, and then Weiss stormed off to the center of the clearing. She opened her small back-strap security carrier and pulled out an object that she placed on the ground. Pulling at a thin metal rod, she extended something that resembled an antenna.

A faint moan from M'Ekar diverted Dahlia's interest back to him. "Are you awake, Hox?" she asked, and bent over him. She removed her jacket and placed it around him, even if she realized he needed to cool off. It was unbearable to watch him shiver like this.

"Madame Diplomat," he whispered huskily. "I am not worthy of your attention."

"Hush. Conserve your energy. I just wanted to see if you were conscious."

"So thirsty."

"There's no more water. I'd look for berries if I knew what was edible in this damn forest. Not that they'd let me."

"You are too kind." He coughed, and to her dismay small droplets of foamy blood streaked the corners of his mouth. She wiped them away with her shirtsleeve.

"Just rest. Help will come." She was telling the truth, she thought with gallows humor. If a search-and-rescue party didn't get here, then Weiss's backup would arrive. Either one would bring medication and water.

"I brought this upon us." M'Ekar spoke hoarsely. "My hunger for vengeance destroyed me. And you."

"Shh." Dahlia couldn't believe the twinge of pity that filled her when she witnessed his remorse. He was too sick to fake it, she thought, and like so many other people, he didn't recognize the truth until it was too late. Even she was losing faith in her rescue and expected Weiss's backup to descend from the sky any minute.

"It's true. I gambled. I thought if I took you back to Onotharat with me, they'd reinstate me as ambassador, perhaps even promote me to a higher rank. I spent all my days and nights on Jasin planning with young Desmond. He's dead." M'Ekar coughed again, and more blood foamed around his lips. "I saw the same ambitious hunger in him as I did in myself at that age."

It was all true. Dahlia couldn't contradict him, and she couldn't forgive him for his actions either, but part of her pitied him.

"Quiet. I'll go ask Weiss if any of her crew can look for signs of water around the clearing."

"Thank you." M'Ekar closed his eyes. He still trembled, but his body seemingly didn't possess even enough energy to keep that up.

She rose and walked on shaking legs over to Weiss, where she stood with two of her crew members. Nobody stopped her, but Dahlia saw White shift her weapon on her lap, pointing it directly at her.

"What?" Weiss looked impatiently at her.

"Since nobody has any water, and we actually don't know the ETA of your backup," she said, careful to infuse disbelief in her voice, just enough to make Weiss glare at her, "could you let a couple of your crew scout for water close to the clearing. Surely a brook or something must run through here. Everything is so lush, and we more or less walked in water mixed with mud the last few hours—"

"Get back to where you were sitting," the man next to Weiss snarled.

"Wait. She has a point, actually," Weiss conceded. "Take two crewmen and as many bottles as you can carry and go look for water. I don't think we have very long to wait, but it's good to be prepared."

"Aye, Captain," the man said, taking his frosty glance off Dahlia.

He waved to one young man and one woman, and they began to gather bottles from the rest of their shipmates.

"You have your moments," Weiss said ironically. "I can't quite grasp why you'd bother to worry about M'Ekar, though. He's meant nothing but trouble to you."

"True. I suppose that's the difference between you and me, Weiss. I may have a reputation as a tough bitch and instill fear in quite a few people who've had to deal with me in negotiations, but ultimately I have a code of conduct, a humanitarian point of view that you lack. Granted, I've seen faint glimpses of something resembling humane traits, but you quickly shed them. Only your cohort in crime, White, surpasses you when it comes to being ruthless."

"Really." Weiss snorted. "You're very perceptive."

"White can't help herself. She's a sociopath. You are not, which makes your actions even more reprehensible. If you think it's strange that I pity M'Ekar, you shouldn't. He's as twisted as White, a product of his upbringing and disposition. You are calculatingly committing these actions out of greed, or perhaps even lust for adventure, I'm not quite sure which. You aren't pitiful, Weiss Kyakh. You're worthy of nothing but contempt."

Dahlia turned and walked back to M'Ekar. Sitting next to his stretcher, she wiped his chin and cheeks as he coughed. She didn't know if the trauma he'd been subjected to or the gangrene eating away at his body caused his inner bleeding. But she was sure that if help didn't arrive soon, it would be too late for him.

CHAPTER TWENTY-FIVE

Rae stopped and instinctively raised her fist. Behind her, Kellen, Owena, and Emeron stopped also. Listening intently, she motioned for them to step away from the wide path and into the dense undergrowth. Next to her Owena scanned the immediate area. She held up three fingers and pointed northeast.

"Weapons?" she mouthed inaudibly, knowing that Owena's scanner could detect faint traces of plasma-pulse residue.

Owena ran another scan and nodded solemnly, holding up three fingers again. She acknowledged the signal and reached for the scanner, which Owena handed over so she could examine the readings. The three individuals were about fifty meters away and not as closely grouped together as she would have assumed. They moved in what had to be a search pattern, and for a moment she allowed herself to hope that her mother had escaped. But if that was the case, surely more than three people would be out looking. Dahlia was their treasure trove.

"All right," Rae whispered, "here's what we'll do. We'll split up in pairs. Kellen, you and Owena start in from the left flank, Emeron and I from due south. Let's find out why these people are so far away from the rest of their gang. I'd like to apprehend them without a single shot and without them alerting their associates. All right?"

"Yes, ma'am," the other three echoed.

Before Kellen and Owena left Rae and Emeron, Kellen looked pointedly at her without saying a word.

"I know," Rae said quietly. "I know. And you too."

"Yes. See you soon."

Rae and Emeron returned to the forest path, since walking along the wide trail would create much less sound than forcing their way through the tall grass and bushes among the trees. Emeron used a scanner Leanne had given her, since the EMP had incapacitated her own earlier. It wasn't as elaborate as Owena's, but it showed how well Owena and Kellen progressed.

The three green dots that indicated the location of the enemy kept nearing, veering off farther to the east. The clearing was yet another fifteen minutes away, and a larger yellow dot showed where the rest of the mercenaries, and presumably her mother, were. At this point, Rae could care less if they apprehended M'Ekar. She was only interested in rescuing Dahlia.

When they were ten meters from the location of the three mercenaries, she and Emeron slipped into the undergrowth, careful not to make a sound. Ducking, they sneaked up on the closest one. A young man, dressed in black, dusty coveralls and carrying at least ten bottles slung over his shoulders, walked along a smaller path, looking back and forth, obviously searching for something.

Emeron gestured toward the man and mimicked drinking. Rae nodded. She'd already figured out he was searching for water. The possibility that her mother had been without water for quite some time, something that hadn't even occurred to her before, enraged her. Emeron gestured to her, her weapon ready and set to heavy stun. She nodded and ducked out of the way, allowing Emeron to take aim.

Five seconds later, she heard a faint thud. The mercenary lay on the ground, the bottles scattered around him. Emeron scanned the immediate area again and nodded. "The others are thirty meters to the northeast," she whispered.

"Good. Let's take care of this one."

They ran over to the man and Emeron grabbed some thin restraints from her belt. She secured his hands and feet and connected them behind his back, then pulled out a roll of bandage and pressed some of it into his mouth before she wrapped the rest around his head, to keep the muzzle in place. Rae made sure his airways were clear, grabbed his legs, and with Emeron's help dragged him into the dense shrubbery behind two fallen trees.

Another scan later, Emeron smiled broadly at her. "Second one down," she said quietly, and held up the scanner. Another green dot had stopped, apparently immobilized by the two blue dots that indicated friendly forces.

"Perfect. Let's go help them with the third."

They crept forward, ducking when the trees temporarily grew

farther apart. She checked Emeron's scanner and saw that Kellen and Owena were approaching from the north.

"Arrto? Where did you go? Arrto," a female voice called, startling Rae since it sounded so close. She tugged Emeron with her and ducked behind a tree.

"Arrto? Belliaz?" The woman started to sound worried, and if she yelled any louder, the mercenaries at the clearing would descend upon them. Rae knew she couldn't wait any longer. Stepping out on the path, right in front of a young woman, she smiled politely. "Hello. Lose someone?"

"Who are you? Where's Arrto?" The woman's eyes grew wide. "You're SC." She raised her weapon, but Rae fired first. Another beam singed the air from behind the woman, who slumped to the ground where she stood. Kellen appeared behind the female mercenary, looking sternly at Rae.

"I thought you agreed to be careful," she said.

"I did. And I was. I actually think I stunned her first." She checked the woman's pulse. "Oh, dear. I don't think she'll be a problem for quite a while. She's been double stunned, and that's a bit too much for such a small creature."

Emeron used her restraints again and they hid her like they had the others.

"She recognized the uniform instantly," Rae said. "But before she saw me, she acted very casual."

"In other words, they don't have a clue we're on their trail," Emeron said. "And we can safely say they have no scanning capability. We would have seen some action from the clearing by now if they did."

"I agree," Kellen said. "I suggest we stay divided and approach the clearing from two directions."

"Good idea." Rae thought quickly. "Kellen, Owena, you have the better scanner. Circle the camp to the east side and remain there. Emeron and I will reconnoiter from here and also connect with the base team when they're in position. If you notice an approaching backup ship or anything else that dramatically changes our plan, break radio silence and page me and the base team."

"Understood." Kellen and Owena climbed a small ledge and began to circle the clearing at a safe distance.

Rae motioned for Emeron to follow her, and they stepped off the main path, careful where they placed their feet. Birds chirped and the sun was now so low the trees created long shadows that efficiently hid them. Her heart picked up speed as they approached the clearing. Something was in the air, something tense. She could practically smell it. Was it her own fear of what she would find when she reached the place where her mother was held captive? Shrugging off the ominous feeling, she ducked under some low branches and sneaked up behind a dense thicket. Emeron joined her with the scanner ready.

"All mercenaries within the clearing," Emeron mouthed. "The protector and Commander Grey halfway to their position."

Rae nodded briskly and carefully parted the thin branches of a bush. The sun bathed the people clustered at the south end in a warm golden glow. It was hard to distinguish individual features at this distance. The group of mercenaries was about seventy-five meters away. She took out her binocular specs and made sure they were set on anti-reflection mode. She certainly didn't want to send flashes of light from the bush they hid behind.

After pulling on the binocular specs she adjusted the magnification. People were standing or sitting in groups, and at first she couldn't detect any familiar faces. She adjusted the sharpness of the binocular specs, and this time it took only a moment to find Dahlia.

❖

Dahlia watched White stalk back and forth, glancing at her chronometer. "Something's wrong." She stopped in front of Weiss. "They've been gone too long."

"I agree." Weiss stood and waved two of her crewmen over. "Go check out the situation. Don't separate."

"Aye, Captain." The young men walked toward the tree line and soon were out of sight.

Dahlia looked down at her lap, where M'Ekar's head was resting. She'd convinced Weiss to place his stretcher farther toward the tree line, for more shade. When he moaned with every breath, Dahlia couldn't ignore him. No matter what he'd done, it wasn't in her to remain indifferent while another person was in such agony.

"If they're not back with water soon," she said to Weiss, "M'Ekar will slip into a coma and we won't be able to get any fluids into him."

Weiss knelt next to them and gazed closely at him. "He's in bad shape," she agreed. "Damn it. What's keeping them?"

Dahlia wasn't sure if Weiss was talking about the people she'd sent to look for water or her backup.

"I could shorten his agony," White said, hovering over them with her weapon slung over her shoulder.

"Harness your helpfulness, White," Weiss hissed. "They'll be back soon with water, and we're not performing euthanasia on anyone just yet."

"Fine." White resumed her pacing.

Dahlia shifted to shield M'Ekar's eyes from the rays of the setting sun. Her own mouth was parched and her lips were beginning to chap. Licking them didn't help. She estimated that she hadn't had anything to drink for eight hours. During normal circumstances that wouldn't pose such a problem, but sweating profusely during their march through the forest had dehydrated all of them. Weiss looked remarkably unaffected, as did White. Had they hidden bottles of water that they didn't share? Dahlia wouldn't put it past White, but Weiss somehow possessed some "honor-among-thieves" characteristics. She probably wouldn't betray her own crew that way.

Time went on, and Dahlia was so tired she lost track of how long it had been since the two crewmen left to search for the others. Only when Weiss stood and looked in the direction they had gone did Dahlia realize that the two men were probably missing as well.

"What's going on, Madame?" M'Ekar whispered huskily.

"I don't know. People are walking into the woods and apparently not coming back."

"The forest has predatory animals?" He coughed from the exertion of talking.

"I don't think so. Not big enough to take down five people."

"Then it should be obvious."

"What do you mean?" Dahlia leaned down to catch his broken words.

"You shall see...very soon, I think." He closed his eyes. Apparently talking had worn him out. His breathing was shallow and ragged, and his thin lips looked bluish.

Dahlia tipped her head back against the tree, trying to make sense of what he had said. She was exhausted and her entire body burned and ached. Stars began to appear in the sky, and she tried to focus on the beauty of dusk.

Suddenly she noticed what looked like a meteor streak so close it startled her. She blinked and tried to grasp what she actually saw. The streak in the sky was green, a space phenomenon she'd never heard of. Only then did her brain process what her eyes saw, and she realized someone was firing on them.

❖

Kellen and Owena huddled behind a low-growing bush, about thirty meters from the group of criminals, who seemed exhausted. Behind them, two men lay unconscious, tied up with vines Kellen had cut from a tree. They had easily spotted the two individuals on Owena's scanner, and Kellen had knocked them unconscious without having to use any weapon but her rods.

"I see Dahlia," she whispered, and tried to remain calm. She wanted to go in weapons ablaze, but maintained radio silence and waited for Rae's command.

"What's that noise?" Owena mouthed, looking up. "What the hell—"

"Gods of Gantharat." Kellen stared in dismay as a fleet of bots entered the clearing from all directions. Whirling, they glittered in the last rays of the setting sun.

"I don't understand." Owena spoke louder. "The scanner's not picking up anything this time either."

Kellen tugged the communicator to her mouth. "O'Dal to Jacelon. Come in."

"Jacelon here. We see them, Kellen. Mogghy and Leanne just got here. Move in. Move in."

Owena and Kellen leaped to action, and Kellen had only one thing in mind. They had to get to Dahlia.

CHAPTER TWENTY-SIX

Emeron ducked as she dashed along the tree line, firing at the bots. They swarmed around the cluster of people at the east end of the clearing, and she laid a volley of plasma-pulse discharges to draw attention away from Jacelon's mother, who had to be among them.

Mogghy suddenly showed up behind her. "The civilians are safely tucked away, ma'am," he informed her, slightly out of breath. "We found a place behind some massive trees— Watch out, ma'am!" He pushed her sideways.

Four bots flew toward them, firing blue and orange beams, which missed her by a few centimeters. Rolling to her side, she aimed at the nearest one and fired. At first nothing happened, which made her fear these bots had impenetrable shields. Then smoke billowed out from between its antennas and it began to whirl in a crazy pattern. It collided with another one and both exploded in a cascade of sparks.

Mogghy shot the remaining two that now hovered above them, but suddenly he collapsed next to her, grabbing his left shoulder. "Ah."

"Mogghy." She took aim, furious at the mindless machines that kept appearing and threatening them, injuring them. She kept her finger on the sensor, spreading a wide ray of plasma-pulse fire, and watched with satisfaction as the bots exploded. Scorching debris hit her, but she reveled in the heat, knowing she'd taken them out. Mogghy slumped beside her.

"Mogghy, let me see. Let me see." She tried to pry his hand away.

"I'll be fine, ma'am. Go on. They need you. I'll cover you. Go on."

She stared at him for a few seconds, then began to advance toward the clearing. Jacelon crouched behind a large rock about fifteen meters in front of her, with Ensign Noor. They were fighting the bots that hovered over the group of mercenaries by the tree line. The mercenaries were defending themselves, but not all of them were armed and some were too injured to fight.

Emeron crawled to Jacelon. "Have you located your mother yet?"

"I think she's over by that tree—covering someone with her body." She raised binocular specs. "Damn it, if I didn't know better, I'd say it's M'Ekar, on a stretcher."

"Do you have a headcount of those bots?" Emeron fired at a group of three that hovered just above the tree that sheltered Dahlia Jacelon.

"Noor did a visual and we have at least fifteen active ones right now."

"Damn it, how did they manage to deploy so many of them, and why the hell don't they show up on sensors?"

"Creative shielding harmonics," Jacelon suggested. "Look, that tall dark-haired woman in the center of the group. The one who's firing standing up. She's the leader. She matches Ayahliss's description."

"Should I take her out?"

"No. She's doing a good job firing at the bots, and we need her in that position." Jacelon gazed around her for a moment. "But she's not enough. Only four more of them are firing at the bots, following her example."

Suddenly six of the bots veered southwest. The others still hovered above the clearing, but had ceased shooting.

"What the hell's going on now?" Jacelon muttered. "Where are they going? I... Oh, Gods."

"What?" Emeron rose to her knees, following the disappearing bots.

"They're moving toward where Mogghy and Leanne hid the civilians."

"Dwyn." Emeron's heart constricted and she thought it would never be able to pump her blood through her body again. "Where is she? Where did they hide her? Does she have a communicator?"

"Yes, but she won't break radio silence unless they're in direct danger. We can't page her. The bots might track the signal. Jacelon to Leanne, come in," she barked.

"Leanne here, Admiral. I see them. I'm on my way." Leanne's breathless voice echoed over the communicator.

"Go with her, Commander, when she gets here, but don't tip your hand. They might not find the civilians. Wait for backup."

"What backup?" Emeron was cringing where she knelt, wanting nothing but to ensure Dwyn's safety.

Jacelon didn't answer, but grabbed her communicator off her lapel. "Jacelon to Oches. Contact SC headquarters. I repeat, contact SC headquarters."

"Aye, ma'am. Already have them standing by."

"Excellent. Jacelon out." She gazed out over the clearing again. "Looks like they've ceased firing for now. Go on, you two. Make sure the civilians are safe."

"Yes, ma'am," Leanne said, and disappeared down a narrow path. Emeron followed her and, as they passed Mogghy, saw that he had managed to put an emergency bandage in place. He made an encouraging gesture and she nodded in response, thinking of no one but Dwyn. Obviously the bots had nothing to do with the hostage situation and everything to do with Dwyn's presence in the forest.

The foliage became denser, and when Leanne suddenly stopped, Emeron was surprised that they were on the edge of a small ravine. Leanne pulled out a scanner.

"I can't see anything, but that's expected." She spoke quietly. "Look at that small indentation, almost a cave, in the bedrock wall of the ravine. Dwyn and the guides are tucked in there, and I covered the entrance with tons of branches and rocks."

"If the bots have better scanning features than their predecessors, that won't be enough." Emeron closed her mouth so quickly her jaws ached. She wiped cold, clammy sweat from her forehead.

"Let's hope they don't, but prepare for the worst. We have to go in, but before we do, we need to warn Dwyn. You know her better than I do. Tell her that she and the Disians need to stay completely still, unless we tell them to start running."

"All right, I—" Emeron had begun to reach for her communicator when three bots whisked by, their humming sound now all too familiar. They played spotlights from side to side across the walls of the ravine. It was almost dark, and Emeron pulled out her night-vision visor, then snapped it in place around her head. The bots slowed down and began to shoot randomly at the bedrock wall.

"Damn." She tugged Leanne down with her, pulling her behind some trees. "They've located her."

"Page her. We know the bots aren't very accurate in their aim, and if she and the others run, they have a better chance of getting away. If they stay, the bots will find them by elimination. They'll be sitting ducks."

"Emeron to Dwyn. Get out of there, run eastbound through the ravine. Come on."

"Affirmative." Dwyn's voice, breathless and husky, echoed from the communicator, as clear as if she'd been standing right next to them.

Emeron stared between the trees into the ravine. At first she couldn't see anything except undergrowth and rocks, but then three individuals burst through what looked like solid rock and began to jump and run, all the time gazing upward in all directions.

"Three bots just passed your position, Dwyn," Emeron continued. "Three others are on the prowl for you. Try to get to our position. Leanne and I are waiting three hundred meters east of you, up the ledge to your right."

"Understood. It's hard to walk this fast in the dark down here." Dwyn gasped, and Emeron knew this activity had to take a toll on her damaged lungs. She prayed her inhaler wasn't empty.

She poked her head out from behind the trees and saw how Dwyn ran behind Trom and Yhja, making sure the innocent were taken care of. Her protectiveness made Emeron's eyes burn.

"Oh, no," she heard Leanne gasp. Snapping her head up, she saw all six of the bots converge on Dwyn and the others. Blue, purple, and orange beams tore up the dirt around them.

"Dwyn," she moaned, and leaped into action. "Dwyn."

❖

Dahlia moved sideways and slid off M'Ekar's still body. Lights flickered against the purple-black sky, indicating the position of the hovering machines. She had no idea where they came from or who had sent them, but they were clearly as hostile toward the mercenaries as to her. Weiss still stood with her weapon raised, her face set firmly as if chiseled in marble.

"M'Ekar," Dahlia whispered, carefully nudging him. "M'Ekar." He didn't stir, and his breathing was rapid and shallow. She felt for his pulse, but could barely find it on his wrist. She tried his neck, and it was more palpable there, but erratic. She closed her eyes and groaned.

Suddenly more fire aimed at them lit up the sky, and once again she flung herself across his head and chest. Metal pieces began to rain on them, scorching her. At first, she couldn't fathom what was happening, then realized someone firing from the tree line was taking out the hovering machines. Rescuers? Weiss's backup? She closed her eyes and prayed. *Perhaps this was what M'Ekar tried to tell me before. Please let it be SC military.*

"Who the hell..."

Weiss growled behind her and Dahlia's question was answered. Suddenly energized, despite being dehydrated and exhausted, she slid off M'Ekar again and began to tug his stretcher out of the clearing. If there was a standoff between Weiss, the machines, and whoever was approaching from the forest, she didn't plan to be caught in the middle of it.

She dug her feet into the ground, for the first time in days grateful that she wore boots with thin heels, and yanked the stretcher. The branches it was made of nearly gave way, but slowly she managed to drag the unconscious man toward the shrubbery behind her. When the stretcher finally broke, she knelt and put her arms under him and pulled. "Come on," she begged, "help me out here, *Ambassador*. Wake up and push."

All the time, she kept her eyes on Weiss, who was pressing up along the group of trees, shooting against the machines and also returning the fire coming from the forest.

Finally, Dahlia hid M'Ekar behind a large rock located near some bushes. She broke off some large branches and placed them over him, hoping they would be enough. She had to circle the clearing and find out who was attacking the mercenaries. Surely it was a search-and-rescue party sent to bring her back.

It was completely dark now, and she could make out her surroundings only when the blasts from the plasma-pulse weapons and the beams from the machines lit up the area. She stumbled along the path, stubbing her toes constantly against roots and rocks, clenching her fists hard enough to dig her nails into her palms. This was the only way she could remain quiet. She was lightheaded and reluctantly admitted in a bout of dark humor that she wasn't twenty-one anymore.

Another blast, this time causing an ear-deafening explosion, lit up the forest around her. She froze in place when she spotted the shadows of four or five figures running toward her, then stepped off the path, since she couldn't tell if they were her captors. Forcing herself to hold her breath, she heard her pulse thunder in her ears.

The figures were closing in now, and only the dim red light from their weapons gave away their position. Dahlia knew enough about weapons to realize they were probably SC-issued. She was also savvy enough to know that pirates and mercenaries had stolen many such arms over the years. She wanted to let these people know who and where she was, but having marched for days with rifles directed at her every second, she wasn't keen to be subjected to them again.

❖

Dwyn moved as fast as she could, grateful to have Trom and Yhja running even faster in front of her. Emeron's voice over the communicator had sent her flying out of the damp, cold cave. Trom and Yhja had realized the severity of their situation immediately and not questioned her orders.

Night had fallen around them like a black shield, and Dwyn knew they would have to slow down soon and feel their way forward. The bots might catch up with them then and kill them with one well-directed beam. Fortunately, so far these machines, as devious as they were, had poor aim.

"Dwyn." Her communicator crackled. "You can't follow the ravine to its end." She recognized Leanne's voice. "It leads back to the clearing, and I don't know if you can hear it, but a major battle's going on there right now."

"I hear it." She gasped. Something tugged at her head, and she realized her hair had escaped its constraints and was getting tangled in twigs and branches. "Ow." She kept moving, her scalp burning where small strands were ripped off.

"What's wrong?" Emeron asked, her voice from the communicator on Dwyn's shoulder sounding so close. "Dwyn, talk to me."

"I'm all right. Just a bit scalped." She slowed down as the darkness became impenetrable. "Yhja, Trom, be careful."

"We are right here." Yhja's voice floated toward her and she fumbled in her direction.

"Good. Grab Trom's hand. We have to stick together."

"Move up the right side of the ravine now," Emeron said over the comm system. "I'll guide you."

"She can see us, Dwyn?" Yhja asked, sounding amazed.

"Night-vision technology." She began to cough. Afraid to admit how much her lungs burned, she dragged Yhja behind her up the ravine wall.

"A little more to the left, there are roots to hold on to. Keep climbing."

A large explosion sent tremors through the ground. She had to let go of Yhja, but urged her and Trom to stay immediately behind her. Her hands slipped on the roots that were covered with something sticky, probably old sap, but she kept climbing, one step at a time, hauling herself up.

"Good, keep going," Emeron said. "Just a little farther."

"I should let Yhja and Trom go first. I'm too tired." She rested her forehead against the bedrock.

"No. Yhja, Trom, can you hear me?"

"Yes, Imer-Ohon-Da." Yhja wrapped her arm around Dwyn's waist. "I will not allow herona Dwyn to fall behind. She is very tired, but we will make it up the ledge."

"Don't let go of her." Dwyn could hear the anguish in Emeron's voice. "Just don't let go."

Trom joined in and mimicked Yhja's grip from Dwyn's other side. Together they pulled themselves and Dwyn up along the bedrock, tugging at roots, clinging to small bushes. She tried to help, but her arms were too heavy and she could hardly move her feet. The strong, young arms around her waist were painful and constricting, but she knew if they let go, she'd fall to the bottom. "Thank you," she whispered. "I'm sorry—"

"You're almost there," Emeron said encouragingly. "A few meters, that's all. You can do this. Dwyn, just let them help you."

It seemed like a lifetime, but eventually a new set of strong arms hauled her over the edge and up on soft grass. Yhja and Trom collapsed next to her, and she looked up in time to see Leanne kneel next to Yhja and hug her.

"You made it." Emeron embraced her and buried her face in her hair. She groaned as her scalp burned, and Emeron flinched and let go. She protested wordlessly by hiding her face at Emeron's neck, trying to catch her breath.

"You're injured," Emeron said hoarsely. "There's blood in your hair."

"Some branches caught it."

"Want me to tie it back for you?" Leanne asked. "I have a spare clasp."

"Thanks." Dwyn whimpered almost inaudibly as Leanne quickly braided her hair.

"Rest a few minutes and drink some," Emeron said, as she stroked her back. "We have to get away from the bots' trail here. They'll be looking for traces of you the next time they pass the ravine. They lost track of you when you veered off up the wall. It's just a matter of time before they return."

"Can we repeat the EMP?" Dwyn asked, breathing a little easier with each new breath.

"Not advisable, since we risk disrupting any backup that Jacelon's called in."

"Damn."

"Exactly."

"Sorry, but you've rested long enough. We need to leave." Leanne sounded casual, but it wasn't hard for Dwyn to sense the sincerity and professionalism behind her words. "The bots haven't fired as much on the northwest side of the clearing. I say we move carefully to that side, preferably without bumping into any of the bad guys."

Emeron helped her to her feet. "Lean on me. Yhja and Trom, you follow me, and Leanne will come last. You okay to walk, Dwyn? I can carry you."

"You can*not*," she said firmly. "I can walk."

"Okay." Emeron kept her arm around Dwyn. "Let me know if that changes."

"All right."

They crept along small, winding paths, Emeron's night-vision visor enabling her to lead the way. Dwyn heard shouting and firing in the distance, and once they had to duck and play dead for several minutes while two bots circled them like vultures. They finally flew away, and she shivered so violently that Emeron had to feel it.

"Why don't they see our body signatures?" she asked. "The others we came across seemed to."

"The plasma-pulse charges must have jumbled their sensors. Smell them in the air? The slightly phosphorous scent?"

"Yes. That could mask us?"

"My best guess."

They kept walking and Dwyn thought they would reach Jacelon and the rest of their team any minute. Perhaps SC backup had already arrived?

A loud explosion sounded not far from them, followed by a blinding light. She pressed herself against Emeron and clung to her weapon harness. "*What* was that?"

"I have no idea." Emeron stood still. "I thought I saw something."

"Where? More bots?" Dwyn froze and looked frantically around her.

"No. A shadow. A person over there?" Emeron began to walk toward it, dragging her with one hand and holding her weapon ready with the other. "You. Show yourself. Damn if I'm going to pass you and let you shoot us in the back."

There was silence for a moment.

"Let me check it out." Leanne pulled out a scanner. "I'm getting erratic readings. There are a lot of disturbances. Can you see them?"

"I think they're behind the trees five meters ahead of us, ten o'clock."

"Come out," Leanne demanded, raising her weapon. "If you don't, we'll be forced to shoot."

Another bout of silence, then a soft rustle of leaves.

"I know that voice," a woman said, sounding tired but with obvious command in her tone. "D'Artansis?"

Dwyn blinked. Who—?

"Diplomat Jacelon?" Leanne said, her voice reverent. "Dahlia?"

"Oh, Leanne, for stars and skies," the woman they'd been sent to rescue said as she stumbled toward them. "If you're here, so are Rae, Kellen, and Owena." She stood before them and Dwyn could barely make out the contours of a tall woman. "And while we're on the subject, what took you so long?"

CHAPTER TWENTY-SEVEN

K ellen placed her plasma-pulse rifle in its harness on her back
and dislodged her gan'thet rods. The familiar cold rage at the
sight of an oppressor, or in this case, a hardened criminal, a murderer,
engulfed her, and she tore across the clearing. Many years of training
kept Kellen's fury at the exact level she needed to perform at peak
efficiency. She was determined to find Dahlia and kill M'Ekar and
the female leader of the mercenaries. Her night-vision visor tinted
everything faint green, which gave the situation a ghostly glow.

Rae and Mogghy covered her, firing repeatedly at the bots and the
criminals, and as far as Kellen saw, none of the mercenaries dared poke
their heads up, except a small blond woman who stood straight up in
the middle of the huddled and wounded.

"Ahh." Kellen pivoted when she saw the woman raise her weapon.
Plasma-pulse beams singed the air next to Kellen's head, but she
maintained her trajectory, whirling in an evasive pattern that her father
had taught her. Ducking and twirling at the same time, she launched
one leg sideways, hitting the blonde in the back of her knees.

To Kellen's surprise, the woman fell, but not all the way to the
ground. Her arms were thin, but she placed one hand on the ground and
somersaulted, came full circle, and was about to redirect her weapon
toward Kellen when Rae or Mogghy shot again, hitting the blonde's
rifle. It flew out of her hands, and she cried out as it broke against a
tree trunk.

"Damn you to hell," she screamed, and produced a knife. Her
left hand hung useless from the elbow down. The laser-blade hummed
to life, and Kellen crossed the rods in front of her in a deceptively
defensive stance.

"I know you," the blonde said, gasping, perhaps from pain, but

Kellen doubted it. Something in the other woman's eyes, something bordering on insanity, made Kellen think she probably didn't even feel the pain.

"Really. You have me at a disadvantage." Kellen closed in slowly, menacingly. She heard Rae and Mogghy lay down cover fire and saw out of the corner of an eye how the mercenaries retreated.

"You are the protector. Her daughter-in-law."

The mention of Dahlia sent a jolt through Kellen, but she disregarded it. "Then you should be concerned."

"Should I?" The blonde smiled sweetly. "I'm not famous like you, but I can hold my own against anyone." She sliced the knife through the air in a slow pattern.

Kellen didn't have to guess. "You are known as Ms. White," she said, circling her.

White looked taken aback for a few moments, only to produce the same sickly sweet smile as before. "I'm flattered." She rocked from side to side, looking up at Kellen with burning eyes.

"Don't be. You're a pirate turned mercenary. Hardly an accomplishment, especially since you and your cohorts in crime failed so blatantly in your last endeavor." Kellen saw movement reflected in White's eyes and leapt to her left.

A bot, with black smoke billowing from underneath, spun past her toward White, who jumped to the side, but not soon enough. The bot struck her, and her unrestrained cry confirmed what Kellen saw—it had knocked White's shoulder out of its socket.

She watched without feelings as the woman fell to her knees, dropping her knife as she clutched her upper arm. Kellen calmly took the knife from where it had fallen and switched it off, then tucked it into her harness next to her own.

"Where is Dahlia Jacelon?"

"Not here, obviously." White grunted.

"I see. Where have you hidden her?" Kellen lifted her foot and placed it on White's injured shoulder. "Where is she?"

"I don't care where she— Ahh!" White cried out again when Kellen shoved her onto her back and stood over her, her gan'thet rods ready to give the final blow.

"I will not ask again." Kellen could hear her own frozen rage.

White, now looking like she was about to throw up from pain, stared at her with unabashed hatred. "I don't know. All of a sudden she was gone, and so was M'Ekar, and he's dying from his injuries. She must have taken him."

Kellen had to struggle to hide her bafflement. In her opinion, White was telling the truth. She was in far too much pain, and too furious, to fabricate something so implausible. Kellen judged that she wasn't going to learn anything more from the blond sociopath. Raising her gan'thet rods in the classic pattern, she spoke words in Gantharian that revered life and welcomed death.

"Stop it, Kellen," Rae said from behind her. "We're doing this by the book." She shot at White, and Kellen knew her weapon was set to heavy stun. "No unnecessary blood on your hands, darling."

Kellen bowed and tucked her gan'thet rods into her belt before she grasped her rifle again. As if she'd slipped into her lieutenant-commander skin and tucked away her nature as protector with the rods, she nodded briskly. "Aye, Admiral. White said that Dahlia ran away and took M'Ekar with her. Apparently he's badly wounded, perhaps dying." She tried not to sound too pleased.

"The mercenaries have regrouped farther south in the clearing, so it should be safe to conduct a quick search of the immediate area," Rae said. "If Mother pulled M'Ekar out of here, she can't have dragged him far. She's tired and he's probably dead weight."

Mogghy came up, pale and obviously in pain. Kellen admired the way he still carried himself.

"Report," Rae said.

"The bots have disappeared from the clearing, at least for now. We can't detect them with scanners. It's disturbing that they just vanished, and I hope that doesn't mean they've located Dwyn."

"I do too." Rae pointed at the unconscious White. "Tie her up. We don't want her to cause any more trouble. Are the other mercenaries we took care of secure?"

"Aye, ma'am," Mogghy said. "Commander Grey and Ensign Oches put two of our junior officers on that. Apprehending criminals is their area of expertise."

"Good." Rae looked around. "I need you to establish a perimeter around this part of the clearing, Lt. Mogghy. Commander O'Dal and I will search along the tree line. Keep an open comm line, Lieutenant."

Mogghy nodded and began to issue orders, and soon Kellen could see the marines and several of the Cormanian junior officers approach from the forest. Ducking, they ran toward Mogghy.

"Come on, Kellen." Rae attached her rifle to her back and pulled out a sidearm. "We don't have much time. Weiss Kyakh is undoubtedly regrouping at the other end of the clearing, now that the bots aren't here."

"I agree." Kellen's scanner beeped quietly as she flipped it open, and she was stunned to get a reading immediately. "Rae. Faint life signs to your immediate left."

Rae lit a small light on top of her sidearm and went down on one knee as she searched the bushes next to her. "I can't see any—wait—oh, gods, I see a hand."

Kellen knelt next to Rae and they began to pull away the broken branches. Soon they stared down at the body of an emaciated man they both knew so well. M'Ekar, their nemesis, lay still and white on the ground.

"He's alive. Barely." Kellen spoke quietly and felt nothing for their ancient enemy. "His body is shutting down one organ after another. This isn't a medical scanner, of course, but unless I'm reading it wrong, he has high levels of toxicity in his blood."

"Sepsis. He's dying." Rae sighed. "And we have no way to care for him. Damn it."

"You want to heal this person, the one responsible for all this?" Kellen asked incredulously. "You should rejoice in his failure. This is, how is that saying, literary righteousness?"

"You mean poetic justice." Rae corrected Kellen without her usual smile when she got Earth sayings wrong. "Trust me, Kellen. If I let myself off the hook, professionally, even for a second, I'd snatch those gan'thet rods off your belt and break his neck. But I can't. And, really, death is too mild a punishment. I want him incarcerated."

"I don't understand, but as an officer I will abide by the SC regulations." Kellen had never found it so difficult to restrain herself, to respect the rules. She was ready to kill M'Ekar, but knew she wouldn't.

Rae grabbed her communicator. "Jacelon to Mogghy. Come in."

"Mogghy here, ma'am."

"Is Commander Grey there yet? We're only a hundred meters due east of your position and we've found M'Ekar, half-dead. Send the marines to retrieve him and take him inside the perimeter you're establishing."

Mogghy confirmed that Owena had joined him, and within seconds, she arrived with the marines, who carried M'Ekar over by the large trees.

Then Rae and Kellen followed the winding path that led away from the shrubbery. Kellen kept an eye on the scanner readings and also looked among the treetops, in case the bots tried a sneak attack.

They had walked for five minutes when the scanner signaled another presence. Just as Kellen began to report to Rae, their communicator came alive again.

"D'Artansis to Jacelon. Admiral, this is Leanne, do you read?"

"Leanne. Glad to hear you're all right. Are Emeron and Dwyn with you?"

"Aye, ma'am, they are. And we've added another member to our group."

Rae gripped Kellen's arm. "Go on."

"Rae, this is your mother. I'm in one piece."

Kellen could barely make out the tears in Rae's eyes, but they glittered where they hung on the tips of her eyelashes.

"Mother," Rae said huskily. "Did they hurt you?"

"A few bumps and bruises, but otherwise, no. Leanne gave me some water, which helped."

Kellen circled Rae's waist. The shared strength would rejuvenate Rae like nothing else could. Rae stood still for a moment, clutching Kellen and breathing evenly as if that were her only way to regain her equilibrium.

"I'm so glad, Mother," she said, her voice barely more than a whisper. "So very glad."

"Child..." Dahlia's voice drifted off, only to return with a sharp undertone. "What's that sound? That faint buzz. Damn, those machines are back."

The communicator went silent, and Kellen tapped the sensor several times before it became functional again. "Leanne, Emeron. Go back to the southeast end of the clearing. Mogghy and Owena have set up a perimeter there."

Static sizzled from the communicator, and then Leanne's voice returned. "We're on our way. Six bots are performing a search grid and we can't take the shortest route. We have to maneuver under the densest foliage."

"Affirmative. Keep the civilians safe, Commander."

"Naturally. D'Artansis and D'Artansis out."

Even Kellen had to smile at Leanne's attempt at humor, which she took as a good sign, since Leanne was normally facetious only if she was in an optimistic mood. Rae, on the other hand, tended to use the humorous approach when circumstances were horrible.

"All right. Let's return to the clearing. Owena and Mogghy will probably need all the help they can get to keep both bots and mercenaries at bay." She began to walk, but stopped suddenly and gazed at Kellen with eyes turned silvery gray in the twin moonlight. "We found her. We found her, Kellen."

"Yes, we did. And now we have to hang on to her and keep her safe until backup arrives, then take her back with us." Kellen wanted to embrace Rae, but knew this wasn't the time or the place. They could indulge themselves later, when they were all safe. Kellen touched her gan'thet rods, taking comfort in their presence. She was an expert with all types of weapons, but the rods never failed her.

"Come on, then." Rae smiled faintly. She had opened her mouth to say something more when the now-so-familiar whining buzz drowned out her words.

The bots were back.

❖

Dahlia forced her heavy legs to keep running, following in Leanne's erratic zigzag pattern to try to fool the machines, which the others called bots. The large orbs buzzed around them, and sometimes the noise they made was pierced by colorful beams that burned holes in tree trunks and set more than one bush on fire. The forest lit up, making it easier to see where they were going. Dahlia was afraid, however, that the light might also make it easier for the bots' ocular sensors to determine their position. So far the zigzag method seemed to work, but she wasn't sure she could keep up much longer.

The young woman with the long blond hair, Dwyn, seemed even worse off. She needed the Cormanian law-enforcement officer, Emeron, to help her keep her balance. They were last, and Leanne kept glancing back to check on them.

The path they were on widened and now Leanne picked up speed, running more in a straight line than before. "We'll be there soon," she said, gasping, "just a few more minutes."

Dahlia began to think she wasn't going to make it. Her legs felt completely uncooperative and each new step was like wading through syrup. The smoke around them made her cough and she was desperately thirsty again. She had emptied all of Leanne's water, but it wasn't nearly enough.

They rounded a cluster of trees and Leanne stopped, holding up her hand. She placed a finger over her lips as she pulled out her scanner. Emeron and Dwyn caught up with them, and Emeron flipped open her scanner as well.

"The mercenaries are still grouped in the far southeast corner. Our people are fifty meters away, approximately, to our left. Let's get behind the tree line. You up for it, Dwyn?" Leanne asked. "I'd rather not leave you behind and risk not finding you later."

"Dwyn wouldn't be alone," Emeron said starkly. "If she can't make it, I'll stay with her." It was obvious to Dahlia that Emeron harbored strong feelings for Dwyn, who in turn shook her head determinedly.

"Let's go," she said, and would have sounded more convincing if her voice had been more audible.

They moved slowly the last fifty meters. Dahlia could still hear the bots, but they weren't coming any nearer and she wondered why. What were they waiting for? It was obvious that the people behind them wouldn't give up. Another few steps later, their small group ran into one of the marines patrolling the perimeter. He saluted and guided them to the tall group of trees that provided some protection from the bots.

Dahlia looked around, trying to make out her daughter's features, but couldn't find her. She had turned to Leanne to ask, when a hand on her shoulder stopped her.

"Mother...Mom?"

Dahlia pivoted, exhausted, and would have fallen if the strong arms of her daughter-in-law hadn't caught her. Kellen stood next to Rae, who in turn was smiling tremulously. Dahlia, the master of rhetoric and negotiations, found no words. Standing there, looking at her only child, she realized at times during these last few days she'd thought she'd never see her family again.

"Oh, Mom." Rae wrapped her arms around her, kissing her cheek tenderly before she hugged her tight. "I've sent word to Dad, but I don't know when he'll receive it." She pushed Dahlia back at arm's length and looked at her closely in the light of the moons that were rising above the treetops. "Are you all right? *Really* all right?" She held Dahlia tight again.

"I'm fine, Rae. I'm tired, and as I said, a bit sore, but I'm fine *now*." It was true. Suddenly her exhaustion, thirst, and fear meant nothing. Her daughter was in her embrace, and her new daughter, Kellen, was standing next to them, smiling. Dahlia extended an arm and Kellen willingly allowed herself to be hugged for a few seconds.

Rae finally let go. "As much as I'd like to revel in our reunion longer, we have things to take care of. I'm not sure how long reinforcements will be, or if they'll come at all, since communications in and out of this forest are dicey at best—"

"Ma'am, look," Leanne said from where she stood with Owena's arm discreetly around her waist. She pointed toward the sky where a band of lights indicated an approaching vessel.

"Is that our backup?" Dwyn murmured. She was propped against a tree, breathing shallowly.

"One ship?" Rae said slowly, and Dahlia knew her well enough to be concerned about the wrinkles marring her forehead. "No. I don't think so." She pulled her plasma-pulse rifle from her harness and flipped down her visor. "Saddle up, people," she called. "Prepare to engage the enemy."

CHAPTER TWENTY-EIGHT

Dwyn stared at the lights in the night sky. Corma's two moons highlighted the ship's sharp edges, and the piercing lights around its belly hurt her eyes. Blinking away tears, she stood as the SC military unit and Emeron's team got into position.

"Dwyn. Here." Emeron tossed her a smaller rifle, a short-barreled energy-destabilizer. It was as powerful as a plasma-pulse weapon and had a longer reach. "Keep Yhja and Trom safe. Take Diplomat Jacelon too and hide behind the trees, and don't let them out of your sight."

Dwyn coughed as she gripped the weapon. Yhja and Trom had already crawled behind the cluster of tall trees that formed a semicircle, hiding their heads against their pulled-up knees. Dwyn regretted that they had needed to bring the youngsters, but she was determined to keep them safe or die trying. Dahlia joined them, a sidearm in her right hand. She nodded at Dwyn, looking worried.

"Are you all right?" Dahlia asked. "Let me know if you want to switch weapons. That one looks heavy."

"Thanks, but I'm fine, ma'am." She suppressed another coughing attack.

Two junior officers carried M'Ekar to a safer spot next to Yhja and Trom. The former ambassador didn't stir, and Dwyn wondered if the skeletal man was already dead.

The vessel hovered briefly, but nobody opened fire. She suspected the ship's shields were too impenetrable for mere plasma-pulse rifles. She stood half-hidden behind a tree, watching Emeron as she prepared for battle. Dahlia took position on the other side of the trunk.

Tall, and with her hair like blackbird wings around her cheeks, Emeron stood at the front of the SC unit, her weapon raised and ready. Dwyn knew that as long as Emeron was able, she would carry out her duty to protect her and the others.

The ship touched down on struts that looked deceptively fragile. A ramp opened, and the mercenaries ran half-bent toward it. Rae gave the order to engage, and two of them fell.

"They're getting away, ma'am," Owena yelled over the noise from the ship's propulsion system.

"No. They're about to engage," the admiral answered. "They're not giving up." Looking back at her mother, she barked orders. "Make a ring around the civilians. Don't let these criminals anywhere near them."

The marines and the junior Cormanian officers changed positions, standing in a semicircle in front of the trees. Oches stood between them and the forest to forestall a stealth attack from behind.

Some of the mercenaries had entered the hovering spaceship now, while some stood on the open ramp located at the aft section. The noise from the vessel increased and it seemed to tremble impatiently where it stood, and then it ascended, only a meter off the ground. Slowly it advanced toward them, and Dwyn drew a deep breath. Was it going to ram them or shoot at them? Surely they couldn't protect themselves against such an assault?

"Stand your ground," Jacelon roared. "Open fire."

Plasma-pulse rays coursed through the night, bouncing off the vessel's shields in a cascade of white flashes. The ship neared and pushed Jacelon and Emeron's unit back against the trees.

"No. Stand your ground," Jacelon shouted again. "Aim for the sensitive technology on the roof."

Dwyn knew that many smaller vessels had less shielding around their sensor array, since a dense shield bubble could give false readings. Larger ships didn't usually suffer from this dilemma, but this ship was smaller than the one that had crashed into the Disian village.

She suddenly straightened her back so quickly it snapped, making her fully alert. The strange lull of fatigue that had clouded her mind for the last few days because of the lung injury disappeared. She looked at Oches, who kept firing upon the ship, his normally jovial face austere and focused. Trom and Yhja huddled, and Dahlia was shooting at it as well, clinging to the tree as she did so.

Suddenly Dwyn had an idea, born from a childhood memory when she, her parents, and their entire collective had been stranded on a mining planet for weeks because an electrical supercharge had accidentally incapacitated their vessel. If she could copy the circumstances, she could possibly disable this ship. If it didn't work, only quick intervention from the SC could save them. But it didn't seem as if that would come soon enough.

She ducked and ran just inside the bordering bushes, trying to travel far enough to get behind the ship. Apparently, the mercenaries focused all their attention forward, on the SC units. The vessel tore up grass and dirt as it used its propulsion system to remain horizontal. She estimated that it now hovered approximately two meters off the ground. She prayed it would keep that distance, or she would be crushed. Even now she risked getting caught in the turbulent air, which could easily propel her into the nearest tree or, worse, slam her into the fuselage.

She crouched as she ran, squinting at the whirling dust. She coughed and knew this might be the last straw for her lungs. The possibility of Emeron being killed, together with her new friends, who'd risked their lives to keep her safe from the bots, ignited her. She tugged at her collar and tried to pull it up over her mouth, to filter some of the dust out. It still filled every crevice on her face and found its way into her nose and mouth.

Afraid she'd miss this chance she slipped under the spaceship's starboard fin, where the air was hot and turbulent. She struggled to remain on her feet, clutching the weapon in her cold hands. If she dropped it, she wouldn't get a second chance.

The downdraft sent her almost to her knees, and she blinked furiously in the whirling dust that stung her eyes. Finally she reached the center of the ship's belly and looked up. Six narrow struts were still extended, and Dwyn knew the ship's captain would land soon.

To her right, one of the struts came at her faster than she'd counted on. The ship was turning, directing its port ramp toward the SC units. She threw herself to the ground and rolled onto her back with the weapon directed straight up toward the vessel's underbelly. When the strut passed above her, she blazed at it. The shields held, but she kept her finger on the trigger sensor, hoping the weapon was fully charged. The destabilizer beam chewed away at the shield, and she thought she could see the typical dark outlines that were sometimes visible when a shield was about to be compromised. Blackish-purple sparks rained over her, scorching her hair and prickling her face.

Suddenly the strut base began to crackle and she smelled burning electronics. A hydraulic hose severed and, seeing that she was actually causing damage, she kept firing. Her arms ached and she could barely see, but she refused to stop.

At first she thought the hum in the air and the sense of high density around her had resulted from what she was doing. She greedily drew new breaths, but the air had become almost liquid. Panting, she fought to keep the destabilizer weapon up, even if it was now radiating so much heat her hands hurt.

The explosion began as a loud whirring sound, coming from deep inside the belly of the ship. She dropped the weapon and, pinned to the ground, saw the fuselage begin to crack. Before darkness descended upon her she saw the jagged edges of the crack in the fuselage separate in an explosion of blue-green flames.

❖

Emeron thought she glimpsed something. Squinting, she raised her rifle, wondering if any of the captured mercenaries had escaped their restraints. She narrowed her eyes further as she saw a long, blond braid flutter in the strong gushes of the ship's downdraft. *Dwyn.* She groaned. What was she doing? Dwyn raced toward the ship and ducked underneath it.

"What the hell is Dwyn up to?" Jacelon shouted next to her. "Keep firing, Commander. We can't help her any other way."

"I can pull her out." Emeron was ready to run the same route Dwyn had taken.

"Negative. We need all the firepower we can get."

She tried to spot Dwyn underneath the ship, but the dirt and grass whirling around the vessel made it impossible. Tears of fury and disbelief rose behind her eyelids, but she refused to break down. She needed to be on top of her game and keep the mercenaries occupied long enough for Dwyn carry out whatever she had set out to do. She hoped she hadn't gone in without a feasible plan.

A high-pitched tone echoed in the air, and for a moment Emeron thought the bots had returned to join the party. She looked around, ready to act, but even as the tone became increasingly louder, no bots appeared. She sniffed.

"Do you smell that?" she shouted to Leanne, who stood to her left, continuously firing on the ship.

"Smells weird, doesn't it?" Leanne yelled back. She stopped firing for a second and stared at the bottom of the ship. "Stars and skies, is that Dwyn?"

Emeron shifted to the left and tried to make out what Leanne saw. "She's under the ship, but I can't see her. Where is she?"

Leanne opened her mouth to answer, but a great explosion interrupted her and sent them both flying. Emeron landed in a short tree and, at first, she had no idea where she was. The branches pierced her uniform, and one sharp twig perforated the palm of her left hand. She yanked herself loose and cradled her hand as she slid down the tree. Standing on unsteady legs, she found that the explosion had tossed her more than five meters.

Around her, the teams were staggering to get to their feet. A quick glance at the cluster of trees where they had placed the civilians showed that the trees were intact. She couldn't make out Dahlia or the Disian young people, but hoped they were all right.

Shaking off the dazedness, she suddenly remembered Dwyn's position. She stared in horror at the wreckage, all that was left of the ship, which had broken into three major parts with debris scattered all around it. She couldn't imagine how Dwyn could have survived. A cry of outrage and sorrow broke from her, and she called Dwyn's name repeatedly as she ran toward the downed vessel.

"Dwyn." She sobbed as she waded through the debris. "Dwyn."

"Emeron. I thought I saw her being tossed right through the explosion." Leanne was suddenly by her side, her temple bleeding from a deep cut.

"You're injured," Emeron said hollowly.

"It's nothing. We have to secure the area. The mercenaries were thrown in all directions." Leanne picked up a rifle and pressed it into her hands. "We'll find her. We'll find all of them."

One by one, Emeron and Leanne located their teammates. The protector was the first to appear, climbing over the rubble to reach them. Emeron had never seen her look this way, disheveled and dangerous and with her hair in wild disarray around her face. "Report," the protector barked.

"We are assessing the situation and locating our people,

Commander," Leanne said. "I was standing right next to the admiral. I haven't seen Owena."

"Ma'am?" Oches came running toward them, three plasma-pulse rifles under one arm, pressing a torn piece of fabric to his neck. "The admiral is over by the bushes. She's fine, but needs help with one of the Disian youngsters, who was hit by shrapnel. We need a derma fuser. She's hemorrhaging badly."

Emeron glanced around for any of their back-strap security carriers. Unlike the people, the packs had been sitting low enough to avoid the shock of the explosion. She ran to the bushes behind the trees and, as she bent to retrieve two of the carriers, she heard a faint voice to the left. "Commander?"

Pushing the branches aside she saw Ensign Noor sitting on the other side, cradling one of her junior officers. "Noor, hang on, we'll get to you."

"We're all right, ma'am," Noor said, and coughed. "She's breathing and her pulse is strong."

"Good. You're protected where you are. Just stay there."

Noor acknowledged and Emeron pulled the carriers out, rummaging through them. She found a med kit and pulled out a derma fuser. As she hurried back, she ran the fuser over her hand, patching herself so she could use it. The repair job would probably need reworking, but for now it would have to do.

Oches showed her where Jacelon sat, pressing her fingers into Yhja's inner thigh. The fabric of Yhja's pants was torn and her femoral artery was clearly severed.

"Oches, help the protector and Leanne localize our people. I'll assist the admiral."

Oches nodded and took off.

Emeron set the derma fuser to a deep-blood-vessel setting and ran it over the wound. Yhja seemed unconscious, and all the blood on her clothes and Jacelon's made it clear that she would need a transfusion soon. After closing the rift in the artery, Emeron let the derma fuser work on the tissues, then finally closed the skin wound.

"There," Jacelon said. "Do you think you can carry her back to the others? We need to regroup and get a head count."

She lifted Yhja and shuddered at how boneless she seemed. "She needs a MEDEVAC, ma'am."

"It should be on its way. I have no idea if Oches's communication center survived or why there was such an explosion. Nothing we did could have caused such a blast."

"Dwyn was firing from underneath." Emeron held Yhja tighter. "Who knows what she hit."

"No matter what it was, the blast was completely out of proportion."

"Perhaps the mercenaries were moving explosives in their cargo bay?"

"That's one theory. We'll see." Jacelon ran up to Kellen and held her face in her hands. "You are all right, darling?"

"Yes. And you?"

"I'm fine. Now. Report."

"We've located nearly all of our people, including Dahlia. She's over there, taking care of M'Ekar."

"She's what?"

"Tending to *him*." Kellen made a wry face.

"And Dwyn?" Emeron asked, putting Yhja down next to Trom, who pulled her into his arms and closed his eyes.

"I'm sorry. There's no sign of her."

Emeron looked at the clearing and sensed that Dwyn was out there, under the wreckage.

"The mercenaries?"

"Several dead. We're gathering the survivors and giving first aid to the injured. The ones in the ship died, I believe, though some of the ones on the ramp made it."

Emeron joined the members of her team who were sorting through the debris. She pulled at scorching pieces of fuselage, shoving what had once been seats and cabinets out of her way.

"Ma'am, over here," Mogghy called urgently. "I found her."

She stumbled across the debris, cutting her shins on sharp metal edges, but ignoring the pain. Mogghy was kneeling next to a big piece of the ramp, trying to move it.

"Dwyn. Is she...?" She knelt next to Mogghy. All she could make out of Dwyn was her long blond braid. "I can't see a thing. I need to get under there."

"I don't recommend it, ma'am. The metal's still hot."

Disregarding Mogghy's advice she dropped to her stomach and crawled in next to Dwyn, who didn't stir. It was dark under the ramp, and very hot. She wiped at the sweat forming on her forehead. Finally, she managed to reach Dwyn's head, and she fumbled for and prayed there would be a pulse in her neck.

She found the pulse, faint and thready, but it was there. She crawled closer and listened to Dwyn's raspy breathing. "Dwyn, come on." She felt with her hands but couldn't judge if Dwyn had internal injuries, which she suspected. "Mogghy, I need a medical scanner."

"I know. I don't have one. I have no idea where the main med kit is." Mogghy murmured something inaudible, and she realized he was talking to someone outside. Suddenly the ramp above them shifted. She crawled on top of Dwyn and shielded her from falling dirt and rubble.

Mogghy knelt next to them. "Do you think she can be evacuated?"

Desperate, she shook her head. "No, damn it, I don't. Look at her, she's hardly breathing." Jacelon, Kellen, and Leanne had joined them, and Owena was approaching behind them, carrying two blazing branches.

"We need some light here," Owena said, and drove the branches into the ground. "Here, help me make more." She handed several limbs to Leanne, who lit them with a quick blast of a sidearm.

Jacelon knelt next to Emeron and gently palpated Dwyn's stomach. "I think she's bleeding internally. Oches signaled the SC headquarters several times before the blast, and I can only hope the MEDEVAC teams get here in time." She touched Dwyn's cheek. "She's so brave."

"She's braver than any of us." Emeron choked on her words, feeling utterly helpless. Fury rose inside her, as did the bile in her throat. "Dwyn..." she whispered to the motionless figure on the ground. She wanted to pull her into her arms, cover her with kisses, and coerce her life-force to return to her. Dwyn was so cold, but so deeply unconscious she didn't even shiver. Emeron didn't want to imagine what might have happened to her brain, and spine when the blast threw her and the ship halfway across the clearing. A small, persistent voice repeated that Dwyn was dying, that help was once again coming too late, and she could do nothing about it.

"Imer-Ohon-Da?" a faint female voice said, startling her. She snapped her head around and looked at Yhja, who stood on uncertain legs behind her with Trom holding her up. "We must hurry, Imer-Ohon-Da."

"Yhja, you shouldn't be on your feet." She motioned for Mogghy to take the young woman away, but Yhja raised her hand in a commanding gesture. "Listen to me, Imer-Ohon-Da. You are the daughter's daughter of Briijn. You possess the knowledge and talents of her bloodline. You don't recognize this, but now you have to use all the courage your grandmother gave you when you were a small child." She stumbled up behind Emeron and placed her hand on her shoulder. Trom did the same, and their touch was warm and vibrating. "If you don't, Imer-Ohon-Da, we will lose Dwyn. Only you can save her."

CHAPTER TWENTY-NINE

Emeron was about to object, fiercely, that Yhja would even suggest she should engage in the Disians' pseudo-magical thinking. She'd once hoped that the Disians would be able to save Briijn, but had soon realized that her Cormanian relatives were right. It was useless gibberish.

"You cannot allow your doubt to stand in the way of Dwyn's life and happiness." Yhja spoke softly, but her voice grew stronger with each word. "You blame the Disian culture for the death of your grandmother, this is no secret. And Pri warned Trom and me that you were too wounded to determine the truth."

"I need a medical scanner. And she needs a MEDEVAC to a hospital in Corma," Emeron cried.

"Dwyn needs you. She needs the wisdom and knowledge that run through your veins. Trom and I cannot perform the ceremony, but you can. With our help, through you, you can do this, Imer-Ohon-Da."

"Try, at least," Leanne sobbed. "If I can do anything to help, Emeron, I will. Don't believe the cold-hearted socialites and careerists that make up most of the women in our family. Believe in Briijn. Believe in the woman you adored and who loved you unconditionally. Don't throw away your heritage. If you don't try..." Leanne drew a trembling breath and clung to Owena. "You'll never forgive yourself if she dies."

"Leanne." Emeron wanted to explain just how preposterous the possibility was when suddenly she visualized a half-naked Dwyn sitting on her bedroll in their tent, waiting patiently and faintly smiling as Emeron ran the sanitizer rod along her hair and body. She trembled and looked up at Yhja. "All right. What do I do?"

"You know the songs your grandmother sang by the fire?"

"Yes. Those were lullabies."

"Yes. They are also the key to the gateway to healing. This is how parents and grandparents keep their families, especially their children, healthy."

Emeron stared down at Dwyn, and for a terrifying moment, she thought it was too late. "All right." She cleared her voice and glanced around, seeing the dirty and scratched faces of her unit and Jacelon's. Except for the two marines guarding their captive mercenaries, they all stood around Dwyn and her in a circle, and their presence gave her strength and courage. She placed her hands around Dwyn's ribs.

"*Megos hordos maitele, megos hordos nove oso nenne taghest...*" *I will help you, darling, I will help you and you will feel no pain...* Emeron sang the guttural song that Briijn had crooned to her so many times. Yhja and Trom's hands rested on her, sending a near-burning sensation down to her own hands and out of her fingertips. She sang the four lines over and over, and with every new cycle, she felt as if her knees sank farther into the dirt as she became one with the forest around her. Beneath her fingers, Dwyn lay still, and the only thoughts in her mind were to save her, to give her back her future.

Emeron was aware of the others around them, but only vaguely. She drove herself and Dwyn farther along the path of healing each time she repeated the chant. Her own torso was warm, despite the cold ground she knelt on, and she wanted to give all that abundant warmth to Dwyn. Envisioning her own soul entering Dwyn's system, flooding it, finding everything that was injured and healing it from within, Emeron heard her voice sink half an octave.

For the first time since Emeron had returned to the forest, the life-force of the *Umbra* coursed through her, strengthening her as she chanted, and she felt safer and stronger than she'd ever been. She knew she could help Dwyn. The chant mesmerized her, and she trembled. The Umbra simmered just beneath her skin, sent shock waves of an unimaginable force through her, and she abandoned the last remnants of her fear. Throwing her head back, she stared with unseeing eyes at the starlit sky, well aware of the people nearby, but at the same time focused only on Dwyn.

The low murmur continued as of its own volition, and eventually she began to fall, but she refused to let go of Dwyn. Gentle hands helped her lie down and only then, when she lay next to Dwyn, her face buried into the amazing blond hair, did she let go. Exhausted, she closed her eyes. She still hummed the chant, even as she began to black out. She struggled hard to carry on her chant, forcing every word over her lips.

"*Megos hordos maitele, megos hordos nove oso nenne taghest...*" *I will help you, darling, I will help you and you will feel no pain...*

❖

Rae gazed down at Dwyn. Emeron had chanted for more than forty-five minutes, until her voice had failed and she had passed out. Trom and Yhja were now on their knees, looking almost as exhausted. Dwyn lay still, and Leanne crouched next to her, feeling her carotid pulse. The moment Leanne touched Dwyn, her eyes snapped open and she drew a deep breath, then another.

"Emeron."

"Dwyn, Dwyn," Leanne said, and tried to keep her from sitting up. "Listen to me, you're wounded badly. You have to stay like this."

"No, I'm fine. I'm fine, but where's Emeron? Oh..." She stared down at the woman next to her. "What's wrong? What's wrong with her? What happened?"

"Nothing's the matter, Dwyn, lie down." Dahlia joined Leanne's attempt to keep her immobile. "You look better. In fact, much better than before. And it's because of Emeron."

"What do you mean?" Dwyn looked at Leanne and Dahlia.

"She healed you," Leanne said reverently. "She chanted a Disian chant for the longest time, the same verse over and over, and finally she...well, I don't think she actually fainted, rather fell asleep. From exhaustion."

"She healed me?" Dwyn blinked several times. She took two deep breaths, without coughing, Rae noticed. "My lungs. They feel fine. Help me up." She extended a hand to Owena, who stood next to Leanne. Owena helped her to her feet, slowly, and she stood first on one leg, then the other, stretching. She smiled. "Whatever she did..." She fell to her knees in the dirt next to Emeron and pulled her up into her arms. "Whatever you did, Emeron, it worked. It worked." She cried now, large, crystal-clear tears that moved Rae enough for her to step closer to Kellen and place her hand on the small of her back.

"What's going on? Dwyn?" Emeron looked up, dazed. "Dwyn."

Rae motioned for Kellen and the others to follow her to the group of restrained prisoners. Dwyn and Emeron needed a chance to make sense of what had just happened. Rae looked at the row of eighteen dead mercenaries, most of them the crew of the crashed vessel. Suddenly she stopped and raised her head. At the same time her communicator came to life.

"Alex de Vies to Jacelon, come in. I repeat, Alex de Vies to Jacelon, come in."

Rae tugged her communicator to her lips. "Jacelon here. Good to hear your voice. What's your ETA?"

"A minute or two, Admiral. We received a delayed message via the old communication system only forty-five minutes ago. We've been trying to pinpoint your location since then. I've never come across such magnetic disturbance. It threw all our sensors off. If you hadn't set off that explosion, we'd still be looking for you."

"Well, glad we could oblige."

"Is everything all right, ma'am? We understand from your previous transmission that you have Diplomat Jacelon safely in protective custody?"

"Affirmative. Have you let my father know yet? And Armeo?"

"Yes, ma'am. And you should be able to see the first hovercraft by now. I'll land first and have my tactical team make sure the area is secure before the MEDEVAC teams arrive."

"We have secured the mercenary enemies, but we haven't determined who is sending bots to kill Dwyn Izontro. We have wounded on both sides and need the medical teams ASAP."

Rae and Kellen looked up as the night sky became bright. Two large hovercraft landed and marines streamed out, quickly assessing the clearing and the surrounding forest. Alex de Vies joined them, inspecting the wreckage area.

"You took down this vessel with plasma-pulse rifles?" He looked dumbfounded.

"Not really. We're not sure how it happened, but we have Ms. Izontro to thank for it, I think. There have been some extraordinary events here tonight, and honestly, I'm not sure how to phrase them in my report." She knew they might never know how Dwyn could have caused such an explosion with a mere energy-destabilizer.

Six of the larger MEDEVAC hovercraft landed in the center of the clearing, and the medical staff jumped out and began to run toward them. Dahlia stood a few feet away, watching the arriving backup. She swayed a little and Rae was immediately at her side, her arm around Dahlia's waist. "Hey, Mom, easy. Let's get you a stretcher."

"I'm all right, Rae. I need to make sure M'Ekar goes on the first hovercraft out of here."

"You're going to have to explain why you care what happens to that callous bastard later. Right now I want *you* out of here. No objections. I'm pulling rank."

"I'm not one of your soldiers..." Dahlia began haughtily, then softened and smiled. "Very well. Send M'Ekar and me on the first one."

Rae shook her head. "All right. If that's what it takes. You'll both go directly to the infirmary aboard the *Dalathea*. Father, Armeo, and Ayahliss are there. It's the safest place for you right now."

"I doubt I'm in danger now that M'Ekar and Weiss Kyakh are both helpless."

"I'm not taking any chances, Mother." Rae didn't intend to back off. "Father would never forgive me, nor would I, if anything else happened to you."

"If you insist. Honestly," Dahlia said, and leaned against her, "I'm ready for a nap."

❖

Dwyn helped Emeron to her feet, taken aback by the intensity in her eyes. SC forces examined the wreckage and scanned the clearing as well as its surroundings. She had so many questions, but Emeron's slightly dazed expression told her they would have to wait.

"Thank you," she said quietly. "You saved my life."

"Only after you saved mine, and everyone else's." Emeron hugged Dwyn. "We should get you to one of the MEDEVAC hovercraft and have you checked out immediately."

"No need," she insisted. "You healed me. Don't minimize or doubt what you just did. My lungs are fine, and whatever injuries I sustained in the explosion are healed too."

"But you had extensive internal bleeding," Emeron said. She placed her hand on Dwyn's stomach. "You were swelling up and..." She quieted.

"No swelling now. Nothing. I'm fine." She smiled. "I promise. I wouldn't lie to you."

"I know. I also know how persistent you are, and determined to put your duty above yourself." Emeron looked thoughtfully at her. "All right. Stay close to me while we wrap things up. I don't want you out of my sight."

"Okay. I can do that." She winked, feeling lighthearted and giddy merely to be alive.

They joined the rest of Emeron's team, and Dwyn walked among them, making sure they were all right. Mogghy had his cut seen to by an SC nurse and seemed well enough to flirt ruthlessly with her. Dwyn stopped when she saw Ensign Noor, who sat on a rock holding her knee. "Noor. What happened?"

"It's embarrassing." Noor sighed. "The blast didn't hurt me, but then I tripped over Lt. Mogghy's back-strap security carrier and twisted my knee." She looked miserable and Dwyn fought to hide her smile.

"Anyone seen to you yet?"

"No, no. I can wait. There are people with worse injuries that need medical attention."

Dwyn wouldn't have expected any less of a member of Emeron's team. She remembered how disdainful of babysitting an environmental activist Noor had originally been.

"We should ask Emeron to hold your knee and chant," she deadpanned, but began to laugh at Noor's horrified expression. "I'm kidding. A little touch-up with a bone knitter will do the trick."

"You shouldn't scare a poor soldier that way, ma'am," Noor said, with a relieved grin. "It's one thing to see the commander bring you back to life, but—"

"Another matter to have her tend to a sore knee. Got it." She sat down next to Noor. "Mind if I keep you company? She healed me, but to tell the truth, that wore me out."

"I bet." Noor looked at her with half a smile. "I owe you an apology, Dwyn."

"Whatever for?"

"I treated you badly those first days. You were merely doing your job, and I shouldn't have been such an idiot about it."

"Apology accepted. I don't think I made it easy for you either. I can really get wrapped up in the importance of what I do. Guess it's called arrogance." She shrugged. "It's easy to fall into that trap, and I'm sorry too."

Noor lit up and extended her right hand. "We've reached consensus," she said brightly.

"I agree."

Dwyn was amazed by how quickly the SC troops worked the area, and she watched as they carried the surviving mercenaries one by one aboard the MEDEVAC craft. Emeron explained they would go to several different prison facilities, depending on their injuries.

"Will I be able to retrieve my samples?" Dwyn asked when it was time to leave. "We went through quite a bit because of them. At least that's what I assume."

"I'll send in a well-armed unit to retrieve our hovercraft and your samples right away," Emeron said. "Now that the SC forces are dealing with the aftermath of the hostage situation, I can go ahead and do what I do best. Police work." She reached out to Dwyn. "Time to go."

"All right." Dwyn took the proffered hand and stood. "Do you have teams coming in to clear out the debris?"

"The SC forces have people who will recover everything here and examine it thoroughly. It's part of the chain of evidence against the kidnappers, and I'm sure it'll tell quite a tale about pirates in general."

"And the Disians. Will they get help? I mean to rebuild, that sort of thing."

Emeron's smile softened. "I'll make sure that help is offered, at least. Whether they'll accept it, I don't know. A unit of SC marines will escort Trom and Yhja back to the village. Yhja is doing all right, and it was clear they want to go home. Poor kids, they look exhausted."

"I bet they are. We've taken them for quite a ride." Dwyn found she was still clinging to Emeron's hand. A little embarrassed, she let go. "So where's our ride? I don't know about you, but I'm ready to get out of here and go straight to my hotel and have a long bath."

Emeron laughed. "Sounds like a good idea. The bath, I mean." It was her turn to look flustered. "And our ride is over there, with Captain de Vies."

They joined the protector and Jacelon, who stood talking to Owena and Leanne outside the hovercraft. Dwyn climbed inside and took a seat near a small round window. As the hovercraft ascended, she looked down and was amazed at how far the wreckage had scattered. It seemed to cover almost the entire clearing.

Something glistened at the far eastern corner, and she shifted in her seat to take a better look. The sparkling object moved, and soon more followed it. Like six deadly projectiles, the bots streaked across the clearing. Dwyn gasped. "Raise shields," she shouted, drowning out the conversations around her. "Captain de Vies, maximum shields. They're headed right for us!"

CHAPTER THIRTY

S hields up," Alex de Vies commanded. "Evasive maneuvers. Damn it, these things don't show up on sensors."

"They're shielded somehow." Rae, buckled in next to him, looked furious. Kellen saw the familiar signs that she was running out of patience. Her thin lips were pressed even tighter together, and her eyes were so steely gray, they were almost black. Angry red spots glowed on her cheeks.

"I'd sure like to capture a 'live' one," Alex said. "Whoever constructed these little devils has some serious money and brains behind them."

"I have my guesses," Emeron said. "You said capture one, sir?"

"Yes, but right now we have to stay clear of them." Alex gripped his armrests as the pilot made yet another neck-breaking turn, this time sending the hovercraft ascending at almost a ninety-degree angle. Kellen's head pressed into the backrest and she too had to hold on, despite being strapped in. Hovercraft didn't employ any inertial dampeners while they were operating within the planet's atmosphere.

"Any suggestions, Commander?" she asked Emeron.

"Protector, I know this type of hovercraft well. My team and I use them often. They come with quite the setup. The propulsion system is in the back and underneath, obviously, and between the nacelles are shield-enforced compartments."

Kellen thought she knew where this was going.

"Oh, for stars and skies, I know that look," Rae groaned. "I see it on Kellen and now on you too, Emeron."

Kellen studiously ignored her wife and focused on Emeron. It was obvious she was a kindred spirit, and Kellen wanted to hear more.

"Those compartments are intended to transport anything that needs protective shielding, such as biohazard materials, unstable chemicals, explosives, even people heading for quarantine." Emeron leaned forward, continuing eagerly. "If the pilot descended on one of the bots, which would of course be the tricky part..." The hovercraft jerked again, this time in a quick hairpin maneuver that made them all clutch their armrests.

"I see your point. I need to take the helm. Permission, Captain?" She looked expectantly at Alex.

"You're going to capture one of those things and bring it aboard the hovercraft?"

"Yes, Captain. It's our only real hope to find out who's behind these attacks. At first Dwyn was their target, and I suppose she still is, since they waited to attack until a craft with her aboard took off."

"And once we've tucked it away in this compartment, how do you propose to keep it from firing?"

"Once it's inside, the fortified shields will take care of that."

Alex turned to Emeron. "You certain they will hold?"

"Yes, sir. We can release liquid nitrogen to put a damper on them, so to speak. The compartment is fully capable of this."

"Your call, Admiral," Alex said finally, raising an eyebrow toward Rae.

"As crazy as it sounds, I think it could work. Kellen, take the helm. Emeron, you ride shotgun."

"Aye, ma'am," Emeron said, and unbuckled her seatbelt.

Kellen and Emeron struggled to change places with the pilot and co-pilot, which wasn't easy as the craft was now under fire and was reeling constantly.

After Kellen slipped into the pilot's seat, she quickly buckled up, then lowered the visor from the ceiling and reviewed the list of readings that flickered by.

"Adjust the sensors to detect the bots as early as possible the next time they shoot." She flipped switches and punched in new commands. She was in her true element, though this wasn't an assault craft, a vessel to which she was more attuned. "Affirmative. Sensors calibrated."

Kellen switched to manual and took the hovercraft in a wide semicircle around the clearing.

"I want to try and spot them visually." She could see three of them now, on a direct trajectory toward them. "Here we go." She pushed the controls first one way, hoping to fool the bots, and when they lined up along this new course, she flipped the controls back, sending the hovercraft into a dive and then climbing sideways, with the craft's belly turned toward the bots.

"Open the compartment hatch."

"It's open."

Kellen didn't take her eyes off them. They were preparing to ram them, and if she didn't hurry, all three of them would hit in rapid succession. "Any sign of the other three?"

"Yes. Farther away, ten o'clock."

They had time to worry about them later. Kellen shoved the controls away from her, sliding the narrow buttons along the console and making the craft lurch and nearly stall. She heard gasps from the passenger compartment, but couldn't worry now. "Here we go," she murmured as she gave full throttle. The propulsion system screamed underneath the hovercraft as it forced itself into an almost impossible angle, defying gravity.

A faint clunking sound, more like a bouncing metallic noise, told her what she needed to know. "Close the hatch."

"Closed. Fantastic, Kellen. You got two of them," Emeron said, sounding reverent.

"Two. How about that?" She focused completely on outrunning the remaining bots. No matter what state-of-the-art technology the machines sported, they shouldn't be able to keep up with a hovercraft. She let the craft climb straight up, squeezing out every drop of power its propulsion system had to offer. Once she gained enough altitude, she let it slide into a shallow dive and picked up more speed than the craft was normally capable of as she whizzed back toward the capital. They passed the outer tree line within minutes and, so far, no one attacked them from behind.

"Perhaps we scared them off when we took a few of them prisoner," Emeron muttered, making Kellen grin.

"You think they're sentient beings?" she chided amicably.

"I wouldn't put it past them," Emeron said, and shrugged. "They were like relentless Banatax leeches. And we need to find their weak spots ASAP. If they go after the Disians as a means of revenge..." Emeron's expression darkened.

"You won't allow that," Kellen said. "You'll find a way to protect them and the Thousand Year Pact."

"I will." Emeron looked out the window. "They are my people, my responsibility."

"That kind of belonging, that passion, will help you find a solution."

Emeron blinked. "Yes, I suppose it will." She looked introspective as she slumped back. "One way or another, I have to."

❖

At the Supreme Constellations headquarters, Dwyn insisted they drive her to her hotel and maintained she'd be perfectly safe there. Emeron tried to convince her that she needed to remain in protective custody, since they still didn't know who was trying to kill her.

"All right. Assign a couple of your most trusted people to guard my door. But I am going to have that bath and eat a proper meal, then sleep in a soft, cozy bed. Nothing you can say will make me change those plans for a stay in the sparse cells you call protective custody."

"Sounds like you've been through that before," Rae said.

"I have. I've been threatened and had attempts on my life. This is more on the high-tech side, but ultimately it's the same situation."

Emeron looked displeased. "I'll come and check on you after I've given my report and made sure our best people are dealing with the bots."

Dwyn shuddered. They'd heard the bots rustle around in the compartment below their feet several times, and she had sensed that they had tried to find a weakness in their prison and, like live entities, tried to escape. She'd be happy to distance herself from the bots, definitely having had enough of them.

"I look forward to it," she answered Emeron, not wanting to give too much away in front of the others.

"See you then." Emeron's eyes were dark, filled with unspoken emotions, and suddenly Dwyn felt those familiar internal tremors again. Her face burned and she had to clear her throat twice before she told the rest of the team good-bye.

"See you soon, Dwyn," Rae said softly. "Rest up."

"Thank you, Admiral."

"Rae."

"Rae."

Emeron gestured for two ensigns to join them and issued strict orders not to let her out of their sight until she was safely in her room. They were to report to no one but her.

The ensigns guided Dwyn to a smaller hovercraft and immediately took off toward the center of the capital.

❖

The bath rejuvenated Dwyn in a way she wouldn't have thought possible. The hot water nearly lulled her to sleep several times. Sipping some Cormanian coffee, she inhaled the aroma of the hot beverage mixed with the soft scent of the soap. Very few things had ever felt as blissful. She tried to figure out how long their ordeal in the Disi-Disi forest had lasted, but couldn't. She only knew she wasn't eager to return soon.

Humming, she started the underwater jets and let them massage her tired muscles. Emeron had healed her, but she was still weary from the constant stress. As she washed her hair, she was relieved that it wasn't as badly damaged from the blast as she'd thought, even if her scalp was still sore.

She stayed in the bathtub until her skin began to wrinkle. The conditioned air felt cool as she stepped out of the water, and she opted to use the thick towels and rub herself dry, instead of the automatic drying sequence, which was less sensual. Wrapping herself in a robe of the same luxurious material, she entered the living room of her suite.

This wasn't her original room. In fact, it was a suite on the Supreme Council floor usually reserved for active members of the SC Council. She wondered who had pulled some strings with whom. When she had tried to object, the female ensign assigned to protect her suggested that anyone trying to harm her would have had all the time in the world to booby-trap her former room while she was gone. The ensign's words made sense, and though Dwyn gladly would have used any of the normally priced rooms at the hotel, she was too tired to object. Besides, the desk clerk said that her luggage was already being transferred.

Her security detail had examined the suite and luggage meticulously and left her to enjoy her bath only when they were fully satisfied. Now, she plopped down on the couch and grabbed the control for room service. She was starving for real, fresh food and practically salivated as she perused the menu. When she saw they even had an Earth selection, she ordered vegetable soup, walnut bread, and blueberry pancakes for dessert. The food arrived within twenty minutes and the female ensign brought it in.

"Enjoy your meal, Ms. Izontro."

"Thanks." She inhaled the food and sat back, licking her fork before she put it back on the tray. Suddenly feeling cold she tugged a blanket over her. Then she slid down and worked at the pillows until she was comfortable. As tired as she was, she couldn't relax. Images, painful flashbacks of the bots, of how Emeron had been hit and how the mercenary vessel had moved in on them, kept coming and going, and eventually she gave up and pressed the command to open the large view screen over the fireplace. Still cold, she pressed a sensor on the remote control to start a fire as well.

"Let's see. News." Dwyn opened the first channel of the Cormanian broadcasting system. An elegant news anchor looked seriously into the camera as she read her report.

"...and this is the interview our reporter got from an eyewitness."

The view shifted to a hotel lobby where an eager middle-aged woman stood next to a tall male reporter.

"I'm standing here with Mrs. Exxer, who witnessed what transpired here only a few days ago. Why don't you tell us what happened?"

"I certainly will." Mrs. Exxer hijacked the microphone from the interviewing reporter. "I was just window-shopping when I realized who was standing by the toy-store window, only a few steps away. Prince Armeo. Completely unguarded and open to an assassin or a kidnapper."

"What did you do then, Mrs. Exxer?"

"Well, I realized the dangerous circumstances, of course, and fulfilled my duty as a Supreme Constellations citizen by offering my protection. He had a friend with him, a rude young woman who nearly broke my arm."

"What preceded her attack?"

"Eh, well, I don't know. I was merely being helpful, and he is such a cute boy."

"Didn't you try to touch him?" another voice asked, and a hotel security guard appeared. The woman paled and sat up. This was getting interesting.

"I did nothing of the sort."

"Only because the young woman stopped you. You saw the prince, and instead of calmly offering your assistance, you drew attention to him, which attracted a big crowd. The prince wasn't in any danger before that happened."

Mrs. Exxer looked stricken and for a moment Dwyn felt sorry for her.

"I plan to press charges anyway," she finally said triumphantly, which effectively erased Dwyn's pity. "That girl gave me these." She held up her arms where five distinct bruises were visible.

"Good luck," she muttered, and changed channels.

"...and the authorities in charge are certain that these findings will have repercussions throughout our government, as well as among some of our high-profile businessmen and women. The news that the Thousand Year Pact has been violated, and people injured because of it, will no doubt reverberate throughout our system for years to come." The news anchor went on to describe the Thousand Year Pact, but Dwyn stared blankly at the view screen.

How could things be revealed this quickly? She stood and began to pace, until the answer hit. "Damage control. Of course." The reporter had mentioned repercussions for both politicians and top business tycoons. Perhaps even the local Cormanian military. Dwyn tried to harness her thoughts. It wouldn't do to become paranoid.

She sat down at the desk where a security guard had placed her computer bag, pulled out her computer, and accessed a flow-sheet software. She began to fill the chart with everything that had happened since she received her assignment from Aequitas. When she finished, she followed the different timelines and names with her finger and began to slowly relax.

Her initial reaction was correct. The people responsible, and the people who in turn had turned a blind eye to the ones responsible, must have heard that Kellen and Emeron had successfully captured two bots. And something in the bots' systems would lead the law-enforcement agencies directly to the ones in charge, or at least indirectly responsible. Yes, she decided, indirectly. Since these people wouldn't take the fall for the ones who commissioned the construction of the bots, everyone was now trying to cut deals, offering up the ones lower in the food chain.

Dwyn curled up in her chair and yawned. This last brainstorm was too much for her poor body. She needed to sleep. Reluctant to leave the cozy fire, she returned to the couch and clicked off the view screen. She was sure Emeron would fill her in when they saw each other and hoped she had found some time to clean up and rest. She would definitely be busy now. Testifying, helping to sort this mess out, and, on a personal level, trying to figure out where she stood regarding her ethnic affiliation. She hoped Emeron would have a little time for her. Hugging this hope to her, Dwyn yawned again and embraced a pillow as she huddled under the blanket.

❖

Emeron stood watching Dwyn sleep. She had brought two other ensigns to relieve the ones at Dwyn's door and let herself in quietly. She told herself she just needed to make sure, to see with her own eyes, that Dwyn was safe. At first, when she wasn't in the bedroom, Emeron had panicked. Hurrying back to the living room, she found Dwyn asleep on the couch, barely visible among the blankets and pillows.

"Emeron..." Dwyn whispered, and crawled beneath the blanket. "Mmm... Yes."

Suddenly hot, Emeron unbuttoned her collar and stared down at Dwyn. Her hair flowed over the pillows and the armrest, almost touching the floor. What was she dreaming? Was she having a nightmare?

"Yes, there. Mmm..."

That didn't sound like a nightmare. She knew she should leave and return to her quarters and finally get some sleep. But she couldn't take her eyes off Dwyn.

Suddenly Dwyn awoke. "Emeron?"

"Eh, hello." She placed her hands on the back of the couch and tried to look casual. "Just checking on you."

"Emeron?" Dwyn sat up, wrestling a little with the blanket that engulfed her. "You're really here? I mean, already?" Her voice had a husky, sleepy tone, which sent ripples of pleasure through Emeron.

"As I said. Checking. On you."

"That's nice. Can I get you anything? Room service here is very fast." Dwyn seemed unaware that her robe was open, though the blanket still covered her from the waist down.

"No, no, thank you. I ate at headquarters."

"No more of those awful ration bars?" Dwyn's disgusted face made it clear she wasn't kidding.

"Admiral Jacelon sent out for food during our debriefing. It took quite a while."

"What time is it?" Dwyn checked the chronometer on the coffee table. "Oh. Six in the morning. And you haven't slept?"

"Not yet. I'm on my way home." Emeron's exhaustion was nearly suffocating her.

Dwyn jumped up and took her hand. The robe fell open completely, treating Emeron to the enticing view of Dwyn's breasts and the triangular shadow between her legs.

"Oh. Sorry." Dwyn let go of her and secured the robe around herself with the belt. "All right, come on, then." She guided her toward the bedroom. "Here. Undress and I'll use the computer to make you some underwear."

"It's all right. I can sleep like this." She fell into bed and knew she'd be asleep within seconds. She wanted to stay awake longer, to look at Dwyn, perhaps hold her, but she only managed to kick off her boots. She thought she felt soft lips on her forehead and her mouth, and she was certain that a soft voice said, "Sleep well."

CHAPTER THIRTY-ONE

Emeron woke slowly, stretching her arms toward the ceiling where a crystal chandelier created an intricate light pattern. She flinched. A chandelier. She'd never stayed at a place with something so luxurious. She sat up and discovered that she was naked. Looking around, she saw no trace of her clothes, and now that she began to recognize her surroundings, she realized Dwyn wasn't there either.

An object on the nightstand caught her attention. A sanitizer rod. Was that a not-so-subtle hint that she smelled bad? She sniffed her armpit discreetly and ran a hand through her hair. In fact, she smelled of Dwyn's personal scent. Had Dwyn run the rod over her as she slept? She vaguely remembered being led into this fantastic bedroom last night, or morning. She checked the chronometer. Two in the afternoon. She jumped out of bed, pulling the sheet around her. She had to locate her uniform and return to headquarters immediately.

"You have the day off. Well, at least you have the afternoon off. You're to report in at 2000 hours. Captain Zeger's orders." Dwyn stood in the doorway, dressed in a white tunic and light blue pants. Her hair was down and she looked healthy and rested.

"I...you sure?" Emeron felt silly standing there with the sheet wrapped around her.

"I'm sure. You can double-check, but that really isn't necessary. Captain Zeger and Admiral Jacelon promised to let us know right away if something comes up."

"Ah. I see." She sat down on the side of the bed and watched Dwyn approach, her lips curving in a half smile, so familiar by now. "Are you all right?" she asked, fully aware how husky she sounded.

"I'm fine. Thanks to you." Dwyn stopped in front of her. "And I'm so happy that you're doing fine also." She stroked Emeron's face.

"So, very...very glad." She kissed Emeron's forehead slowly. Her heart seemed lodged somewhere in her throat and pounded painfully.

Now she was certain she hadn't dreamed the kisses before she went to sleep. Dwyn kissed a trail down her nose, skipped her lips, and kissed her chin. She raised her head and looked intently into Emeron's eyes.

"I've dreamed of having you to myself without interruptions."

"You have?" She closed her eyes briefly, trying to get herself under control. "I want you." She opened her eyes and returned the unwavering gaze. She had to know that Dwyn, innocent in so many ways despite her worldliness, knew what they were talking about. "I want to make love to you."

Dwyn blushed, a fresh pink color that enhanced her elfin beauty. "I want that too. I've never wanted it before, never thought those feelings...*these* feelings were meant for me."

"What feelings are you talking about?" She pulled Dwyn onto her lap. She wanted her to feel safe and cared for, certain that she'd never want to hurt her. "Tell me."

"You know that the only indulgence in my life has been listening to music." Dwyn leaned against Emeron and nuzzled her neck. "I thought I was too unfeeling, too wrapped up in the causes I was involved with, and that wanting more was selfish."

"So at times you wanted more?"

"When I *dreamed* of more." Dwyn curled up and Emeron kissed the top of her head.

"I'm here. I'm prepared to give you more. As much as you want." The words, so unlike her, came easily to Emeron. "Or as little as you want."

"What do you mean, 'as little'?" Dwyn peered up at her.

"Well, I want you. That's rather obvious, but I understand that you might want to go slowly. And truthfully, even if it has been quite a while, I'm still in full control of myself. I won't hurt you." *At least I hope I'm in control. The way you smell, maitele, could drive anyone crazy.*

"I don't want that," Dwyn said, crushing Emeron's hopes until she continued. "I don't want you to be in control of yourself. I want to feel everything. I want you to let yourself go and remember that I'm not made of crystal like that chandelier." Dwyn pressed her parted lips to Emeron's in a clear invitation.

She groaned into the kiss and met Dwyn's tongue with her own. The kiss deepened. Soft whimpers told her that Dwyn was far from unaffected by the kisses, and she eased them both onto the bed. At least Dwyn would lose her virginity on the finest of beds. Then she flinched and pulled away far enough to look into Dwyn's eyes.

"You don't have to make up your mind now, and you can tell me to stop any time you want. I'm just asking, are you sure? I—"

"Shh." Dwyn placed a finger across Emeron's lips. "I'm sure. But thank you." Dwyn raised her arms and tugged off her tunic, then her pants. To Emeron's surprise, Dwyn didn't wear any underwear.

"Oh, maitele."

"Show me?" Dwyn pulled the sheet away. "Show me how to caress you."

"You did fine when you touched me in the tent," she managed. "Just to feel your hands against me is heavenly." It had been so long since she'd been stroked by a lover, and even back then, it hadn't felt anything like when Dwyn slid her hands from her waist to beneath her breasts.

"Nipples?" Dwyn asked hoarsely, clearing her throat. "This good?" She rubbed her thumbs across Emeron's aching hard nipples.

"Yes." Arching, she couldn't get close enough. "Like that."

"Or like this?" Dwyn kissed the skin between her breasts, a hot burning trail to the left nipple, which she sucked into her mouth, just hard enough to make her cry out. Dwyn let go instantly. "Did I hurt you?"

"Only if you stop."

"Oh." Dwyn took the other nipple gently between her teeth and flicked her tongue over it.

"How do you know?" Emeron's head was spinning and her toes curled as wetness pooled between her legs.

"I watched a few instructional films this morning."

"What?" Dizzy, she tried to focus on Dwyn and what she had said.

"Well, they were in the hotel database. Under 'cultural exchange.'"

She barked out a short laugh and rolled Dwyn over on her back. Lying half on top, mindful not to crush her lover-to-be, she looked down at Dwyn, half-laughing, half-scowling. "You *studied* while I was asleep?"

"Yes. I didn't want to appear a complete moron."

"Oh, maitele, you could never seem even remotely like a moron. If anyone, I'm the moron for not seeing you for who you are from day one." She ran her hands over Dwyn's body, trying to feel all the satiny skin at the same time. She was greedy and about to lose the control she'd vowed she could maintain. Burying her head between Dwyn's small breasts, she pressed one leg between hers. "I want you so much. You're so sexy, so precious—"

"Emeron, yes, yes." It was Dwyn's turn to arch, and she pressed Emeron's head against her, guided her toward her breasts. "Taste me. Please. I want you to, so much."

Emeron knew then that she couldn't turn back. No matter what she'd told Dwyn, if Dwyn changed her mind, she'd have to direct a weapon at her or kick her where it hurt for her to stop now.

❖

Dwyn spread her legs, hoping the fact that she was completely soaked wouldn't become embarrassing. Self-conscious, and more turned on than she had ever thought possible, she held her breath as Emeron's hand shot down between them. When it made contact with the sparse tuft of hair between her legs, Emeron groaned loudly and hid her head against Dwyn's neck. "You're so wet—"

"Yes, I'm sorry." She squeezed her eyes closed. "I know why. But—"

"Don't ever be sorry. This," Emeron said, and ran a finger lightly along her sex, "is for me."

And it was. She knew it and so, obviously, did Emeron. "It is." Dwyn, trusting Emeron with her life, spread her legs farther, pulling one up to her chest.

"So willing." Emeron spoke huskily and parted her folds. "So trusting." The gentle fingertips examined the moisture and spread it farther. Every time they brushed over the small protrusion of nerves, she flinched, which made Emeron chuckle and sound very pleased. "So responsive."

Two could play this game, she decided, and sneaked a hand down between them. If she was wet, Emeron turned out to be positively drenched. She slid her finger easily in between Emeron's folds, and now she realized why such wetness wasn't embarrassing at all. The scent of their lovemaking aroused her, and when she found Emeron's entrance, more or less by mistake, Emeron raised herself above her.

"Not yet," Emeron rumbled, the tenderness in her eyes contradicting the feral tone in her voice. "First you, maitele." She spread Dwyn's legs wide and kissed her way down her stomach. Dwyn gasped and clutched the sheets, then Emeron's hair. Hot, burning her mercilessly, Emeron kissed, sucked, and licked her way down toward her swollen folds. Trying to prepare for the onslaught of emotions, she still had to clench her teeth around a scream of pleasure when Emeron plunged her tongue against her pulsating ridge of nerve endings.

Emeron was merciless in an excruciatingly pleasurable way. Her tongue, silken and coarse at the same time, never stopped moving, and finally she focused all her attention on that aching part of Dwyn that would explode very soon. When Emeron pinched one of her nipples, something toppled her. The orgasm hit, and the way it took her breath away and made her cry out should have frightened her, and in a way it did, but mostly, she felt Emeron slide up, pull her into her arms, and ride the waves with her.

"Imer-Ohon-Da." She sobbed. "Oh, Emeron, oh—"

"I know. I know."

She sobbed as the convulsions began to ease and clung to Emeron's neck, certain that Emeron and how she made her feel had created this amazing orgasm.

A few minutes later, Emeron lifted her head and looked down at her with almost black eyes. She could read all about Emeron's arousal in their bottomless depth. Emeron needed her touch, and she was eager to provide anything that would give her relief.

She rested her free hand between Emeron's breasts. "That was something," she said, and kissed Emeron with all the tenderness she felt.

"I'm glad. That it was something." Emeron breathed evenly, but she kept her eyes on Dwyn's lips. "Very."

"Your turn."

"Yes?"

"Tell me. Show me."

"Anything you want to do with me, to me, is fine." Emeron looked a little flustered, and it took her a few moments to realize that Emeron was embarrassed. Intrigued, she knew she had to investigate.

"I'm sure you know yourself much better than I do." She infused as much innocence as she could into her voice. "I really want to do this right and make it as pleasurable as possible for you."

"Oh. Yes." Emeron drew a deep breath. "I...eh...I like to...I mean, if you lie on your back." Now she blushed profusely, probably because this was about her, Emeron, and not about introducing Dwyn to pleasure.

She lay down next to Emeron, flat on her back. "Like so? And now?"

"Raise one knee."

She pulled up her left knee. Emeron rose onto her hands and knees and straddled her raised leg. Trembling, she began to slide her sex up and down Dwyn's thigh, coating it with her own moisture, blending it with hers. Not about to torment Emeron with any more questions, she held Emeron's breasts and tweaked her nipples, wanting her to feel what she herself had just experienced.

Emeron moved faster, pressing down harder, and as she did, her right thigh rubbed against Dwyn, over and over, reigniting the flame that had never really died down. "Dwyn, Dwyn. Just like that. Oh, maitele."

Emeron lunged forward and kissed her hard and deep. Her body shook and then began to convulse like her own had. Dwyn wrapped her free leg around Emeron and suddenly felt one of Emeron's fingertips at her opening.

"Yes." She opened up as much as she could, certain this was what she wanted.

Emeron went gently inside. There was so much tenderness in the way she did it, and no pain at all. Dwyn had never felt so full, or so taken, in the best sense of the word. Her body knew what to do when she didn't. Another orgasm, not as forceful, but deeper, pulled Emeron's finger farther in, and she contracted around it until she was spent.

Emeron rolled onto her side and gently extracted her finger before she tugged Dwyn with her. She covered their sweaty bodies with a sheet and kissed Dwyn repeatedly.

"Oh, Emeron." Dwyn sobbed. "Emeron."

"Did I hurt you?" she asked, sounding appalled.

"Not at all. I've never felt so loved. The way you touched me. Do you love me, Emeron?" She looked into Emeron's eyes, needing to know the truth instantly. If this was merely a physical reaction after having been in constant danger for days, she needed to know now.

"I—"

"Zeger to D'Artansis. Come in." The distant male voice from Emeron's communicator cut between them like a laser-blade knife, and Dwyn pulled back with a small gasp.

❖

Emeron looked at Dwyn, tormented, before she reached for the device. "D'Artansis here, Captain."

"You need to come in earlier. Several ministers have demanded to talk to you, as a representative of the Disian Nation."

"The what, sir?" Emeron didn't take her eyes off Dwyn, who seemed to shrink where she lay naked. She backed up, just enough for their bodies not to touch, but the movement was obvious. "There's no such thing as a Disian Nation, sir."

"There is now. Apparently the ministers have had emergency meetings all day, and your name came up more than once. I will have a hovercraft at your address within half an hour."

"I'm going to be a little longer, sir. I'm not home right now, and I need to go back to my place to change."

"Very well. Two hours then. Formal attire, D'Artansis," Zeger said shortly. "Try to make us look good. Zeger out."

"Make the military look good? I thought I was representing the Disians," she muttered.

"I suppose duty calls," Dwyn said brightly. Too brightly.

"In a manner of speaking." She gazed down at Dwyn, who valiantly struggled to seem casual. "Would you come with me?"

"What? To your place? I'm not sure. I should get my notes in order—"

"To meet the ministers. You asked me a very important question, and I've never wanted to strangle my boss as much as I did just now. And trust me, there have been several occasions." She paused. "Anyway. I'd like to answer this question when we're really alone and have plenty of time to follow it up appropriately."

A careful glimpse of hope lit up Dwyn's eyes. "You would?"

"Absolutely. So, do you have a dress, or something else that's kind of posh to wear?"

"I always bring one dress."

"Then let's clean up and get out of here. We have things to do and

I want to finish them quickly, so I can show you as well as tell you why you never have to ask me that question again."

Dwyn's eyes filled with tears, but she jumped out of bed and headed for the bathroom immediately. When Emeron joined her in the ionic-resonance shower, Dwyn slid promptly into her arms. Emeron kissed her softly and tipped her head back so she could meet her eyes.

"You already know, don't you, when you think about it?" she asked tenderly.

"Yes." Dwyn trembled, but her smile was the most beautiful thing Emeron had ever seen. She was certain Dwyn loved her. It was there, beaming in her eyes, and she hoped that one day Dwyn would be able to read her just as easily.

Chapter Thirty-two

"Kellen, Rae." Armeo ran along the corridor on deck four aboard the *Dalathea*. He threw one arm around each of them and nearly knocked them down in his eagerness. Rae held him tight, and so did Kellen, and Rae was happier than she'd been in a long time. "You're back," Armeo continued. "Where's Grandma?"

"Here, son." Dahlia stepped from behind Kellen and smiled at him. "You look like you've missed me."

Armeo's mouth fell open at her words, but then his sense of humor obviously kicked in and he grinned at her. "A little," he said, measuring half a centimeter between his thumb and index finger.

"You little devil," Dahlia said, and hugged him. "I've missed you too." She looked over at her husband, who had just caught up with Armeo. "Hello, love. Sorry I'm late."

"Dahlia." Ewan took two long steps and wrapped her in his arms.

"Hey, Granddad. Let me out first." Armeo freed himself of his grandparents and stood next to Kellen, one arm around her waist.

Ewan kissed Dahlia tenderly and embraced her one more time. He kept one arm around her, looking at her with so much love it was palpable. Finally, he lifted his gaze. "Excellent job, my daughter. And Kellen, what would we do without you?" For a frightening moment, Ewan seemed as he might shed the tears that glazed his eyes, but he cleared his throat and remained in control.

"We're glad to be able to deliver her, at last," Kellen said. "We meant to bring Dahlia and M'Ekar back here immediately, but M'Ekar's condition worsened and Dahlia made the MEDEVAC pilot stop by a local hospital in the capital. That saved his sorry life," she continued darkly, "and they're admitting him to the infirmary aboard here as we speak."

"I assume under heavy guard?" Ewan asked.

"Of course," Rae said. "He's very ill and probably will lose his legs, but I'll keep him alive to stand trial again. No pun intended."

"I thought Commanders Grey and D'Artansis were joining us?" Ewan asked.

"They were, but they took the opportunity to continue their honeymoon at the hotel a few more days. They might join us here tomorrow or the next day."

And speaking of missing people, where is Ayahliss?" Dahlia asked, glancing around. She paled. "She isn't injured more than you said, is she, Rae?"

"No, Ayahliss's injuries have healed," another familiar voice interjected as Judge Beqq joined the happy reunion. "She's in my quarters. Hiding."

"What?" Kellen stared at Judge Beqq.

"Why is she hiding?" Rae asked, nonplussed.

"You're welcome to join me for lunch, and you can talk to her yourself. She's got the wrong idea about a few things, and I don't think she'll be all right until she's spoken with the two of you and Diplomat Jacelon. The admiral and I have tried, but..." Beqq shrugged.

Rae didn't like the sound of this. Ayahliss had come so far since they took her to Earth, and to learn that now she was going through something they knew nothing about disturbed her.

❖

Judge Beqq's dining-room table was beautifully set, and Ayahliss was still fiddling with details, trying to occupy her mind as well as her hands, when the door to the corridor hissed open.

"Ayahliss, they're here," Armeo called, and she knew she couldn't hide any longer. She walked slowly to the door and stood there, determined to meet their eyes no matter how much disdain they showed. Dahlia was the first to approach her. She stopped and held her gently. "You brave girl. I'm so relieved you're all right." She kissed her on both cheeks, then led her over to Rae and Kellen. The other three made themselves busy, and Ayahliss stood there, shaking, as she faced the two women who had taken her in and given her a new home.

"I'm glad you're back," she whispered. "We...I mean, Armeo was so worried and he missed you very much."

"We felt he was better off since you and his grandfather were here with him," Kellen said. There were no accusations in her voice, but that meant nothing. Kellen could sound calm even when she was very, very angry.

"Now, what's all this about hiding from us?" Rae asked. She sounded more confused than angry, and Ayahliss didn't know what to say. "Ayahliss? Please?"

"I failed you. I failed you and then I began to resent babysitting Armeo. He's safe aboard this ship, with his grandfather, and I needed, I mean I *need* to do more. I love him. But..." Hateful, revealing blue tears ran down her cheeks. "I need to go back to Gantharat and continue the fight."

❖

Rae didn't know what to say. She looked at Kellen, whose eyes had narrowed, not usually a good sign.

"Why do you think you failed us?" Kellen asked, and guided Ayahliss to Judge Beqq's study.

"I let Armeo go exploring at the hotel when he was bored."

"I know that. When I returned I saw a broadcast about that woman whose arm you nearly broke." Rae spoke lightly. "I also talked to the security officer there, who told me exactly what happened. It wasn't a smart move, but we know Armeo, and if you hadn't gone with him, he might have decided to go alone. He's growing up, and sometimes he thinks he knows best."

"But, I—"

"If for a moment I thought you'd failed us," Kellen said, "I wouldn't hesitate to let you know. You have my word. Now the other part, of resenting not going on a mission, of babysitting. That's something we need to discuss, but you don't have to hide anything from us."

Rae could see that Ayahliss was about to cry again and wanted to spare the proud young woman the embarrassment. "Listen, why don't we just rejoice that M'Ekar and two of the mercenaries are incarcerated, with no chance of escape, and enjoy Judge Beqq's good food?"

Ayahliss nodded, seemingly relieved. "They're here? On the *Dalathea*?"

"Yes. M'Ekar, Weiss Kyakh, and the infamous Ms. Smith. I believe you tossed that woman into a wall," Kellen said. "Well done."

Ayahliss looked at them with a new light in her eyes. "Yes, I did. Let's do exactly what you just suggested. Reena's a great hostess."

Rae wasn't sure she liked the glee with which Ayahliss spoke, and she noted also that she was entitled to use what had to be Judge Beqq's nickname. A lot had obviously happened in their absence.

"Are you coming? The food will get cold," Ewan called. They took their seats in the dining room, and it warmed Rae's heart to witness Armeo and her father's happiness over their safe return.

Judge Beqq raised her glass and looked at all of them, one by one. "Here's to happy endings and new beginnings," she said, toasting them. Everyone echoed her words, and Rae wondered if she was the only one to pick up on exactly how Amereena Beqq had gazed at Ayahliss when she spoke.

❖

Weiss slowly opened her eyes, groaning because of the searing pain in her side. She had been slipping in and out of consciousness since the blast, and now she tried to determine where they'd taken her.

"You're awake. Good," a throaty voice said from her right.

She turned her head slowly, daggers piercing her skull. "Who are you?"

A small woman with fiery red hair regarded her solemnly. "I'm Admiral Rae Jacelon. I believe you've met my mother."

Shit. "Yes. Charming woman."

"She can be. Kidnapping her was probably the biggest mistake you've ever made, right after getting in bed with Hox M'Ekar."

For a moment, Weiss thought the admiral meant what she said literally. "I can see why you would think so," she muttered.

"Another mistake was teaming up with the lovely Ms. White."

"Is she dead?"

"No. In fact, she's right here. In the bed on the other side of the alu-glass wall."

Weiss opened her mouth to speak, but pain hit again, tearing through her side. She refused to show any signs of discomfort.

"If you had any idea what memories this situation brings back," Jacelon said. "Nurse," she continued, raising her voice. "Is it all right if I up her dosage of painkillers? She's in agony."

"Sure, Admiral. Just press the sensor twice," a male voice said from afar.

The admiral did as told, and after a few moments, Weiss could breathe again. "Thank you," she said quietly. She looked up at the only woman who had ever chased her down. "Why are you here?"

"Because I've spoken to my mother, and she thinks there's more to you than meets the eye, in a manner of speaking." Jacelon placed both hands on the bed railing, to which Weiss noticed her own hands were chained. "I'm not convinced, but my mother is seldom wrong."

"You'd lock me up and throw away the key if you had your way, wouldn't you?" she snarled.

"That's one option."

"What's stopping you?" She coughed, closing her eyes, furious at the tears of pain that rolled down her temples into her hair.

"My mother's conviction that there's hope for you. White will be transferred to a maximum-security prison while she awaits trial for her impressive list of crimes. She's had a knack for killing off her bosses, thus taking over their business, so you might want to count yourself lucky that we intervened."

"I knew her reputation and had an eye on her," she said huskily. Her head was spinning, perhaps from the upped dosage of the pain medication. She also might be trying too hard to make sense of Jacelon's words. She sensed that the admiral disliked her and wouldn't trust her for a second.

She tried to remember what she had done or said to make any sort of positive impression on Dahlia Jacelon. She was a wanted criminal, had teamed up with the archenemy, M'Ekar, and kidnapped a distinguished diplomat. Granted, she'd resisted White's demands to leave the injured M'Ekar behind, but that hardly warranted any feelings of forgiveness on Dahlia Jacelon's part. She groaned. This was too much. Such thoughts hurt her head. "So, what do you want from me? Why are you really here?"

Jacelon was silent for a moment, looking like she was debating whether to speak again. She tapped her fingertips against the bed rails, then glanced at the imbulizer pump. "Medication helping?"

"Yes. Thank you." It hurt to thank this commanding woman who could have her locked up and make sure nobody remembered she ever existed.

"Good." Jacelon towered over the bed, looking directly at her. Her eyes were an unusual shade of gray, bright and piercing. "I'm prepared to cut a deal with the SC Council, as well as with Judge Beqq, and have you transferred to a special facility."

"What?" She shook her head. "I know I'm looking at many years in prison, but I want my day in court. You're not throwing me into any *facility*."

"You don't understand." Jacelon smiled joylessly. "I'm not talking about a facility within the penal system. I mean a training facility."

Now she was sure she was too high on drugs. "What the hell are you talking about, Admiral?"

"You have two choices, as I see it." Jacelon straightened and folded her arms over her chest. "Either you 'have your day in court' and serve the rest of your life in prison, or you take the offer I make you while it's still on the table. If you do, we will transfer you to a covert SC facility. Once there, you'll start by recuperating and regaining your health. After that, you'll undergo a thorough mental and emotional evaluation. If you pass, you will attend extensive training and education classes."

"Training? Trained to do what?"

"Become a covert operative for the SC."

"You're kidding," she exclaimed, the words gushing out. "You must be out of your mind."

"I may be, but I trust my mother's judgment. She's seen qualities in you that I have yet to discover and has suggested this option." Jacelon looked like she thought she never would see any redeeming qualities in her. "You have until tomorrow morning. The *Dalathea* embarks at 0900 hours and we need your decision by then, since a small medical shuttle would have to rendezvous with us once we've broken orbit, to transport you to your destination."

Clutching her forehead, Weiss tried to think. Her life would be forever altered no matter what she decided. "I'll let you know before the ship embarks."

"And if I find that you've discussed this with anyone, the deal's off." Jacelon sounded cold and relentless, far more ominous than White.

"You have my word," she said quietly.

"Time will tell how much that's worth. I'll come by tomorrow morning." Jacelon turned and walked away.

Weiss's eyelids grew heavy. Her mind reeled with questions that she was now formulating, but she couldn't stay awake and focus on them. It really didn't matter. Relaxing into drug-induced sleep, she already knew what her answer would be.

CHAPTER THIRTY-THREE

D wyn stared at Emeron. She had never been so taken aback or seen anything so beautiful. "Emeron," she gasped.

"Yes. Eh...it was my grandmother's." She gestured at the outfit, looking embarrassed. "I meant to throw it away so many times, but kept it in a box hidden deep inside my closet. It was hers, Briijn's, when she was young. She married my other grandmother in it, so I simply couldn't discard it. I suppose I needed *something* that represented my heritage, no matter how disdainful or conflicted I was." She smiled uncertainly.

"I chose it since I'm not going to meet these ministers in my role as a commander of military law enforcement, but as a representative of the Disians."

"The Disian Nation," Dwyn corrected. She hardly recognized her lover. *My lover.* Emeron wore a long, golden straight skirt, with deep blue metal threads interwoven in the fabric. Under a gold mesh short jacket, woven in elaborate patterns, an intricately cut blue shirt left her waist bare. Only a golden chain with a multitude of charms covered it.

Emeron held out the headpiece that went with the outfit. "Help me with this? It's supposed to sit perfectly straight." The same type of gold mesh as the jacket hung from the back of the blue, triangular headpiece. Emeron sat down on a chair in her simple living room, and Dwyn placed the hat on her head. The mesh that reached to the small of Emeron's back reminded her of an old-fashioned wedding veil.

"You look fantastic. Incredibly beautiful. I don't have words to describe you."

"Thank you." Emeron looked at her in the mirror and took a deep breath. "And you look very different. Beautiful, always, but the way you've put up your hair makes you look regal, maitele. It's like a crown."

"Really?" She felt the braids twisted high on the top of her head.

"You're glowing."

Her cheeks warmed at Emeron's tender scrutiny. "And you're radiant."

Emeron smiled. "Well, why don't we go meet the ministers? They must have something very urgent to tell me."

"Then we should hurry." She pulled Emeron to her feet, then wrapped her arms around her neck. "Wait. Just one kiss."

Emeron smiled, the first full, broad, and happy smile she had ever given her. She returned the smile, knowing that no matter what happened at the ministry, she would stand by Emeron's side in the battle for the Thousand Year Pact.

❖

The large, rectangular room featured a long table where ten ministers sat, all facing the door that Emeron had just stepped inside with Dwyn. The ministers rose and Emeron recognized the Minister of Domestic Affairs, Garon Nerposs, who bowed politely.

"Welcome, Emeron D'Artansis of the Disian Nation," he began ceremoniously. "As one of the few of Disian descendants living and working outside the Disi-Disi forest, you have been selected as liaison. We regret the lack of communication between our two people for many years."

"Thank you." She bowed discreetly, surprised at how calm she felt even though she was the center of attention. Dwyn's presence next to her wrapped her in a blanket of complete loyalty and affection and helped her find her footing among these dignitaries. "I am still at a loss, ladies and gentlemen. Has any representative contacted my grandmother's people and asked if they *want* to communicate via a liaison? Or have you merely assumed this?"

Minister Nerposs looked taken aback. "But, Ms...eh, Commander D'Artansis, why wouldn't they? They need to have someone speak for them and look after their interests."

"If that's what you're after, you should give a couple of them seats in the parliament."

"Unheard of," another minister said.

"So is this meeting," Emeron responded. "I am ready to hear your motives for appointing me as representative for my own people, and I will relay anything you have to say to the Disians. If they choose to further communicate with the Cormanian government, and if they want me to speak for them, I will gladly serve as liaison."

Garon Nerposs cleared his throat, suddenly looking uncomfortable. "Well, Commander D'Artansis, we have summoned you here today because of the unfortunate events that took place during Ms. Izontro's assignment in the Disi-Disi forest." He looked around him, and the other ministers nodded solemnly. "My department secretary and spokesperson has stepped down from her position as a result of a preliminary investigation. She is suspected of having shared classified government details with nationwide companies wishing to exploit the forest. She has also used the parliament stamps to covertly approve illegal exploitation and thus facilitated preliminary underground work that reaches beyond the borders established by the Thousand Year Pact."

"One woman did this?" Emeron knew her disbelief was obvious.

"No, of course not. She was a pawn in a vast collaboration among conglomerates, many of them funded by off-world interests."

"So, she was the gate in and you didn't know anything?" Emeron didn't believe this for a minute. A handful of people couldn't possibly pull off such a complicated operation. The department secretary was most likely the scapegoat, paid to take the fall for people higher up. She was furious, and one glance at Dwyn confirmed that she was too. "What do you suggest we do about the damage that has already been done?" she asked, as she willed herself to calm down.

"Restoration is already the first topic on the department's agenda." Garon Nerposs smiled with practiced reassurance. "We won't rest until confidence in the pact is restored."

Dwyn crossed her arms and looked angrily at the ministers as she spoke. "And the conglomerates? What punishment will they receive?"

"They will of course be fined."

"Fined," Dwyn spat. "They could probably buy and sell Corma twice over. You need to incarcerate the guilty as an example of what happens when companies attempt to kill an entire planet and its inhabitants."

"Please, Ms. Izontro, going down that road is hardly constructive." Garon Nerposs frowned. "We cannot disrupt the Cormanian economy because of this incident. That will benefit nobody."

"And their attempt to destroy the ecosystem isn't disruptive enough?" Dwyn took a step forward, and Emeron placed a hand on her arm to stop her from throttling the condescending Nerposs.

"I see that politics still reign," Emeron said calmly. "I am prepared to work as your liaison on a few nonnegotiable conditions."

Nerposs pulled his bushy eyebrows into a homogeneous black line. "Conditions? Explain."

"You will find out who *personally* sent the high-tech bots after us and punish them for attempted murder. I'm sure you're aware that the SC forces possess two of those bots, and it wouldn't look very good if they beat you to it, would it?"

"I have already told you—"

"*Personally responsible*, the person who gave the actual order," Emeron demanded.

"Very well." Nerposs was obviously seasoned enough not to reveal his annoyance at being ordered around.

"Second, Ms. Izontro plans to present her report to the SC Council on behalf of her employer, and you will personally ensure her safety, by any means necessary, before, during, and after she's written it."

"I cannot be responsible for what happens to Ms. Izontro once she leaves Corma," Nerposs objected, clearly irritated.

"Hopefully, Ms. Izontro will use Corma as her home base from now on, so you will have plenty of opportunity to ensure her safety." She was careful not to look at Dwyn as she spoke. They hadn't talked about the future, at least not in that many words, but she wanted nothing more than for Dwyn to stay with her.

Nerposs looked ready to implode at Emeron's last statement. "Very well. Of course Corma will benefit from having a person of Ms. Izontro's courage and expertise."

Dwyn coughed, and Emeron was briefly afraid that her lover would explode into a fit of laughter at the minister's forced words.

"I will shortly return to the Disian village that the crash devastated," she said. "I will convey your thoughts and ideas to the elders."

"Commander D'Artansis," a woman to the far right said, "let the Health and Social Department know when you go back. We would like to send whatever aid you might require." This minister sounded both caring and sincere.

"Thank you. I will." Emeron nodded gratefully. "The Disians are a formidable people, but they need help."

"You can page my office any time you require assistance."

Emeron listened to a few more polite niceties, but knew she had gone as far as she could this time. She would gradually grow into this new role, and with Pri's help, she would also be able to embrace her Disian legacy. Briijn had taught her many things, but she knew she had only begun to understand the mysteries of her culture.

They told the ministers good-bye, and once outside the impressive structure, Dwyn drew a deep breath. "Politicians," she muttered.

"I know." Emeron walked toward the commercial hovercraft where the pilot waited. Inside, she pulled off the headpiece, grimacing as she rubbed her neck. "Not quite used to wearing this stuff."

"You look stunning." Dwyn kissed her softly on the lips. "Absolutely wonderful."

"Thanks." She leaned into the gentle caress. "Normally, I could care less about exterior beauty, but your compliments mean something."

"That's just it." Dwyn smiled. "Your inner strength and beauty make it possible for you to do justice to garments like these. You seem proud of your heritage for the first time."

She sobered. "Yes. I've failed my grandmother and all she taught me for so many years."

"Don't." Dwyn shook her head vehemently. "You needed time to let things fall into place. We all live our life at our own pace. This is your destiny, and you've assumed this role with grace. All the knowledge of the intricacies of Cormanian and SC politics you've gained during your years as a commander will be an advantage."

"And I won't resign my commission."

"Smart move." Dwyn rested against her as the hovercraft circled the block in order to reach the air corridors. "Now that we've settled that, what about the fact that you told the ministers you hoped I'd work from Corma in the future?"

"Yes."

"If my imagination isn't playing tricks on me, that answers my earlier question, doesn't it?" Dwyn sounded certain, but still looked worried.

"Yes." She tipped Dwyn's head back. "Dwyn. I love you. I can't imagine life without you." The words were simple and direct, but Dwyn's tears were all it took for her to realize how strong Dwyn's own feelings were.

"I love you." Dwyn threw her arms around her neck. "And I don't ever want to leave you."

"Good. Then stay." The hovercraft ascended to the tenth-level air corridor above the clouds, and the sun's rays poured over them. Dwyn's hair ignited with highlights of silver that made it shimmer like a live entity. Emeron stroked the silken tresses. "Stay."

"Oh, Emeron. Of course I'll stay." Dwyn held her even closer. "For as long as you want me to."

"Forever."

"Yes. Forever."

EPILOGUE

Kellen was sitting in bed when Rae returned to their quarters, propped up against the headboard with a portable computer console on her lap. Rae stood still just inside the doorway, for a moment enthralled by the beautiful, strong woman who was her wife. She had never met anyone quite like her, and she knew with complete certainty that she never would.

"Writing your report already, darling?" she asked as she began to unfasten her uniform jacket.

Kellen smiled faintly. "No. I've already done that. I checked my correspondence from Revos Prime. It's very encouraging. The Gantharian refugees are making great progress, and several teams are considered deployable already."

"Excellent." Rae slid her pants off and hung them on a chair by the view port. "Ayahliss and Armeo asleep?" The domestic normalcy of the question struck her as slightly surreal after everything that had taken place in the Disi-Disi forest.

"Yes. Armeo had a hard time settling down. He chatted about every topic he could find until I told him he wouldn't have anything left to share with us tomorrow unless he went to sleep." Kellen tucked her computer away on a table next to the bed. "Ayahliss was probably completely drained. She retired right after dinner."

"So, it's just us old folks?" Rae winked and removed the rest of her clothes.

Kellen looked at her with darkening eyes. "Old? Who's counting years when you do that?"

"Do what?" Rae feigned innocence and slid into bed. "I'm tired, but not *that* tired." She pulled Kellen on top of her and kissed her with all the passion and love in her heart. Kellen's hands roamed along her body, igniting small flames on her skin.

"I'm so happy," Kellen whispered. "So happy we're all together again."

"So am I. It frightened me to think I might lose my mother just when we were...you know—"

"Beginning to know each other as mother and daughter, rather than merely as accomplished women."

"Yes." Rae was thankful Kellen rarely needed extensive explanations. She lovingly caressed Kellen's smooth skin and laced her fingers through her hair. "Now, what are you thinking about? You have that certain look in your eyes. You're brooding, darling."

"I..." Kellen sighed. "I'm concerned about how long I'll be able to harness this urge, no, this need for revenge. When I'm in this environment, with a clear command structure, it's not difficult to stay in control. But down on Corma, in the forest, it was a different matter."

"How so?"

"I acted on impulse, and when I fought White, I didn't want merely to win, but to finish her. I try to teach Ayahliss the art of self-restraint and yet my feelings rampage in me, especially when you and Armeo are in danger, and I have hardly any control." Kellen lowered her face, then met Rae's gaze again.

"You're not being fair to yourself. You've come a long way since you fired on my ship a year ago. You've gained a commission as a lieutenant commander on your own merits, and nobody has had anything but good to say about your conduct." Rae held up her hand to forestall any protests. "I know your demons haunt you. I know that better than anyone else. You're handling them, darling. You are. And it will get easier." Rae brushed her lips over Kellen's. "Trust me."

"I trust you."

"Good. I'd never lie to you."

"I know. You're very honest." Kellen kissed along her neck, murmuring words between the caresses. "And I want you. Now."

"Oh, my." Rae knew she didn't want anything more than to give herself to Kellen, let her take her to that place where they forgot everything except each other. "I love you."

"And I love you, Rae." Kellen moved in between her legs, making her whimper, a sound nobody but Kellen had ever heard from her.

This moment was theirs alone, and for these precious minutes of ecstasy, nothing was wrong anywhere in the universe.

❖

Kellen sat up, hearing the door to the living-room area hiss open. She hadn't fallen asleep yet. She kept mulling over the reports relayed from the SC Command. As their Gantharian subject-matter expert, she had spent the last three days on the *Dalathea* studying the intel she had missed regarding her homeworld.

The resistance movement on Gantharat reported that the Onotharians had instituted worldwide sanctions against the Gantharian population. Medication and food rations were in short supply as it was, and this development was alarming, if not surprising. Kellen knew that dictatorships customarily employed this punishment, and she worried for her world.

Now she rose, concerned as to who might have entered their private quarters. She quickly pulled on pants and a shirt and entered the living area, which was empty. A quick glance into Armeo's bedroom showed the boy asleep, his feet on the pillow and the blankets on the floor.

She glanced into Ayahliss's room and found it empty. The bathroom was empty too. Frowning, she ran barefoot into the corridor just in time to see a lithe figure turn a corner at the end of it. Kellen sprinted after her, nonplussed at what she might be up to, but when she turned the same corner, Ayahliss was already inside the quick-lift. Kellen called her name, but the doors were closing. Checking the computer console next to the lift, she saw that Ayahliss was going to the twenty-second floor. She frowned, wondering what she might be up to, and as she caught the next lift, she knew the answer. *M'Ekar.*

Kellen had no weapons, but she was grateful she still wore her ID bracelet. It would identify her to any of the guards and make it easier, she hoped, to catch up with Ayahliss. Why was she doing this? Was it because of her perceived helplessness at the kidnapping, or because she had felt useless while Rae and she were in the Disi-Disi forest rescuing Dahlia?

The lift stopped at the twenty-second floor, and Kellen knew she was at the right one. An unconscious guard lay just outside the lift. She checked his pulse and respiration quickly and determined that he was merely knocked out. Cursing Ayahliss under her breath, she ran toward the prison infirmary. Another downed guard by the door leading into the outer perimeter told of Ayahliss's presence. This guard was also unconscious, and Kellen kept moving forward through the corridors. A nurse on duty poked her head out. "Yes? Can I help you?"

"Have you seen a young woman, a civilian, run through here?"

"A young woman? Here? Of course not." The nurse looked almost offended that Kellen would ask such a question.

"I am Lt. Commander Kellen O'Dal. Let me through the doors to the locked area. She must have sneaked in there."

"I most certainly think you must be wrong, Commander... Did you say O'Dal, ma'am?" The nurse stopped gesturing and looked more closely. "Oh, ma'am, I'm so sorry. I didn't recognize you."

"Now that you do, will you open the door?" She tried to remain calm, when all she wanted was to open the first weapons' locker available and blast a hole in the door unless the nurse didn't stop gushing over her and open it.

"Of course, of course, ma'am...Protector." The nurse pressed her ID bracelet against a sensor and performed a retina scan. The door clicked open. "When I think of it, if this person of yours was sneaky, she could have hidden behind the orderly who went inside to help restrain a patient just a moment ago."

"Thank you. I'll take it from here. Carry on."

"Yes, ma'am."

The door closed behind Kellen and she ran, her feet growing colder by the second, hoping to get to M'Ekar before Ayahliss did. Luckily she knew where the former ambassador's room was and Ayahliss didn't.

Or so she thought. Around the next bend, a heavy-set man lay unconscious with several colleagues gathered around him.

"Did you see who did this?" she demanded as she approached them.

"No. We found him this way when we came out of a patient's room."

Kellen wanted to groan aloud, but then she glimpsed something. A quick movement and a red lounge suit. Ayahliss. She dove in her direction and managed to pin her to the wall in the next room.

"What do you think you're doing?"

"He doesn't deserve to live."

"No, he doesn't, but that's not up to you."

"Armeo is my responsibility. You placed him in my care. This man endangered him on the Keliera station and hurt Rae's mother. He nearly took Dahlia from you, from us, and he had no right." Large blue tears of what Kellen determined was true fury ran down Ayahliss's cheeks.

"Dahlia gave me something nobody else ever has. She made me feel like I belonged. Like I deserved to belong. When he stole her, kidnapped her from her family, he took that feeling away from me, as well as my purpose. I couldn't save her when the kidnapping took place..." Ayahliss gasped for air, over and over, unable to speak.

"You decided to create your own sort of justice and kill a man that Dahlia fought so hard to keep alive when they were in the forest?"

"She was dehydrated, hurt from the crash, and apparently not thinking clearly."

"She wasn't incapacitated in any way." Kellen spoke firmly. "She was trying to—"

Blaring alarm klaxons drowned out Kellen's words, and for a moment she thought the unconscious guards had been found and the authorities were looking for the culprit. The klaxons became a little quieter, even if they were still active, and a dark female voice spoke over the ship-wide communication system.

"All hands, this is your captain. All SC military personnel, take your battle stations. All civilian passengers, move to secure facilities in the center-ship corridors. The SC Council has declared a state of emergency. Onotharian forces are attacking our borders. I repeat, Onotharian forces are attacking SC borders."

Kellen and Ayahliss stared at each other in silence. Then Kellen whispered, "It's happening. It's finally happening and we will now have the chance to free our homeworld."

"And vengeance." Ayahliss's eyes challenged Kellen to contradict her.

"The Onotharians will find out what justice means," Kellen said hoarsely, "but not from any of us. We will return and do our duty to our *people*. Nothing else matters. Vengeance is for people like M'Ekar and his likes. Don't lower yourself to their level. You are a Gantharian. Understood?"

Ayahliss had paled and now nodded slowly. "Yes, Kellen. Yes."

"Good." Kellen knew her impromptu speech was true and reflected her innermost feelings. As she looked up at the ceiling, the communication system hummed again.

"Gamma VI and SC headquarters have confirmed more incursions of our borders," the captain announced. "Thus, I regret to inform you that the Supreme Constellations are now officially at war with the Onotharian Empire."

About the Author

Award-winning author Gun Brooke lives in a Viking-era village in Sweden, where she writes romance and science fiction full time. When she isn't working on her latest novel, Gun enjoys training her dog, a German Shepherd mix, and plans to buy a Labrador puppy this summer. Gun spends part of the brutal winters in Texas, and it is during these journeys that she collects her characters and goes looking for sceneries and locations for future stories. Another recent love is creating digital art, a hobby that Gun finds inspiring since she can create the images of her characters on her computer. Her romance *Sheridan's Fate* is a 2007 Lambda Literary Award finalist.

Books Available From Bold Strokes Books

Falling Star by Gill McKnight. Solley Rayner hopes a few weeks with her family will help heal her shattered dreams, but she hasn't counted on meeting a woman who stirs her heart. (978-1-60282-023-4)

Lethal Affairs by Kim Baldwin and Xenia Alexiou. Elite operative Domino is no stranger to peril, but her investigation of journalist Hayley Ward will test more than her skills. (978-1-60282-022-7)

A Place to Rest by Erin Dutton. Sawyer Drake doesn't know what she wants from life until she meets Jori Diamantina—only trouble is, Jori doesn't seem to share her desire. (978-1-60282-021-0)

Warrior's Valor by Gun Brooke. Dwyn Izsontro and Emeron D'Artansis must put aside personal animosity, and unwelcomed attraction, to defeat an enemy of the Protector of the Realm. (978-1-60282-020-3)

Finding Home by Georgia Beers. Take two polar-opposite women with an attraction for one another they're trying desperately to ignore, throw in a far-too-observant dog, and then sit back and enjoy the romance. (978-1-60282-019-7)

Word of Honor by Radclyffe. All Secret Service Agent Cameron Roberts and First Daughter Blair Powell want is a small intimate wedding, but the paparazzi and a domestic terrorist have other plans. (978-1-60282-018-0)

Hotel Liaison by JLee Meyer. Two women searching through a secret past discover that their brief hotel liaison is only the beginning. Will they risk their careers—and their hearts—to follow through on their desires? (978-1-60282-017-3)

Love on Location by Lisa Girolami. Hollywood film producer Kate Nyland and artist Dawn Brock discover that love doesn't always follow the script. (978-1-60282-016-6)

Edge of Darkness by Jove Belle. Investigator Diana Collins charges at life with an irreverent comment and a right hook, but even those may not protect her heart from a charming villain. (978-1-60282-015-9)

Thirteen Hours by Meghan O'Brien. Workaholic Dana Watts's life takes a sudden turn when an unexpected interruption arrives in the form of the most beautiful breasts she has ever seen—stripper Laurel Stanley's. (978-1-60282-014-2)

In Deep Waters 2 by Radclyffe and Karin Kallmaker. All bets are off when two award winning-authors deal the cards of love and passion… and every hand is a winner. (978-1-60282-013-5)

Pink by Jennifer Harris. An irrepressible heroine frolics, frets, and navigates through the "what ifs" of her life: all the unexpected turns of fortune, fame, and karma. (978-1-60282-043-2)

Deal with the Devil by Ali Vali. New Orleans crime boss Cain Casey brings her fury down on the men who threatened her family, and blood and bullets fly. (978-1-60282-012-8)

Naked Heart by Jennifer Fulton. When a sexy ex-CIA agent sets out to seduce and entrap a powerful CEO, there's more to this plan than meets the eye…or the flogger. (978-1-60282-011-1)

Heart of the Matter by KI Thompson. TV newscaster Kate Foster is Professor Ellen Webster's dream girl, but Kate doesn't know Ellen exists…until an accident changes everything. (978-1-60282-010-4)

Heartland by Julie Cannon. When political strategist Rachel Stanton and dude ranch owner Shivley McCoy collide on an empty country road, fate intervenes. (978-1-60282-009-8)

Shadow of the Knife by Jane Fletcher. Militia Rookie Ellen Mittal has no idea just how complex and dangerous her life is about to become. A Celaeno series adventure romance. (978-1-60282-008-1)

To Protect and Serve by VK Powell. Lieutenant Alex Troy is caught in the paradox of her life—to hold steadfast to her professional oath or to protect the woman she loves. (978-1-60282-007-4)

Deeper by Ronica Black. Former homicide detective Erin McKenzie and her fiancée Elizabeth Adams couldn't be happier—until the not-so-distant past comes knocking at the door. (978-1-60282-006-7)

The Lonely Hearts Club by Radclyffe. Take three friends, add two ex-lovers and several new ones, and the result is a recipe for explosive rivalries and incendiary romance. (978-1-60282-005-0)

Venus Besieged by Andrews & Austin. Teague Richfield heads for Sedona and the sensual arms of psychic astrologer Callie Rivers for a much-needed romantic reunion. (978-1-60282-004-3)

Branded Ann by Merry Shannon. Pirate Branded Ann raids a merchant vessel to obtain a treasure map and gets more than she bargained for with the widow Violet. (978-1-60282-003-6)

American Goth by JD Glass. Trapped by an unsuspected inheritance and guided only by the guardian who holds the secret to her future, Samantha Cray fights to fulfill her destiny. (978-1-60282-002-9)

Learning Curve by Rachel Spangler. Ashton Clarke is perfectly content with her life until she meets the intriguing Professor Carrie Fletcher, who isn't looking for a relationship with anyone. (978-1-60282-001-2)

Place of Exile by Rose Beecham. Sheriff's detective Jude Devine struggles with ghosts of her past and an ex-lover who still haunts her dreams. (978-1-933110-98-1)

Fully Involved by Erin Dutton. A love that has smoldered for years ignites when two women and one little boy come together in the aftermath of tragedy. (978-1-933110-99-8)

Heart 2 Heart by Julie Cannon. Suffering from a devastating personal loss, Kyle Bain meets Lane Connor, and the chance for happiness suddenly seems possible. (978-1-60282-000-5)

Queens of Tristaine by Cate Culpepper. When a deadly plague stalks the Amazons of Tristaine, two warrior lovers must return to the place of their nightmares to find a cure. (978-1-933110-97-4)